SILENT WATERS

Also By L.V. Matthews

The Prank
The Twins

SILENT WATERS

L.V. MATTHEWS

WELBECK

First published in 2023 by Welbeck Fiction Limited,
an imprint of Welbeck Publishing Group
Offices in: London – 20 Mortimer Street, London W1T 3JW &
Sydney – Level 17, 207 Kent St, Sydney NSW 2000 Australia
www.welbeckpublishing.com

A CIP catalogue record for this book is available
from the British Library

Paperback ISBN: 978-1-78739-919-8
Ebook ISBN: 978-1-78739-920-4

Printed and bound by CPI Group (UK) Ltd., Croydon, CR0 4YY

10 9 8 7 6 5 4 3 2 1

To my husband.
You are the rock in the storm.

ONE

Something wakes her; perhaps it's a bird's cry in her ears, or the pink of the sun that's edged over the horizon and into her eyes. Or maybe it's pain; her feet are hurting. She blinks, looks down and realises that her feet are bare and submerged in the cold shallow silt of the riverbank. She's dressed herself in leggings and a jacket, but has removed her boots and socks, which are placed next to her on the wooden boardwalk. She took care, obviously, not to get them wet, but on closer inspection, they look muddy. She puts her hand to the pocket in her leggings and feels a key – she has brought it, thank God, but she hasn't got her phone.

She knows where she is at least. For years, the water-meadows were a favourite place to come; a patchwork of wild-flower-rich grasslands and woodland, criss-crossed by waterways. When they were young she and her brother used to come to throw sticks into the water, watch the birds that would stalk through the reeds, and pick at the flowers that dressed the meadow like jewels. As teenagers, they used to swim further down, in the deeper part of the river opposite the farm, but those days are all long gone.

She needs to get home, quickly, before anyone sees her. She lifts her feet cautiously, wary not to disturb the riverbed any more than she has already done so. People throw anything into water and assume that whatever they wish to be hidden will be concealed forever, but she knows almost anything can be found beneath the surface if you're trained in how to look for it.

She sits on the wooden boardwalk to try to get the worst of the dirt from her feet before shoving her boots back on, and then walking fast, squinting against the rising sun which stains the sky gold. The wind rushes through her hair, and the bulrushes, and there's a humming in her ears, distant and insect-like. She wraps the jacket tighter around herself, starts to jog. She needs to get back to Sam before he notices she's gone.

'Mum?'

She's woken him by enveloping his little body in her arms.

'You smell of the outside,' he says.

'I know.'

She's washed hurriedly, is wearing her pyjamas now, but he can tell that she's been out. They share the same love of fresh air, of water, of the outdoors. Sometimes they talk about the smell of the grass, the sea, the soil. He shares her very soul too. She wishes she could jar the scent of him now; the damp sweetness of his hair.

'And you're cold,' he says.

'I know, sorry,' she replies, but she doesn't move her arms. She couldn't even if she tried because he's hugging them tightly and he doesn't want her to move them – she's never usually a 'cuddly' parent, so he's milking it for all it's worth.

Thank God, she whispers in her head. Thank God that she remembered to lock the door before she left the flat. She knows that there could have been anyone who had happened to step out of their flat at the same time as she had, and taken advantage of an open door. Because she *has* left it open before and this *is* the kind of place where a stranger might take the opportunity. She berates herself – all the locks on the property and for what? Her treacherous walking has her travelling open-eyed yet totally blind to the fact she's left the only precious thing in her life, six-year-old Sam, alone.

'Go back to sleep,' she says softly and kisses him on the cheek.

'You take Piggy,' he says.

'OK.'

She lifts the toy cow that he calls Piggy from beside him, and then she creeps out, goes to the kitchen. She's starving, is always hungry after sleepwalking. She opens the cupboard, makes herself a Pot Noodle and then takes a carrot from the fridge, eats it raw, to balance the E-numbers.

The walking is nothing new. When Jen was around eight, her mother regularly used to find her standing by the fridge blankly eating bread and drinking milk straight from the carton, or in Bill's room seeming to read books which were never even open. For a while, they all found it funny, but then Jen started walking further; round the block to her best friend's house, to the park. When she was eleven, a neighbour just happened to find her walking up the middle of the road, wearing her pants and a hoodie and nothing else, and delivered her back, both of them in a state of absolute panic. Their mother started taking it more seriously after that, but however many locks she put on the door, however many obstacles she put in the way for Jen to potentially trip over and wake up, Jen continued to walk.

When she was thirteen, her brain found a loop it liked – through the little streets of the town, then following the lanes up into the belt of trees, out to the fields and past the big house on the hill, through the water-meadows and following the river, past the farm, and then back again. It's where she thinks she's gone tonight, but she's never woken *in* the water before. She could almost laugh that even in her supposed sleeping hours, she had found the water again. She's called to it like a lover. If she was a poet or writer, maybe she'd attribute her love for it as being an unconscious memory of her mother's womb, but she's not a poet and her mother is very much not in her life any more, so to hell with that theory.

The morning light now slices through the kitchen window and she's thankful that she's got Sunday ahead of her with Sam, with no jobs to respond to yet because she just came off one yesterday – only nine hours ago. She'll take him to the new climbing wall in the next town, and for a burger after. She prays Idris won't text her.

But in less than forty-eight hours, he will text, and everything will change.

TWO

The message comes in as it always comes in – his name in capital letters on her phone screen, with the minimal, yet crucial, details.

> *Caucasian woman, blonde, 5'7", 34, declared missing this morning. Suspicious sighting in the river by member of public an hour ago – matches description. Come to base.*

It's five in the evening on Monday and Jen needs to leave the flat as soon as she can. She flits between the kitchen and the bedroom, sorting the rest of the week's school uniform for Sam and, with her phone clamped between her shoulder and chin, trying to sort childcare. Sam's father is an impossibility, and her best friend Kerry isn't answering her phone, but, to be fair, she's looked after Sam enough over the last few months. Jen calls her brother even though she'd rather not because Bill's stressed at the moment with the build he's managing, and he stresses her out in turn. She has, however, limited resources, and clearly she's stressed anyway because she's sleepwalking.

'Can you watch Sam for a bit?' she says when he picks up. 'It's for a job.'

'Hi,' he says pointedly because she always forgets the pleasantries.

'Yeah, hi,' she says. 'Is that OK?'

'How long for?'

She looks at Sam, who watches *Transformers* and eats dry Shreddies from a bowl on his lap.

'I don't know, obviously.'

He pauses.

'Bill? Is that OK?'

'I'm sort of busy,' he says. 'The site, you know . . . but, no, it's fine. I can help out. Where's your job?'

'Local apparently. A woman was declared missing this afternoon.'

The town and neighbouring villages are built on a complex system of waterways and it's not uncommon that people fall into them by mistake or when drunk. She hasn't dived here for a job for a year or so, though. Doubtless there will be a lot of wading tonight.

Bill asks her more questions, none of which she can answer, before there's a bang on the door. She jumps, even though she knows it's him.

'Fuck's sake,' she says, and opens it. 'You'll take the door off the hinges.'

'Not with the amount of locks you've got on it,' he grins.

The phone is still at his ear, but now he drops it to his side. There are definite benefits to living minutes away from Bill, but there are also definite drawbacks. He comes over drunk at stupid hours of the morning, vomits on her sofa, but, most annoyingly, he tries to set her up with his friends.

She looks to the living room, to Sam. 'Keep your voice down.'

Bill was the one that suggested adding locks to her front door to prevent her from sleepwalking when it started up again nine months ago, and she did, but she opens them all in her sleep anyway – a padlock, a combination lock, a latchkey and a security chain.

'Maybe I should lock you in from the outside,' he muses. 'Like a safe room.'

'Sounds more like a prisoner.'

He wanders through to the living room and sits down, a Rottweiler of a man, next to her small son.

'Thanks, I owe you one.'

'You owe me so much more than one,' he says.

It's true, she does.

'How long?' he asks again.

She picks up her bag by the front door. 'I really don't know,' she says. 'Could be days? Could be a week? Depends what happens first – we find a body or we run out of the money funding the search.'

'Hmm.'

'I'm sorry.'

'I'll work it out. With Kerry or whatever.'

'Yeah, or Denise,' Jen says. Denise is one of – actually, the only – school mum friends Jen has. She literally doesn't have time to make any others. 'I'll email the school and ask if they can take him in for after-school club for a while.'

'That would be good, yeah.'

'And I'll buy you a lot of beer. Actually, no, you drink enough. I'll buy you chocolate.'

'Right, give me high cholesterol instead.'

She smiles and thinks, not for the first time, that the closest person to her has always been, and will forever be, her big brother. The one person that she can call on night or day, the one person that would have her back in a fight even if she'd already lost it. The one person who understands her for all that she is.

'You work out in the gym every day.'

'Not because I want to,' he says. 'I hate the gym and all the tossers in it.'

'It's because they're young.'

'Fuck off,' he mouths before turning to Sam. 'What's this, Samster? Optimus Prime? Awesome.'

'OK, I'm going.'

'Wait,' he says. 'You got any cash?'

She pauses. 'Oh, I— Sure.'

He looks sideways, at her bookshelf. 'For if I want to take Sam out or whatever? It's not payday for ages.'

It's his tell when he doesn't meet her eyes. He's never got any money, even though he earns probably three times what she does. Sometimes she asks him about it, other times she knows not to. Today is not a day to start talking about debts – not when she's in his.

'I'll transfer some money into your account for some food and bits.'

He looks back at her then, flashes a smile. 'Thanks.'

'Love you,' she says to the both of them and she kisses the top of Sam's head. She feels the immediate crushing guilt for leaving him and for keeping such odd hours, for sending him to Tea and Toast Club in the mornings and to clubs after school, for asking her brother to pick him up, or Kerry to have him. 'Be good for Bill, OK?'

'Love you, Mum,' he replies, but his eyes don't leave the screen and she's glad of it. Let him live in a world of *Transformers* able to save the day.

It's all about touch. Under the water where a diver goes, there is little to no visibility at all. You are alone in the black and in the cold, often pitted against tides or risk of entanglement and knocking debris, and you can't even rely on your own eyes to help you. A diver recovers things with their fingertips: lost property, sunken vehicles, weapons, bodies.

'If you've got an overactive imagination, you'll be in trouble,' one of her dive instructors had laughed, and in the years since, that's proved definitely true. She's lost count of how many branches or reeds under the water have touched her on the shoulder in the blackness and she's almost freaked out.

Jen would make for an interesting dinner guest, if she ever had time for it – she could tell people about the time a letter was found in a bag that had lain for three weeks underwater and a laser was able to read fingerprints on it, how she uncovered a murder weapon, a knife that, despite being underwater for two months, had samples of the victim's blood on it. It didn't wash away. The truth rarely does.

She would never recount what they think they want to know about – the times where she's dived for bodies.

'Come on, you can tell me,' Bill often says. 'I've seen loads of shitty things.'

But she doesn't, and she won't. Even Bill, with the tattoo on his back, the highest grading in karate, a man who prides himself on being unshockable, wouldn't be able to stomach Jen's experience with the little girl who fell overboard from a barge and got caught up in a motor. He wouldn't want to know about the teenager who was playing dare with friends and got swept away down a weir. He wouldn't hear about the baby who had drowned when a car went over a bridge. No, Bill wouldn't want to know any of that. Who would?

Jen has been a full-time police diver for nine years – qualifying after the expected two-year stint on police First Response. She never wanted to be a normal police officer, the goal was always to be in the water because she simply loves it: the variety of environments, the variety of cases. She's never involved in the 'whys' of an investigation, only the hunting of what's crucial to solve them. Divers do a job and then they move on, rarely finding out the resolutions of a case they've searched for, and Jen likes it that way; she likes being part of the police force but minus the relentless and depressing day-to-day grind.

That's not to say that they don't become emotionally invested *whilst* on the job. She doesn't forget the bodies and she often dreams about the first time she was called out to find one. There was a fire at an abandoned mill where five kids had escaped the flames they had started by jumping out of a tall, glassless window into a fast-flowing river below. The dive team searched for hours, and found them all in various places down the river – one boy was found alive, mute with shock and cold, and clinging to rocks. When they were done, they went to the fire station with the fire crew and they all slept on the floor. Jen remembers crying until dawn broke while one of the firefighters stroked her hair.

There's nowhere underwater you can think of that a diver hasn't been or won't go: the sea, in lakes and rivers, canals, sewers and wells. A police diver is someone who craves a very particular type of challenge, and who has a deep drive for success against the odds. A person who is comfortable being claustrophobic. Jen's unit covers a vast area, so she's away a lot, which she loves and hates in equal measure since having Sam. She aches with the decision of if she should change to go to a part-time unit elsewhere, or go back to being a regular police officer and work in a less demanding role.

'But then you wouldn't be Superhands,' he's said before when she's asked him. 'I like telling my friends about you. Their mums do boring jobs: you're the coolest one.'

She loves his pride in her.

'Make us a cuppa, Jen?' Joe says when she steps up into the dive lorry.

She rolls her eyes. 'You think you can treat me like you treat your long-suffering girlfriend?'

He laughs.

'Are we waiting for Gareth?'

'When are we ever *not* waiting for Gareth?' Idris mutters.

Gareth is on his third marriage and this one is looking perilous too. It's only been three months, but they're taking bets on when he requests an MSD – a Marriage Saving Day. When she first joined the force, she thought an MSD was a joke. It's not. Lord knows this is a tough job to do while you're married, not that Jen would know.

'And me,' Oliver pipes up. 'Extra sugar.'

'I'll take one and all,' adds Liam.

'Joe's volunteered himself,' Jen says.

Joe sighs, gets up, but makes it only a step to the kettle before Gareth crashes inside the lorry.

'Sorry, sorry.'

'Tea is off the menu, boys,' Idris says.

He always calls them all boys, forgets Jen isn't, but she doesn't care. These men have all seen her naked when they've been changing in the lorry, seen her at her absolute physical and mental and emotional worst, just as she's seen them at theirs. They're all immune to one another, in the way family are immune to the bad bits. Like Bill, they've become her brothers, and they take her the way she is.

She knows so much about her team – she knows that Amir's wife makes him coconut pancakes every Saturday morning when he's home, she knows Joe cheats at cards because she's been on the receiving end of it too many times, she knows Idris is in training for his fifth Ironman, she knows Gareth wants to write a fantasy book, Liam writes software in his spare time and that Oliver's sister has a guide dog called Pebble. But they all know very little about Jen. Men don't ask, they assume anything worth voicing will be voiced, and she's fine with that. She doesn't particularly want them to know her because she's got a past she's not especially comfortable with.

They strap themselves in and the lorry starts up. She listens to them talk about what they'll do when this job is done – if another isn't already lined up, which it mostly always is. Joe wants to build a climbing frame for his nephew; Liam wants to patch up the chicken coop; Amir is going to smoke a bass on his new barbecue. She feels a pang of jealousy at hearing of their summer plans in their gardens. Her flat doesn't have a garden so she takes Sam to the park. What she wouldn't give for even a scrub of grass for him to play in. It was always her intention to move out and find a place with more space, but the closest she's ever got to it is scrolling Rightmove.

'Why would you ever want to leave?' Bill always says. 'My flat is round the corner and we're right in town!'

But above her flat is a couple who fight, and on the other side is a teenager who plays computer games all through the night. Sometimes she allows herself to think about Sam's father – simultaneously a rose and a thorn in her backside – and what it might feel like to live with him; to lie in his feather-down bed, to walk barefoot in the fresh-cut grass of his garden, to sit at the kitchen breakfast bar with a glass of expensive wine and watch him make dinner with the food he has delivered from M&S, but a man like him doesn't end up with a woman like her – she should know that by now. But there's always a what if, isn't there?

Every time she sees him over that one coffee once a month, his eyes, gemstone bright blue, pluck at the strings of her heart and she dares herself to imagine that someday he'll tell her that they should be a family. But these are daydreams; she's not likely to move in with him, or anywhere else at this rate, she thinks. She'll always be Jenny from the block. She almost laughs out loud.

'All right, Jen?' Idris says.

They're all staring at her. Maybe she *had* laughed out loud.

'Yup.'

The lorry stops.

'Short trip?' Liam comments.

'Listen.' Idris ignores him and looks at his phone for the report details. 'As I said in my text, a dog-walker saw something "ominous" at the river at four, phoned it in.'

'Where?'

'Near Cowell Farm, where the river splits into three channels.'

Jen blinks. 'Cowell Farm? That's near where I live? Are we at Cowell Farm?' She can't see out of the lorry because there are no windows.

'We're diving at night for "ominous"?' Joe mutters.

'It coincides with Control Room having had a report of the missing woman who lives about thirty minutes' walk from here straight up and through the water-meadows. Caucasian, thirty-four, five foot seven, blonde. Matches the description of what the dog-walker thinks they saw. And we have a name.'

They all fall quiet, expectant.

'Claudia Franklin.'

The breath leaves Jen's body like she's been punched.

'What?' she asks after a second. 'I . . . I didn't hear the second name.'

'Franklin. Claudia Franklin.'

Idris starts reading Claudia's profile out loud, but Jen can't hear him because all she can hear is the rush of her heartbeat in her ears. She has a split second to say something – to declare a conflict of interest, because she knows Claudia. More than knows her.

She keeps her mouth shut.

THREE

It's been twenty-four hours since the news broke and Bill hasn't been able to tear himself away from updates. He sits in the office, the blue of his phone screen glowing back into his eyes with the headlines shouting: *Missing: Claudia Franklin.*

The words and all the connotations they bring spin around and around in his head. There are divers out at the river looking for her – what the hell does it all mean? He wills Jen to contact him; he's called her countless times, but she's not picking up.

He watches the news reporter on screen, outside Claudia's childhood house, sees the summer wind whip her hair back. He can almost hear it, the song of the wind through those tall birch trees. He knows that house, knows the grounds of it like the back of his hand.

The reporter starts to talk.

'A report was made by a member of the public yesterday afternoon of a suspicious-looking object in the water, prompting a dive search for local woman Claudia Franklin. Claudia moved back with her husband, Mark Mason, to her childhood hometown of Bourne after twelve years spent in Chicago and, later, Boston. She was last seen by Mr Mason at home here, at Oak House, at five on Saturday evening before he left – alone – to go to his parents overnight.'

The video cuts to the appeal made this morning by her husband, who looks gaunt and red-eyed.

'It's completely out of character for her not to be here, or not answering any calls. I just want to know that she's safe.'

The reporter continues: 'Claudia Franklin's bank accounts have not been used since Saturday morning and her phone signal was last picked up at Oak House on Saturday evening. Her husband has confirmed that Claudia's belongings remain at their house except for her phone and laptop which are missing. Police are appealing to anyone who knows Claudia, or who might recently have seen her, to please come forward.'

The video is spliced once again by Mark Mason. 'She's a bright and brilliant woman. We're meant to leave for Paris in two weeks for the Olympics and she's been so excited about it.'

Bill turns off the phone, chews his nails. It's a disgusting habit but one that he can't seem to break because it's a nervous tick, something to do with his hands when he feels out of place. He's done it since he was a child and phones weren't invented to distract his fingers.

'Bill?'

Bill looks to the door of the portable office, where Andy, the site manager, stands.

'The steel's going in on the last house,' Andy says. 'I know how you love a steel.'

Bill nods. 'I'll come.'

He's always present for the final steel of a house going in: besides, he needs the distraction. He almost missed one earlier in the construction and was clammy with sweat when he finally reached the site. He berated Andy for not waiting longer for him and Andy laughed because he doesn't understand the tradition that Bill holds in his own head. No, it's more than tradition – maybe it's superstition because if he misses one going in, what will happen to the house? Perhaps it'll fall down, perhaps someone will be crushed. He's obsessive about site safety, is constantly gobbling up stories online about accidents: people falling from heights, defective equipment and vehicles overturning.

Last night, while at Jen's house when Sam was asleep, and Bill was blissfully innocent at the time about Claudia's missing person report, he'd read a post about a concrete stairwell collapsing, which crushed three workers beneath it. It took hours to hook up a crane big enough to help, and when eventually it started to move the rubble, the pull snapped and it dropped the stairwell straight onto another worker who had gone in to try to recover one of the men underneath. Bill wanted to gag. He tells himself that he reads all these things because he can prepare for every eventuality and make notes on safety procedures, but it's not only that – it's a need for gruesome detail and it's become addictive, horrible, fascinating. It's like self-torture. It's like gambling.

There are some days he's wanted to jack in being a foreman and work for someone else so they can shoulder all his anxieties. He's even gone so far as interviewing for other jobs – he went for one recently for a multi-million-pound business, wore a suit and tie, but hasn't heard back yet, and maybe he never will. Maybe he doesn't want to work for someone else anyway, because Andy is a good and fair boss, but Bill is on borrowed time with Andy, though Andy doesn't yet know it. Bill prays he never will. He's reminded that he needs to sort the email that came in earlier from the client who's bought house number two – he's now paid a large deposit on the build and Bill needs to carefully cipher this away for a week.

He crosses the site, looks up to the crane which holds the steel and watches it raise its arm. For the last nine months, his team has been working on the twenty luxury houses which have views of the South Downs. Most of them have been bought off plan already, and he covets one of the left-over three, but he doesn't have three million in the bank. He has about three hundred because he's a spender, oh man, is he a spender.

'Yup,' he says to everyone and no one in particular. 'Good.'

His phone bleeps from inside his pocket, makes him jump, and he snatches it out hoping it might be Jen, but it's an alarm telling him that he needs to pick up Sam from school again. Jesus, why did he say yes to looking after Sam?

Bill is aware that his nephew is talking to him since he barrelled out of the school gates, but he luckily seems oblivious to Bill's distraction. They walk past the town's many gift shops and hair salons, past the M&S and the bookies on the corner that has become a regular haunt but Bill doesn't really see any of it. Only Claudia's face in his mind's eye.

There's a tug at his sleeve. 'Uncle Bill?'

'Hmmm?'

'Am I staying at Kerry's tonight?'

'You bet,' Bill says and smiles at his nephew.

Poor kid is continually confused because he's continually passed like a baton between friends' houses, Bill's, Kerry's. But he's robust, adaptable, and the apple of Bill's eye.

'We missed the turn to Tea For Two,' Sam says.

'Oh.'

They turn around, walk back ten yards and go through the cobbled mews and courtyard towards the cafe that Kerry works in.

Sam opens the door to the cafe, runs to Kerry, who sits at the table waiting for them. The cafe is big, wide and open. Crudely varnished wooden tables and fake plants and flowers on shelves, and art that has faded over time. Tinny music plays from speakers on the walls.

'All right, babe?' she says to Sam but also to Bill.

Kerry and Jen have been unwavering best friends since high school, but Bill's relationship with Kerry has been trickier to navigate. Kerry has always made it obvious that she likes Bill in a way that's not platonic and, God help him, she is beautiful, with thick, dark hair and cherry-red lips. He did slip up one night when they were in their mid-twenties and he'd kissed her after a boozy evening at The Hare, but he'll never love her like she wants him to.

'I got us all The Epic,' Kerry says.

Bill sees Sam's eyes light up at the enormous glass vessel in front of them – countless scoops of ice-cream, drizzled with chocolate sauce, squirted with whipped cream, decorated with hundreds and thousands. Wafers, flakes and three silver spoons stick out of the top of it.

'And this,' she says and produces a magazine for Sam.

'Lego! Thank you, Kerry!'

Jen has brought him up with manners, Bill thinks. He's such a great kid.

Sam grabs a spoon and starts to eat, simultaneously turning the pages.

'I thought we could all do with a treat,' Kerry says to Sam, but it's Bill's eyes that she holds. 'Thanks for dropping him here: I can't get away for another hour.'

'Yeah, no trouble,' Bill says. 'Thanks for having him over tonight. I've got a meeting tomorrow that I should really do some prep for.'

'Sure,' she says. 'Are you doing OK?'

'Yeah.'

'Have you heard anything from Jen?'

'No,' he says. 'She's diving.'

He swallows. Diving for Claudia. What the actual fuck. He looks to Sam.

'Is that good, Sammy?'

'So good!' Sam says with his mouth full.

'Are you going to show Kez how to play that Minecraft game later?'

'Yeah!' Sam grins.

Kerry passes Bill a spoon. 'You look like you could use some sugar.'

'I'm fine—'

'I know she meant something to you,' she says quietly. 'Claudia did.'

His gratitude at her kind words snags when he registers the use of the past tense.

'She's not dead.'

'I didn't say that. I said she meant something to you.'

'Yeah.' He tries to smile but can't manage it. 'OK. Thanks. Once, a long time ago. But don't be talking that way, yeah? No one knows what's happened, do they?'

Claudia's face swims in front of his eyes once again – that elfin face and that wide, childlike smile that links to his own boyhood.

'You think her husband did something?'

He frowns. 'I really—'

'It's not every day someone from round here goes missing and is on national TV though, is it?' she says. 'Especially someone like *her*.'

'Shall we talk about something else?'

'If you want.'

They sit in silence, with only the sounds of the pop music blaring, and the rattle of Sam's spoon in and out of the glass.

'Sorry,' Kerry says.

'Sorry,' Bill says at the same time.

She reaches for his hand again, and it's then that he has an idea that makes his stomach churn with guilt.

'It's your birthday coming up, right?'

'Yeah,' she says and smiles, obviously happy because he's remembered – though, of course, he *should* remember because they've been friends for long enough. 'Next week.'

'You doing anything?'

She shrugs. 'Depends who's around. I've not organised anything.'

'We should go out. You, me, Jen. A couple of the guys maybe? To The Black Rat.'

She raises her eyebrows. 'The Black Rat? Really? You're paying?'

'I would pay your share. Not Eddie's, he'd eat everything on the menu if he thought someone else was paying for it.'

She laughs. 'I'm in.'

She looks so happy and surprised at his suggestion that she doesn't notice the falter in his smile. She bends down to Sam, gives him a kiss on the head, and Bill exhales. He needs people – good people like Kerry who will vouch for him.

'Dig in,' she says.

He gulps a ball of ice-cream so fast that it burns down his throat.

No one knows, he thinks. No one knows that he's seen Claudia since her move back to Oak House, that he has been in contact with her.

No one knows what he knows.

FOUR

It's been seventy-two hours and the police are running out of time to find Claudia Franklin alive. Everyone knows the statistics – that the first forty-eight hours are critical in a missing person's case because that's when investigators have the best chance in chasing leads, before people's memories start to fade. After seventy-two hours, the trail begins to cool, and after a week, the objective of finding a live person switches to trying to locate a body.

The dive team's objective is different from the police team on land and always has been – they've always been looking for a body. They've been searching relentlessly, but the river and its many miles of arms is difficult to navigate. The added complication is that if there is indeed a body, it can still move around in the water, depending on the stage of decomposition. It can lie dormant, snagged on a root or in reeds, but if the water is disturbed, the build-up of gases inside can mean it's propelled elsewhere.

The divers have found some things – have been bagging pieces of material and other objects that are foreign to the water, in case of connections, and analysis on these will be timely, and no doubt futile, but they do it nonetheless.

'Lean in.'

Idris surveys the map unrolled on the floor of the dive lorry and they all squat over it.

'This is the old pipe between the marsh into the river,' he says, pointing. 'It wasn't on the original waterway plans we were given because it was cut off a while ago, but, it was never removed because it runs under West Road and it would have been too difficult to close the road to dig it out. There's a grate over it, but maybe it's somehow been displaced, so we need to look.'

They all nod. They know how unlikely it will be that the grate will be loose, let alone that Claudia Franklin will be anywhere near it, but they will leave no stone unturned. A disappearance so close to their town makes them feel worse that they haven't found her.

Guilt gnaws at Jen's insides; she should have declared straight away that she knows Claudia. Failure to declare a personal connection which she knows could have an impact on the investigation could lead to being investigated herself by the professional standards team and she could be suspended. But every chance she gets to rest, every chance she thinks she should tell Idris – which is only an hour or so at a time, and never alone – she justifies keeping the truth to herself that being here with the team is a good thing, that they need her here. If she were to be pulled out of the investigation, the dive team would be short, and therefore less efficient, and therefore the chance of finding Claudia would be narrowed even further.

Besides, she thinks, her history with Claudia was a long time ago and they have nothing to do with each other now. They knew each other for a short, intensive time, and always in the context of water – playing out in the river, in the pool where they used to swim together, and in the kitchen of Oak House with the art installation on one side of the room, a cascading of water which flowed in tiny rivulets down one of the walls. Water had brought them together, but it was also the undoing of their friendship.

Possibly it is also the undoing of Claudia's life.

Idris's voice jogs her out of her thoughts.

'Jen,' he says. 'You're OK to check the pipe? It's small and you're the smallest.'

'Yeah.' She nods.

She gets ready in the lorry. Liam is in charge of her equipment and clothing and he tugs at the zips of the drysuit, wrenches her backwards. He needs to be tough – it's to ensure no water can get in because no one wants to get into the water only to have to come straight out again and waste twenty minutes and a complete change of diver. He fits her mask, her fins, her gloves, everything – it's like being a catwalk model or a child.

'OK?' he says eventually.

She nods and he helps her walk out – the kit on her back is heavier than her entire body weight. Gareth will be her attendant in the water, has already waded out and is waiting for her. Together they will go to the lip of where the marsh falls away into the stagnant pool so she can submerge and locate the entrance of the pipe. Idris and the others look on from waist-deep in the water.

'Good to go?' Idris asks.

Jen nods again, takes the jackstay – the line they use when they're searching – and then submerges. As the water closes around her head, she is immediately transported into the 'other world', as she calls it. Her head, her hands through the gloves, and her ears become wet, but everything else remains dry. When she first started diving this was a strange sensation, but it's normal now after so long in the job. She drops down to the bottom of the pool – it's only a little over six foot – and feels the long weeds below snag at her legs. She knows the team are all up there, watching her bubbles, watching the lifeline, but she's alone now and she likes this part the best – when she can only hear herself breathing and it becomes a new rhythm, like a heartbeat.

Usually, she loves water; the depth and the murk of it, the smoothness of it around her body and its rhythmic calm. She loves how the light plays on the surface of it, but conversely loves the darkness of it, too – in its blackest corners, she imagines that it's a winged horse galloping through the night and she's flying alongside it. She would give herself up to the water if that was ever her last option. People say that drowning is a horrible way to go, but for someone like her, who lives it and loves it, it would be the only way to end things.

Today, however, being in the water makes her lungs constrict with panic. Because she doesn't want to find Claudia down here. She wants Claudia alive and well, because what would it mean if she were dead? Murdered? The victim is almost always killed by those nearest to them and the nearest person to Claudia is her husband, Mark Mason.

Focus.

According to the council plans, the entrance to the pipe is to her right. Jen feels blindly around, soft touches along the bed, and thinks of Sam.

'Don't they give you torches?' he asked once.

'It would be like putting car headlights on in fog,' she explained. 'A torch is useless in water.'

She locates the grating easily, feels the rust of the metal cross-hatch and the slime of the grasses that have been pulled in and have then webbed around the squares. She pulls on the lifeline to tell the team she's found the entrance, and then she puts her fingers into the squares to check it's secured. She knows before she pulls that it's not.

This isn't what she wanted to find – she wanted to feel it taut and bolted, but it swings loose and she knows she must open it out wider so she can fit into the pipe. She pulls the line again and goes inside. There's a loud clanging in her ears as her equipment scrapes the inside of the concrete and the sound frightens her for a moment. Sound travels four times faster in water than it does in the air and it makes her diving sharper, but it can also make it confusing – sometimes you think you hear things that aren't there.

She knows that the pipe is twenty feet along; it goes under the main road before it's cut off. Her fingers graze along the metal. She could be upside down and she'd not know it for the blackness surrounding her. She must be especially careful down here; if the grate has been loose for a long time, there could be a whole collection of things that have made their way inside.

Through the thin gloves, her fingers feel the skeletons of leaves and twigs, feel the algae and clumps of vegetation. There are coins here, pieces of broken glass, a syringe. She's ten feet into the pipe now and can feel vibrations from vehicles passing along the road above her. Sometimes she wonders if she'll ever be crushed underwater doing this job, but there's no point worrying about that now. Her breath is steady, her fingers still caressing the pipe, and then her head bumps into something.

Something is lodged in the pipe, centimetres from her face. Her heart starts to pump wildly and she reaches out to touch it.

It's rigid but simultaneously pulpy under her fingers and she knows from years of practice that this thing she's found was once alive. There are bones – small and delicate – and then she feels herself relax because she knows what this is now. She moves her fingers to feel broken feathers floating in the dark, a long neck, a beak. It's the carcass of a huge bird, perhaps a goose or a swan which has been here for God knows how long. She needs to move past it – just in case – but that's a tricky business.

She manipulates its enormous body and squeezes past, tries not to think that its eyes might be open and that it might be watching her in death. One of its feet brushes her arm, feels like the splayed hand of a child stretching for her, as she goes deeper into the pipe.

But there is nothing else to find.

She comes up out of the water, doesn't say anything to her team, but doesn't need to because they know already that she didn't find Claudia. Thank *fuck*.

She's escorted by Liam to the back of the lorry to be hosed down before she can change out of the suit and get dry. Amir makes everyone tea – they drink a lot of tea in this job – milky, sugary tea that they call 'shock-victim tea'. Idris makes more calls, makes more plans for another dive, and the others sit at the table, three aside.

She pulls clothes out of her rucksack, a heavy-knit jumper over jeans. She can smell the filth of the pipe still on her, wishes she could swim in a chlorinated pool to cleanse herself of it because she loves the chemicals, likes to feel she's not only clean but bleached.

'What now?' Joe says and they all look to Idris.

'We eat,' he replies.

Oliver collects takeaway from the local chippy and they sit in the lorry with the comforting smell of grease and with mugs full again. Gareth texts his wife, whispers the words he's spelling, 'sorry, sorry, I don't know when'. Jen eats in silence, lost in memories of Claudia swirling, dreamlike, around her head, while the others talk around her.

The sun has bled out into the sky now, it'll be dark in the next hour, and Jen wonders what Sam's doing. Has Bill found the bolognese she left in the fridge for the two of them? She forgot to mention it to him and she thinks that maybe he might have taken Sam for chips tonight, and that's OK because she's had the same too and for a moment, she feels closer to the both of them.

'Here,' Gareth says, nods at his phone. 'Mason is doing another appeal for witnesses.'

Jen leans in to watch Gareth's screen, sees the name Mark Mason appear below the image of Claudia's husband. The transformation from his first appearance on Tuesday morning to now – two days later – is unreal. He looks like a completely different person; his face pallid, skin taut against cheekbones. His mouth and the lids of his eyes look weighted, everything pulled downwards to the hell of the unknown, and that's always the hardest thing, Jen thinks, the not knowing. Claudia's family are all stuck, fighting against a tide that's dragging them out to a bottomless, answerless, sea.

'Have the investigative team discounted anyone yet?'

'If they have, they've not told me what's going on,' Idris says.

'If not the husband,' Joe remarks, nodding to the footage, 'then who's done it?'

'*If*,' Jen says. 'If she's dead.'

Joe guffaws. 'What, you think she's gone on holiday and forgotten to tell anyone? Taken none of her stuff?'

'The phone and laptop are missing,' Oli says.

'Right, so she's gone with no clothes but her tech? Come on.'

'If the dog-walker was right about seeing something, maybe she slipped in?' Amir says. 'Maybe she was drunk?'

'She didn't drink,' Jen says and they all look at her.

She swallows hard, realises her mistake.

'I read it about her – in one of her interviews.'

'If she's left out of her own accord, no one in her circle of friends or family seem to know anything about it,' Idris says. 'Not that she had many friends, having lived away so long, and by all accounts, her mother lives abroad.'

Jen nods slowly. She knows that Victoria Franklin had emigrated to Canada years ago and forgot – or, more accurately, discarded – the child that had needed her so desperately.

'Does she know?' she asks.

'Her mother? I guess?'

'I don't trust Mason,' Joe says.

'Why not?'

'Looks shifty.'

'I feel for him,' Amir says. 'If he's innocent in all this, he's got the world watching at exactly the wrong time.'

'No one is officially a suspect, remember,' Idris says. 'There's no body. And even if there is one eventually, our job is then done. We don't investigate. We dive, we find. We move on to the next job.'

Jen gets up, walks out of the lorry, and goes to lean against one of the trees that lines the lane. She's desperate to call Bill or Kerry, for them to give her some stability. Both of them have been lighting up her phone for days, the notifications stacking up like building blocks. She knows Bill is worried about Claudia, like she knows Kerry wants to gossip, but of course, she can't call them back.

She closes her eyes, summons the mantra that she repeats from the app she uses, Tranquil.

I will take on any challenges with a calm head, with rationality.

She needs the headspace to think about the one person she's worried most about in all this. It's not Claudia, it's Mark Mason, Claudia's husband.

Sam's father.

Mark has called her numerous times from the phone that he uses for texting her, one that doubtless he hasn't let on to the police about having, but he hasn't left Jen any voicemails or messages, and she's thankful for it, because although she longs to hear his voice, she can't. For one thing, she's on a job and can't be distracted. For another, she's become increasingly worried that Mark has somehow got something to do with Claudia's disappearance, because what else could have happened? And if he has, what would that mean for her, and for Sam? She's mad that Mark doesn't respect that she can't talk to him and yet at the same time, it's beyond frustrating that she can't just pick up his calls and judge for herself if his voice sounds different, if he seems 'off'.

She's known Mark for years and although her heart is one hundred per cent confident that he would never hurt Claudia, her police head knows that anyone, if pushed to their limits, can tip into a state where primal emotions are unleashed. She's witnessed the switch enough times during her first years on response.

Her police head also reminds her that Mark has only been back in her life for nine months after years of being away, and in those years she's changed, so obviously he must have done.

But she's *seen* him every month, she says to herself. He's still the same magnetic, charismatic, man, isn't he? The question mark floats above her head, the answer for now unknowable.

She hears footsteps behind her and she turns to see Idris is out of the dive lorry and walking towards her.

'You OK?' he asks.

'Yeah. Taking a moment.'

'You mind company?' he says.

'Sure.'

They stand together, both leaning against the coolness of the huge tree. She knows Idris doesn't expect conversation – he's happy enough to be quiet with her. She steals a look at him, feels terrible that she's inadvertently lying to him by keeping her silence about Claudia.

'Guv says we've got until the end of the week and then the money runs out,' he says after a while.

She blinks. 'We're stopping?'

'Either she never went into the water, or she did and now she's moved because of water disturbance and we've missed her while we've been looking elsewhere. We can't continue this indefinitely because of who she is.'

'We'll get some flack for stopping if we don't find her, won't we? She's all over the press.'

'That's because she's beautiful,' he says.

She nods. There's no denying that the beautiful ones always get more airtime – the injustice of beauty privilege.

'Not only because of that, though,' she says.

'No, I know. She was famous, I get it.'

'She was an Olympic diver, and she goes missing two weeks before the next Olympics. It's big news. And fucking weird.'

She swears too much, even within her internal monologue, but it's the job and the men that she works with. Cussing has become a way of releasing all the bad things they see every day and it's cathartic, it's collective bonding, and now she can't seem to stop.

'But we've looked, haven't we?' Idris says. 'We've been out for days. Nothing is fairer than having done our best.'

'I know.'

'And since when did you ever care what people thought?'

'I don't.'

He grins. 'Getting soft in your old age.'

'I'm fifteen years younger than you, Idris.'

He scoffs. 'Haven't seen your name on any of the Ironman boards.'

'Because I'm an Ironwoman,' she says.

'That you are. You want another brew?'

'Thanks,' she says and he nods, and leaves.

She tilts her head up to the branches above her, exhales, and thinks about Mark, and the swan mangled in the darkness of the pipe. She thinks also about the early pink of that Sunday dawn, waking at the water-meadows.

FIVE

Every evening, Bill is the last on site to lock up the offices and the gates that give access to the road, but on a Friday he leaves with all the other men and they go out for a drink at The March Hare. On the way tonight, a few of them – including Bill – stop at the bookies and Bill wins eighty quid on the virtual horses, and then loses a hundred. He's twenty down but feels fine about it. Jen tells him, often, that he's a dick for gambling.

'It's a spiral,' she says. 'That goes straight to the fucking bottom.'

Jen, the solid, stable one out of the two of them. It shouldn't be like that, should it? He's older by two years. But how can Bill explain it to her? The fizz of his heart transcends anything else as he guns for the win. It's living in the moment, it's pure in the way that a drug high is, and wouldn't they rather he was putting the odd tenner down than doing drugs? Christ, he thinks suddenly, what amazing life choices he's given himself.

'I've lost too much,' Jonny says. 'Let's go.'

Bill nods his agreement, but right now he'd rather be anywhere else than walking to the pub. He wants to be with Sam in Jen's flat. Sam is with Kerry tonight, though, and they're probably watching a movie.

He'll have one or two drinks, he thinks, as they approach the pub. He'll go to the bar afterwards, to look normal, and then he'll slip away.

The March Hare is a squat building nestled between the Tesco Express and the garage. In the front is a well-kept lawn, tables with umbrellas, where they usually order burgers from the barbecue, but it's started to drizzle, so today they'll all go inside and eat nachos.

Andy goes straight to the slot machines. Jonny sits back with two of the older guys and they watch some of the younger lads play pool. Bill sits with his pint, stares at the TV for the news, even when the channel is firmly on sports, and tries not to think about Claudia, but, of course, by trying not to think about her, he's thinking about her, willing her into existence.

By rights, they never should have crossed paths. She went to a private all-girls school a few miles away where they all wore dark green blazers and boaters with the school-colour ribbon around them, little patent buckle shoes and knee-length white socks. He and his friends saw groups of them in town on Friday afternoons and it was his friend Jackson who pointed Claudia out to him.

'That one,' he'd said with an appreciative whistle.

She carried a little satchel around with her, battered tan leather, and she always wore it across her right shoulder. Bill watched the way the light played with all the colours of her golden hair, he studied the way she laughed with her friends, and he lay in bed imagining that those eyes would one day be made at him. He overheard people use her name and thought it was the most beautiful name he'd ever heard. He wrote it on his wall behind his bed, in black biro. He wanted to draw a heart around it but thought Jen would laugh at him for it.

Claudia's life was a repetition of pony club meets, swimming galas and sampling different hummuses, whilst he came from the estate, rode a grubby second-hand bike and genuinely believed that the limp gherkins in his McDonald's burgers would see him through his five a day. She didn't have the hard weight of finance pinning her down like he did, but instead of resenting her for it, he'd always loved that about her – she was like something otherworldly, and the very thought of her was his own piece of escapism.

He still remembers the first time he talked to Claudia properly. It was the sixteenth of April 2004, when they were both fifteen, and she'd dropped a book she was carrying and he'd shouted out to her before his brain told him not to.

'Hey, Claudia!'

She'd turned, looked at him, and he'd picked up the book and waved it at her.

'Oh,' she said, stepped towards him and smiled. 'Thanks—?'

'Bill.'

'Thanks, Bill. How did you know my name?'

'Every boy in this town knows your name.'

She smiled. 'Do they?'

'Yeah.'

'Well,' she said, 'now I know yours too.'

That was the entire exchange, but the sound of his name on her lips, and the brown of her eyes meeting his, kept him high for a week. From that day, he would engineer his schedule to try to bump into her in town after school on a Friday, pass her house on the weekends even though it was a forty-minute walk away, but it was six long months before he drew up the courage to ask her to the river at Cowell Farm.

'Do you like swimming?' he said.

She was alone outside a cafe in town, her gaggle of glittery friends having already filtered inside, and he'd seized the opportunity.

She had frowned. 'What?'

'Do you like swimming?'

'Actually, I prefer diving. I used to be a county champion,' she said.

He blinked. 'Serious?'

'Yeah,' she shrugged. 'For Sussex, when I was nine. Before my granddad died and we moved to Oak House.'

'Wow,' he said.

'You weren't expecting that, were you?' she replied with a wink.

'I . . . no,' he said and then laughed. She'd taken the wind out of his sails – something she would do for many years to come. Constantly surprising him. 'Why did you give it up?'

'There were other things I got interested in,' she said and then left a beat. 'Boys, mostly.'

'I'm a boy who swims,' he said. 'That counts as double points.'

'Does it?' She grinned.

'Sometimes I go swimming down by the farm.'

She cocked her head. 'That's near my house.'

'Is it?'

'Are you asking me on a swimming date?'

'I'm asking if you want to come swimming,' he said. 'Totally different thing.'

'In October?'

With every question she asked, he sank deeper into the quicksand of doubt. He hoped she wouldn't see that he was beginning to tremble with the effort of appearing casual.

'It's not too cold,' he said.

She paused. 'Sure. Why not?'

And she came. On the Saturday, she waved to him from her bike, dressed in leggings and a thick jumper – a rich olive wool – and then she'd stripped off in the sharp coldness of that morning to reveal a hot-pink, high-legged one-piece.

'Put your tongue back in,' Jen had said next to him in the water, because she had come too, and some of his other friends also, because Bill hadn't wanted to scare Claudia away. He'd wanted her to feel at ease with him, see him for what he really was – a boy with freckles on his face, who loved the water and spending time with friends, and making jokes. A boy that she might think was worth spending time with.

'Look at her, though,' he'd breathed. 'She's like one of those siren things we read about in English.'

'Oh my God, Bill, you're such a dick,' Jen had said, and she dipped backwards in the river and laughed into the water.

But what a vision Claudia was in that pink costume, like some sort of exotic bird. She was an excellent swimmer too, graceful and deft. When her back was turned to him, he would marvel at the way her hair fanned out in blonde ribbons in the water, soak in the perfect arch of her feet when she jumped the banks. She was game to rock-hop further upstream, to race against the pull of the current, to laugh freely with people she'd never hung out with before, and he thought that was her attraction – that she was totally and completely herself, apparently, with anyone. God, he'd never been as enchanted by a person before or since that moment.

Obsessed, Jen called it, but she's always been able to call out the truth, especially his. He wonders now what might have happened to him had he never invited Claudia that day.

'It's eleven,' Jonny says, ripping him from the memories. 'We all going to O'Neill's or what?'

'Yup,' Bill replies.

Jonny calls over to the younger lads and there's a resounding cheer from them, and for a second Bill almost believes that this is an ordinary Friday night, where he can go out and get wasted and then in the morning can go to the gym and sweat out all the booze. But tonight is not ordinary. Tonight, when all his workmates will have drunk enough to provide him with an alibi at the bar, he'll be somewhere else.

It's close to midnight and he's come to Oak House, Claudia's home. He knows from Jen that the resources for stationing cars outside properties are nil and this is only done in films. Nevertheless, he doesn't dare scout out the front of the house to see if there are indeed any police cars in the drive or up the lane.

He's come on foot, confident even in the dark, because he knows which fields to cross, which trees to pass, where to slip through the thick conifer hedgerow, through to where the fence panel isn't quite secure, and then he walks in the blackest of shadows down past the red-brick summerhouse. He glances at it as he passes, reminisces that this is where he used to meet Claudia sometimes when she asked him to. It's also where he came sometimes when she *didn't.*

He walks on, heart banging, towards the stable door that leads into the boot room as Victoria Franklin grandly named it. He can get in without making noise. He's a builder, he knows how to open doors when they lock unexpectedly, when they're stuck. He sidles up to it, takes a pick and the lock gives way immediately. He pushes it with gloved hands and walks right in.

He knows that Mark will be out tonight at a function, an hour away by car, and was due to stay in a hotel overnight, but that assumption was made before everything was turned on its head – when mistakes were made and everything went to shit, and so Bill has to confront the possibility that Mark *could* be at home and what will he do if he is? But Bill is desperate. He needs to find this envelope, needs this money.

He wonders what sort of man he is now, to be breaking and entering a house where a woman is missing, rumoured dead. What sort of a man is he now, to be gambling with something that's gone way over his head.

The boot room smells of mud and earth, of wellington boot rubber and of running trainers. The floor is stone, slippery, and he almost turns his ankle on a piece of folded cardboard recycling that's out of the box by the floor. Bill catches himself before he stumbles and then hastily switches on his phone for the torch light. He cautiously opens the door to the kitchen, pushes it.

The layout hasn't changed, that same beautiful quartz stone kitchen island, the duck-egg blue Aga with the oak beam above it. The décor is largely the same too, but there are new pictures – lots of modernist artwork and black-and-white photography. Lots of pictures of water. The cascade is still there, the noise of it comforting, soothing, and rhythmic. He wants to pause time and allow himself to recall the carefree and languid days that he came here with Jen when they were teenagers. He used to think how strange it was that Claudia opened her home to the two of them; thought initially that it was because she was a lonely only child, or that it was in quiet rebellion to her mother and stepfather to invite people from the 'town' and not of their own social standing, though that turned out not to be true, because Victoria and Henry couldn't have been nicer to Jen and Bill. God, he can't think of them now without a pinching sadness.

On one wall is a picture of Claudia, a black-and-white photograph of the back of her head, with droplets glinting on her hair and shoulders and, in the background, a sheet of water, flat like glass. It was taken when she was on holiday in Ibiza, Bill knows. She was heavily into the Olympic training regime by then, but Victoria and Henry had insisted that she take a week's break and holiday with them. He remembered that he laughed when Claudia told him that she was worried about going, said he couldn't imagine anything worse than his mum begging him and Jen to go abroad and enjoy a five-star, paid-for holiday. Claudia had squeezed his arm then. 'Sorry,' she'd said. 'I know I sound like an ungrateful bitch. But Victoria . . . she's being so shitty with me, honestly. I just want to stay here and train. Why don't you stick a wig on and go as me?'

'Fuck off,' he'd said. 'I don't do blonde.'

He walks slowly out of the kitchen and into the stone-tiled hallway. There was never an alarm system in place when he used to visit, but that was years ago, so he needs to be cautious. But with every step, there's nothing that tells him that anyone is alerted to his presence. He glances out of the window of the hallway. Mark's car isn't in the driveway and Bill breathes a sigh of relief.

Bill passes the large redwood grandfather clock under the huge staircase that he recalls having a conversation about with Claudia a long time ago that every time the clock stopped, someone in the family died – a shared joke that doesn't seem to be funny any more.

It's not stopped now though. It's ticking an angry beat, like it knows he's there, trespassing.

He goes to the study, to the one place that the envelope could be – the safe.

He's prepared for the study door to be locked, but it isn't. Perhaps with the police having been in and out over the last week, Mark has left everything open for transparency, for ease, but whatever it is, it's luck for Bill. The room is large, with a high ceiling and panelled with white wood, and the starkness makes him feel vulnerable even though the curtains are drawn and the lights are off.

He opens the low, unassuming cupboard where the safe is kept and kneels next to it. It's highly possible that the police have cracked into this already, but they would have needed special permission for it and he's banking on the fact that it's only been four days and Claudia is still only 'missing'.

The safe is a huge black matte box with a six-digit code, and he taps in the code – 211298 – the date her beloved first cat died. He wonders who else knows this combination. Does Mark? The lock turns, making a mechanic whirl that sounds like a drill in the silence. He opens the door, looks inside.

There is a stack of papers and he removes them, sifts through the pages, but there's no envelope between them like there should be, and the hope in his heart plummets. He goes through them all again, slower this time, because he might have missed it, but he knows that it's not there. Frustrated, he locks the safe up, and then stands, stares around the study. What if she had removed the envelope? What if Mark knew the code and has removed it? If so, where might he have put it?

He goes to the desk. Claudia's stepfather, Henry, used to work in here, but his old heavy writing desk has been replaced by a sleek white wooden one with a white monitor and keyboard on top of it and a framed picture of Claudia in a swimsuit. Bill pauses at this before pulling open drawers, fingering through files, and paperwork and receipts, but there is nothing, nothing, and he starts to get more frantic, more worried, less quiet. If he can't find it, then all of it will have been in vain. But after ten minutes at the desk, and then another five minutes sweeping the shelves for box files, the feeling of despair is overwhelming.

It's not there. And then he thinks, was it ever? Was it a trick?

He can't risk searching other rooms, but he does need to secure one thing – he walks quickly to the dining room and, from the oak Welsh dresser drawer, he takes the key to the back door. He will need to try again here, when he can. Just like old times, he thinks, and he shouldn't force the lock too many times.

Suddenly, a rectangle of light cuts through the dining-room curtains, and roves across the ceiling, and he can hear the undeniable crunch of tyres on gravel driveway. Is that Mark back from the dinner? Bill can't pause to find out. He races through the house, unlocks the back door and bolts through it, relocking it with shaking fingers, and then he's out and away, back through the fence panel and into the belt of trees.

SIX

Bill meets Kerry at Jen's flat at midday so they can swap Sam. It's the worst timing ever but Bill, of course, can't say no to looking after him because everything has to look normal.

'You look like a zombie,' Kerry says when he opens Jen's door. 'Heavy night?'

'You know the lads on a Friday night.'

'Sam, you might need some sort of a mask to breathe through Uncle Bill's fug.'

'Urgh,' Sam says, but he smiles and slips through the door to go to his room and empty out his toys from the overnight bag on the floor.

Bill looks at Kerry, suddenly feels the need for familiarity. 'Will you stay for a bit?'

Kerry shakes her head. 'I can't, Ricky has a new coffee machine he needs to show me before my shift starts.'

'Oh.'

'I know, that man has all the moves. He asked me out again last week.'

She waits a beat, waits for Bill to react and he knows why she wants a reaction from him. She wants to know that he feels strongly about her going on a date with someone, but everyone knows that Ricky is a dick and literally *no one* should go on a date with him.

'I said no, *obviously*.' She grins and then reaches for his arm. 'It's . . . well I remembered that it's Fiona's birthday tomorrow. Or, it would have been. I know Jen usually makes a cake to mark it. Can you two do something? I'm sorry I didn't have time this morning.'

Fiona's birthday. His mother. It hits him like a cold slap in the face, which Kerry appears to see. She leans in to kiss his cheek, and he knows the gesture is meant to soothe, because every year this day stings. Fiona is cold in the ground.

'Thanks, Kerry. You always remember.'

She squeezes his arm. 'Of course.'

Here is the moment he has needed to ask her what he needs to.

'Kerry,' he says. 'Before you go.'

'Yeah?'

'Last Saturday.'

Her eyes narrow. 'What about it?'

'It was the day that Claudia was last seen. I was working late at the site.'

She pauses. 'OK?'

'I . . . shit, this is going to sound really fucking weird.'

'What?'

'I need to ask you a favour.'

The cake is on the kitchen counter and Bill stares at it, wants to eat a slice. He and Sam spent the afternoon making it to mark yet another birthday Fiona won't see – a chocolate monstrosity – and then they licked the bowl and spoon clean, danced around the kitchen to Capital FM, before Bill complained he didn't have the knees for it. He put Sam in the bath and bet on a football match while Sam splashed around with toy sharks, and then put him to bed. It had been a normal day when Bill doesn't feel normal at all.

His phone pings and he looks at the screen.

Love you, Kx

He feels bad for asking Kerry to help him, but it's necessary. It's the only way to tie any loose threads together or, if the worst comes to the worst, to stall investigation before he has a chance to get away with what he needs to.

He replies back, as he always does to Kerry's effusive messages, with text speak – *Luv u2!* because it's somehow less meaningful and diluted. Though the chances are that she'll read more into it than ever.

He opens the fridge because Jen always makes nice stuff for Sam, and Bill is a self-confessed lazy arse with no culinary imagination. He eats when he's worried, which is most of the time, and that's why he's always at the gym pumping weights. The fridge light pings on, dazzles him momentarily before he spots a bolognese at the back. He gets a fork from the drawer and eats it cold from the dish, simultaneously thumbing through the post on Jen's sideboard which is stacked in a precarious tower. He starts to sort the promotional flyers from the letters that she actually needs to read – they used to do this for their mum and so it's habit now, that they do these things for each other, little things that keep the other's world turning. He knows she keeps his world on the right axis more than he keeps hers, though. She's got him out of many holes before now, out of trouble, out of debt, though not even his pragmatic and sensible sister will be able to get him out of the trouble he's in now.

He bins the junk mail and then places the neat bundle by Jen's row of cookbooks. She's got a new one – a new Jamie Oliver that probably promises creating a masterpiece in under sixty seconds – and he pulls it out. He likes looking at the spreads of Jamie and his family because they look wholesome and carefree. Jen's also got the Jamie Christmas book somewhere and he remembers that in 2018 they poured over those spreads, both of them drunk and wearing paper crowns that wilted on their heads. He thinks that was his favourite Christmas in a long time, the three of them: him and Jen and Sam, watching *The Gruffalo* and *The Highway Rat* and eating handfuls of Celebration chocolates in the matching onesies that Jen had got custom made for them all. Sam's read 'Captain Awesome' on the back, hers was 'Superhands', and Bill's read 'Dickhead', and they had all laughed until their eyes streamed. Sam had been so young that he didn't know why he was laughing, but that's the beauty of young kids, isn't it, Bill thinks. Kids find laughter in everything.

He finishes the bolognese without realising it – definitely not tasting it – and puts the empty dish in the sink. He won't fill it with hot water because the tap running might wake Sam and also because he can't be bothered. That'll annoy Jen, he knows, but he's charmed by her scolding. He tells her so regularly.

'Why are you such a child when you're older than me?' she always sighs.

He sits in front of the TV, more specifically the news, but doesn't watch it properly when there's nothing on about Claudia, so he gets up again and checks on Sam even though he knows he'll be exactly where he's been since seven-thirty. Seeing Sam's face with his duvet tucked around his shoulders floods Bill with warmth; he's so young and so full of potential and sometimes Bill can't help but imagine himself as that little boy – with a bright unblemished future rolled out before him like a map. He wishes he could be six and have the chance to do things differently, do things right. He wishes he'd never met Claudia all those years ago.

He exhales, goes back to the kitchen, tries not to stare at the cake. It'll be OK, he thinks. It'll all be OK.

There's a sudden sound coming from the front door that causes Bill to look to it, expectantly.

'Jen?'

But there's no one turning the handle. He goes to the door.

'Who's there?'

He can hear someone outside, a sudden shift of feet, and then the clang of the letterbox. His heart rate increases. An envelope has been pushed through and for a second his heart flips, because what if it's *the* envelope that he's been searching for? But, of course, it's not, because no one else knows about it, and if they did, they certainly wouldn't be delivering it to him like a goddamn fairy. He takes the envelope, sees that it's blank. It's nine-thirty at night, so who's posting at this time?

He pauses, debating if he should open it because he's not at his house, obviously, he's at Jen's. But the anonymity of it causes him to be suspicious and Jen's had this kind of shit before. People know she's in the police and have baited her for it. He's lost count of the times people have posted things through her door or written on it with markers, and called her a 'pig', and worse. Ignorant arseholes.

'Not one of these fuckers could do the job I do,' she says every time, and although she smiles, throws the notes away, or scrubs at the door, Bill can see the marks they each leave on her. They are yet another reason that she wants to move away from this place, and although he can't bear the thought of her leaving, he gets it. If he didn't spend so much money, he'd escape this town too.

There's also another reason he wants to open it. People have sent her messages before about cases she's been assigned to, and all of them have been discounted or written by nutters, but what if this is something that holds information about what happened to Claudia? Bill doesn't know when Jen will be home, it could be days still, and perhaps this is a vital clue or evidence. He tears it open and exhales in relief at seeing a flyer for an estate agent. Stop being paranoid, he tells himself. He sits down heavily on the sofa once again, picks up his phone and plays another game of cards, and loses another fifty pounds.

In irritation, he switches to another web page, where he searches for a new name. Marie Cadorna, seventeen, bronzed, with loose dark tresses and a body that is toned to perfection. The new British diver, the nation's obsession.

SEVEN

It's Sunday, and six days since Claudia was declared missing. The dive unit have no choice but to declare a negative search, and disappointment and frustration ripples through the team. The thrill of diving is finding the thing that's missing and they haven't found it – no body, no Claudia Franklin, only a random assortment of bits that are likely to be completely unrelated and therefore discounted.

Idris has taken them all for breakfast – even though it's four-thirty in the afternoon – and Jen has ordered a full English, because it's what she usually orders, but when it's put in front of her, it makes her want to vomit. She's sick from worry about Claudia, but also about Mark, and she's grimy and slick with old sweat from all the days spent on the lorry. She longs for a hot bath and some privacy because Claudia's face bangs around her head and the dead swan keeps drifting into her mind's eye. Her past is coming up – literally surfacing from murky waters – around her. She gets out her phone, stares at the news. She's checking every moment she has in case the media have found out anything quicker than they have, but there are only theories, speculation, and nothing else.

'The army decompresses in Cyprus, and we decompress in Wetherspoons,' Joe muses.

'If you joined the army,' Oli says to him, 'I'd be happy for you, and also for all of us.'

'Go to hell,' Joe retorts, but with good humour. 'You'd miss my wit and sparkling banter.'

'Nope.'

'First thing I'm going to do is take a hot shower and get changed without Jen staring at my dick,' Joe says.

He looks to Jen expectantly, who looks back at him blankly.

'You didn't rise to my bait that time.'

'Was it something about your dick?' she asks.

'Of course.'

'You'd never bait me with that,' she says. She turns to Idris. 'What now?'

'We've got other jobs to do that are stacking up. We've got a search that came in a couple of days ago which we need to get to. Missing property in Sutton Common—'

'I meant with the case,' she interrupts. 'Sounds like the investigative team is being as shit as we've been in trying to find her.'

'All I know is what we all know from watching the news. Anyone close to her has been taken in for questioning and for statements. The team will carry on with investigations and hope that someone, somewhere, might know something. We've done what we can in the water and we've sent whatever we've found off to the labs for swabs.'

'That's all going to be useless,' she dismisses.

'We don't know that.'

'You think that dog-walker just got the wrong end of the stick? What they said they saw – material in water, a "body". It could have been anything, right?'

'You've got the bit between your teeth with this one, Jen.'

She shuts her mouth before she outs herself. She wants to know that Mark is out of the picture, and not a suspect, wants to know that her trust in him isn't completely and nightmarishly misplaced.

'Have they found her phone and laptop yet?' Gareth asks.

Idris shakes his head. 'Apparently not. And the last track on the phone was from the road outside the house at ten-thirty that night. So either Claudia was at her home then, or someone else was there with her phone.'

'Who saw her last?' Jen asks.

'Until any one else comes forward, I guess Mark Mason did.'

She wants to vomit but manages instead to nod.

'You eating that sausage?' Joe asks, spearing it with his fork before she answers.

'Take it all,' she says, and shoves the plate away from her.

She opens the door with her numerous keys, and the codes that only she, Bill, Kerry and Mark know. It feels strange now that Mark has this kind of access to her home. She told him a few months ago, in case of emergencies, but it feels stupid, foolish to have even contemplated this, let alone given them to him. At this point in time, Mark feels like a stranger.

'Hello?' she calls tentatively.

'I'm here,' Bill answers.

She walks the few steps to the living room to see her brother on the sofa in front of the TV, beer in hand. Sam is nestled up to him, asleep, and covered with a faux-fur throw and her heart thuds.

'You didn't find her?' Bill asks.

'Oh yeah,' she says, brightly. 'We found her!'

His expression darkens. 'Dick.'

'Well, of course, we didn't find her, you prick. It would have been all over the news and I'm assuming you're watching it?'

'Obviously.'

She sits down next to them, resists the urge to move Sam to place him against her side. Instead, she puts a hand to his back, leaves it there a moment, feels the heat of his body through the blanket and then looks at Bill. The weight of all the unspoken questions between them is heavy.

'You stink,' he says.

'Remember how I told you we shower?'

'Like, you don't?'

'Exactly. Because we have a hosepipe at the back of the lorry. And no toilet. So, of course I stink.'

'OK, so I'll just put up with the smell,' he says, picking up his beer.

'Yes, you fucking will.'

She often wonders what people think if they knew that the dive unit doesn't even have access to a bathroom, a working toilet. Most of the time, they deliberately dehydrate themselves so they don't need to go too much.

She motions for the beer and Bill obligingly passes it over.

'How was Sam?' she asks.

'He was great, as usual.'

'You got the money I sent over?'

'Yeah. Thanks.'

She wants to grill him again about his finances, but there are too many other things going around in her head.

He smiles at her, but it's tight and unnatural. Jen sighs.

'Can you help me take Sam to his bedroom?' she asks.

He nods, picks Sam up like he's a feather, kisses him on the head. He's so natural with him. Jen remembers that she would ring her brother in the middle of the night, howling with pain when Sam fed, howling with frustration when she couldn't wind him, howling with exhaustion when he wouldn't settle. Eventually, Bill just moved into her flat for six months and became a surrogate dad, and Jen realised that it wasn't ever going to be Mark at her bedside, but Bill.

Bill lays Sam down on the bed and Jen covers him with his duvet.

'Thanks,' she whispers.

Bill replies with a shrug and they go back into the lounge together. He flops back onto the sofa and she sits beside him.

'Are you OK?' she asks finally.

'Sure.'

'Liar. Claudia was always your "one that got away".'

He laughs thinly. 'Except I never had her. She went on to better things. I'm fine. Promise. Neither of us have spoken to her for years and I've moved on. Do you have any idea what's happening in the investigation?'

'Idris is the dive supervisor so he knows parts of it, but he gets told the things that we need to know. I've been asking all I can, but I can't ask too much. I've been looking at the news, same as everyone else. She's gone without any of her belongings except her phone and laptop. No one knows where she is. It's fucking weird.'

'What about Mark?'

She stalls. 'What about him?'

'You think he's being interviewed?'

'Yeah, of course,' she says, colour rushing to her cheeks. 'I don't know anything about that, though.'

She's desperate to, of course.

'Have you said anything to your team? That you knew her?'

'No.'

'You don't think they'd go digging into . . . what happened then?'

She knows he's thinking about the barn and she puts a hand to his arm, to steady him, although they're both sitting down.

'We buried all that shit, OK? It's not related.'

Bill nods and she mirrors it. That day is forever burnt into her mind's eye, as she's sure it is into Bill's, but it's been an unspoken dark cloud over their past for eighteen years and she sure as hell isn't bringing it all up now.

'And you haven't seen Claudia,' she says. 'Neither of us have seen her.'

'Or Mark.'

'Right,' she says hurriedly. No one needs to know that she's seen Mark. She changes direction. 'Fuck me, I'm tired.'

She takes a gulp of his beer again and then he takes it back from her, stares back at the TV. She can feel that he's watching her.

'What?' she asks.

He shakes his head. 'Nothing.'

'Spit it out.'

'I . . . actually, I need more money,' he says.

'For what? I literally just sent you some.'

'I can pay you back.'

'Can you?'

'Yes, of course I can,' he says and looks cross. 'Can you get me cash?'

'I can transfer you some over.'

'No,' he says. 'It needs to be cash.'

She scowls. 'Like, notes? Why?'

He glowers at her. 'Because I'm out of it, OK?'

'You've been on those sites again, haven't you? Delete the apps, Bill, for Christ's sake.'

Like this is what she wants to be dealing with right now. Her older brother's addictions. As if she hasn't got enough to think about.

'Just delete the apps,' he says quietly. 'Like that's all there is to it.'

She's pissed off that she hasn't she seen the signs before now because she's been too wrapped up in work, in herself, in Mark, in Sam. But those things are *her* life. She shouldn't be responsible for Bill's. For all the love she has for him, sometimes, he completely enrages her. But today she's bone-weary, and she can't yell at him, it's too exhausting.

They sit in silence for long moments and she stares around her living room, seeing it anew. It needs tidying, hoovering. Everything is messy. Her eyes land on a hounds-tooth black-and-white jacket slung on the back of the chair. The pattern makes her eyes swim.

'You need help, Bill.'

'Maybe I should try your woo-woo app?' he says sarcastically.

'It's *not* woo-woo. It's a self-help app. It's called Tranquil.'

'I know what it's called. You go on about it all the time. It's extreme woo.'

'Extreme woo?'

She bursts out laughing and reaches to whack him, grateful that even though she's worried to the hilt in this dire situation, he can still cause her to smile.

He gets up. 'I'm going to go.'

'You could stay over if you like. I can go in with Sam.'

'Nah, you're all right. Your bed is too soft for me anyway, it gives me backache.'

'Sorry, Goldilocks.'

'Fuck off.' He grins and goes to leave.

She catches his arm. 'I love you.'

'I love you, too,' he says. 'Soppy cow.' He's smiling at her now. 'And listen.'

'Yeah?'

'It's Mum's birthday.'

She forgot. With everything with Claudia, with her fear around Mark, she's lost track of the date. She hugs Bill tight, and she feels him relax, feels the bear weight of him, and his arms around her.

'Mum would be proud of us,' she whispers.

'She wouldn't be proud of me,' he says. 'Not any more.'

She pulls away. The smile is gone from his face and there's a look in his eyes that she knows. A panic, an anxiety.

'Don't ever say that. Why do you say that?'

He shakes his head.

'I can help you out. With the money, I mean. OK?'

'It's fine,' he says and he grabs at his coat, leaves before she can say anything else.

Jen sits by Sam's bed, watches him sleep, and can't help herself but touch his cheek, his hair. No one – not Bill, not Kerry, and definitely not Sam – knows about Sam's parentage, but all of a sudden Jen is desperate to talk about it, scream about it, and knowing that she can't makes it even worse.

Jen takes in that Sam's hair needs cutting and that he needs new school shoes and trousers too – she hasn't had the time to properly acknowledge that he's grown a bit over the last few months. He looks so like her – a heart-shaped face, with thick brown hair and brown eyes – and nothing like Mark. She wonders for how much longer Sam will blindly accept that there is no dad in his world, or in the drawings the teachers ask him to do at school. When will it be that he demands to know who his father is? When his friends have their dads on pitch sidelines, in audiences at school plays? She'll owe it to Sam – his parentage is part of his identity – and when that time comes, perhaps she will have to start answering the questions she's managed to skip around for so many years.

They were never supposed to have him. He was an accident but turned into her miracle. Nearly seven years ago, on Jen's birthday and, coincidentally, on a rare day where she wasn't called to dive, Mark had come over from Boston, 'settling some things' he'd said, and he'd messaged her. She doesn't know why, she still has never asked why, after so many years of silence, he called when he was supposed to be in America with Claudia, but she said yes to meeting him. Of course she did, because she's always felt an ache, a physical pull, of wanting him that is almost otherworldly.

She remembers the elation at seeing him again after so long, the joy of him wordlessly handing her a helmet to join him on his dad's ancient motorbike, and taking her to the coast. They'd spent two hours walking the cliff edge and watching the gulls circle the sky, listening to the crash of the waves below as they came in, and the shimmering of the shingle when they drew away again. She had told him that when she had been a girl, she'd sat on these cliff edges and imagined a winged black horse that galloped beneath the waves of the sea. It was talking to her, and only her, from beyond.

Come away, it said. *To the midnight blue of the sea shelf. Drop away to where you can feel nothing.*

'Heavy,' he'd said and he'd laughed, but she hadn't.

Instead, she'd looked to the horizon and remembered how tempting that voice had been, how at eight years old she had been completely ready to give herself up to the sea. She knows why now, with the beauty of hindsight and some reading up on psychology – it had been the year that Fiona had been diagnosed with early-onset dementia, the year Jen had realised that nothing would ever be the same again. It was also the year she started to sleepwalk.

'Let's go get some food,' he'd said.

She'd allowed him to take her hand, to lead her down the path towards the kiosk, where he'd bought them chips and 99s with flakes. He'd taken her chin in his fingers as the wind whipped her hair across her face, and the sea air salted their lips. He'd kissed her, looked into her eyes in the way that had always made her stomach flip.

'This,' he'd said. 'This is freedom, isn't it?'

'Is it?'

'I needed to get away from everything. Things have been difficult . . . at home.'

Notes of excitement and anticipation had raced through her heart as she thought of what that meant, what it meant about *Claudia*. Where was Claudia at the very moment that Mark was talking to Jen like this? Perhaps she was sitting pretty in her Boston house, painting her nails, or at a day course trying her hand at pottery, or maybe trying on some costume jewellery in a boutique store with friends. Claudia, who walked through life with a red carpet unfurling with every step she took. And yet here was Jen with her husband.

'With you it's different. Even though—'

'Don't say it,' she'd said because she knew he was referencing a night long ago.

'Come with me,' he'd said. 'Back to my hotel.'

And she'd said yes. It had been the first and only time they'd been physical together and it was everything she thought it would be, but the aftermath definitely wasn't. She found out that she was pregnant and he ghosted her. So why, why, why does she still want his love so desperately? Perhaps it's because her own father left them when they were tiny and she never experienced a family unit. Perhaps she's never quite got over the feeling of Mark's rejection all those years ago.

She shakes her head, can't think of the years past. She watches Sam's chest rise and fall in sleep, and in innocence, and she puts her arms around him.

His eyes are suddenly open. 'Mum?'

She jumps. 'Yeah. I'm back now. Sorry I woke you.'

'Did they let you come home for Nanny's birthday?'

She smiles. 'Not specifically for that reason.'

'We made a cake,' he says. 'Me and Uncle Bill. To celebrate her. That's what you do, isn't it?'

'You made one?'

'Yeah. We did eat some, though. A little bit. Mostly it was Uncle Bill.'

'He's such a pig.'

Sam laughs, delighted.

'Thanks for doing that, bub,' she says and kisses him on the head.

'Did you find what you were looking for in the water?'

'No. But that's OK. It'll turn up.'

She makes finding a body sound like a lost shoe, a piece of costume jewellery, but Sam wouldn't understand if she explained to him that she's been looking for a dead woman. Or, maybe he would, but it might frighten him. Or maybe he'd think it was cool – you can never tell how a six-year-old might react.

'Sometimes it's better *not* to find the thing you're looking for,' she says. 'That means there's hope elsewhere.'

She can tell by the frown on his face that he's confused, because she routinely tells him that to find things underwater is her absolute favourite thing – the prize, the reward.

'Never mind, it's OK,' she says. 'Go back to sleep.'

He closes his eyes and she listens to his breathing until it becomes slow and rhythmic, and then she tiptoes out of the room.

She's desperate to call Mark now she's alone, but she stops herself. Lord knows that she really shouldn't be calling or be anywhere near him, given the enormity of what's going on. What is he feeling? she wonders. Is he going out of his mind with worry? What does *he* think might have happened to Claudia?

She looks back at Sam. 'There's nothing bad in you,' she whispers. 'Mark hasn't done anything to Claudia.'

But uncertainty bites at her heart. She goes to the living room and watches the news for information, but falls asleep on the sofa within minutes.

EIGHT

Jen wakes to a rush of liquid filling her nostrils. She flails, panicked, before her brain kicks into gear and she begins to tread water, spluttering out the taste of minerals and peat. She looks up and sees the towering shadows of bulrush against the black sky and knows immediately where she is.

She's back in the water-meadows, where they meet the depth of the river.

She's walked her loop again and, unconsciously, has stepped across the boardwalk and into marshland, through the reeds and moss mounds, and has slipped in, and submerged herself. She could have drowned and the thought completely terrifies her.

She swims back towards the bank until the water becomes swampy and swimming becomes laborious through the reeds. She winds knots of long grass around her fingers to drag herself forward, the stench of the water overpowering, from bird muck, and other creatures. She eventually reaches the boardwalk, and heaves herself out, breaking a nail in the process of trying to get her fingers around a gap in one of the wooden planks. She lies down, shaking with cold and dread and panting heavily from the effort, her vision sideways.

She feels about in her water-soaked pockets for her keys, her phone. She has her phone – waterproofed in a bag, of course, from years of experience, but she's not got her keys. And if she hasn't got her keys, does that mean she didn't lock the door? Is Sam OK? She's a bad mother, the worst. What kind of a mother leaves her child unattended in his bed? She's unfit to be a parent, she's always known so. Or perhaps she did have the keys and they've fallen out into the water. She hopes for this, as annoying as that might be to replace them all.

She calls Bill and her voice is loud, even as a whisper, in the silence of the marsh.

He answers at once. 'Have they found Claudia?'

'No,' she says. 'I've . . . I've gone walking.'

If there's one person who will understand this and not judge her – ever – it's Bill.

'I'll check Sam,' he says.

'Thank you,' she says and there's a rising choking shame in her voice. 'I'm sorry. I know you've only been back in your flat for like . . . a few hours.'

'I'm not there.'

'What?' She doesn't think she's heard right.

'I mean – I am here. Where are you?'

'I'm on my way back. My hands are fucking freezing, I can't hold the phone properly.'

'OK, go.'

She hangs up, wrings out her clothes the best she can so she doesn't chill on the walk home. It's summer, but the nights are still cold. She worries that someone might see her at this time if she walks the quickest route through town. The locals are rightfully watchful and nervous now that Claudia has gone missing and what could alert police attention more than seeing a dark, wet figure traipsing up the high street at night? She decides that she'll skirt the centre of town and risk the quieter residential streets and the sports fields before she gets to her road.

The reeds at the edge of the boardwalk feel like spikes closing in on her until she reaches the end of the water-meadows, to follow the river that flanks Cowell Farm. She instinctively turns her head at this point, sees the silhouette of the old barn.

Don't look there.

A bad thing happened there.

She picks up her pace and her footsteps thud on the baked-mud pathway, disturb something – an enormous swan raises its neck, the whiteness of it is like bone in the darkness. It looks at her with blank black eyes and a shiver dances across her skin as she passes it.

She thinks about the mangled swan in the tunnel, and at the same time she remembers that that's how they described Claudia when she dived into the water – graceful, elegant, swan-like.

Bill used to call her 'swan'.

NINE

Bill looks around Sam's bedroom door, sees that he's there of course, because where else would he be? Jen had locked the door, she always seems to, but Bill can appreciate the crippling fear that must come with finding yourself out of bed, out of your own house.

He thinks about how weird it is that his sister sleepwalks. When they were younger, he used it over her like a bargaining chip, but that was when she went no further than downstairs to eat the bread and chocolates she wasn't supposed to, or to their mother's bathroom and used all her cosmetics. There would be times where he would have entire conversations with her at night and in the morning she wouldn't remember them. He'd rib her for it, tell her that she'd admitted to something embarrassing and she'd really go for him, but now he's more careful with what he says to her. He knows that she only ever sleepwalks when she's stressed and he knows that it's frightening, disorientating.

When he was twelve, he'd woken to the sound of the front door opening and he'd known instantly that Jen had left the house. He'd hurriedly thrown on joggers, a hoodie, trainers, grabbed a spare jumper to put on her in case she'd gone without and had run down the stairs after her.

She was ahead of him down the road, in her pyjamas, her silhouette black against the midnight darkness and he followed her cautiously. He knew not to wake her, knew he needed to coax her home again and put her back to bed, but there was also a part of him that was intrigued by her sleepwalking – he wanted to know how far she would walk and where it was she would go to.

She walked half a mile to the local park she takes Sam to now, opened the gates, went to the copse of trees, stopped between a solid oak which was due to be cut down due to storm damage, and an elegant chestnut. She stood there for a long time, unmoving like a girl in an eerie horror-movie poster, before moving towards the oak, putting her hand to its bark and leaning her head against it. One of its storm-wrecked branches hung low, like an arm cradling her.

'Oh, Mum,' she was saying as he approached her. 'Mum, you're not right.'

Her words had startled him. In sleep, she was trying to make sense of their changing world – Fiona's dementia – and it broke his heart.

'Jen,' he called softly. 'Come away.'

'How can I make you better?'

'Sis,' he said, and touched her thin shoulder.

She turned, her face blank, her eyes glassy and dark, and it scared him, but he put his arm around her.

'We have to save her,' she said.

'Come home.'

'No, I can't leave her. You can't leave.'

'That's not Mum—'

She opened her mouth then, screamed a scream he'll never forget. Animal-like, and desperate, which went right through him like an electric current.

He put his hand over her mouth and then she started to bite at him.

'Wake up!' he shouted, fearfully. 'Wake up!'

'We need to save her!' she cried, and then as quickly as the anger came, she fell down against him and lay on the grass that was wet with dew and was fast asleep.

Bill's heart hammered in his chest. He didn't know what to do – he couldn't lift her. So he lay down beside her and put his arms around her.

He shakes the memory from his head. Thankfully, she found her loop. At least he knows where she goes now.

He sits on her sofa, picks up the remote and channel-surfs before he subconsciously flicks to the YouTube app. The screen goes blue and white, there's someone talking, and then it's filled with the picture of Claudia's face. It's only then that he realises what he's absently typed in—

Claudia Franklin, diving, Beijing Olympics 2008.

He remembers watching all those years ago on TV as fresh-faced, twenty-year-old Claudia walked the steps to the diving board the first time. He drank in the sight of her in that blue swimsuit, and saw the nerves in her face as the camera zoomed in, because he knew every muscle in it. Along with the rest of the nation, he held his breath as she contemplated the water below and he thought then that it was the beginning of something special for her, a turning point after all the shit that had happened in the years prior, but then it all went wrong.

He knows how it went after that first dive, but still he watches, video after video, dive after dive, until it hurts to keep going. He types in another name and a link pops up immediately.

Marie Cadorna, 10m backwards double-somersault.

It's an amateur phone video which tracks the dive poorly, but Bill can still see the skill that the young woman possesses. Marie's body is strong, tucked, perfectly angled, and he watches as the video zooms on the girl's face as she resurfaces. There's no smiling even when it's a good dive. Marie is clearly serious, determined. Bill wonders who took the video – a family member, a friend perhaps, or a boyfriend. Maybe Mark Mason, her coach.

There's a knock at the door and he quickly switches off the TV before going to the door. He puts his ear against it.

'Who's there?'

'Me.' Jen's voice sounds cross through the door. 'Who do you think?'

He unlocks the door, and she steps inside, closes it.

'Why are you wet?' he asks. 'It's not raining.'

'The river.'

He blinks. 'Like, you fell in?'

She smells of soil and silt and of the wheat smell of the reed that grows tall in the summer.

'You did the loop?'

'Yes. I guess so but I . . . I went into the water.'

'You've been searching for Claudia. That must be it, right?'

She looks so wretched that he goes to her, hugs her close to him.

'What's the matter with me, Bill?' she says into his shoulder. 'Why do I do this?'

'You need to see someone about it.'

'And risk losing my job? No way.'

'You wouldn't,' he says. 'It doesn't affect your work.'

'But there must be something . . . wrong with me. Right? And if I'm diagnosed with psychosis, what then?'

'Nothing. Nothing will happen. You're not psychotic, OK? You're a normal person who happens to walk around semi-conscious from time to time.'

'I don't think anything about either of us is normal.'

He smiles. 'There it is. A sense of humour from a woman that's just stepped out of a swamp in the middle of the night.'

She smiles back. 'Thanks for looking after Sam. Again.'

'Do you need me to stick around?'

She shakes her head. 'Thanks, but no. I'm . . . I'm OK.'

He moves past her, twists his feet into his trainers and puts his hand to the door.

'Bill?'

He turns. 'Yeah?'

She's looking at him strangely.

'What?' he says.

'Can I . . . I need to . . . Where were you?'

He frowns. 'Where was I when? When you called me? At home.'

'No,' she says. 'I mean, where were you when Claudia went missing?'

A bolt of panic somersaults inside his stomach. He doesn't want to look at her, but he knows he must.

'Why are you asking me that?'

She shakes her head. 'I don't know – I . . . Swans.'

'*Swans?*'

'We found a swan on one of the dives and you used to call her that. You used to call Claudia a swan. When she swam.'

He frowns, confused. 'What's that got to do with anything?'

'I just want to know where you were. I think it's the barn, it's everything coming back up again. I went past it tonight . . .'

He must think carefully about how he answers this. He licks his lips.

'I was at the site that night and then . . . then I saw Kerry in the evening.'

The relief on her face is visible and he is immediately ashamed. He's lying to Jen.

'Great. Sorry. I know that was a weird thing to ask. I just—'

'You want to know we're safe.'

'Yes.'

'Well, now you know,' he says with a tight smile.

'Yeah.' She sighs. 'Sorry. I know we already had the conversation about the barn . . . I know you haven't seen her either and . . .' She sighs deeply. 'I need to get out of these clothes.'

'OK. See ya,' he says and he steps outside into the concrete corridor, leans against the wall.

An acute smell of weed inhabits his nose from one of the neighbours downstairs and he wishes he could have some to dull the pain in his heart, but he needs to be alert.

He'll go tonight. There's no time to waste.

TEN

It's midnight and Bill locks up the house. He's paranoid he's left a light on, or a door open somewhere, or that the fridge-freezer he brought in won't work and will puddle on the floor, but he needs to be back at his own flat now.

It's a beautiful house. This one has already been bought, is one of the houses with an inside basement pool, a double garage, and white stone porch columns, and Bill loves this one most of all because it's the last one on the site map with a garden that overlooks both the woodland and the South Downs Way.

Inside it's nearly finished and the clients are now in the process of customising the rest of the interiors – or rather, their designers are. Through the empty windows, he can see into the hallway, past the grand staircase that sweeps upwards to yawning bedroom doorways, and through to the kitchen. The immense white marbled island shimmers in the pale moonlight that filters in from the enormous windows and he thinks how nice it'll be for the owners to look out that window to the garden. They'll drink coffee in expensive cups and read the papers. The turf and trees and blooming flowers will be put in next month, ready for effortless-looking house-warming barbecues and champagne parties. How the other half live. It's how *Claudia* used to live. He thinks that this house is exactly the type that he would have liked to have built for her if life had worked out differently. He imagines a life where they might have married, and had kids. An impossible hope.

He walks back across the site. It isn't floodlit at night and the silhouetted diggers and bulldozers look like sleeping monsters in the dirt. It's not unusual for him to do odd jobs on site in the middle of the night; he often likes to stare around and tick off any potential hazards of a job while no one else is there, but tonight he hadn't come to tick off hazards. He'd come to collect something he stashed at number ten but now needs to get out – a laptop which is smooth and cold, and now under the crook of his arm.

He gets into his truck, puts the laptop on the passenger seat and drives off, stopping again only to lock the site gates behind him. There is no room for error. He's made enough already.

He drives back to his flat but hates the silence of it. He wishes he had stayed at Jen's. Then he could have avoided her sleepwalking, could have avoided lying to her about where he was that night. He wishes he could turn back time on a lot of things – how far back would he go? Perhaps to the day Claudia came to the river for the first time? Perhaps before that?

He sits on his sofa with a packet of crisps and the laptop on a cushion seat next to him. He doesn't open it. Instead, he absently taps on his phone, the screen glaring the red and blue of the betting website, and he transfers one hundred pounds into a poker game and mouths, silently, a prayer to the leprechaun sitting, at the end of a rainbow. Claudia promised Bill money but never made good on it and now it's all gone to shit.

He loses eighty, wins two hundred pounds, and for a stupid moment he thinks maybe he can do it, maybe he can get out of debt without falling into any more trouble.

A loud ping causes him to drop the phone, before he realises it's an email notification and not an alarm, or a siren for that matter.

Bill, we need to talk, Mark.

Bill's heart starts to race. Mark Mason wants to meet him and he can't refuse him for long. He turns the phone off, wonders what the hell he's going to do.

ELEVEN

It's three in the morning and Jen sits in her dressing gown, her hair wet down the back of it, post-shower. Is Bill right that she was there, in the water-meadows, because she's spent most of the week there, hunting fruitlessly for Claudia? Or is it because her feelings around both Mark and of Claudia are so complex that her brain is trying to process it by walking her loop? She's only started walking it again since they came back to the U.K. What about the fact she woke on that Sunday morning? Might she have seen something at the house as she passed it? Heard something?

She wants to negate the deep discomfort in her stomach. She looks at her phone, scrolls the internet for Claudia's name to trawl through speculation theories but there is no new news – no developments, no statements issued. Every time, she hopes to hear something about Mark – that the police have declared his innocence – but she's met with silence. Jen has to remind herself that technically Claudia is still *missing* because there is no body but it feels like a vague hope now.

She puts her phone down and stares at the TV, puts on *Midsomer Murders* because it's an easy go-to and always appeals to the police officer in her, and watches two episodes. As the second finishes with the theatrical flourish that she loves, the screen asks 'Are you still watching?' which annoys her and she deliberately presses 'No' and clicks into another app which won't judge her amount of screen time. A whiteness dazzles her eyes and she realises she's put on YouTube. Little squares of things Sam has historically searched for ping up – *Pokémon*, Ryan playing with Lightning McQueen toys, *Transformers*, and a square with a tutorial on smoky eye make-up when Jen went out with Kerry last month. There's another square, however, that she doesn't recognise. A brilliant bright, swimming-pool blue, with the caption underneath.

Claudia Franklin scores 44.5 Beijing Olympics 2008, 10m.

Jen frowns. She hasn't been looking at this footage, so it could only have been Bill. She clicks into it, and watches Claudia's dive. She remembers watching it live on TV with Kerry – remembers how they both screamed at the screen because they wanted Claudia to fail, but at the same time Jen secretly wanted her to succeed. Feelings are so conflicting, so contrary.

The screen fuzzes in front of her – she needs some fuel to make it to the end of the night. There's the cake Sam made so she gets up, cuts herself a slice. The sugar melts on her tongue, is an immediate physical hit of relief and pleasure after the gruelling hours she's had. Fiona's birthday is so conflicted for her and for Bill.

Her thoughts drift again to Claudia's mother, Victoria Franklin, and Jen wonders how she might be feeling tonight.

Jen knows first-hand that there's nothing more terrifying than a missing child, she's witnessed enough on her job. A body becomes preferable after days of anguish, because without it, the mind goes to terrible places – imagining the worst scenarios: abduction, rape, violence, torment.

Victoria was never Vicky, because 'Victoria' sounded stronger and like a woman who takes no shit, she used to say. Jen remembers that Claudia used to give her mother plenty of it during childhood just to test the theory, but it was correct – Victoria never did take any shit. She had had a strict upbringing herself and like hell was she ever going to go off blueprint. She would always speak her mind, even when she knew her words would bite, would dress up criticism as being constructive, and had an opinion on all topics. She played a tug of war with Claudia when it came to giving her maternal support because, to a woman like Victoria, displays of open feelings were distasteful. Claudia once told Jen that her mother had trained as a classical dancer and was used to managing any sort of vulnerability. Strangely, however, Jen got on well with Victoria. Perhaps because she was as straight talking as Victoria was, perhaps because there was no pressure on their relationship. Perhaps, Claudia had said with a laugh that Jen couldn't quite read, because Victoria simply liked Jen better.

Jen clicks back on the app, the rest of the cake balanced on her knees. She doesn't want to see Claudia diving again, but the app jumps, and there's another dive now, a video uploaded from last year of the new dive sensation, Marie

Cadorna, diving a perfect backwards double-somersault. Jen skims the comments beneath.

Marie Cadorna, the new golden girl of British diving.
Tipped for the Olympics next year.
OMG she's amazing! Defo one to watch.
This girl looks dead behind the eyes imo.
LOL!

Marie Cadorna is indeed in the Olympics diving team this year and due to be flying to Paris in a week or so with the team, and both Mark and Claudia. Did Bill watch this also or was it a recommended video that popped up after he'd searched for Claudia?

Jen wipes the history from the app, and waits for the dawn. Her head is humming with angst.

Sam holds her hand tight at the school gates.

'Do you have another job today?'

'Not the job I was on,' she says. 'That's up to the investigative team now.'

'What job are you on today?'

'A boring one.'

'The boring ones mean you'll be back for tea!'

'I hope so,' she says. 'Otherwise Kerry will pick you up after football club, OK? Or Denise if Kez isn't free.'

He looks delighted because Denise is Miles' mum and Miles is his best friend and any time they can spend together is like gold dust to him.

She kneels down to him. 'I love you,' she says, and kisses his forehead.

He holds out his fist for a bump. 'Bye!'

Jen waits until he's vanished inside the building, and then checks her watch. It's seven-forty and she could – and probably should – take the hour to rest before the search up the coast but calculates that she has time to go for a swim.

In the car, she listens to the news, but there's nothing on Claudia, so she switches to the app on her phone, Tranquil, which plays through the stereo. It always helps settle her heart rate. She puts it on, selects 'Rain on a window', and repeats the mantras.

'Contract to myself – I will no longer wake up anxious. I promise to reclaim my mornings, my joy of the sunshine, of laughter.'

It's not the waking up that's the problem, she knows, but the going to bed, the promise of sleep, but nevertheless it all helps.

'I will no longer fear what the day may hold.'

Except that she does right now, and will until she has answers to Claudia's whereabouts.

'I will look forward to the day, and I will take on any challenges with a calm head, with rationality.'

She pulls up at the side of the road, walks with purpose through the wooden gate that leads down to the river of Cowell Farm, five minutes away. This is where she ran through last night after calling Bill in a panic, and now she's come again, in the light, to try to make sense of what her subconscious is trying to claw at. With Claudia's disappearance, she's submerging herself – literally – with worry.

She hasn't swum here in a long time. She walks down the grassy knoll to the river. There's no one here at this time of the morning and she's grateful for it; there are signs that say not to wild swim here because there's a strong pull, but some chance it. Jen's fit enough to fight against it, she *likes* to fight it.

She pulls her jumper and T-shirt over her head, shrugs off her jeans and removes her shoes. Underneath, she's already in her swimsuit and she slips from the bank into the water and is embraced by the cold, immediately feels the pull of the current against her body, tightens her muscles against it. She won't need her mask on to know if there's anything nasty in there because the water is clear, but, in any case, they've already searched here for Claudia and found nothing. Nothing, nothing.

She recalls one of the days she came here as a teenager, with Bill of course, and with Claudia when she started to join them. It was early autumn, a clear day with a cloud-scudded sky, and they had leapt into the water, their skin kissed by silver bubbles. They raced each other against the current, up to where the weeds stood tall, suspended in fronds, and the newly fallen leaves glowed like jewels from the bottom of the river until they then let themselves be taken all the way back to their piles of clothes. Jen got her foot stuck in the front of Claudia's swimsuit, couldn't remove it at the speed they were going and she remembers how they both gurgled their laughter into the water. Afterwards, they all lay together for the afternoon, and talked about summer jobs, and future plans, and nothing at all, until the sky turned red with the sun sinking behind the trees.

'We should check on Mum,' Jen said.

'Humm,' Bill said. 'We have nothing for dinner.'

'You should come over to mine for dinner,' Claudia said simply. 'You can take some back for your mum.'

Although Jen had historically prided herself on avoiding 'posh, pretty' girls that went to the private school, Claudia was – admittedly – funny, and clever, and Jen liked her. So they had gone for dinner, and to her surprise, Jen had also liked Victoria – her matter-of-fact mannerisms and her effortless hosting (made easy, she supposed, given their housekeeper made their meals), and Henry too with his loud laughter and the smell of cigar smoke that clung to him like a second skin. Claudia had put a generous portion of stew in a Tupperware for their mum. After that night they started having dinner with Claudia and her family once a week and Claudia would always dish a portion for Fiona.

'You don't have to do this,' Jen said once.

'I know,' Claudia replied. 'But I want to.'

Jen started talking about Claudia at school to Kerry, and was surprised at how jealous of Claudia Kerry appeared to be. Kerry never came swimming at the stream, disliked the water, but there were a couple of times that she seemingly forced herself there, each time sitting on the black stones at the edge of the river with her arms folded and a scowl on her face.

'It's because Bill likes her, isn't it?' Jen laughed at school afterwards.

'It's because she's a bitch.'

Jen had exploded with laughter. 'Oh my God, Kez. You've met her *twice*.'

'And that's enough for me. She knows she's got him on a hook.'

'They both like the water. We all like it. I've told her she should try out at swim practice.'

'Fucking fish,' Kerry muttered.

'Give over,' Jen said with a gentle nudge. 'You know you're my one and only bestest.'

'Even when I'm not one of the Three Musketeers?'

'Fish can't hold swords,' Jen grinned.

But Kerry hadn't laughed, and hadn't spoken to Jen all the rest of the day, and after that, Jen decided not to talk to her about Claudia at all because it wasn't worth the aggro. Kerry *was* her best friend and would always be and it's proved true – Kerry has always been a constant. Jen's relationship with Claudia grew at the river, it fused at the barn, then it soured. Died.

Jen shakes herself free of the memories, puts her head down against the current, and cuts through the water, in a fast front crawl for ten minutes until she lifts her head to find herself level with the old barn. She didn't mean to come this far up; she usually avoids it, but she's been thinking about it – maybe she always intended to come back here.

She pauses to look at it, turns over in the water so she can half-drift and take in its majesty. Once, it was a place of childhood games and memories as sweet as the twitch grass and the wild flowers that grew around it. Now it's charred, derelict, but still such a beautiful part of the landscape.

A movement by the side of it catches her eye, a brush-stroke blur of a person, or perhaps an animal – though it would have been a big one. She stops drifting and turns herself upright in the water.

'Hello?'

She has to throw her voice for it to carry because it's a long way away.

'Is anyone there?' she shouts again.

Her heart is thudding in her chest. There's no reply and no more movement, but she's spooked now. She allows herself to be carried back downstream and then gets out, shivering as she strips and quickly dries. There's no one here, she thinks to herself, but the feeling of caution lingers and she's always told herself to trust her instincts.

She checks the time on her phone because she needs to be at the base for the property search dive, but there's a notification on the screen that spikes her heart rate. A BBC News alert.

Mark Mason, husband to Claudia Franklin, the former Olympic diver, has been cleared for travel with the dive team for the Paris Olympics in a fortnight's time.

Jen gasps. After days spent avoiding him, worrying for him, he's now cleared and she throws caution to the wind, dials his number. He picks up immediately.

'Jen.'

'Does this mean . . . ?'

'I didn't do anything to Claudia,' he says in a choked voice and then he's crying down the line and so is she. 'The police have cleared me.'

The relief is insurmountable. Because even if Claudia *is* dead, then Mark has had nothing to do with it.

'Tell me everything,' she says.

TWELVE

When he wakes in the morning, Bill runs through the list in his head of the plates he's spinning. There are so many that he's still counting them off in the shower, brushing his teeth, getting dressed, driving to the site.

He is sick with shame that Andy trusts him when he shouldn't. He's horrified that he's hiding the truth from Jen. He's lying to every single person he knows, about everything. This level of deception is exhausting.

As he parks up, there's a beep from his pocket. Mark has emailed again.

We need to talk about The Corner House Cafe.

Bill swallows. He saw on the news that Mark has been officially cleared for travel to Paris, so what does that mean? Is he clear of being investigated in what's happened to Claudia? There's only one thing about this that Bill is relieved about – the police clearly aren't accessing Mark's emails, and thank fuck, because then they might have Bill's name too and Andy's company because that's how Mark has found him.

He crosses the site to the office – he has a full day before he can get to Fording Hill, the only other place he's thought that the envelope could be. He spends it obsessing over the architect's plans for the stone courtyard that they will build in a month's time, defusing a fight between two of the workers who have found out recently that they're dating the same woman and making tea badly for one of the contractors that he doesn't like. Andy chats away to him consistently, and gives him a headache. At lunchtime, to break up the day and his never-ending thoughts of doom, he hedges some money on a new betting website he's found, and wins seventy-five quid.

He manages to leave at five-thirty, and drives the forty minutes to Fording Hill, puts rock music on the radio to try to drown out his anxieties, but his heartbeat punches in his ears alongside it anyway. He needs to break into a home. He's fast racking up counts against himself. He parks some way down the road from the address, and then walks to the front door.

The flat is part of a newly built block – sandstone and white windowsills and a pretty, well-maintained hedge at the front of it. He presses the bell – second from the top – and then stands back and squints against the sunlight to look at the window he presumes is the number he wants. He presses again, two, three times, to make sure, but the door remains unanswered and his heartbeat steadies. He can do this.

He peers closer to the mechanism on the central door lock and knows that he can open it with no problem. As he opens his wallet for a card, a noise startles him.

'Hello?'

It's a voice from the speaker and he drops his wallet, bends down quickly to retrieve it.

'Who is it?' The voice is female, sounds young.

'It's maintenance,' he says, thinking quickly. 'I – there's been a call logged about condensation in the bathroom windows. Was it you?'

'I don't live here. The landlord will be back in a minute if you want to wait.'

Shit.

'What's your name please? So I can say that I've come?'

'Marie Cadorna,' she says.

He gasps internally. Marie Cadorna, the diver. He hasn't found the money, but he's found *her*.

'Thanks. I'll try another flat first and then come to you later on if I have time?'

'OK,' she says.

'Great.'

He stays there for a couple more minutes, pretending to call other flats, praying that the homeowner doesn't return, and then he walks away, head down, in case Marie is looking out of the window.

In the car, his phone vibrates.

What time tonight? Who's coming with us?

'Shit,' he says aloud.

He'd forgotten that he'd told Kerry he would take her to The Black Rat this evening. He hasn't even booked it, has forgotten to ask any of his friends, and never mentioned it to Jen either. He doesn't have the money, or the energy, to face Kerry and all her expectations of him, but he must muster both. He rings the restaurant.

Kerry sits across the table from him wearing a new dress.

'I bought it for tonight,' she says.

She's styled her hair in dark waves over one shoulder and her eyes are made up with a sparkly copper which accentuates the green of her irises. Her lips are lined in a perfect bow of red, and he thinks that she always makes herself look like a present to be opened. To be loved.

'You look beautiful,' he says, because she does.

'I was thinking I'd wear my shell suit but decided to leave that for a *really* special occasion.' She raises her glass to his. 'Cheers. This is so nice. Thanks for taking me.'

'No problem,' he says, but he feels strange sitting here with her.

The wine is white: crisp and fresh and expensive, like everything else on the menu. The restaurant is situated in one of the more unique and historic houses in the town and its character is charming, and off the charts with romantic atmosphere. Low-beamed ceilings, candles on the walls and the tables, herringbone wooden flooring, Tiffany stained-glass lamps. He's wearing a polo shirt and good jeans but feels underdressed.

'Are you still giving free buns to that stitch and bitch group at the cafe?'

'They're three old biddies making a quilt for their church,' she says. 'But yeah, I give them freebies when Ricky's not looking. They're so cute.'

'Bet they bitch as hard as the rest of them.'

She laughs, takes a sip of wine. 'Have you heard anything from that interview you had?'

He is surprised that she remembers – he must only have mentioned it in passing a few weeks ago – but Kerry tends to remember things: people's birthdays, family member illnesses, where a teenager is looking to apply for college. She is a people person, a carer. Bill sighs, thinks how Kerry is like sunshine, but at the moment there are too many clouds in his sky for her rays to reach him.

'To be honest, I'd forgotten about it. It was two weeks ago, so I don't think I've got it.'

'Ah, come on,' she says. 'Don't be defeatist. I bet you were great. You should call them tomorrow and ask for feedback.'

'Maybe,' he says but knows he won't call them because he'd felt so uncomfortable the entire time he was sat there, shivering as the nervous sweat beneath his shirt was blasted by the air con.

The waiter brings their starters – salmon for him, crab cakes for her – and he picks up his cutlery.

'I don't know if I want to wear a suit and tie every day anyway,' he says when the waiter leaves. 'It's not very me.'

'Why not?'

'I don't do suits. I felt like a bit of a cock.'

She takes a bite out of one of the crab cakes. 'Shut up, you'd look good.'

He thinks that there's a huge difference between looking and feeling good. The suit he bought for the interview was a Ted Baker, charcoal grey with a scarlet lining, and he wore a tie to match, which Jen had to fix for him because his hands were shaking too badly. What a joke. For all his easy banter and extrovert bravado, he hates small talk and he finds being sociable utterly exhausting. He read the other day that an extrovert gains energy when interacting with people, and an introvert is drained of it. Bill has a big personality, but he's still an introvert and he doesn't have the confidence in himself to pull off being the corporate hustler.

'How's the site going anyway?'

'It's fine,' he says. 'But it's a big site. I can't fuck it up.'

'What makes you think you would?'

How could he begin to explain the money he owes, the games he's being forced to play.

'You need to channel all that nervous energy,' Kerry says. 'Maybe book in a massage.'

He looks at her and she's smiling that coy smile she does whenever she wants him physically.

'I'm offering,' she purrs.

'Roger that,' he says in a low voice and they both laugh again, but he knows he can't play with her like this.

He steers the conversation back to people in common, work, new books she's into, because she's always reading, always learning, always fucking brilliant. So. Why. Can't. He. Love. Her.

The waiter comes to collect their plates, replaces them with their main courses.

'Is Jen doing OK?'

'She's fine. She's on another job now,' he says, like Claudia disappearing is old news. The lamb loin is beautiful, melts in his mouth, but he can't taste it. 'Sleepwalking.'

'Really?'

'Are you surprised?'

'No. I'm guessing it started when Mark and Claudia moved back.'

'I . . . Yeah. I mean, maybe? Why do you say that?'

'All that history between you all.'

He looks at her and wonders for a brief second whether Jen has told her about what happened at the barn. But how could she have done, given that Kerry is here, with him? If she knew about what he did that day, she would never be able to look at him. She'd be horrified, disgusted by him, because that day at the barn is the defining thing about him, the thing that has shaped who he is now – a coward.

'I'm guessing Mark Mason is worried as hell,' she says.

'He's been cleared to go to Paris, did you see?'

'Yep. So, that's good, right?'

'Is it?'

He sees her raise her eyebrows because his tone is gruff. She continues with eating – she's delicate with a knife and fork, like Claudia, and he internally chastises himself again for making her comparable to the girl on his pedestal.

'You never liked him, did you?'

'Not really. He's a rich and manipulative arsehole.'

Mark is doing well in acting the concerned partner, likes the limelight of the news cameras. He's used to an audience, used to being adored. He fools people, Bill thinks. Mind you, Bill's been doing exactly the same thing for the last few months too. It takes one liar to know another.

Kerry puts down her cutlery, knife and fork on each side of her plate. 'What, and Claudia wasn't those things? Rich and manipulative? If you ask me, they belonged together.'

He blinks in surprise at the venom in her voice. 'Claudia was nothing like that.'

'Wasn't she? Then I remember her differently. I remember that Jen could have been great but wasn't because of Claudia.'

'What do you mean by that? She's great doing what she does. She loves being a police diver.'

'But she could have been an *Olympic* diver if Claudia and her whole entire family hadn't fucked her over.'

He puts his hand to his head, pushes back his hair. 'Kez, please.'

'What? They did! And we all know it. Jen could have made it all the way, you know that. If she'd been on that platform, she would have scored high. She could have made a medal for sure.'

'I did say he was an arsehole.'

But Mark is an arsehole who knows something big about Bill, and Bill can't afford to misstep and upset him. Which, ironically, is exactly what he's doing by not returning his emails.

'We don't know that—'

'Why didn't you fight for her?' she says. 'When she could have reached the top?'

He's surprised into silence by this question. The truth is that he *should* have fought for Jen to stay on the dive team, but he didn't know how to.

Kerry picks up her wine glass. 'You know what? I'm going to say it. I'm glad Claudia has gone because she's been a blot on Jen's life all these years. And yours.'

Rage rises up Bill's throat like lava. He wants to overturn the contents of the table onto Kerry's new dress, throw the wine into her face, because she has no idea – no *idea* – what Claudia has done for him, the sacrifices she once made. Instead, he puts the white napkin beside his plate, swallows down his anger. To pacify Kerry is all he can do because he needs her. He needs her to lie for him, like she agreed to, if the police come knocking.

'You're right,' he says. 'She wasn't good for Jen.'

'Or you.'

'Or me.'

She nods, confirming that her opinion is the right one, and they carry on eating.

Bill lies in bed, clicks into his work emails. There's been a new payment made by one of the new clients – seven thousand straight into his personal bank account which lifts his spirits but sinks his moral compass simultaneously. He emails a friend about hiring a van, and then he books a holiday cottage on the fifth credit card he's taken out in as many weeks. Life has become too complicated and the only way to figure out his next move is to get some breathing space – away from everything and everyone that might ask questions of him.

His phone bleeps as the transaction confirms and then bleeps again with a message. He tips the screen so he can read it. But it's not a text but a video from Jen and as he clicks it open, he's greeted with the sound of Sam's laughter.

'Look, Uncle Bill!'

The video is of Sam learning to skateboard. Jen has taken him to the skate park at some point today – the same one where he had learnt as a kid, the same one where he laid on wet grass next to her when she hung on to that big old oak tree.

'I'm going to do the tricks! I'm going to be like you!'

Don't grow up to be like me, he thinks.

He watches the video, watches how Jen comes into view.

'All right, bro,' she says. 'He's doing well, right?'

Her smiling face in this point of his own personal crisis brings tears to his eyes. He wants to tell her everything. He was a kid who did a stupid thing, he thinks, gambled to make it all right and wanted it to be all behind him. Instead it's become more tangled, more complicated.

He emails Victoria Franklin in Canada.

It's done.

Everything now hangs in the balance. New secrets traded against old ones.

THIRTEEN

They're waist-deep in the water. Jen is supposed to be watching Amir because he's under the water and trying to locate a key chain for a lock-up the police have intelligence about, but her mind is on the news article she read this morning. The Olympics is now less than two weeks away and Mark will soon leave for the Olympic Village with the team and the other coaches. The picture that accompanied the news report was of all of them together, all of them smiling, arms around shoulders. Mark's arm around Marie Cadorna's waist.

The New Queen of British Diving.

Jen thinks about the YouTube clip she found of Marie on her TV, and allows herself a moment to think about the past; that, at one time, *she* could have been exactly where Marie Cadorna is now – on the cusp of greatness.

Jen can still recall, like it was yesterday, the moment she first looked into Mark Mason's eyes. She had just dived ten metres, a two-and-a-half somersault, tuck combination, and she had known it had been perfect because she'd heard the 'rip' sound that every diver covets, the entering of the water without making a splash. She came up out of the water, smiling to herself and rested by the side of the pool to catch her breath and watch the water glitter with the dawn of summer through the large-pane windows when a shadow fell over her.

'Hello.'

She looked up to see a man crouched above her. She put him at late-twenties and he had dark hair and jewel-like blue eyes, and his thigh muscles bulged from his sports shorts. His white T-shirt had been splashed and now clung artfully to his honed frame.

'That was a great dive,' he said.

She removed her goggles, frowned because he had an accent. 'Who are you?'

He smiled with his perfect teeth. 'I'm Mark Mason,' he said, 'and I'm looking for Olympians.'

That sentence launched a thousand butterflies in her stomach. There she was, a young girl of fourteen, now with a thud of a glittering future knocking on her heart.

Under his watchful eye, Jen trained every hour God gave her, and allowed herself to believe that she could make something of herself, make something for her family. But it was only four short months before that illusion was shattered so spectacularly. Because Jen met Claudia Franklin through Bill at the river, and became close with her. It was *Jen* who told Claudia to try out for the dive team, never imagining that Claudia might turn out to be a rival, and she was good. Fuck, she was good, and she was also beautiful.

'Excuse me?'

She startles, her vision suddenly sharp. Joe is beside her in the water. 'What?'

He rolls his eyes. 'Exactly. You're not listening.'

'I am listening.'

'Liar.'

She looks to where Amir should be and momentarily panics that she can't see him before she spots him, now above water, and talking to Idris.

Get a fucking hold of yourself, Jen, she says to herself. I will take on any challenges with a calm head, with rationality.

'What did I say then?' Joe asks.

'I don't know. But if it was *anything* about your penis, then it's not worth repeating.'

'It wasn't actually. I said Amir has picked up the keys. Pay attention.'

Idris wades towards them. 'Tomorrow we drive two hours up to the coast – we're needed for a weapons search in the Hamble. Two knives in connection to a stabbing.'

'Juicy,' Joe says.

'Oh, and I got a heads-up from the team that are investigating Claudia Franklin.'

Jen's ears prick. 'What's happening?'

Idris reads from his phone. 'The husband is out of the frame and cleared for travelling for the timeline she went missing.'

'I saw that on the news.'

'Apparently, there's confirmed CCTV of his vehicle driving to his parents' house early Saturday evening and it doesn't come back until the following day. His parents have a camera on their driveway and his car didn't move all night.'

Jen knows all this, of course, because Mark has told her everything that was in his statement to the police.

'Why don't CID think she went missing on the Sunday? Where was Mason on Sunday?'

'She could well have gone missing on Sunday, but the last place her phone was on was at their house at ten-thirty, so that's when the time-frame opens. Mason left his parents' place on the Sunday morning, and went straight to the diving pool. Then he went to a bar and dinner with friends and slept over with one of them, returning home on the Monday, at lunchtime. It was then that he rang in that Claudia was missing because he couldn't get hold of her.'

Joe makes a face. 'Fuck's sake.'

'But, and this is the first interesting development, CID have found blood on one of the garden fence panels. It matches Claudia's DNA. But there's DNA from someone else on it too. As yet unidentified, but *not* Mark Mason's.'

Jen's heart is hammering. 'Jesus.'

Idris puts his phone back into his pocket. 'Yup.'

Sam is sitting at the table they always sit at, with a school-book open in front of him. Kerry is behind the counter, serving someone, and gives Jen a wave.

In the moments before Sam notices her come in, Jen looks at him and her heart swells with love, but her head swarms with questions. What does it mean that Claudia's blood was on a fence panel, and who else's DNA is on there?

'Mum!'

She focuses on Sam, reminds herself firmly of Tranquil's mantra. The present is where her attention needs to be.

'Hi, bub,' she says and sits down in front of him and reaches her hands across the table for his, wants to feel the warmth of him, wants his realness to ground her. 'Did you have a good day at school?'

'Mrs S told us about Nibbles.'

'What's her crazy hamster been up to now?'

Sam's eyes glint. 'She said that he turned the oven on in the middle of the night to make chips, but then he set the fire alarms off and Mrs S had to ring the fire brigade.'

Jen smiles, is thankful for all the people who bring out the joy and imagination in her son. 'That joker.'

'Hi, babe.'

Jen looks up to see Kerry coming over, the white pinny smeared now with rainbow-coloured butter icing and sugar dustings.

'Usual?'

'And whatever you're having,' Jen nods.

'Totally. I'm due a break now anyway.'

Jen nods, looks down at the wooden table, at her son's book and then catches sight of an indent on the table next to it – the faded engraving made years ago with Biro ink that's now washed out – *I was here. Take the moment. J & K.*

Jen and Kerry.

Kerry sits opposite, sets down a tray.

'Thanks for picking him up the last couple of days.'

Kerry shrugs. 'You know I love him.'

'Oh, I forgot, I've got your jacket at home.'

'Did I leave one? Sorry, I'm always shedding at your place.'

'Are you like a snake, Kerry?' Sam asks.

'You think I look like one?' she teases.

'Only when you're mad.'

'Do I get mad?'

'Only at Uncle Bill.'

'Shh!'

Jen laughs.

'There's Miles!' Sam exclaims.

Jen turns to see Miles and his mum, Denise, walking in.

'Can I go and talk to him?' Sam asks.

Jen mouths to Denise, 'That OK?'

Denise nods as they sit down, and Sam goes to join them.

Kerry takes a bite of her bun, and leans towards Jen. 'You OK, babe? It must have been so horrible looking for Claudia.'

'It's more weird that we didn't find her. And that no one has any idea what's happened to her.'

'From what I'm reading in the news, it sounds like the police are out of leads?'

Jen nods. Usually, she can tell Kerry some of the details about her jobs, but not this time. She can't tell her about the phone, the blood on the fence panel, none of it.

'All I know is that Mark Mason has an alibi.'

'I thought perhaps he might have got in touch with you actually. Mark.'

'Why would you think that?'

'Because of . . . well. You know. Your connection to the diving. Shared history.'

'No,' Jen lies.

Kerry sips her latte. 'Bill says you've started sleepwalking again.'

'Yeah.'

'It's because of them, isn't it? Since Claudia and Mark came back, you've been nothing but stressed. That's why you're walking.'

'I—' Jen considers denying it, but Kerry knows her better than anyone. 'I don't know. But I'm OK. Everything is strange right now, obviously.'

'Maybe you should go to the doctor for stronger sleeping tablets?'

'But I'm always on call. There's no way I could knock myself out completely. Idris would freak if he knew I was even taking the other stuff.'

'Maybe it's time for another lock on your door then.'

'Don't, Kez,' Jen says with a grimace. 'You sound like Bill.'

There's a pregnant pause and Jen chastises herself, because she shouldn't have mentioned Bill to Kerry because Kerry's obsession over him is a complete head-fuck for Jen.

'You think Bill is doing OK about this Claudia situation?' Kerry asks.

'He's worried. We both are. But we didn't find her, which means she's still missing, so I'm hopeful.'

'Really?'

'No one knows. Anyway, you've seen more of Bill than I have. How do *you* think he's doing?'

'He's been distracted. But I saw him earlier this week and he was on good form. We went out to The Black Rat. That's got to mean something, right?'

Jen says nothing – it's safer not to feed her friend hope. She's also working out how Bill could afford a restaurant like The Black Rat. She hopes it's not from another loan, but then a betting windfall would be no better. In fact, that would be worse.

'He's my lobster, Jen.'

Jen smiles despite herself. 'Fuck's sake. Happy birthday, mate, though. I'm sorry I've been rubbish.'

Kerry leans across the table. 'I love you both, you know that?'

'Of course I know. And I love you back.' Jen sighs. 'If anyone comes to talk to you about me . . . you know, about before . . . about the diving . . .'

'Listen, all that was so long ago. It would have come up before now, right? So don't worry about it.'

'I can't lose my job, Kez,' Jen whispers.

'You won't,' Kerry says. 'Why would you?'

'Because I haven't declared my connection.'

'You're not connected.'

We'll always be connected, Jen thinks. Through Mark, through their history of diving, and the barn. Through Sam. As if on cue, her son bounces back over.

'You're a hero in my eyes, you understand?' Kerry says to Jen, turns to Sam. 'Isn't your mum a legend, babe?'

'She's Superhands.'

'She is. What you do every day, Jen, is nought short of amazing. The likes of me fanny about making people cups of tea, and doing bridal hair and make-up on the side. That's all surface stuff. You're the real deal.'

'People need their cups of tea and their make-up doing. People need to feel happy. You give happiness.'

'They sure do, babe,' Kerry says. 'But they need people like you more.'

Jen smiles and thinks how lucky she is to have a best friend like Kerry. For years, they've sat at this very table; painted their nails together and done their homework, planned nights out, and nights in. There have been tears shared at this table, laughter, frustration and secrets.

It feels strange to remember that Jen used to sit here once upon a time with Claudia, and not Kerry. It had been Claudia who had etched out – *I was here. Take the moment.* It was something Mark used to say in training and they used to laugh about it.

Stand on the edge of that platform, take the moment to look at the water. Tell yourself you are here, *that you can do this.*

Perhaps it was Mark's pep talks that kick-started Jen's self-help addiction.

It was years later when Kerry added a scratch to make the 'C' a 'K' instead when Jen's friendship with Claudia was so damaged. Kerry believes that it was when Claudia won the British Championships, which led to her becoming part of the Olympic diving team, but it was months before that – the fire at the barn.

FOURTEEN

Jen knows Mark's schedule because she's had to learn it from all the many secret meetings they have managed to negotiate in the last few months, but she's never interrupted one of the training sessions before. It's Thursday, seven in the morning, and no one else is here at the dive pool except for the team. No one is usually allowed to be there at any time because it's off-putting for the divers, but Jen flashes her police badge at the receptionist, who immediately opens the glass doors for her without question, and she walks upstairs and slips through to the viewing gallery.

She hasn't been here for years. It's a purpose-built deep pool for training, with a tower of three platforms of varying heights and a water depth of five metres. She used to jump from all of them. She sees three girls are in the warming pool, talking, but she can't hear what they're saying over the agitator – the spray of water that distorts the surface of the water, ready for divers to enter. That used to be her and Claudia and the other girls she's lost touch with.

She looks up the board, sees that Mark is up on the ten-metre platform with one of the girls – recognises her immediately as Marie Cadorna. From what Jen knows, she lived in Wales and then relocated a hundred miles away so she could try out the career and see if it suited her. With his coaching, it looks like it fits her perfectly.

No one has noticed Jen, so she takes a moment to watch, enjoy the drama of the sport. She misses the discipline of perfectly positioning her body, and the thrill of getting it right, the thrill of potential disaster if she didn't. Free-falling through the air at thirty-five miles an hour is not for the faint-hearted – diving is a collision sport, put in the same category as boxing, football and ice hockey, and the force of hitting the water can break bones and dislocate joints. As well as the constant risk of injury from entering the pool at the wrong angle, divers suffer similar issues as gymnasts – overusing their muscles with jumps, arches and twists, but God, it was all she wanted. Her fists involuntary clench, her short nails making tiny crescents in the flesh of her palm. Another life, she thinks.

She focuses on Mark. The mess of her relationship with him started up when he and Claudia returned from Boston. Jen had bumped into him in the leisure centre pool, where she goes as often as she can, where Sam has his lessons. That day, she'd come up out of the water to rest and check the time because Sam would be finishing and she needed to get out to meet him. But as she looked to the clock on the wall, someone was standing below it and staring right at her.

She heard the hitch in her breath as she registered him – Mark.

'Jen?'

She could have dived back into the water to escape him, but she was so shocked that he took the split second of her paralysis and walked over to her. He knelt down to her, just like that first time when she had been fourteen, when he'd told her that he was looking for Olympians.

'What are you doing here?' she had asked coldly.

She *wanted* to feel angry, she wanted to slap him round the face and yell at him for having ghosted her since their night at the hotel. Yes, she'd learnt to live without him, had hardened her heart to the fact that he was not hers and would never be, but, here he was now, in front of her. Older, more lined but tanned and still handsome.

'We came back from America.'

She got out of the pool, glanced behind her to make sure Sam was still engaged in his lesson. 'Why did you come back? Are you here to stay?'

'Yes. We moved back three weeks ago. My career opportunities are here. I'm training with the UK team again, back at the dive pool. My parents have been here for years, if you'll remember; my dad grew up around here.'

'You're living with them?'

'No, Oak House.'

She shook her head, trying to land all this information. 'But Oak House is rented?'

'Was,' he corrected. 'We're there now.'

She could only nod, numb, but knowing that his return was going to be her undoing. How would she avoid everything he had once meant to her if she saw him in town, or at the pool again like this? How *dare* he move back here without contacting her first?

'I have to go,' she said and she turned to walk away. Sam couldn't see Mark here. Here, anywhere.

He grabbed at her hand. 'Wait, Jen. I wondered how'd you'd been. If I'd ever see you again.'

She snatched her hand back. 'I've always been here.'

'I'm sorry for the silence.'

'I should go,' she said, glancing again at Sam – saw his was head down, practising his front crawl.

'Are you here with someone?' he asked, turning his head to the direction she looked in.

'I . . . no.'

She should have said yes, should have told him that she was here with a boyfriend, or husband. In the early years after Sam was born, when she was bone-weary with night feeds and sleep deprivation, she had imagined Mark's heartbreak at thinking that she could have moved on and was with someone else. She craved him to be angry that she could have other romantic interests, wanted him to sit at home and worry. She wanted him to match the nights that she'd spent imagining him with Claudia and their happy life together, while she was impotent to change the situation she was in.

'Your body is the same,' he said, looking her up and down. 'Strong.'

To anyone else, that might have sounded inappropriate, rude, but her body and all its potential had been the reason he had picked her out for training all those years ago. The body, in sport, no longer belongs to the individual, but to the team.

'I have to keep fit for work. I'm a diver, remember?'

He looked at her quizzically. 'You're diving again?'

'For the police. I was in training when I saw you that time . . . when you came back from Boston.'

'That's pretty something.'

She glanced again to the learner pool, saw that Sam was now getting *out*. In panic, she started to move away from Mark, chastising herself that she'd let herself talk to him for too long.

'I've got to go,' she said and made to pass him.

He stepped forward. 'I'd really like to see you again.'

He was obscuring her vision, she craned her neck to try to see Sam. 'I don't think so—'

'I feel so bad. After . . . after we left things.'

She looked at him then, dead in the eyes. 'After *you* left *me*.'

'I know I did.'

'Mum?'

The breath left her body. *Not like this.*

Sam was by her side, stood beside her, with droplets running down his arms and legs. He beamed up at Mark.

'Hello,' he said. 'I'm Sam.'

Mark looked from Sam back to Jen and she saw the moment it landed – the shock, horror, anger, hurt – so many emotions played out across his face, before he plastered on a smile.

'Good to meet you, buddy.'

Sam pulled Jen's arm. 'Can I go and play?'

'Two minutes.'

Sam bounded off towards the jet sprays and the bright Styrofoam wheels of the splash area and Jen dragged her eyes back to Mark, who looked like he was about to cry, about to rage.

'He's mine, isn't he?'

'He's yours.'

'But . . . but I didn't think that you'd keep it.'

Her fists clenched. '*Him*. His name is Sam. You got my messages then. That I was pregnant.'

He looked shamefaced. 'I got your messages.'

'You ignored them.'

He looked over to Sam, whose dark hair was slick to his head, his eyes shining with delight as his fingers wove through the tickling water of a fountain.

'God, Jen. I'm sorry. I was trying to make a life.' He stops, realising his words. 'He . . . he looks like a real nice kid.'

'He *is* a nice kid.'

'*Fuck*.'

'I don't want anything from you, Mark. I don't *need* anything. We've done fine without you.'

She went to go, but he caught her arm.

'We could have a coffee?' he said quickly. 'Don't we *need* to talk about this? This is . . . this is huge.'

'It was huge when I found out I was pregnant.'

He watched Sam. 'I know, but he's . . . he's real now. He's my son. What's his birthday?'

'New Year's Day.'

'Shit.'

'Yeah. That was a fun New Year's night,' she said and betrayed herself with a smile at the memory.

'Does he know anything about me?'

'He doesn't think he was conceived by immaculate conception, if that's what you mean.'

Mark flushed. 'But does he know my name?'

'No one knows you're his dad.'

'No one? Not Bill or your friends?'

'No.'

She couldn't read his face at that moment. Was there relief there? Hurt?

'Will you give me your number?' he asked. 'I can cancel a session next week, OK? Please?'

'My number is still the same. It hasn't changed. If you had called me in all these years, you would have known that.'

'I'm sorry,' he said. 'Really.'

'I have to go.'

'Next week – let me know when is a good day, or an evening, and we'll talk. Spend the day with me and tell me about him.'

His urgency caught her off guard. Here he was and he'd met their boy, their *Sam,* and he hadn't run away. He wanted to talk about Sam, know him.

She let him programme her number into his phone and he texted the very next day with a date to meet. Now it's a regular meeting and her stories about Sam pour out of her because their kid amazes her, and she wants to – no, more than that, *needs* to – pass this pride on to Mark. He has to know what a great boy Sam is – that at six years old he can ride his bike one-handed, that he's learning to skateboard, that he sings pitch-perfect, that he loves Santana. She wants Mark to also know and respect what a good mum *she* is. That although her work is demanding and she's time-poor, her bond with Sam is fierce. She knows when he's unwell before he does, knows what dinner he wants before he asks, knows his insecurities, his joys. It seems that Mark does appreciate all this, and in gratitude – and perhaps to alleviate his guilt – he has set up a trust for Sam as a way of a thank you. At first, she didn't want it, but it carries a princely sum and she would be foolish not to accept it. She wants big things for Sam and the trust will deliver it.

Jen studies how Marie walks to the front of the board, confident and elegant, before turning around so she's facing Mark and with her back to the water below. He nods at her and she edges to the end of the platform, placing her feet precisely so that she can stand up on her toes. She holds her arms out wide, like a bird, for balance, before she then lifts them to propel her body up and rotate herself backwards.

Jen holds her breath as she tucks her head to her knees and holds her legs which are extended and rigid into pike position. It's a difficult triple pike, with a quick unfolding into an arrow before entering the water, but she executes it effortlessly. Jen hears the rip, feels the satisfaction of the dive wash over her as if she herself had done it. Bubbles rise to the surface of the water and then Marie breaks it, her face expressionless – a refusal of acknowledgement that it was a good dive – as she gets out of the pool.

'Excellent!' Mark yells down, a smile wide across his face, and his praise echoes around the pool.

It's then that he notices Jen in the viewing gallery, and his smile vanishes.

'Shall I go again?' Marie asks. Her voice has the distinctive beautiful Welsh lilt to it, musical, but it seems at odds with her grave disposition.

'No. Get in the warming pool. I'll come down.'

Jen watches as Marie tracks Mark's eyeline and she spots Jen.

'You know what, girls? We're done for today, OK? Sorry to cut it short, but I've got to speak to this woman here.'

Mark's shoes thud on the metal stairs as he comes down. The girls get out of the pool, pick up their shammys to dry themselves, and Jen looks at the little towels with nostalgia, knows that they are a diver's comfort blanket – used so a diver can dry off between dives, and to keep them warm, and to ensure that their bodies don't slip out of position in their next dive. Jen watches them file into the dressing room. Marie is the last to leave, and she turns back to Jen, seems to stare right through her.

Mark bends down to turn off the agitator and the pool goes silent, the water settling into glass. Jen steps over the white chairs and hops over the low white wall so she's standing poolside with him.

'What are you doing here? I'm teaching. I don't want the girls going back to their families and telling them the *police* interrupted our session. You're lucky none of the other coaches are here.'

'I'm not in official uniform,' she says. 'And even if the girls did know I'm police, I didn't come here in any sort of aggressive manner. If anything, they might tell their parents that I was friendly. I'm on your side. Because I am, OK? And I wanted to reach out in person – after everything that's gone on.'

'Thanks,' he says quietly.

'She's good. Marie, I mean.'

'She is.'

'A bit dead behind the eyes, though,' she says with a grin, remembering the comment she read on the YouTube clip.

Mark doesn't laugh. 'She's been through the foster system, she's got a chip on her shoulder, but this is her chance for something big. She's serious about her career. And thank God. Because a lot of them are, I don't know . . . being weird with me now. Different.' He looks hurt. 'It's like they think I've done something to Claud, Jen. I've not touched her. The police need to issue a proper statement.'

She puts a hand to his shoulder, squeezes it.

'The Olympics are around the corner,' he says, 'and Claudia decides to go and disappear and cause a scene.'

She's surprised at his anger, his dismissal that it can't be something more serious than Claudia having upped and left him. Jen thinks that he can't know that CID have found traces of her blood on the fence panels.

'Cause a scene? You actually think she's somewhere safe? With none of her belongings with her? Her phone off?'

'I don't know.' He looks around the empty pool.

'Has Victoria been tracked down yet?'

'She's not responded to my calls, or the detective's, but then I'm not sure why I'm expecting it to be easy to make contact. Claudia had no correspondence with her for years. We don't even know her address.'

'She should be here.'

'I know.' He sighs. 'I feel like I'm doing it all on my own. Why can't the police do a better job of this?'

She understands his frustration, his grief, but to hear it directly from Mark punches her in the gut; no one goes into the police wanting to be the bad guy. She shouldn't rise to the challenge, but she gets heated when people blame the police for perceived lack of progress. Every step of the way through an investigation, there's criticism, there's balancing the media and public opinion, and then a stretched budget on top of that.

'You can go screw yourself if you're going to go off on one blaming things on *us*,' she says. 'Why don't *you* know where she is?'

'Can I account for her every move?' he snaps. 'I was at my parents. How can someone disappear like this? Someone like her? I'm here carrying on with the training, but should I be here? Should I be at home the entire time in case she shows? Should I be out looking for her? I'm going out of my mind.'

'The investigative team will be handling it as best they can. You concentrate on the Olympics. It's a good distraction.'

'It's more than that, it's a *commitment*,' he says. 'To the team. To myself.'

'I get it. Just keep passing any information to the police that you think might be useful or relevant.'

'I know you're not involved in the day-to-day running of this case, but I wanted to talk to you about something. I wanted to tell you before, but I . . . didn't know how to. But with every day that passes and with no sign of her, I think you need to know.'

'Know what?'

He pauses. 'I saw Bill with Claudia, a couple of weeks ago.'

Jen's winded by this. Bill told her he hadn't spoken to Claudia, let alone seen her. 'Seriously? Where?'

'The Corner House Cafe. I was due to be out that day, but my meeting was postponed so I went to town and I saw them there, through the window.'

'Right. I . . . OK. Have you told this to the police?'

'No, I'm telling you. I thought he might know something about Claud.'

'Why? Did she look like she was telling him where she was planning on going on the twenty-ninth of June?'

She's being defensive, sarcastic, but she can't help it.

'I thought he might have told you something about their meeting,' he says. 'I tried to email him but he hasn't emailed back.'

'You didn't ask Claudia about it at the time?'

'No?'

'Why?'

'I guess I was surprised she hadn't told me she was meeting him. I was a bit taken aback.'

'I'll ask him about it,' she says.

'Word it carefully.'

She frowns. 'Carefully? What does that mean?'

'Because, Jen, I'm sorry to say it, but I've never fully trusted him. Not after what happened at the barn.'

Fury ignites in her chest. He's never once used that day against her, against Bill. 'You think Bill would have anything to do with Claudia having gone missing?'

He's silent.

'Mark? Do you? He would *never*.'

He raises his hands in a defensive gesture. 'I'm telling you what I saw. You should ask him before I'm forced to mention it higher up.'

Her eyes widen.

'I'm trying to protect him,' Mark says.

'Call me if you think of anything else *useful*,' Jen says and leaves the pool.

She gets in the car, slams the door closed and thinks hard. Five minutes pass and then ten, and then she punches out a name in her contacts, an old friend from First Response who now works in Fraud. Travis answers on the first ring and she thanks God that he works early and works hard.

'Jen Harper. To what do I owe this pleasure?'

'Trav, how you doing?'

'I'm cool, yeah. How you doing?'

'You know. Smelling of roses in the shittiest of places.'

He laughs down the line.

'I wondered if you could do something for me, Trav? It's really stupid. I don't even want to ask you, but I said I'd make some enquiries.'

'Sure?'

'Can you see if there are any CCTV cameras on Bereweeke North? My friend lives there and thinks someone keeps taking her bin.'

He pauses. 'Her bin?'

'Yeah. Look, I'm sorry. I know this is a waste of your resources, but it's the third time it's happened and I said I'd look into it. She's worried someone's targeting her or something.'

The lie trips off her tongue so easily, even though it's lame. She should have thought of something better, but it needed to be something forgettable.

'First-world problems,' Travis says.

'Right? I told you it was a waste of your time.'

'What date?'

'The twenty-ninth of June. Afternoon.'

'You want me to send you a file when I've got it? Tomorrow?'

'Can you? Thanks, Trav. I appreciate it.'

'Hope your friend gets her bin back.'

'She's pretty shaken up,' she says, accidentally talking about herself. Understatement of the year.

FIFTEEN

Another day has passed. It's Friday and Jen's had a day in the water, fishing for knives in the Solent, and it's seven-thirty in the evening now. She wants to be at home with Sam, but instead she's in base, told Idris that she wanted to complete some mandatory online training before tomorrow, but the real reason is because she wants to log on to her emails.

She makes conversation with the few people left – they share the helicopter base and a few of them are always on call – and then, when she's satisfied that everyone is settled, she logs into one of the computers. She knows she shouldn't have asked Travis to do this for her, but she has to know, has to discount her own mounting fears, that Bill might have lied to her about his whereabouts that Saturday night. And if he has, then why?

Travis has already sent her the file and she puts it on speed motion, skimming through the footage from the entire twenty-four hours of the day that Claudia Franklin apparently disappeared. With each passing hour that ticks down in the bottom right-hand corner, Jen's heart rate increases, because not once does her brother appear on the street where Kerry lives, not once does her best friend open her door.

She deletes the email immediately and, with a sickening dread, she steps out of the base to call Bill.

'What's up?'

She can hear music in the background. He's at The Hare because it's a Friday.

'You need to come over,' she says, bypassing 'hello'.

'What's happened? Is it something to do with Claudia?'

'You tell me,' she says and hangs up.

It's nine in the evening when Bill walks mud and clay into her flat. Jen sighs, pointedly, and he rolls his eyes, but then begrudgingly takes off his boots.

'You know how long these take to lace up?' Bill mutters.

'Get ones with Velcro.'

'Fuck off.' He laughs.

She didn't mean to make a joke, but it works in her favour because she needs him to sit down and feel comfortable. *She* also needs to feel comfortable in order to question him like she knows she has to.

She walks into the kitchen and he follows her, sits at the small table. There's a sandwich waiting for him.

He looks up at her. 'You made me a sandwich?'

She leans against the counter, folds her arms and then unfolds them. She doesn't know what to do with them suddenly.

'I always make you food,' she says.

'No, you always make food for the fridge,' he replies. 'And I eat it. There's a difference. What's the matter?'

She glances to the door, although it's locked and bolted and Sam is asleep in bed.

'Why didn't you tell me that you'd seen Claudia?'

His mouth slackens. 'What?'

'Mark told me he'd seen you both in town a while ago.'

'Mark – Mark Mason?'

'Yes.'

'Where? The cafe?'

'Yes.'

'Did he . . . did he tell the police he'd seen us?'

'Not CID, but *I'm* police, so what do you suggest I'm supposed to do with this information?'

'I did bump into her once.'

'What did you talk about?'

He curls his top lip. 'What's this, an interview?'

'I wouldn't make you a fucking sandwich if this was an interview,' she says. 'Just answer the question.'

'Is it a crime that I saw her? I hadn't seen her in years and there's history . . . obviously.'

'Why didn't you tell me?'

'I . . . It slipped my mind.'

She is furious. 'Slipped your fucking *mind?* Are you insane? What did the two of you talk about?'

'It was a catch-up.'

'A catch up sounds like you're in contact regularly. Were you?'

'No – a couple of times since she came back.'

'You just said *once*. Why were you meeting with her?'

'Jen, really,' he says and he looks away.

He's deflecting again by not meeting her eyes.

'It was nothing. She wanted help with something.'

'What something?'

He still doesn't look at her. 'House stuff. She wanted to sell Oak House. I said I'd ask around for her. Andy has a client list. She asked me for help. Like I was going to tell her no?'

'And what time did you go and see Kerry the night Claudia went missing?'

'I told you,' he says. 'I went over in the afternoon and stayed overnight.'

'No, you didn't, you liar.'

Now his eyes snap up. 'What did Kerry say?'

'She didn't say anything. *I* looked at the CCTV of her road today from that night, and guess what I saw? Not you. You didn't go there and you lied to me. So where were you?'

He's silent.

She sucks at her top teeth. 'Don't make me—'

'Make you what? *Accuse* me of something?'

'Are you in trouble?'

'Are *you*?' he counters.

She's taken aback by this question. 'Me? Why do you say that?'

'Oh, I don't know,' he says, rolling his eyes. He stands up, pushing his chair back. 'Coming back from God knows where, sopping wet?'

'That's nothing new—' she starts.

'You said it yourself,' he interrupts. 'You've never gone in the water before when you walk the loop. Never, not once since you started doing it.'

'Whoa, whoa. Don't you turn this back on me.'

Bill reaches for his boots, shoves his feet inside and stands up. The laces are trailing, and make him look like the teenager he once was.

'Where are you going?'

She grabs his collar, wrenches him up to face her.

His eyes are wide like saucers. 'You have to give me time, OK? Just buy me some time.'

'Time for what? If you know something about what happened to Claudia, you need to tell me!'

'Let me make things right,' he says. 'Let me pay off my debts.'

'Is this about your gambling? What's going on, Bill?'

'I can't compromise you. All that you've worked so hard for, OK?'

'*What?*'

'You have to trust me. I owe people money and . . . Claudia said she'd help me, but she couldn't and now . . .' He shakes his head. 'I have to go.'

She lurches for him, but he moves before she can reach him.

'Where do you think you're going after you've told me *that*? Sit the fuck down! I can help you with money—'

He's at the door. 'You haven't got the money I need.'

'Wait—'

But he's gone, has opened all the locks and the door is shutting behind him.

'Bill!'

She grabs the door just before it catches, shouts out of it, but he's gone.

'Shit, shit!'

She stands, uselessly, heart thrumming. Why would Claudia want to sell Oak House? Did Mark know about it? She assumes not if Claudia sought out Bill to talk to, the one person she would have known would do anything for her. If he wasn't with Kerry on Saturday night, where was he? Jen thinks about the blood on the panel, the DNA unidentified.

SIXTEEN

Bill needs to kill time. Not too much time that anyone – namely Jen – can go looking for him, but enough time to set everything in motion. Since he left her flat, his sister has called him over a dozen times, but he's ignored her and has driven out of town to Cowell Farm.

He stops the engine, and sits in the truck for a while, gathering all the mental energy it will take him to walk to the water's edge to stare beyond the river to the skeleton of the barn. After a moment, he sets out, opens the gate and walks through the rough grass, following the water until he reaches the barn on the bank opposite. The air is fresh, birdsong the only sound permeating the noise of the river.

They first discovered the barn as kids. They would clamber over the old rusted machinery that was housed inside, or climb the ladder to the old hayloft. They'd talk about school, tell each other jokes, funny stories about people in their classes. And later, sometimes they would talk about their mother's spiralling demise. He remembers vividly a time that Fiona hadn't been herself and threw a glass against a wall which smashed all over the floor. When she had eventually fallen asleep, Bill had crept out of his room and cleared it up, but he'd missed some shards and Jen had trodden on a piece the next day, barefooted. He'd never seen so much blood, was horrified at his mistake. He'd taken Jen to the bathroom, washed out the cut, plastered it, and then they'd cycled to the barn, the one place that was safe for them on a weekend morning because school was closed.

When they were teenagers, often Bill would come alone. Just as Jen had her sleepwalking, he had his day-dreams. He would lie on the planks of wood in the hayloft and close his eyes to imagine Claudia, imagine peeling back the wet straps from her swimming costume, place his hot fingertips to her breasts.

But despite so many memories of this place, there's one that dominates the rest. Every time he smells a bonfire, he is transported back to that day. He hates going to country pubs that have open fires and he avoids fireworks night even when three-year-old Sam cried for him to go. Now Sam knows not to ask – thinks Uncle Bill doesn't like the loud noises, like a dog.

He wasn't even supposed to be swimming at Cowell Farm that day.

A bird flies past his eyeline. He sees movement by the timber.

'Hello?'

There's nothing but shadows.

'Come out!' he yells.

But he knows there's no one there. He's screaming at ghosts.

It's eleven at night when he drives his pick-up to the site. A branded company truck coming at this time might attract the odd glance from still-awake neighbours who may think it's late to be working, but arriving in the dead of night – as he so desperately wants to – would tip the scales into suspicion.

He parks the truck and then switches vehicles to the nondescript black van that has been delivered by his scatty friend who doesn't bother with paperwork. Bill told Andy that they might need it for extra pick-ups from suppliers, but it was a lie. He uses it now, and parks it up outside number ten, and opens the garage.

No one is here to see what he's doing, but even so, he looks around to check before climbing on top of a mini forklift to collect the fridge-freezer and the generator from inside the garage, carefully elevating them, and placing them into the back of the black van and securing them. He's lucky it hasn't rained recently – there will be no evidence of him having driven up, but even so, he puts the forklift back exactly where it was before. His heart is racing as he drives out of the site, jumps out of the van, and locks the gate again.

He drives to the end of the road before stopping and taking out his phone.

'Andy?'

'All right, mate?' Andy says. 'What's up?'

'Sorry it's late, but I've got to go away for a while, OK? Family emergency. You all right to hold the site for a week?'

There's a pause. 'A whole week? I . . . Sure. Everything OK?'

'Everything's fine, but I need to get away for a bit. I'll check in, OK?'

'The last steels go up next week. I know you hate to miss them?'

'I know,' Bill says and wonders how many houses he might jinx in not being there. But what more could go wrong now?

'Hope everything is OK, mate.'

Bill says goodbye and rings off. He needs to disappear. He's going north and he's going right now. Fridge-freezer and all. He switches off his phone and begins the drive to Cumbria.

SEVENTEEN

It's Sunday, two days now since Bill pleaded with Jen to trust him, but he's given her no reason to.

'Why are we at Uncle Bill's?'

She looks down at Sam, who stands beside her outside Bill's flat.

'We need to see if he's OK, bub. He's not answering my calls.'

All the time she's spent worrying over Mark and what he might have done, when she should have been worrying about Bill.

'Oh,' says Sam.

Bill lives minutes away in a red-bricked block that could once have been pretty and sought after but now is run-down and poorly maintained. He could afford so much nicer and bigger if he was better at saving money, but she knows his gambling addiction has been present in both of their lives since what happened at the barn, and then worsened a year later when their mother died. The apps are the result of a swirling black mass of guilt and grief and shame in his heart that he harnesses into self-destruction, but whenever she tries to address it, he laughs it off, and then manages to claw himself back from the precipice. But he's balanced on a knife-edge, she knows.

Aren't they all.

She thinks that maybe she could help him with money now that Mark has set up the trust for Sam. She's a trustee and can draw from it whenever she likes, but even if she did so, it's not what Bill needs long term. He needs years of therapy.

Don't they all.

The key is smooth and cold in her hand. She opens the door and as they step inside, Jen's nostrils are hit with the smell of damp washing, and the citrus tang of Bill's expensive aftershave.

'Bill?'

She walks the footprint of the flat.

'He's not here, Mum.'

'No . . . Can you do me a favour, bub? Can you see if Uncle Bill left any food in the fridge? He's always got chocolate in, hasn't he?'

Sam wonders through to the kitchen happily and Jen starts to leaf through all the dog-eared books, looks behind the sofa cushions in the living room. She doesn't know what she's looking for, but she's a police officer, a specialist at searches, and there are clues everywhere to a person's mental state of mind, if nothing physical.

'I found a Twix.'

'My favourite. One finger each, yeah? Do you want to put the TV on while I tidy up for him a bit?'

Sam nods and she smiles and when he's engrossed in a programme, she goes to Bill's bedroom, turns cupboards upside down, takes out all the linen in the trunks and removes the top of the toilet to look into the cistern. She riffles through his bathroom cabinets, tries to ignore how many packets of pharmacy pills and prescription Prozac packets he's got stacked up. She checks under the bed, strips it, turns the mattress over, goes to the wardrobe and checks on top of it, and inside it. A suit hangs on the wardrobe door, the suit he wore for that interview. He'd sent a picture of himself in it because she'd lent him a tie. He looked good and she told him so, but that pride in him is now uncomfortable.

She leaves the bedroom, opens all the kitchen drawers, tips up the cutlery tray, pulls out the plates and the bowls. She looks in the larder, the fridge, the freezer.

Nothing, nothing. She stands, hands on hips and thinks. He wouldn't be at the barn, would he? He sometimes liked to camp out there, but she knows now he only associates it with bad feeling. He wouldn't be there, but where the hell is he?

'Come on, bub,' she says.

'Aren't we waiting for Uncle Bill?'

'I don't know when he's coming back,' she says and then chokes on her own words.

She locks up.

'What now?' Sam asks.

She looks down at him, feels the swell of guilt wash over her. She can't go to Bill's site, no one would be there anyway, and she can't break in.

'Now I take you to the park like I promised, weeks ago.'

Flowers are out with their heads tipped up, paying worship to the midday sun. There are other kids here from school, but Sam won't play with them yet – not while Jen is here and he has her all to himself. He's excited to be with her, he's always excited to be with her, and she knows she should treasure this time, even though she's exhausted, because there will be a time, not too far in the future, where he won't let her pull him in for a cuddle whenever the whim takes her, won't let her muss his hair, or let her read to him.

'Look, Mum!' he cries.

He's on the high climbing frame, standing right at the exposed edge, and it sets her heart on fire, but she doesn't rush to tell him to step back. He grins at her and then flies down the metal slide and she exhales.

'Nice one,' she says as he goes again.

'Put on your stopwatch,' he says and races to the obstacle course.

She obliges, sets her watch, and shouts go. There are two mums near the swings that have kids in Sam's year and she thinks maybe it would be nice to speak to them, strike up some sort of interaction, if only for Sam's sake, but she can't because her head is completely filled with worry. Where is Bill? Where is Claudia?

'How many seconds?'

'Twenty-three! Go again.'

She finds a free bench to sit on, one that's not covered in coats and bags like a sunbed on holiday, and takes her phone out to scroll the news pages again for something to do, to feel like she's trying to navigate this mess, even when she's in a children's playground, for God's sake.

'How many now?' Sam shouts.

'Twenty-one,' she calls, flashing him a smile even though she hadn't been watching.

Sam beams and runs off to the climbing frame. She watches him for a while and then looks to the copse of trees behind the playground. She and Bill used to play in this park. There is the chestnut tree standing slightly apart from the rest. It used to have a partner, an oak tree that had been storm-wrecked over the years, but it was cut down a few years back. Bill told her when the council had wrapped tape around it; he said he wanted to warn her that it would be taken down because he thought she might cry about it. She remembers that she had laughed at that because she'd never thought much about that tree, but when it was cut down, she'd been devastated. She didn't even really know why. But he'd known before she did that she would be sad about it and that was her brother all over. He cared about her, he loved her. And she loved him – *loves* him – so she has to trust him now.

The air is cool on her face, she wants the wind to whisper in her ears like a conscience, and tell her what to do to make all this better. She looks for Sam, sees him at the top of the slide with a young woman next to it, her head tilted upwards and talking to him. Jen gets up and starts to walk over, but as soon as she does, the woman walks swiftly out of the park gate.

'Who was that?' she asks.

'One of the childminder people,' Sam replies, running round the climbing frame to go down the slide again. 'She's nice. She comes every week.'

Jen looks over towards where the woman walked, but she's disappeared in a throng of other parents and children.

'What was she asking you?'

'She asked if were you a police officer.'

'What did you say?'

Sam grins at her. 'I said you were better than a police officer. I said you were a police *diver* and I call you Superhands.'

She doesn't want her son targeted because of what she does, but perhaps she's been naive to this – the police and the investigation into Claudia's disappearance are the talk to the town, of the nation.

'We don't talk to strangers,' she says.

'But she's not, though,' he says, and then he pulls her arm. 'Your phone's ringing, Mum.'

She answers it before reading the screen. 'Bill?'

'It's me,' Idris says. 'You need to get to the base. It's about Claudia Franklin.'

She looks at Sam.

'I'll come in now,' she says and she touches Sam's cheek gently because she sees it – that whisper of sadness that crosses his face before he stoically rearranges it again into a smile for her.

EIGHTEEN

The holiday let is a remote, old farmhouse with views over Eden Valley, and with no neighbours for miles. It's perfect. In the lemon light of the afternoon, Bill steps outside and drinks in the towering hilltops beyond the stone-walled garden, soothed by the knowledge that this vast landscape cloaks all within it.

Inside, he is equally reassured there is invisibility. There are heavy blackout curtains to aid sleep, white walls so everything feels clean. There are spotless mirrors, plants in ceramic pots in every room, and a dog basket. Bill wishes he had a dog, feels like he's a man that should have one, a Lab or a setter or another sort of big hound. But right now all he has is the view and the sounds of birds calling and the warmth of the rising sun on his skin.

He thinks back to what Kerry said to him at dinner, how she accused him of not fighting for Jen when she had missed the British Championships and, if he's being honest with himself, her words hit a nerve, because they were true. Jen had missed one competition, but forfeiting it had closed all the door to the Olympics for her. Mark had made up his mind, and set his sights elsewhere, on Claudia, and by that time, after what happened at the barn, neither Bill or Jen were in a position to challenge it.

After that missed event, Jen faded into the background of the swim club, like a burnt-out star. Once showered with praise from Mark, and then dismissed. It was impossible for Bill to ignore the increasing hurt on her face when they cycled the ninety minutes home again from the diving pool together. Her hurt was like something physical – a needle stabbing him in the heart.

'Hey,' he said one day. 'You're better than what Mark has done to you. You deserved to have been picked.'

Her face changed then and she was angry. 'What would you know about it? Mark is the coach, the everything. *My* everything, but I wasn't good enough for him.'

Her words stunned him, surprised him, and he stopped cycling. 'He's not the "everything",' he said. 'Maybe you should stop diving now, sis, it's making you sad.'

Jen stopped too, and turned back to look at him. 'You don't get it, Bill. Diving is the only thing I know how to do well and it was the only thing that could have changed things for us. Proper care for Mum, a better life for her when—'

He made a sharp noise to cut her off. 'Don't say it.'

'I *will* say it. Proper care for when she gets worse. Because she *is* getting worse – she's so bad now.'

'Leave Mum to me,' he said firmly. 'I can look after her. Just promise me you'll think about other things you're good at. Focus on other things other than diving, aside from Mark. You could be a swimming instructor?'

'I have to be *in* the water, not out of it.'

She went on, of course, to join the police and specialise in the murkiest of units. But the lure of the water wasn't why she joined. No, it was the guilt that she carried – that she *still* carries. As does he. He sighs into the stillness and a bird flits from the hedgerow and onto the stone wall in front of him. He knows that he'll need to check in with Andy at some point, but he can't turn his phone on yet because he's worried about being tracked. He'll have to drive elsewhere to look at it, in case someone thinks to check on his location.

God, it's all such a mess.

He took a leap, he thinks, and it was for love, but love makes people do stupid things.

NINETEEN

Jen steps up into the dive lorry, dumps her bag on the floor. The others are already all there – even Gareth.

'I called you an hour ago,' Idris says, in a tone that's tells her he's pissed off.

'I had to wait for Kerry to say she could pick up Sam for me,' she says, in a tone that tells him to back off.

'Fine,' he says, in a tone that tells her he won't.

He doesn't get it, she thinks, none of them do. How can they possibly understand how hard it is to raise a child as a single parent, and keep focus on this job. She puts her hands on her hips. She loves her job, loves being a police diver, but being a parent at the same time takes all the energy she has. She's wrung dry from so many moments of heartache, of guilt. And now Claudia on top of it all.

'Sit down,' he says. 'We're going.'

'I'm fine standing,' she replies, a tiny rebellion of his command.

'Fine, but you'll fall over,' he says.

The lorry makes its guttural splutter and starts to move. She's immediately unbalanced, tuts loudly and straps herself in.

'One of the pieces of material that we bagged is back from the labs and it's got Claudia's DNA on it.'

'Shit, really?'

'Her husband's DNA is on it, too.'

Jen's heart sparks.

'What does that mean?' Joe asks. 'He's back in the picture again as a suspect?'

Idris gets out his map. 'It could be an item of clothing that's entirely unrelated, but it's enough evidence to inject some funding into a new dive search. Right now there's no more reason to suspect Mark Mason than any other person, but obviously he'll be coming in for questioning again.'

Jen's heart is thumping wildly. She forces herself to breathe.

'What's most interesting is that there are DNA strands from two other people, as yet unconfirmed, but one of them matches the DNA on the fence panel where traces of Claudia's blood was found.'

'Seriously?' Joe whistles. 'That's big progress.'

'The fence backs onto the woods. The woods lead out to fields, eventually out to the water-meadows.'

'We're going back there?'

'Yup.' Idris points to the map. 'The likelihood is that it could have drifted downstream from one of these streams here.'

'What's the item?' Amir asks.

Idris holds up a clear bag and Jen squints to see inside it. There's something small, wound up, red. 'A tie.'

Jen can't trust herself to open her mouth. She knows that red tie. She took it from Mark and gave it to Bill to wear for his interview.

TWENTY

For the two hours that Oli is underwater in the north part of the river, Jen is feverish beneath the blazing sun. She feels like she's in some sort of parallel universe where nothing makes sense, because why would that tie be in the water? Did Bill have it last or did Mark? Bill's DNA will be one of the strands unidentified, so, God Almighty, what would that *mean*? Is it also the DNA on the fence alongside Claudia's blood?

They stop to eat shop-bought sandwiches that Gareth runs out for, drink their shock-victim teas – she has two – and then discuss where to search next. The lorry is hot and humid and stinks. Jen loosens her button on her shirt, catches Joe's eye. He winks and smirks flirtatiously as is his wont, and usually she would mouth a causal 'fuck off' at him, but her mind is preoccupied, flipping over itself with questions. She keeps telling herself that there's been no body so far so why should there be one now? They've dived *here* for her before, haven't they, and they found nothing.

'Jen, you're next in, OK?'

'I . . . yeah.'

'We'll get things ready outside. Amir, can you dress her?'

Amir nods and the others troop out of the door.

'I'll get the kit sorted,' Amir says.

Jen changes swiftly while he hums, retrieving her fins, her mask, her tank.

'Where are her friends in all this?' he says as he bends down for her to step into the suit. 'Her mother?'

'She didn't have many friends,' she says absently.

'I read that too. Perhaps a person like that picks up friends, has them for the moment.'

Their friendship was definitely of the moment, Jen thinks. Cut short.

Amir pulls at the zip of the suit. 'Ready for the tank?'

She nods, already sweating, as he fastens it with precision and care.

'All right?' Idris asks as they step out.

She nods.

'In you go.'

Jen breaks the surface and sinks down, crossing the gateway into the liquid world. She often thinks of a diver being akin to the children who found Narnia through the wardrobe. Both enter worlds that are secretive, magical, but where Narnia was blinded by thick snow, she's blinded by muddy amber water.

The heat of her body embraces the coldness before it's regulated by her suit, and the sound of the water – a gentle humming – replaces the noise above of her colleagues talking and of birds overhead. She slowly follows the jackstay, one hand on it, as she travels along the river bed, breathing steadily, and hunting through the silt and the snarl of reeds and water grass that are like silk threads.

She loses track of time. Her team will be counting the minutes for her, so she needs only to concentrate on finding what they're looking for, but she now doesn't want to find it. The water darkens and deepens the further she goes, changes from gold to a forest green, and the fronds from the bottom begin to cluster, thick and reaching. She parts them carefully, tries not to entangle herself or the equipment, but it's slow progress to sieve through, the visibility is near nil, save for the occasional gilded shaft of light that cuts through from above. As always, she imagines the black winged horse with her, sometimes a friend, sometimes a foe.

And then, all of a sudden, there is something in front of her. A white material that drifts, ghost-like, between the grasses. She jerks backwards, wants to vomit but can't because she'd choke herself. Please, God, don't let this be what she fears it might be. She needs to press beyond the drifting trail of material, needs to know for certain. She's never been so scared in her life, but she reaches forward and her fingers find that there is bulk beneath the white and that's the moment she knows – she knows it's a body. With a sob choking in her throat, and her breath ragged in her ears, her fingers move upwards to feel shoulders, a thin neck, and a woman's delicate head tipped backwards. She makes herself lean forward to see better. Her hand is inches from the woman's head and she can see hair floating with the current on the palm of her hand, like something alive. Blonde.

Claudia. Claudia is dead down here.

Jen wants to scream, her mind spiralling out of control and falling away into dark places. Has Claudia drowned or has someone killed her? Has Bill done something – has he made a split-second mistake – and tried to desperately bury it? Her big brother, the only one who has ever looked after her. Has he *murdered* Claudia?

There's a pull on the rope and a panic seizes her. She's paused here too long. Above water, the team will have seen her bubbles stay in one place and will be wondering what she's doing, what she's found. She has only a heartbeat to decide what she's going to do.

Jen pulls gently back and then swims on, leaving Claudia's body in the black water.

TWENTY-ONE

Everything is shades of grey – all the colour has bled out from Jen's eyes.

'You look like shit,' Joe says to her. 'Everything cool?'

'You were down there ages,' Idris says. 'You need to warm up.'

'I'll get you tea,' Liam offers.

Jen doesn't trust herself to talk, but she manages to nod – or at least, she thinks she does. She needs the shock-victim tea because this time *she's* the victim.

'Here,' Idris hands her a mug and she falls on it, scalds her mouth, but she doesn't care – she needs another feeling to distract from where her head is going. Claudia is dead, she is *dead*.

'How long are we looking for this time?' Joe asks.

'CID have confirmed funding for a while, but it's a complicated area to search, we all know that. And we still don't know if there's a body. There's a tie, yes. But there's no blood on it. It could have fallen in completely accidentally.'

'What does Mark Mason say about it?' Gareth asks.

Idris shrugs. 'I don't know.'

Jen gets up, wobbles. 'I'm going outside,' she says. 'I need the toilet.'

She opens the door to the elements. The sun is still up high, but there's a wind now and the air is fresh. She runs the hosepipe off the back of the lorry and splashes cold water onto her hands and face, grateful there's no mirror here because her skin is grubby, translucent, and her eyes will be ringed by dark circles.

She's lied to everyone by omitting the truth of her dive. All the values she held herself up to as a police officer: morality, order, discipline, responsibility. She's shattered them all. How can she look Idris in the eye again, how can she banter with Joe, after this? She had managed to convince herself beforehand that she wasn't a corrupt officer, but there's no doubt now that she is. She has wilfully neglected to perform her duty and has abused her position, has thrown a grenade through the life that she's built up for herself over a decade and blown it all to pieces. The offence of misconduct is serious and carries a maximum sentence of life imprisonment. What would that mean for her, and for Sam?

She clenches her fists in anger towards her brother. She's desperate to get to her phone, to see if Bill has made contact, but she's beginning to worry that she'll never hear from him again and as the clock ticks down, she has to navigate the very real possibility that Bill may have committed a crime – the *worst* crime. The pain of his betrayal feels cataclysmic.

Claudia isn't a missing person any more, she's a body, but how long will Jen have the luxury of being the only person who knows it? How long will she have to protect her brother, because that's what she's chosen to do, isn't it? Family first. She's chosen him over her job – over the *right* thing to do – but by doing so, could get them both thrown into the fire.

The image of the burning barn at Cowell Farm flashes in her eyes. She leans her head against the back of the lorry. Her vision is swimming and she closes her eyes.

'Mate?' It's Idris.

Jen prises her eyes open. 'One minute.'

She washes her hands, lets the cold water flow over the veins of her wrists to cool the blood. She doesn't know if this ever works: someone told her about it once, Mark perhaps.

'Are you OK?'

'I'm . . . Yeah,' she calls back. 'I'm fine, I'll be a second.'

She wobbles. Her eyes are jumping, the pixels grey and soupy. She staggers towards the lorry door and opens it.

'You've been out there ages,' Joe says. 'And you never take that long – even to shit.'

She can hear that he's smiling, but she now can't see him. He's a shimmering white outline against more white, and before she can step up into the lorry, she reaches out for him because she can feel her legs buckle and suddenly she's whispering—

'Sorry.'

She feels herself fall backwards, hears a thud.

Jen opens her eyes. She's lying on the grass, and Idris is beside her, concern on his face. Joe, Amir and Oliver are standing above her looking confused.

'Shit,' she says, sitting up. 'I fainted.'

'Like a proper girl,' Joe comments, like a proper knob.

Idris ignores him and helps her up. She's embarrassed. She's tough, she's capable, she's *not* this woman. Except she is. She *is* this woman and Bill is a murderer. She tells herself that she can't think like that, not when she doesn't know all the facts. Never assume. In this line of work, there can be no assumptions, everything is done methodically, logically, practically, no guesswork. Guesses can lead to skipping down bad pathways and wasting time, and they all know the sense of this, but sometimes a wild stab in the dark leads to progress. She needs a fucking wild stab at something.

'You OK?'

'Yeah, I . . . Maybe it's sunstroke or something. I don't know.'

'You need to drink something,' Idris says. 'And eat. We'll get a pizza, yeah? I'm calling us done for today.'

'There's got to be something here,' Oli says. 'I can almost smell that we're close.'

'Bloodhound Oli, is that what we're going to call you now?' Joe grins.

'Old Honker,' Gareth says.

'I'm only saying—'

'Nostrils McGee.'

'Clear Passageway.'

'Are we still talking about noses?' Joe laughs and the others fall about.

'Oh, fuck you,' Oli says, but he's laughing too.

Everyone is laughing except Jen. Jen is a shadow of a person, now on the periphery of their unit because she knows something they don't, something she shouldn't know.

'We'll go to the Italian in town.'

'Or that grill up the road. Jen, you want meat?'

How can they think of eating at a time like this? she wonders. Everything would taste like ash.

'Jen likes meat in her mouth,' Joe says.

She doesn't reply and Joe ribs her.

'Come on, princess. Just messing with you.'

The lorry grunts.

'Strap in,' Idris says. 'We'll come back here tomorrow.'

Jen stares at him. 'We're coming back?'

'We've not combed all of it, you know that.'

'OK.' She turns away before he can see that she's trembling.

What if Idris decides to re-cover the same place she found Claudia? They'll know that Jen had found the body and decided not to pull the rope. They'll ask all the questions why, they'll start digging into the past, and she can't let them.

'I need to go home,' she whispers.

'What?'

'It's not far for me. Let me go home and sleep tonight, OK? I don't feel good.'

Idris frowns, but she can see a chink in his expression.

'Please. I'm close by and I need to see Sam. I can be back at six tomorrow morning. Please, Idris.'

He regards her with a tilt of the head and a frown on his face. 'You're not OK, are you?'

'I just want to sleep well,' she says.

'OK.'

Another few hours buys her some time to work out what the hell is going on. A few more hours to find Bill.

TWENTY-TWO

Back in her flat, Jen goes straight to the bathroom. She showers, washes her hair and warms up her bones under scalding water and thinks how on earth Bill has got himself into a situation so deep that murder could have been his only solution? Had Claudia broken the promise they all made each other all those years ago and threatened to tell someone about the barn? Has she *already* told someone and it's backed him into a corner? He said he wanted to help her, repay his debts. Did he kill her in anger about money? Jen's terrified for Bill but suddenly also terrified *of* him.

The hot water runs out, and the cold streaming down her back wakes her out of her thoughts. She gets out, wraps herself up in a towel and then a dressing gown over it and thick socks. She wants to feel like a child, physically wrapped up and protected, even though she knows that, emotionally, this is impossible. She's always been the one who's looked after everyone's emotional needs. Except she's clearly dropped the ball with the person that needed her most.

She calls Kerry, wants to hear the sound of Sam's voice because he will ground her in the now, the present, and this will help her figure out what to do.

'Hi, babe,' Kerry answers.

Jen can hear the familiar sounds of Kerry's kitchen. Spoons in pots, water streaming from the tap. The squeak of the larder door. She can picture Kerry with the phone balanced between her shoulder and the crook of her chin, never a fan of the loudspeaker.

'Is everything OK?' Kerry asks.

'Everything is fine,' Jen says, but panic blisters her stomach. She wants to tell Kerry, but how can she? She doesn't know what's happened, only that it's bad and somehow connected to her. Besides, Bill already asked Kerry to lie for him; Jen can't add that weight of responsibility onto her friend as well.

Sam's voice calls out. 'Hi, Mum!'

'Hi, bub,' Jen whispers and feels like she might cry because she's suddenly desperate for him – the mess of him, the smell of grass stains on his clothes, the stories he tells her about school.

'Shall I put him on?' Kerry asks.

'Yeah, just for . . . just for a second.'

'Mum!'

'You OK? You had a good day?'

'I played football with Hux,' he says. 'And Kerry took me to the park.'

'Aww, that's great.'

'Bye!'

'I . . . Sam? Bye?'

'You on the lorry?' Kerry asks, coming back on the line.

'Is Sam OK? Is he mad at me?'

'What? Course not – he's watching Pokémon. What's going on? Are you allowed to say?'

'There have been developments. It means more diving that can't wait. I've come home just for a bit and I'll be round in a few hours, OK? I'll come round with a bag of clean school clothes for Sam. I've just got to sort some stuff.'

'I've got dinner, can you stay for that?'

'I don't think so.'

'Are you diving again tonight?'

'Not tonight. Tomorrow, early.'

'Do you want to stay over before you dive again then? You and Sam will have to share as usual.'

'Yes, Mum!' Sam's voice pipes up. 'Stay over!'

The combination of this simple invite to her best friend's house – always open – and Sam's excitement brings tears to Jen's eyes. She wants nothing more than to curl up with her boy in a freshly made bed that smells of Clean Cotton Yankee Candle because that's who Kerry is.

'Yes,' she says. 'Yeah, I'd love that.'

'Great,' Kerry says. 'I'll sort everything else.'

'You're like a sister, Kez, you know that, right?'

'I do know that,' Kerry replies. 'We all look after each other. You hear that, Samster? Mum will be back late. I'll read you a bedtime story, OK? He told me he wants a scary one, Jen, and you know I can't tell ghost stories, right? I hate them, even the kid ones. Remember the one about the dog under the bed licking the hand, but it was the killer?'

Is it as bad as the one where she finds the woman underwater that her brother might have murdered? Jen thinks.

'I don't remember that one,' she says.

'You know what my mum said to me when I told her?' Kerry carries on. 'She said she'd get our dog to sleep in my room that night. She thought that might be reassuring! *How?*'

Jen can barely keep all the emotions from spilling over. 'Kerry?'

'Yeah?'

'I appreciate it, OK? Everything you do even when you shouldn't.'

There's a pause. 'What do you mean by that?'

'Looking after everyone,' Jen says. She waits a beat. 'Have you seen him, Kerry? Have you seen Bill?'

Kerry hesitates. Jen hears a door close. 'No, and I can't get hold of him. Actually he's been a bit of a wanker, truth be told. We went out last week, but I've not heard from him since then. I know you're busy with all the shit and Claudia and whatever – but, like, don't I mean *anything* to him?'

'You know you do.'

'I don't, though. That's the problem. If you're looking for him, try Andy at the site.'

It's Sunday night, but she needs to involve other people now if she's going to have a chance to find Bill. She hangs up and calls Andy Bowman.

Jen is let through the gates via the telecom and the sandy gravel crunches beneath her feet as she walks to the office where Bill works in all his chaotic mess.

She knocks on the office door.

'Come in, Jen.'

Andy is sitting at the desk when she opens the door and a rush of warm, biscuity air hits her face. Files are stacked on a free-standing shelf, marked by grubby fingers, and there are coffee cups littering any available surfaces. The strip light flickers.

'Sorry I got you in late, Andy, and on a weekend.'

She closes the door, follows the well-worn dirty boot prints towards him, but she doesn't sit down on the plastic chair that he's nodding her towards. She stands, impatient, but knows she's got to play this the right way.

'It's fine,' he says. 'Like I said on the phone, I've been here all day. I'm a man down, and there's some shit that has come up that I need to deal with. One of the houses has been vandalised over the weekend.'

'Serious?'

'Yeah,' he sighs. 'Is there any more news on Claudia Franklin? I saw on Twitter that you've all been out again.'

'No news,' she says. 'Andy, on the phone, you said that Bill's truck is here.'

'Yeah,' he replies. 'I assumed he'd got a lift with you for this – you know, for the family emergency he told me about.'

She opens her mouth to speak, falters. 'I . . . That's right,' she says. 'I didn't give him a lift though. I thought he might be still here. I didn't know when he was leaving.'

Andy nods. 'Oh.'

She wishes she had spare keys to his truck but doesn't. She wonders if he might have left anything in plain sight.

'Where did he leave the truck?'

'Round the back.'

'OK.'

She stares around the room, wondering how in God's name it's come to this. Her eyes rest on the free-standing lockers behind Andy's head.

'Actually,' she says. 'Bill left Sam something in his locker. A toy car apparently. I should get it.'

'Oh, OK. Sure.'

She walks with purpose to the lockers. She tries Bill's birthday, her birthday, their mum's and the date their mum died.

'He didn't tell you the code?' Andy asks, swivelling his chair so he's watching her.

'He did, but I forgot,' she says.

She moves so his eyeline is obscured by her body and keeps punching in codes, feels the sweat gathering on her brow, and then she tries Sam's birthday and the mechanism springs. The locker is stuffed full of papers and she takes them all out – sees bills, sees bank statements. All in the red. Her heart sinks with dismay. And then a small, random receipt. She stares at the company name at the top of it. She yanks it out.

'Did you find the toy?'

'Yup, thanks' she says, patting her pocket.

'Great,' he says.

'Yup.'

'If you speak to Bill, tell him I need him back as soon as possible, OK? I've left messages.'

'OK.'

'See you then,' he says, busying himself with paperwork as she leaves the office and shuts the door.

Jen waits until she's halfway across the site before she looks again at the receipt. It's from a few weeks back – two coffees from The Corner House Cafe. Sickness steals up her throat. Mark told her that he'd seen Claudia with Bill at this cafe. Is this from the date they met, and if so, why would Bill have kept this receipt? It's obsessive, psychotic. Jen wants to throw it away, burn it. She scrunches it up in her fist.

Before she leaves the site, she diverts round the back to find Bill's truck. There it is, a silent beast with an open back, which she glances into, finds a wheelbarrow, a sack of sand. She moves to the cab, but the torch on her phone can only illuminate so much – packets of crisps in the footwells, crumbs on the tatty leather, Red Bull cans, papers. Nothing out of the ordinary.

She gets back into her car, and then drops the scrunched receipt on the passenger seat and exhales. What the fuck is going on? She glances at it again, watches it slowly unfold, and then realises that there's writing on the back of it. She snatches it up, sees that it's an address and it's written in Claudia's writing. Jen's heart starts to race.

She can't risk searching what this address is or who it might belong to on the police database – she'll be breaking more rules, and given the enormity of what she's dealing with, she can't chance it. She needs to go there herself, right now.

It's a flat, a new-build in Fording Hill which is forty-five minutes from her town. It's yellow brick with white gloss window frames, and a neat little boxy hedge – a somewhat supernatural shade of green – is planted outside of it.

Jen looks at the names on the list next to the door, counts five, but there are spaces for three more. She wonders if the blank spaces mean that no one is occupying them, or that if someone does, they wish to remain anonymous. Does the flat belong to Claudia? *Did*. Did, did, did, because Claudia is dead. Jesus, Mary and Joseph.

If it did belong to her, Jen wonders if the police know about it and if they have it already under surveillance. She bites at the inside of her cheek to stop herself screaming in anger. What is Bill doing to her? Useless piece of shit.

She rings one of the buzzers that has no name, and waits. Nothing. She rings the second two, and nobody answers. She presses the first button with the name 'Jack Strout' attached to it, and leaves her finger on it so long that it becomes aggressive.

'Hello?'

'Are you Jack?'

'I am?'

He sounds old, his voice crumbly.

'I'm sorry to call here late. I'm wondering if you know a woman called Claudia who lives here?'

He pauses. 'Claudia who?'

She hesitates. She hasn't thought this through. To tell Jack Strout anything else may compromise Jen's position even more than she's already compromised it herself. How close does Jen want to skirt in jogging this man's memory if indeed, Claudia did live here?

'I don't know her second name ... She might have changed it. She's blonde, mid-thirties.'

'I'm afraid I don't know any Claudia,' he says. 'There's Paula and Simon on the ground floor. And Tanith? But she's maybe a bit older. Forties, I'd say. Sometimes she invites me in for a cup of tea and we talk about jazz. She's into gramophones, do you like them?'

'I—'

'We play some cards.'

'Who else?'

'Sorry?'

'Who else lives in the building?'

'Sorry, who are you again?'

'I'm a friend of Claudia's,' she says. 'She told me she'd moved to this address.'

He sighs in the slow way only old people who have the time to do so can. 'There are two students on the top floor who go to art college. There's a bloke – can't remember his name – and his daughter.'

'Is there anyone here called Bill? William?'

'I don't know, love. What's your name, and I'll ask Tanith if she knows of the woman you're looking for? Claudia, was it?'

'It doesn't matter,' Jen says. 'I'll find her. Thanks for your time, Mr Strout.'

TWENTY-THREE

The Cumbrian hills have turned black and the sheep are bright white dots against grey grass.

It's easier to navigate the narrow roads in the dark – especially driving the black van. Bill can see headlights approach, but tonight, he's not seen anyone, and he relishes the quiet majesty of the Lake District. Oh, for another life, he thinks wryly.

For the last few days, he has driven an hour from the rental – not always in the same direction – so he can switch on his phone and check in with Andy. He can't risk pissing him off by being away too long without contact. Nor can he be away from his gambling addiction.

He pulls up in a lay-by outside a small village, turns the phone on and immediately goes to click on the betting apps to relieve the tension he feels, but he's taken aback by the phone pinging with urgency as it gains signal. Bill watches with alarm as voicemails stack up – all of them from Andy.

Fear makes his fingers slick with sweat. Andy must have found out that he's been stealing money from the company and now going to throw Bill to the wolves.

With dread, he clicks on the first of the messages left at six this evening and hears Andy's voice.

'I know you have a family thing, but there's been an incident on the site. Someone broke in – I'm guessing Friday night – and vandalised one of the houses. We only just saw it this morning because one of the alarms went off when a bird flew into a window and into the security system; you couldn't make it up, right? Jonny went in fifteen minutes ago, just by chance, to check the tiling down in the pool and found it's been tampered with. When are you back? I'm trying to deal with all the insurance shit, but I could do with you being here.'

Bill sits for a minute, relief flooding through him, but simultaneously trying to work out the best excuse as to why he can't return yet. He dials his number and Andy picks up immediately.

'Before you say anything, I just got all your messages. The signal is crap. I'm sorry I haven't called in person before now. It's been a difficult time.'

'But your family are OK, right? No one has died? I saw Jen literally an hour ago.'

Bill pauses. 'You saw Jen?'

'Yeah. She came looking for you. I assumed you'd been together.'

'No—' He needs to change the direction. 'Tell me what happened to the house that got vandalised?'

'I think some kids must have jumped the gates and went on a bit of a jolly,' Andy says. 'But they avoided the CCTV because I had a quick look and can't see anyone near the gate. I've called the police.'

'The . . . the police?'

'Yeah. Got to get a claim in for it.'

'Which house was it?'

'Number ten.'

Cold dread floods Bill's body.

'There're no obvious signs of entry,' Andy carries on. 'No window smashed, no door forced, but the police will come out sometime tomorrow and look at it, take all the available CCTV and whatever.'

Bill's heart is thudding so loudly that he can hear it in his ears. What if the police take a look around the house, the garage? But why would they? He swallows.

'What happened to the house?'

'Someone scratched into the pool lining with a knife or something. Annoying as hell – we'll have to patch it, or if it's too bad, replace the liner.'

'Just scratches? Nothing else?'

'Well, graffiti. Says, "I was here. Take the moment." Pfft, what the hell does that mean?'

Bill says nothing, is physically unable to. He has a distinct memory of exactly those words. An expression that Mark Mason used to say at dive practice that Jen and Claudia used to fall about laughing over.

How did Claudia manage to scratch that out into the bottom of the pool when he had her at number ten? *When?* It definitely *wasn't* Friday night as Andy thinks it was.

'I'll be there as soon as I can, OK?'

'Right you are.'

Bill hangs up, starts to bite his nails. He has to go back now, doesn't he? He has to cover his tracks, because as soon as the police come, they will have photographic evidence of that phrase, and, with the investigation happening, they may well look at every possibility that this could be something related to Claudia. They might show it to Mark for identification and he, after all, would know its significance.

TWENTY-FOUR

Jen startles out of sleep, but she's not in bed. She's upright, with a cool breath of air in her face. She's done it again, has walked the loop, but she's not in the water, or for that matter, near it either.

Her fingers are curled around cold, black cast-iron railings, and her eyes now focus on a house beyond the gates. With a gasp of recognition, she steps back and lets go of them like they've burnt her hands.

A gravel drive cuts through an immaculately manicured front garden and leads to the enormous detached white square house with a charcoal slated roof and huge wooden front door that seems to whisper a challenge.

Come in.

She used to come here all the time, to the imposing Oak House, but what's she doing here now?

She breathes deeply, tries to soothe the panic in her chest, and concentrates on the birdsong from one of the trees on the avenue. Dawn will soon be here, but right now everything is touched by the blue-grey hue of a heron's wing. Why did I wake here? she wonders. Am I still asleep? There's a feeling of something dark stirring in her heart, a hum in her ears like a hornet, and it's loud, but there's nothing here.

Jenny?

She startles, looks back at the house. There is a shadow at the door – Victoria Franklin, Claudia's mother, stands at the door wearing slacks and a pale blue linen shirt. In her hand is a cafetière. She was always throwing old coffee grounds out onto the soil.

'Victoria?' Jen whispers, though Victoria won't be able to hear her from this distance.

Victoria approaches her anyway, comes to the gates. 'What are you doing here in your nightclothes?'

Jen looks down at herself. She's in pyjamas, a coat, shoes that don't belong to her. 'I—'

'You have to stop coming here. It does you no good, you know. Mark's not the one for you. Look after Bill.'

'Bill?'

'Keep your eyes closed, Jen.'

She frowns. Victoria is speaking in Bill's voice.

'What?'

'Mark isn't here.'

Jen blinks in confusion and suddenly Victoria Franklin is gone. Jen has conjured her up out of thin air, there was no conversation, no coffee grounds. There is only her and the silence of Oak House.

She reaches her hand to the coat pocket, pulls out her phone. Thank God, thank *God*. She starts to run, guilt hammering her heart, and automatically calls Bill, forgetting that his phone is off and that he's gone, before she then dials Kerry.

'Kerry!'

'Jen? What's wrong?'

'I've woken up – I'm at . . . I don't know if I locked my door!'

'Hey, hey,' Kerry says. 'Sam is with me? Remember? Did you leave my flat?'

Kerry's flat, she was staying at Kerry's. She's wearing Kerry's shoes, that's why she didn't recognise them when she looked. 'I . . . Yeah, I did. Check your door. I'm sorry.'

'Are you OK?'

The strange vision of Victoria lingers in her eyes. And Bill's voice.

Mark isn't here.

She looks up the driveway of Oak House. There are no lights on anywhere and Mark's car isn't in the drive. Mark isn't here, so where is he?

'Do you want a drink?' Kerry asks.

'No. I'm . . . I'm fine.'

Jen opens the bread bin because she's starving, exhausted, and so tired of half-truths and the fucking elephant in the room that is Claudia's body she's found and left.

They stand together in Kerry's kitchen, palms around cups of tea. Kerry is in her pyjamas, a hoodie thrown over, and her hair in a tangled bird's nest of a ponytail over her shoulder. Jen is wrapped in Kerry's dressing gown.

Kerry instinctively reaches for the Marmite jar from the cupboard, hands it to Jen. 'I'm worried about you.'

'I know . . . I'm worried about me. God, I owe you, a thousand times over.'

'You don't owe me anything.'

Jen spreads the Marmite, bites into the toast, feels the relief of the salt hitting her tongue. 'I've got to ask you a question.'

'Yeah?'

'Bill told me that he was with you that Saturday night. The night Claudia went missing. Did he ask you to cover for him?'

Kerry stands very still. 'He came at—'

'You don't need to lie to me,' Jen says. 'Don't lie.'

Kerry looks up at the ceiling. 'I don't know why he asked.'

'You would have lied for him if you'd been asked by the police?'

'Yes,' Kerry says. 'I would lie for him, of course I would! I'd lie for you too if you asked it of me.'

'Kerry. *No*.'

'Well, I would.'

'If you know anything to do with what might have happened to Claudia, you have a duty to tell me,' Jen says, ignores the irony of her own situation.

'I don't, I promise.'

'So do you know where he was?'

'You don't think he's done something . . . bad?' Kerry's voice is small, anxious. She wants reassurance that Jen can't give her.

'For the last few days I can't find him,' Jen says. 'He's not been at his flat, his phone is off, and he's not gone to work. And I'm worried. He admitted he's seen Claudia since she's been back from America.'

'He's seen her?'

'Yes. But only I know that. Not the team investigating her disappearance. And, fuck, I shouldn't have told you . . . I'm sorry. But I'm going spare.'

'But so what, right? So what if he'd seen her? It's *Bill*. Bill is one of the good guys.' But even as she says it, Kerry looks worried.

'He's in trouble,' Jen says. 'Financially. He told me. Claudia said she'd help him with money.'

'He owes people money?'

'Lots of it. I don't know who to. Betting websites, I don't know what else. You know the stupid thing, Kez? The stupid thing is that I *have* money. I could have helped Bill, if only he'd asked me. I have a lot of money now.'

'You've won the lottery?'

'Not that. But I have enough for him.'

A sudden bolt of panic seizes her. What if Mark's accounts have been accessed by the police? Would they see that he's made the trust transaction to Jen? She reminds herself that there would have to be lots of permissions needed for this, but it's only a matter of time now there's a body. The body *will* surface at some point and then the police will start linking further back. Would they think to investigate the barn?

Kerry reaches over to her. 'You OK?'

'I want to sleep,' Jen says. 'And I don't want to wake up until the alarm goes, you know what I mean?'

'No sleepwalking.'

'No sleepwalking.'

'You can tell me anything. You know that? I know your work is supposed to be confidential, but you need to be able to share things, right?'

'I wouldn't even know where to start,' Jen says. She hugs her friend. 'I love you.'

'I love *you*,' Kerry says.

Jen closes the door to the bedroom, walks in the darkness to the bed, where she sinks, succumbs to sleep.

She dreams of Claudia, of Mark, of diving. She dreams of a swan beating its wings in the light of a bone-white moon. She dreams of Bill with bloodstains on his fingertips, slipping through the fence panel of Oak House.

TWENTY-FIVE

Bill opens the office door and Andy looks up, appears surprised to see him.

'It's seven in the morning, mate. I wasn't expecting you until about midday?'

'I drove back last night,' Bill says. His voice is low and crackly from lack of sleep and he's exhausted, but there were things he needed to do during the stillness of the night-time hours. There are other things he *still* needs to do.

'You're a legend,' Andy says. 'I spoke to the clients last night. They're pissed at having to delay their move date. I've ordered more liner for the pool, but it's going to take two sodding weeks.'

'When did the police say they'd come?'

'Sometime today,' Andy says.

'You want me to deal with them?'

'Given you have experience with coppers, be my guest.'

Andy has thrown him a bone. Bill could cry with relief.

'OK. I'll just go and have a look at it.'

Andy leans behind him, plucks the key from the board for number ten and hands it to Bill. 'Yeah. See what you think.'

The machinery is silent, the lads won't be here for an hour or so. Birdsong and the wind whistle through the site.

It's fresh today, a welcome relief from the heat, but he's already sweating. From anxiety, stress, from being on the fucking edge.

He lets himself into number ten, walks downstairs and along the corridor from the kitchen, opens the door to the basement where the pool is. He flicks the light switch at the top of the stairs, except it doesn't turn on. Perhaps Andy turned the electrics off. Bill clicks his phone for light and walks down the white stone steps into a plunging darkness, almost tasting the mix of tile sealant and paint.

The houses with pools all have the same finishes – white-wash walls and sky-blue ceilings, a floor of gold and turquoise mosaic, but the pools at the moment are merely pits with shallow steps, hollowed out and smoothed like yawning caverns. An unfilled pool looks a strange thing – eerie and unnerving, especially when the deep end is eight foot down and dark with shadows.

Bill curves his phone around the huge space to illuminate the corners and then he sees some scratches – right at the deep end, scrawled and leggy like a spider.

I WAS HERE. TAKE THE MOMENT.

Stupid, stupid girl.

He walks down the steps of the pool, his steel-cap boots echoing, and he kneels down. He ponders how he'll amend it. He can't manipulate it too much, but enough that it looks different. From his pocket, he takes a Stanley knife, and makes a deeper incision in the liner, enough to disturb some of the writing. "I was here" is fine to stay, it's the other part that might cause Mark Mason to question it if he were to be shown photographs. Bill pulls at the incision, tears a little chunk of it, until suddenly he hears a noise.

'I turned off the electrics. I want to check them in case anything else was damaged.'

Bill whips his head to see Andy coming into view down the stairs to the pool room, drawing his phone also out.

'You see it?'

Bill hides the blade from view against his leg. 'Yeah. This liner is shit, Andy. I just lifted it to take a closer look and it's torn a bit. Can you see? Some of the writing is skewed now.'

Andy shines a torch down on Bill like a spotlight and huffs. 'The whole sodding thing is skewed, thanks to them, mate. Don't worry about it.'

Bill stands up, subtly pulls in the blade and flips the knife swiftly into his pocket. 'Stupid kids.'

'Don't get me started. Let's go have a brew before the others get here then, yeah?'

Bill gives the pool a final glance, satisfied that he's disturbed enough of it, but then realises in horror that he's not only heard those words before uttered by Jen and Claudia in jest, but *seen* them before. He's sat at a table practically every week for nearly twenty years with them written on the table of Tea For Two where Kerry works. He could almost laugh out loud. The sheer work Claudia has made for him is enormous. As if he didn't have enough on his fucking plate.

'Where have you been, stranger?'

Bill smiles at Kerry as genuinely as he can. He's been waiting for the police to come to the site all morning, but they've not yet arrived. In the wait, he's bitten his nails down so much that the skin at the edges of them is raw and throbbing. He's taken his lunch break out, told Andy he needed to nip to town, prays that the police don't come in the next hour.

'How you doing, Kez?'

She glances towards the counter, where the manager – Ricky – is staring at them. She sits down next to Bill.

'Where did you go? Jen's been looking for you.'

'I went to her flat last night. She wasn't there.'

'She was with me. She and Sam stayed over. But she's diving again, Bill. She said there have been developments.'

'Really?'

'She didn't say what, but they're back at the river. Haven't you been watching the news?'

'I wanted to get away from the news.'

'Jen's exhausted, Bill, and she doesn't need you flitting off without a word to her with all this going on.'

'I know. I'm sorry.'

'She knows that you asked me to lie for you. About where you were on Saturday night.'

His heart sinks. 'Oh.'

'Where were you?'

She's looking at him so intently, but he registers a note of suspicion slip across her face, and he suddenly feels so tired. So *sad*. He thinks about the closest truth that he can muster.

'I was trying to sort out a problem,' he says. 'A . . . a gambling thing that I didn't want Jen to know. That's where I've been the last few days.'

She grabs at his hands, laces his fingers with hers. 'Oh Bill! Why didn't you just say? Do you know how worried Jen was when you disappeared? She told me she has money. Lots of it that she can give you.'

He goes to shake his head, but then stops. Jen *had* tried to say she could help him with money when he went over that day, before he went to Cumbria.

'Lots of it?'

'Yes.'

'Where did she get it?'

'Kerry?' Ricky calls from the counter.

'I don't know where she got it. Just speak to her, will you? She can help and then you'll be OK, all right? And you can talk to me any time. You know that.'

'Yeah.'

She leans close to him. 'She said that you'd seen Claudia.'

He blinks. 'I mean – I just bumped into her in town. That was all.'

'Was something going on between you?'

'Definitely not,' he says, though how many years had he wished it?

'Kerry. This isn't your break.'

She grimaces over at Ricky and then squeezes Bill's arm. 'I don't have a break for another hour. Are you staying long?'

'Don't worry,' he says. 'I just wanted to come and see you – I missed your calls and I felt bad.'

'Do you want a tea and cake? We've got your favourite. Red velvet? Or I just finished a walnut and coffee. It's still warm. Do you want a slice of that instead?'

The simplicity of this choice is almost overwhelming and, to his embarrassment, tears spring to his eyes.

'You OK, babe?' she asks.

'Yeah. Something in my eye.'

'Shall I take a look?' she asks with concern.

Her perfume is something floral and sweet. Her dark hair is in a bun on her head, her make-up immaculate, the powdery residue of cocoa and flour a complete juxtaposition on her pinny.

You are one in a fucking million, he wants to tell her.

'Nope. All good,' he says instead. 'I'll have the walnut and coffee, ta.'

'Great choice.'

She walks towards the counter and he watches until she goes into the kitchen and Ricky follows her, of course he does, that lecherous dog.

There are three more tables occupied by people, all of them elderly: a man reading a newspaper with a coffee, two women talking by the window on the far side and three women who have a basket on the table. They are all engaged in something other than him, which is good, because he's not here to sample cake.

He hopes the tinny music from the speakers is up high enough to disguise the noise of the small square of sandpaper that he now removes from his pocket. The words written on the bottom of the pool are the same words here on this table, and in case the police go linking the writing to Claudia, if they were to put it up on the TV or something, he can't have them also investigate who 'J' and 'K' are. He can't get Jen and Kerry in the shit any more than they would be if they come knocking for him.

He crooks his arm and, after a glance around, he starts to smooth out the wood, needs to mask the engraving, even just a word or two. It can't be too obvious that he's gone at it, delicate circular motions, so that it blends with the rest of the table. He'll have to do a few more patches elsewhere on the table too so it doesn't stand out.

After a few minutes, he's bleached out *'take the moment'* completely, leaving only *I was here*. He folds the sandpaper so it disappears as Kerry returns, hides it up his sleeve, like he's some sort of bizarre magician.

'Here you go, babe,' Kerry says and puts the cake down, right on top of the patch. 'Shout if you want anything else, OK?'

She smiles at him and then goes to tend the table of the three old women. He watches her pick up a ball of yarn and marvel at it and he realises that they must be the stitch and bitch group that she's told him about many times.

He wolfs the cake, needs to go back to the site and wait for the police. With the hit of sugar, his body seems to relax, as if the butter icing is smoothing out the jagged shard of stress that's lodged in his skull.

'I've got to go, Kez,' he calls.

'OK,' she says, coming out of the kitchen. In her hand is a plate of buns and the stitch and bitch group start to coo over her as he walks out of the door.

His phone vibrates in his pocket as he gets to his truck.

'Andy? You OK?'

'You done in town, mate? The police just got here.'

'They're there? Now?'

'Pulled up into the site right this second. You coming back to deal with it or what? I've got one of the contractors in.'

'Yeah, yeah, I'm coming right now. I'm three minutes away, OK?'

'Also, when you're back, something looks weird on the books. I can't balance the sale of number two and twelve against what invoices we've been paid?'

Bill's heart thuds. 'Really?'

'Yeah.'

'I'll take a look.'

'Thanks, mate.'

Here it comes, he thinks. Life as he knows it will soon come crashing down around his ears.

TWENTY-SIX

Contract to myself – I will no longer wake up anxious. I promise to reclaim my mornings, my joy of the sunshine, of laughter.

What a joke. Her body is electric with anxiety, with *sorrow*. Bill has killed Claudia and this mantra that's been a lifeline for so long is now a wasp in Jen's ear that she wants to slap out.

'What's the matter with you?' Joe says, gruffly. 'You didn't zip me up right!'

'I'm sorry,' she says. 'I thought it was tight.'

'Well, newsflash, it wasn't, and now my bollocks have fucking shrivelled.'

It's midday and the sun is high and strong. They stand in front of the dive lorry, Joe dripping wet on the scrubby grass and angry in all his equipment. He grabs the hose from the back, starts to get the muck off of him, and sprays her in the face for good measure.

'Hey! I said sorry.'

'You're being a real clown,' he says.

Water drips down from her chin. 'What? No, I'm not.'

'You're not *concentrating*. We just wasted an hour of prep and we'll waste another half getting someone else ready.'

She doesn't know why she's sabotaging the investigation, even more than she already has done. She's buying more time for Bill, but for what? For escaping justice? They've outrun the law once before, twice would be foolish.

'Quit your bitching and get changed,' Idris says, walking towards them. 'You're no use to the team with that attitude, Joe.'

Joe cusses under his breath, starts to strip off.

Idris steps closer to Jen. 'Step it up, mate,' he says softly so only she can hear. 'Joe's right, you're a liability. What's up with you?'

'I don't feel well.'

'That's no use to me either. Go and see a medic. Rule out anything nasty, yeah? Do you think you're OK for one more dive?'

'Yeah.'

'We'll get Gareth in next and we'll keep you surface just in case you've got something. What are your symptoms?'

They're all trained to spot water-related diseases – some can be harmless but inconvenient. Some can be harmful and so even more inconvenient. Her only symptoms at the moment are guilt and acute anxiety.

'Nausea. Dizziness.'

'Keep an eye on it.'

She longs to be back at Kerry's house with Sam. This morning she woke and spent five whole minutes just staring at the back of his head because she wanted a precious moment where she was just his mum – not a police officer, and definitely not the felon she's becoming.

She takes her hair from her ponytail, scrapes it back and reties it. It feels greasy and smells of pondweed and muck even though she's only been wading this morning.

What if she can blame a murder on someone else? But who else *is* there, given the tie, except for Mark? How could she ever do that to him, or to Sam?

It takes another hour before they're all ready again and then they stand by the edge of the water. Idris points to where they were searching yesterday – where Jen went down and found Claudia. Dread tightens her chest.

'Why are we going over this patch again?' she asks.

'Because you weren't on form yesterday,' Idris says. 'So it's worth another look.'

Her skin feels like it constricts against her bones. 'Oh.'

'Let's go.'

They wade in. She watches Gareth sink down and Liam take his rope. Her hearts starts to hammer and everything around her feels amplified – the sound of the flow of water as it navigates around them is hissing and loud, the colours of the river she loves so much are bright and vivid and terrifying, the smell of Joe's sweat next to her is carried over on the air and makes her want to gag.

She closes her eyes, imagines it's not Gareth combing the water but herself. She feels the freeze on her face, reaches out into the dark reeds, trying to find Claudia's arm, anything to hold and haul, but her fingers meet only the slippery long water grass over and over. She imagines swimming further into the reeds, scoping left and right. A shock of white material. She opens her eyes again, sways in the water.

Gareth stays under, his bubbles tracking slowly along, until Jen sees that he's on top of the very spot that she found Claudia entangled by the grass. Unless something has disturbed her body enough for it to move, at any second Gareth will be pulling on the rope because he will see her.

She's unbalanced, unstable.

'You all right? Jen?'

'Has Gareth stopped?' she whispers.

'Has he found a G spot?' Oli laughs.

She's going to pass out, right here in the water. She focuses all her energy in staying upright, her eyes almost burning with keeping them on Gareth. Now, now, is the end. Everything will implode. But Gareth swims on. He goes a metre beyond Claudia's body, and then two metres, five, ten, and she can't hold it any longer. With shock and relief, she vomits into the water.

'Fuck me, Jen,' Joe exclaims, jumping away from her.

'Bring Gareth up,' Idris says.

They pull on the rope, sharp pulls to communicate to Gareth that he needs to surface.

'I'm sorry,' she says; wipes away the sick from her chin.

'We'll go back to the lorry, have a cuppa. You need to go to the medic straight away.'

She nods, but she has no intention of seeing the medic.

Gareth didn't find Claudia, which can only mean one thing – her body has moved. Or *been* moved.

Jen doesn't know how long she'll have. Half a day, perhaps, to fool the team into thinking she's being assessed. She gets back to her flat and locks the door behind her. The first thing she needs to do is steady herself with food, because in among all this chaos, she's forgotten the basics. She goes to the fridge, takes the block of cheese from its wrapper and bites into it, while simultaneously reaching for the bread and grabbing a slice, stuffing it in. A mess of a sandwich assembled and disassembled all at once in the mouth.

There *was* a body, wasn't there? The trail of blonde hair on her palm and the white of a shirt under the water was real, so the only explanation is that Claudia has moved. Jen knows, of course, that there is a chance that the body could have been disturbed by a bird, a dog, and moved through the water due to the build-up of gases. But what if someone else knew Claudia was there? The press and the town know the team are diving in that exact spot, so what if someone moved the body elsewhere because they were worried it would be found?

Jen stops chewing. Something about her flat feels different. There's a presence that she can feel, smell. She tenses.

'Hello?'

'In here.'

It's Bill. A rush of emotion pulsates through her heart and she runs to the lounge, about to throttle him, about to hug him so tight that nothing bad can ever happen to him, or to either of them, but she stops dead before doing either of those things because he's standing, white-faced, and wringing his hands, and on the sofa lies Claudia Franklin.

TWENTY-SEVEN

Jen's going to scream – scream or vomit – but Bill steps in front of her with his palm up and covers her face. His eyes are glassy, huge. There's stubble on his jaw, and there's a smell on him, the bitter stench of dried sweat.

She swipes his hand away. 'What have you done?' she cries, but her voice is hoarse and cracked.

She pushes him roughly to one side so she can see the spill of hair over the sofa, the way he's covered her with one of Jen's throws. The worst thing he could have ever done and it's here, in her living room. How has he done it? When did he move her out of the water?

'I know I've put you through shit, but I needed to bring her somewhere safe—'

But she's stopped listening to him because her brain has caught up with her eyes. Claudia's face is not at all bloated but flushed pink, and her hair is dry and golden, not stringy and rank.

Jen moves past Bill, manic laughter rising in her throat, and places a fingertip to Claudia's hand and feels the warmth of her, can see the familiar shape of the fingernails that she used to paint as a teenager. Jen sinks to the floor beside Claudia, can see her chest rising and falling. *Fucking breathing*. Claudia is *alive*.

'Oh my God,' Jen whispers, but her relief is short-lived because everything is flipped upside down again.

Was there a body in the water or did Jen imagine the whole thing? Was she so stressed at the red tie that her mind played the biggest and darkest trick? But she's not insane; she knows a body when she sees one, when she touches one, doesn't she?

She tastes salt on her lips. Tears have come and make tracks down her cheeks, drip to the floor. Her body is pouring out the strain.

She feels a hand on her arm – Bill's hand – and he takes her into the kitchen and closes the door. 'Are you . . . are you OK?'

'Holy Mother.'

'Surprise, right, sis?'

Jen turns to him, her brother who is grinning at her – *grinning* – and she lunges at him then, because any relief is immediately replaced by a white-hot anger.

'Do you know what's been happening?' she cries, her fingers gripping his polo shirt. 'Do you know what you've put me through, you selfish arsehole?'

'I know, I know,' he says and then he gives a boyish shrug, and this little gesture makes her so furious that she pushes him hard in the chest and he staggers back with the force of it. 'Ouch! Jesus! I'm sorry, Jen, but it was for good reason—'

'Do you know how many people are looking for her?'

'I know—'

'No, you don't!' She jabs him hard with her finger. 'You *knew* we were all searching. You *know* how dangerous diving is! You wanted to put us all in danger?'

'I'm sorry, OK?'

She steadies herself against the kitchen worktop, trying to work out how Bill and Claudia – fucking *Bill and Claudia* – have put her through this together, like they're playing bloody Romeo and Juliet.

'Where the hell did you go?'

'Everything sort of . . . blew up.' Bill reaches for her. 'But Claudia isn't dead, right? She's *here*. We can work everything out, but we need your help.'

'My help? Are you kidding?'

'She needs to get away to Canada, to see Victoria. Start a new life.'

'Are you serious? A new life? What the fuck is wrong with the one she's got?'

How dare Claudia want a new life when she got the one that she, Jen, wanted? The looks, the charm, the money, Oak House, the handsome husband. Jen looks around at her own life, at this tiny flat, where she struggles to find space to hang washing, where she struggles to pin all of Sam's new artworks from school . . . She gasps. Everywhere there are pictures, drawings – evidence of Sam's existence. She starts tearing at the walls, her beautiful treasures crinkling and cracking as she grabs at them.

'What are you doing?'

She whips around to him. 'What have you told Claudia about me? Does she know about Sam?'

He shrugs. 'I told her that I have a nephew?'

'You complete *shit*.'

'Why was that the wrong thing?'

She goes back through to the lounge, starts removing pictures off the walls in there too, more carefully, her eyes on Claudia as she takes down each one. One seems to be missing – the one of Sam playing Lego that was propped by the lamp.

'Why are you doing that?' Bill whispers.

She ignores him, stalks back, her arms laden.

'This is *my* private space. How dare you.'

She shoves all the pictures in a kitchen cupboard and then thinks it's all useless anyway. Sam has a bedroom for Christ's sake. Jen can't erase all evidence of him.

'But it's *Claudia*, Jen. The chips are down and she needs us. She wants to leave Mark, but she was waiting for Paris, when he would be distracted with the Olympics.'

'She wanted to disappear and not tell him?'

'Yes, and she was going to pay me for helping her. I've been emailing real estate in Canada. I've been the one making calls to Victoria Franklin about selling Oak House so Claudia could free the money and move. Victoria isn't too happy about it, but it's the only option.'

'Is that what you meant by Claudia giving you money?'

'From the sale, yeah.'

'But why did she want to leave Mark? Why all this secrecy?'

'You wouldn't believe—'

A bleeping causes her to look down, and she sees that her watch alarm is firing.

'Shit, Sam's school – I didn't sort pick-up for this afternoon . . . God, maybe someone might be able to' – she fiddles with her phone, taps on the screen – 'bring him back here or . . . Shit, shit.'

'Go and get him,' Bill says. 'But we all need to talk. Come back after?'

'And bring Sam with me? Are you for *real*?'

'Can you leave him with Kerry?'

She looks at him coldly. 'You're calling all the shots, are you?'

'I know it's been crap of me to keep you in the dark, but we can't go to the police until we've all spoken.'

'You know what trouble I could be in?' she says. 'You know what I've put on the line with all this? I want you *gone* by the time I'm back.'

'But what if someone sees her coming out of your flat? We have to stay here, Jen.'

She makes a noise, high-pitched, frustrated and torn. 'Why didn't you just *call* me, prick? I hate this. I hate her, and I hate that you brought her here!'

'I tried to leave her in the Lakes.'

'That's where you've been?'

'Not the whole time – just for a few days. A holiday house as far away as I could get for a while. I told her she should stay there, but she wanted to come back with me. She's terrified.'

'Of what? *Sheep?*'

'Of Mark. Anyway, she had to come back at some point. She needs the ID and the money. I couldn't find them when I went in.'

She narrows her eyes. 'In where? You went to Oak House? When? *After* she'd been declared missing?'

'Yes—'

'How did you get in?'

'I went through the garden.'

'Through the fence panel, right?'

'Yes?'

'Jesus, Bill.'

'I know. I feel like I'm hanging on by a fucking *thread*. I had to help her? Don't you see? I *owe* her. Go and get Sam and then come back here, OK? You'll know what to do when we explain it all.'

She wants to kick him in the face, in the bollocks.

'But I *don't* know what to do!' she hisses. 'And I'm tired of being responsible all the time! What have I found in the—'

'Found?'

'You disappeared and I *found* a . . . I thought you'd . . . I thought . . .'

'You thought I'd hurt Claudia? Is that why you were asking about where I was that night?'

'You lied to me, Bill.'

He looks upset. 'You think I would hurt someone? You think I could do that? I've been trying to *help* her!'

'But do you know how reckless you've been? My *God*, Bill.'

'I'm sorry.'

'You're going to be.'

She gores him with a look as she opens the door and then, on the other side of it, she starts to cry.

TWENTY-EIGHT

Bill exhales into the silence.

He feels bad. He knows that Jen's diving is dangerous, he knows too that causing a false investigation like this is a criminal offence. He and Claudia had expected Mark to have declared her missing at some point, but to have a random dog-walker spot something in the river on that Monday elevated everything to a height they could never have foreseen. They thought it would just fade away into nothing and then they could get Claudia safely away to Canada, but instead they watched the news, saw that the divers were called out again, and then again the following week, there were more appeals made for more witnesses. In the quiet of number ten's garage, they talked about coming out to the police, but that would have ruined her chances to properly vanish later. The investigation grew.

There was no question of helping her when she came to him four months ago. After what happened at the barn, there was a debt to be repaid, and a chance for him to prove his worth in repaying it. The added incentive, of course, was the money she promised him – five thousand pounds immediately (in the envelope that he couldn't find in Oak House) and forty thousand from the sale of the house. Enough to cover his financial debts and all the money he's borrowed from Andy without Andy noticing. Christ, it's so much money that he's racked up, a staggering, eye-watering amount, and the stupid thing was that the bigger it got, the less it felt like when he lost a fifty here, or a hundred there. Pittance against the monster of debt already accrued. The thought of it makes his stomach lurch.

He goes into the living room, watches Claudia sleeping. It was a risk returning, but she'd backed him into a corner with her stunt with the pool liner.

'Why did you do that, Claud?' he'd asked her in dismay when he'd returned home from the drive, after he'd talked to Andy.

She was sat still in the armchair of the vast living room of the house in Cumbria.

'Why did you write that in the bottom of the pool?'

'I'm sorry,' she said quietly.

'I put you in that house to keep you *safe*,' he said. 'So no one would be suspicious of where you'd gone.'

She nodded. 'I know. God, I know, and I'm sorry.'

'What did you even use? One of the knives I gave you to eat with?'

'Yes.'

He wanted to shout at her stupidity, her thoughtlessness, but he couldn't articulate it because it was confused – it's *still* confused – with so many other emotions. He loves her, he always has, and he *needs* her for his financial security.

She had put her hand to his shaking shoulders. 'I did a stupid thing. I should have told you about it. When you left me each night, I felt like I was in this weird time warp. Invisible. And I was angry. I was so angry at having to be in that house, alone, with none of my things, and frightened of the future. The night you said we had to go to Cumbria, I had left the garage and just wandered the house and found the pool. It drew me in, I guess.'

She looked at Bill with those beautiful eyes, those thick lashes.

'I had scratched out those words because *he* used to say them to me. And I wanted to tell myself that I *did* take that moment and so I carved it out to tell myself that I was alive and that I was worth something, *despite* him.'

She'd pulled him towards her in a hug, and then she'd cried, huge sobs against his chest so that his T-shirt was wet with tears.

Maybe it's good they've come back, he tells himself. Because Mark will go to Paris soon – he's been cleared for travel, so Claudia can try to get into the house for the passport and money. Possibly this could all work out. Breathe, he tells himself now. Go back to the site, try to sort more of the shit he's gotten himself into with Andy, and then back to Claud, speak to Jen. He also needs to email Victoria Franklin about furthering the sale of Oak House. He has a list of things to do the length of his arm.

He clicks on his emails. Victoria's last correspondence is full of fury, directed not at him, of course, but at Claudia.

Claudia, how dare you even consider selling Oak House, which was my father's beloved project all those years ago?

How dare you contact buyers without my permission?

Claudia has emailed her twice since then from Bill's email account, but she's not replied. Bill chews at his nails. What will happen if Victoria tries to stop the sale? What would happen to his debts then?

With a final glance at Claudia, he grabs the keys to the black van, and locks the door behind him.

TWENTY-NINE

Claudia wakes.

She's lying on a sofa, covered with a fleece blanket which smells of things she remembers; of jasmine, peaches, and of chlorine – Jen's smell. There's safety in the memory of it because it belongs to Claudia's childhood, when life was hopeful and free and not like it is now. Now it's toxic and all the bricks she built her life on are crumbling.

The light has faded and she wonders briefly if it's dusk or dawn before she sees a clock on the wall. It's seven in the evening. She thinks how strange it is to wake like this. She was dreaming again about the diving pool agitator, that when she jumps from the platform, it suddenly turns off, and she's spinning faster and faster into a sheet of water that now looks like glass. She's can't tell where the bottom of the pool is, and she's going to crash into it like it's concrete and her body will break. She's been long used to waking to the immediate sense of dread, she's had years where's she's tried to work out what mood Mark might have been in before he's even rolled over to face her. Even on the good days, she couldn't trust Mark's smiles – they could change very suddenly, like a cloud that turned the sky black.

'Hello?' she calls quietly, but she's met with silence.

She sits up and takes in her surroundings. The lounge is small and compact, with a tall standing lamp in one corner, a mirror, and a huge TV. On the walls are framed pictures of stock internet phrases on well-being – *Believe you can and you are already halfway there* and *Life beats down and crushes the soul but art reminds you that you have one* – and they make Claudia laugh because Jen was always the most capable person Claudia knew, so what on earth is she doing with all this rubbish? Jen was always driven and ambitious and determined – all the things that Claudia wasn't but pretended to be. She can see numerous hooks on the wall too, noticeable gaps where frames should be. Was it that way when Bill brought her in here? They'd driven all night and she was so tired and now can't remember.

There is a bookcase with shelves filled with books with titles like *Into The Deep*, *The Wave*, *Something Beneath the Sea*, and this brings a smile to Claudia's face. Jen, a human whose heart and soul belong in the water.

She's thought about Jen a lot over the years; has wondered who she is now, what makes her laugh, and what makes her cry. She remembers years ago they used to do both at the same time. She remembers a day at the river, where they'd floated along where the water became rapid-like. It had shot them downstream alongside little gathered icebergs of dun foam, beneath a canopy of yellow leaves. Claudia went so fast that she clung wildly to Jen's legs and Jen got her foot stuck down Claudia's cleavage and couldn't pull it free. Claudia thinks that she's never laughed so hard before or since. She wonders if Jen ever thinks of this memory, if she's kept it close to her heart or thrown it away like she did the friendship they had. Or was it Claudia who had thrown it away?

She shivers because she's wearing only Bill's T-shirt and her jeans and she's cold, she wants a cup of tea, or maybe something stronger. She definitely wants a jumper and she wants Bill here, but he's not. She looks around for her bag to see if he might have messaged her on the phone he bought her, but she can't see it by the sofa or, indeed, anywhere. She gets up to find a jumper in Jen's bedroom and wonders what Jen would think of her entering her most intimate space – it feels like something utterly forbidden.

The bedroom is as messy as it has always been. The bed – a simple navy duvet cover and white sheets – is unmade and there are clothes strewn around the floor, books in a stack on the bedside table with a teacup perched on top of it, the remnants of it cold and discoloured. There's a dressing table opposite, with an assortment of cream tubes and cosmetics without lids littering it and Claudia can bet most of them are out of date. On closer inspection, she's right.

Jen was never a girlie-girl. When they were teenagers and they used to spend hours in front of Claudia's vanity complete with Hollywood-dressing-room-style light bulbs, Jen would prefer to make herself up to look like a gargoyle and make them both laugh than try to enhance her features. Claudia used to roll her eyes, thought Jen wasn't confident in her own skin, wasn't brave enough to see the woman beneath the surface of her girlhood, but now she thinks Jen was actually just above it all – she wasn't in a hurry to be something she wasn't. She was always just herself.

Claudia tilts her head, sees a few strips of photo-booth photographs tucked into the back of the mirror and lifts them out. Black-and-white pictures of Jen and Bill, and Jen with a few men she doesn't recognise. There are some too of Jen with Kerry Westbrook, Jen's best friend who idolised Jen and who loved Bill. Claudia never liked her.

She looks for photos of Jen's child – Bill told her of a son – but where is he? Claudia can't imagine Jen as a mother, though she couldn't imagine her as a police officer either. It would be like a dress-up day at school and not real life, not *her* Jen. But Jen hasn't been hers for so long, so what would Claudia know about anything. She doesn't know Jen any more, just like she doesn't know herself. The woman she used to be was brave and strong, and above all, a good person, but she's not brave or strong any more and she's definitely not good.

She goes to the wardrobe, pulls the door. Inside is a jumble of jeans and jumpers on a shelf, and countless shirts immaculately ironed that she realises must be part of Jen's police uniform. She selects a generic, brandless, grey hoodie and puts it over her head, immediately engulfed by the comfort of Jen's smell once again.

Some of Claudia's favourite memories are of the two of them sitting at her kitchen table, their hair damp from practice, and wearing each other's clothes. Claudia thought that it must be like having a sister. It became tradition after every Friday practice, and on Mondays after they'd finished their school days, they would meet in the Tea For Two cafe and swap them back again. They used to order salted caramel milkshakes, talk about their days and then move onto more serious things – their dives, their tucks, the modifications they needed to make to be tighter, better, stronger. Jen always made Claudia work harder, made her want more, push her body more aggressively. But every time Claudia improved at arching, or tightening her tucks, Jen would match it all effortlessly. She recalls Victoria commenting once on how naturally talented Jen was.

'Claudia is as good as me,' Jen would say.

'I think you have the edge,' Victoria would say and Claudia would wilt beneath this degradation.

She turns to leave, is hungry and wants to make herself something to eat, when she catches sight of a small cube on the bedside cabinet. It's a photo cube and in each tiny face are pictures of Jen with a little boy and in that instant she knows. She picks up the photograph, puts it so close to her face that her breath fogs the gloss of the picture. Jen and her son are on a beach with their arms wrapped tightly around each other, and sunshine in their hair. They look alike – so alike that not many people would see what she sees, but she's studied Mark's face for decades. She knows that slight upturn in the lips that this boy has, knows the way Mark's hair falls in a curling lock over his forehead, the same as this boy.

Claudia stalks out, and straight into the boy's bedroom, her hunger forgotten. Like Jen's, this room is messy, but God, it's full of life and vibrancy. Little Lego creations on the windowsill, his clothes messy in open drawers, a toy cow on the bed. On the wall is a drawing tacked up, of a person with three fingers on each hand, hair zigzagging across their head in black triangles, a mouth that is drawn in red and runs literally from ear to ear. She takes it down, stares at it. There's a rainbow, and a thin blue line to represent the sky, except she frowns, because, no, there's blue for the sky and also for the ground and Claudia realises that it's because it's a pool or the sea. It's water, of course. *To my Superhands Mummy*, it reads, *beecos you are like a murmayd and a fish and a shark. love from Sam.*

Claudia is taken by surprise by the emotion that rushes to her heart. She imagines that's what it's like to have a child – that you fall in love with them as you do a partner, except the love is deeper, unparalleled. Your own ego doesn't need to be satisfied when you have a child – you just love them. Or, she imagines, that's how it should be. Her own mother was far from it. Rich in material wealth but not in love.

She puts the picture on the duvet, tries to control the angry heat of betrayal, because this boy is Mark's son, and Mark is a liar, a cheat, and worse. So much worse. When did this happen? She can't remember what age Bill said the boy was, but she places him at about seven.

She exhales. She remembers seeing Mark for the first time – everyone remembers where they were when they first saw Mark Mason, like they can recall the moon landing, the Twin Towers falling, Princess Diana's death, the Queen. Jen hadn't stopped talking about him for months, so Claudia had finally decided to see for herself what the fuss was all about. One Saturday morning, she'd cycled to the pool and had sat with Bill in the viewing gallery, her trainers up on the chairs in front.

'Come on then,' she said. 'Where is he? Jen's obsession?'

Bill pointed. 'There. Ripped as shit and drives an old Nighthawk apparently. Dick.'

She followed his finger to see a man coming into view. She blinked, breath knocked, at the sight of this lean, muscular figure, with dark curls and an olive complexion, and she'd smiled in understanding.

'Oh yeah. What a shitty Adonis he is.'

'Whatever,' Bill said. 'I have beauty *and* youth.'

'He's how old?'

'I don't know, do I? Ask Jen – she'll probably know his star sign and whatever animal he's supposed to be on the Zodiac.'

'I'm a snake,' she said.

'I'm a dog apparently. I don't know what that means.'

She shifted in her seat, and produced a fiver out of her pocket.

'It means you're good at fetching. Get me a strawberry smoothie from the bar and whatever you want?'

'Five whole pounds? Is it Christmas?'

'Shut up.'

He grinned and left – oblivious to what she was thinking or feeling – and she sat back and relished the sound of Mark's voice as it echoed instruction, drank in the way he used his hands when he talked, and the way he brushed the long lops of hair away from his eyes. He was authoritative, strong, supportive. Everything she found attractive, and for the first time, Claudia wanted the thing that Jen had. She wanted to dive again, wanted to take Jen's girlhood crush and make more out of it.

On her way out, she listed her past credentials to the dive club manager, and the following day she was called up and immediately invited to try out at the next diving session. She wore a gold one-piece, high-legged and with thin straps, and she stole the show, because that's what happened when you were Claudia Franklin; a winner of any stage. She remembers surfacing from that first dive, knowing it had been good, but she didn't look immediately to Mark for confirmation of it – no, she looked at Jen, who sat on the bench in her faded blue swimsuit, slicks of hair having escaped from her tired hat and her goggles on. She had worry etched all over her face and was looking at Mark, but Mark – Claudia knew – was looking directly at *her*.

'Welcome to the club,' he said as she'd got out, and he'd winked at her. He'd *winked*. She was sixteen.

For a while, there was safety in the flirtation because she knew nothing could ever come of it. She loved that his eyes seemed to lick at her every time she peeled away her shorts and her shirt to a swimming costume that left almost nothing to the imagination, she loved how he knew every inch of her body. And it was legitimate, because she was a diver. She was doing nothing wrong by teasing him. And, my God, she did tease him. She may have been young, but she was in charge of all the subtleties of her body's movement, of a well-timed smile.

The day that they became more than coach and team member was a Thursday evening practice session. Everyone else had left the pool, but Claudia was still up on the dive board, trying to meet the latest challenge Mark had set for her – a reverse triple somersault in pike position. She'd been practising for months, but she was struggling to get her body wrapped taut enough to build up the speed she needed.

'Tighter!' Mark shouted from below, but time and again, she landed awkwardly, or could only make two turns before hitting the water.

'I'm not going to do it,' she sobbed as she climbed out of the pool. The water was taunting her, coming up at her too quick when she wasn't ready for it, when she hadn't controlled herself, and if there was one thing Claudia hated about herself, it was to show vulnerability and lack of control. Everything had to be immaculate, structured, elegant.

He handed her her shammy. 'You will. Go again.'

She went up the stairs to the top, but her legs were fatigued, heavy with the repetition, her muscles shaking. She steadied herself against the railings, looked down. Usually the feeling of free falling was what she liked the most about diving – air rushing around her body and the water rushing up to meet her – it was like total freedom, like the only time when she could live in the absolute present and not be thinking about the next thing she needed to achieve, needed to master. Diving for her was liberation, even though it demanded so much from her physically.

'I can't,' she whispered and Mark heard her even when her voice was so small. The acoustics of the pool were such that – if quiet – you could sigh in part of the area and someone on the other side could hear it. She sat down, cross-legged, and watched as the remnants of water puddled on the porous board around her.

'Stay there,' she heard him say and then she heard his feet on the tower. 'You *are* going to do it,' he said, when he reached her and he sat down with her. 'Because you're here and you're practising.'

'I can't make it.'

'*Yet*. Listen, you're dedicated and you've got the skill. You've got to hone it. You have the potential to be a success.'

'I thought I did.'

'You do. I can see it. And you have the passion. You *want* it.'

He reached for her then, his fingertips soft on her chin, and gently moving her jaw so that she was forced to look at him.

'You do want this, don't you?' he asked.

She looked at him then, his face so close to hers. She knew that his words weren't related to her training.

'Yes,' she whispered.

They paused like that, faces inches apart, and she could smell the mint of gum on his breath. His finger traced the curve of her cheek.

'You're my best diver.'

'Jen's better than me.'

'But you are more beautiful.'

A thrill and a nervousness coursed through her body.

'Does that mean I'm better?'

He stood up on the platform, held out his hand to her. 'Dive again and show me how good you are. Show me you're the best.'

She stood but didn't go to the edge of the board. Instead she went to him, stood on her tiptoes, kissed him. He kissed her back and that moment was the excuse she needed to ensure she was the last one at every training session, the excuse she needed to wear her shortest shorts at the trampoline, the excuse to smile freely at him. Because she thought she was living a dream – she had a glittering career in reach, and an older, attractive man who believed in her, and desired her.

She closes her eyes, inhales through the complex pain that constricts her lungs. It used to be only Claudia that Mark worshipped physically. They crossed the threshold of intimacy when she was seventeen and one month. They had just finished their diving sessions and he'd offered her a lift back. Except they hadn't gone back to Oak House. They'd gone to his flat and he had pulled her towards his bedroom where they'd had lurid, beautiful, raw sex. Her hair had made a damp imprint in the pillow after and he told her that she was golden and she believed it because, all her life, Claudia Franklin was golden.

Until she wasn't.

Until she fucked up the dives at the Olympics, until she grew older and Mark's eyes started to move away from her. But, God, to her horror, she still loves him, needs him, *wants* him, because he's all that she's ever known – he was the one that stayed when everyone else left.

She blinks back the past, stares around Sam's room, willing away the sting of her own mother's abandonment. She can't imagine Jen ever rejecting her child. God, she wishes for her life to have turned out differently.

Whenever she thinks of her mother, she feels a tightness in her chest so she diverts her thoughts. They catch instead on Henry, his infectious smile and his whistle that was like music, calling his dogs to him when they went for a walk. He came into Claudia's life when she was eleven, years after her own father had died in a car accident, and he was good for stabilising Victoria, for providing some lightness when she was in a mood. He was an academic, unassuming, but never overly warm with Claudia and she craved it – God, she craved a father figure and some warmth.

Daddy issues, she said once to her therapist as a joke, but her therapist had nodded gravely.

She pauses. There was a time, now she thinks about it, that Henry had been particularly kind to her. Claudia had been thirteen and her mother and Henry had come to her school sports day. Claudia had won silver in the hurdles and had jogged over to them to show them her medal, but her mother had rolled her eyes.

'You almost had that, Claudia,' she'd said with a disappointed sigh. 'You were a hair away from gold.'

'Nonsense,' Henry had said. 'Claudia did brilliantly. Silver is excellent. Well done, sweetheart.'

He'd never called her sweetheart in the two years he'd been part of their lives and Claudia's heart had soared with his praise. And then he'd *hugged* her, really hugged her to him, and she'd been enveloped by the woody smell of his study, his old books and his cigars.

'Don't call my daughter "sweetheart",' Victoria had said, so coldly that Claudia and Henry had sprung apart like they'd been caught doing something wrong. Victoria had looked at Claudia. 'Silver isn't good enough,' she had remarked and walked out of the school field and missed all the rest of the races. Henry had followed her and missed them all too, and had never called her sweetheart again after that, and never hugged her either. Lord knows what Victoria might have said to him in the privacy of their bedroom that night.

Claudia grits her teeth. She needs to contact Victoria soon. Bill had been sorting things out for her to get to Canada – the sale of Oak House and possible clients for it. Victoria isn't happy about losing it, but what leg does she have to stand on after all these years of silence, all these years of *abandonment*? God, she hates Victoria. There, she's finally admitted it to herself. She starts to laugh.

THIRTY

Somehow Jen has managed to pick up Sam from school, talked to him about his day – though she can't remember anything he told her – has dropped him at Kerry's, managed to hold a cup of tea and a conversation without shaking, and has dodged Idris's calls. No doubt he's asking her about the medic and wondering why she's not contacted him.

It's seven-fifty now and Bill has been ceaselessly calling her too, but before she goes back to her flat again to confront him and Claudia, she's come to the pool – her place of worship. Let them agonise over where she might be like she's agonised over them.

There are ten minutes left of the session and only three swimmers remaining, but all she needs is a few minutes, because she doesn't want to lane swim, she doesn't even want to swim. She wants to sink, wants to distort the noise in her head and think, because she's utterly confused, disorientated, and doesn't know if she's going mad. Somewhere out there is a body. Or is there? Maybe she did imagine it?

She walks out of the changing room, and the humid breath of chlorine prickles at her skin and the back of her throat. Perversely, it never fails to comfort her. She loves that every day the water is cleaned, and anything unsavoury is filtered away. In water like this she can open her eyes, and though the chemicals sting them, she welcomes the clarity. No bodies.

She walks up to the lifeguard on the tower.

'I'm doing some training exercises,' she says. 'Testing lung strength.'

'OK,' the young man says.

'Don't try to save me, OK?'

He grins. 'Fine.'

She slips into the pool, swims to the furthest and deepest part, and then she submerges herself, allows her body to expel all the air in her lungs and to sink to the bottom. She can stay at the bottom, cross-legged, for ninety seconds with her eyes open and unblinking and it's like meditation – like being in between life and death.

She's far from meditative now, however. A new spark of anger flames up in her stomach at the thought of Claudia in her house, doubtless now awake and picking over all the aspects of Jen's life – all the design choices she's made, all the stains on the carpets, the mess of the bathroom paintwork, the pictures that are hung badly, the choice of books she reads. Jen wouldn't change anything about any of it because they're *her* choices and yet she feels the flush of embarrassment, knowing that Claudia would have chosen better curtain prints, better carpets, and pot-fucking-pourri.

But more than any of the surface-level décor, Jen knows that Claudia will be looking at Jen's life for clues as to who

Jen is now, and Jen doesn't want her to know. Why did Bill not take Claudia to his flat? That *dick*. Whenever it came to Claudia, he was always like a sick kind of puppy.

Will Claudia make the connection about Sam? Bill already told her that Jen has a child – surely Claudia will put two and two together, but maybe not. They've been out of this town for so many years and Claudia has never – to Jen's knowledge – been aware of Mark's affair with Jen. She hates the fact that Bill might have talked about Sam to Claudia, may have told her stories about him, what his first word was, or that his favourite stuffed animal is a cow he calls Piggy.

She thinks so hard that her lungs start to burn with pain, reminding her to feel alive, to fight. Jen has always been a fighter even when she's already lost. She has two choices – either she marches Claudia down to the police station to explain herself and they get into deeper shit, or she waits and gathers any new information as to what the hell has happened and then make a decision. Each option carries risk, guilt. The noise of everyone's problems is like the colour white in her ears.

As the sky turns vanilla with the sun's descent, Jen unlocks the door to her flat. A smell that's both familiar and unfamiliar inhibits her nose before she places it as the perfume of her own shampoo.

'Hello?' Claudia's voice sounds scratchy. 'Jen? Is that you?'

Jen dumps her swim bag on the floor. 'Surprise.'

'I'm in the kitchen.'

Jen walks in and sees Claudia sitting at her table, dressed in pale skinny jeans with designer rips at the knees and Jen's own grey hoodie. Her hair tumbles over her shoulder, damp but brushed through.

She's used all my things, Jen thinks, and she's horrified at this, and yet, it's so utterly normal because they always used to share things – hairbands, shammys, dinners in front of the TV.

'Where have you been?' Claudia asks.

'Oh, that's rich. Where's Bill?'

'He had to go to work.'

'So are you going to be the one to tell me what the hell is going on?'

'I think it's best if we're all together to discuss this. Bill said he'd be back by nine.'

Internally, Jen seethes at this air of authority in Claudia's voice. After all this, and all these years, and Claudia can still make her awkward and unanchored. She moves to flick the switch on the kettle.

'Yes, please,' Claudia says.

'I don't have any white china.'

'I don't need white china.'

It would be petty, Jen knows, not to give Claudia a cup of tea. She pours the hot water into two cups, stirs the teabags around, adds the milk. She passes one to Claudia, who sips at it instantly and then recoils.

'Hot.'

Jen got her petty want after all, but it doesn't make her feel any better.

She sits opposite Claudia and waits, but Claudia sits and reflects Jen's silence. It makes Jen seethe. Claudia has always had this way about her – of being a presence in any room and not necessarily a good one. Atoms have to rearrange themselves to accommodate her.

Jen leans forward, irritated. 'Why, after all this time, are you involving Bill in all your crap?'

It's a strange first question and one that obviously takes Claudia by surprise.

'Because he's a good man.'

'He *is* a good man. And he loves you, he always has.'

'Yes.'

'And what do you feel about him?'

'You know I've always loved him.'

'Right,' Jen scoffs.

'Look, I don't expect you to get it. Or maybe you do. A love affair that happens years after it's all done. Do you know much about that?'

Jen narrows her eyes. Has Claudia guessed about Sam? Jen decides not to comment. In her pocket, her phone starts up. She ignores it.

Claudia sips at the tea. 'Getting in contact with Bill again was, at first, an accident. And then it was a relief. And then it was something that suited both of us. It was an opportunity for us each to grab an offer of rescue.'

'You think Bill needs rescuing?'

'You know he does.'

Jen bristles.

'He owes people money, Jen. Lots of it.'

'Were you going to dish out some cash for him with the silver spoon you've got stuck up your arse?'

Claudia doesn't rise. She regards Jen coolly. 'I was going to help him, yes.'

'And have you?'

'I had some money in the house to give him, but I couldn't get to it before I had to get out.'

'So you haven't.'

'Bill wanted to help me regardless,' Claudia says. 'Because of the barn.'

'You've used the barn against him.'

'He told me himself how terrible he's felt all these years – how guilty and ashamed. Don't the two of you ever talk about it? Clearly he's crying out for help.'

'I *know* that.'

'But you haven't helped.'

'I fucking do help! In every way I can. Jesus, Claudia, you don't get to preach at me, in *my* house, about *my* brother. Why are you even here? Bill said you wanted to leave Mark, leave your life. But travelling the world, opening galas, attending dinner parties and being photographed in *Woman and Home* wearing diamonds around your throat doesn't look like a such bad life at all.'

'I didn't know you kept such tabs on me.'

Jen reddens. 'I don't.'

'I was a child, Jen. A child that became wrapped up in herself after a trauma. Mark was the only one who looked after me.'

'*I* was there. But you pushed me out.'

'You'd already checked out of our friendship by then.'

'No,' Jen snaps. 'I was there for you after the accident at the barn, but you didn't want me. You wanted to concentrate on the diving and I understood that. I understood that being with me after what happened – and with Bill – was too much for you.'

'Of course I wanted you.'

'Tell me why you left?'

'Because I found something out about Mark that tipped me over the edge. And I almost don't want to tell you because you're as much invested in Mark as I was, aren't you?'

Jen's phone goes off again. She pushes it further down in her pocket.

'You have a son. I've seen a picture. He's Mark's, isn't he?'

Shit. Jen knew she couldn't hide it. Claudia has seen Sam's face, and Jen hates this.

'Is that what you found out?' she asks.

Claudia laughs then, a sad little 'ha'. 'No. Not that. I could have coped with that, Jen. That's nothing.'

'Then—'

'But you're a fool.'

Jen scowls. 'Look—'

But Claudia interrupts again. 'How often do you see him?' she asks quietly. 'Does he ever take your son?'

'I . . . No. Sam doesn't know who his dad is. Mark only found out by chance when you both moved back here. I had told him I was pregnant . . . but . . .'

'A child out of wedlock would ruin his image.'

This stings coming from Claudia's perfect rosebud mouth.

'That's cruel of him not to have recognised your . . . predicament,' Claudia says.

'Don't call Sam a *predicament.*'

'I can't believe you let Mark get away with it.'

Jen clenches her fists. 'Oh fuck off, Claud. Mark and I have history, like the two of you have history, right? It's raw and horrible and precious. It's also balanced on a knife-edge.'

'And that's what he's always been so good at,' Claudia says. 'I never realised. But it's a good thing he never claimed Sam as his son. You have to keep it that way. Sam should never know that Mark is his dad.'

'Why not?'

'He can be violent.'

Jen starts to laugh. 'Violent?'

Claudia moves towards her. 'You don't know him like I know him.'

They're interrupted again by Jen's phone ringing like it's burning a hole in her trousers.

'Answer it,' Claudia says.

Jen goes to silence it because she thinks it's Bill, or Kerry, but it's Idris's name on her screen and she clicks to answer, wants to tell him that she was about to go to the medic but had to get Sam. She wants to tell him that Sam is unwell, that she's probably got a sickness bug from him. She needs to lie, tell him anything to shut down his questions. But she doesn't get a chance to say anything.

'We've got a body,' he says.

THIRTY-ONE

Jen's sweating, heart crashing against her chest like waves against rock.

She saw a body, she *did*, and this changes everything.

'Hang on,' she says to Idris.

She mutes the call, looks at Claudia.

'I need to go. When Bill comes back, tell him to call me. I'll meet you at his flat. I want you out of my fucking house.'

She takes the phone outside, leaving Claudia alone because she can't have her overhear this conversation – no way. She gets into her car, grips the phone in her hand so tight that her skin is going white. She clicks to unmute.

'What happened?' she asks.

'We found her,' Idris says. 'She's taken quite a journey.'

'Where? Where did you find her?'

Or rather, *who*.

'Downstream from where we were earlier. Tangled up in weeds but obviously been disturbed. She's in a pretty bad state.'

'Have we had identification?'

He laughs. 'Good one.'

Bile creeps up her throat and she pushes it back with her tongue.

'You know the drill as well as I do,' Idris continues. 'We'll wait for the formal ID, but the case needs to progress and she's become a figure of interest. The team will put out a statement to the media tonight or tomorrow to say we've found a body.'

Jen nods, although he can't see her down the phone. Who did she leave in the water?

'Did you manage to sleep?' he asks.

'No.'

'But you saw the medic, right?'

'No—'

He sounds annoyed. 'Why the hell not? I'm not letting you dive again until you do, Jen. I'm serious.'

'I slept . . . I—'

'I thought you said you didn't sleep?'

'I'll go to the medic now.'

'It's too bloody late now, idiot. Clinics will be closed. Go first thing tomorrow.'

Jen drives without thinking. She should go back to Kerry's house and make sure Sam is OK, but instead she's found herself somewhere she really shouldn't be. There might be a police presence at Oak House right now, but she's left the car in town and walked the back way, followed the river past the barn, skirted the water-meadows and up through the fields. She stops outside the woods, at the back of the house.

There's a possibility that Mark has been called to the police station already. Claudia told her that he has a violent streak, but Idris had called before Jen could get a sense of what that meant. Did she mean emotionally? Physically? Either way, Jen's disturbed by the revelation and thinks of Sam, her wonderful, good-natured boy, and a deep ache of disappointment throbs in her heart. She'd grown to enjoy her meetings with Mark and talking about Sam. She had entertained the thought of introducing them someday, had even imagined Mark sitting at her kitchen table and helping Sam with homework. Perhaps she's been a fool, but when it comes to Mark, she supposes that she always has been. The body found *isn't* Claudia's, but could Mark possibly be involved somehow in someone's death? Or is Claudia, and by proxy and his own stupidity, also Bill?

Jen also used to come in through the panel of the garden fence but she won't dare do that now the police are all over it it. She remembers as a teenager once going through it and finding Henry in a deckchair on the lawn, a cigar dangling between his two fingers and his dogs at his feet. One had stood up at the noise of her coming through, and barked.

'Shit!' she'd said. 'I'm sorry.'

He'd looked at her, amused. 'So this is how you come in.'

The dogs padded over, sniffed at her, and she'd stroked them in turn.

'I didn't know we had a loose panel.'

'Claudia says it's easier to come through this way, otherwise she has to open the gates and everything.'

He laughed.

'I'm sorry I came through.'

'I won't tell Victoria. She probably wouldn't appreciate it.'

She had smiled gratefully, had made to go, but his face clouded and it made her pause.

'Jen?'

'Yeah?'

'Does Claudia bring boys back in through here? Is she seeing anyone?'

'Not that she's told me. We're too busy for boys. Or, that's what I thought.'

'Is she happy? With the swimming? The diving? I know you have the championships next year.'

'She's not nervous.'

'Do you like your coaches? You like the team?'

Jen grinned. 'We all like the coaches. The team is great. She's happy, Mr Barton. I think she's doing good.'

He nodded. 'OK. And how's your mother?'

'She's . . . she's OK.'

'I read in the paper yesterday that Addens Hospital are conducting some new medical trials,' he said. 'For dementia. It might be worth looking into?'

'It's OK,' she replied. 'We can look after her.'

'I'm happy to enquire on your behalf?'

'It's OK but thanks, Mr Barton. I'll ring the GP.'

He regarded her then, silently. 'Claudia is in the kitchen,' he said.

The flitting of a bird in the branches above her snaps Jen out of her memories and she stares at the back of Oak House, which has become dark against the skyline.

She just wants to fall asleep right here, in the shadow of this house where she used to spend so much time, and become oblivious to what's happening around her.

Her phone vibrates and she reaches for it – a message from Bill lights her screen.

We're here at mine. Please come.

She goes to leave, but as she does so, a haze of a dream drifts in front of her eyes. But no, it doesn't feel like a dream but a memory, a retelling. The dream house is dark, black eye-socket windows except one – a bedroom light is on, the curtains are ajar. There is movement, the front door is slammed and someone walks down the driveway and out of the gates.

An image of bulrushes rips across her eyes like spears against the sky. There's a distant humming sound in her ears and her feet are freezing cold.

THIRTY-TWO

Claudia has listened to her at least – she and Bill have left Jen's flat and Jen is purged of that acute sense of vulnerability she felt in her own home.

'Come in,' Bill says when he opens the door to her, but she is rigid in the darkness of the corridor.

'Shit is about to hit the fan,' Jen says.

'Shit is *already* hitting the fan.'

'But the shit that *I* know about is going to drown us,' she says. 'Listen very carefully. I've got to ask you something and you've got to answer me honestly.'

Bill frowns. 'Can't you come in first?'

'No.'

'What's going on?'

'The tie you wore for that interview, the red one. What did you do with it when you'd finished with it?'

'I don't know? I gave it back, right? Why are you asking me about it?'

'Back to who? I can't remember you giving it to me.'

'Didn't I leave it back in your flat? I didn't know where you got it, so where else would I have put it?'

'You've got to think, Bill. Really think.'

'Who has access to your flat apart from me?' he asks.

She pauses. 'Kerry.'

'Would Kerry have taken it?' he says.

'No? Why would she?'

She doesn't say who else has all the passcodes to her flat – Mark. But Mark has never been in her flat without her being there because there's never been a need for it.

'I don't know,' she says.

'Jen, I'm sorry, but I don't remember. I'm fucking knackered, can you just come in and we can explain all this?'

'*You're* exhausted?' she mutters.

'Andy knows I've screwed up,' he says. 'It's only a matter of time until he discovers more.'

'Screwed up?' she says and then the penny drops. 'Bill, you've stolen from *Andy*?'

'Just come in,' he urges.

She steps through, immediately treads on a stray sock. Beyond that, an empty crisp packet and a penny gathering dust where the carpet meets the wall. On a normal day, she'd berate him for the mess, but nothing about this day is normal. She wonders how she's supposed to keep the body a secret from them. She wonders too how she's not already horizontal on the floor from exhaustion.

'Do you want some wine?' he asks as they go through to the kitchen.

'Sure. And some nachos,' she says.

'Jen—'

'I don't want any wine, you knob.'

Claudia is already in the kitchen, leaning against the counter, still wearing Jen's top. She looks better in it too, and this pisses Jen off more than it should. She sits down on the kitchen bar stool.

'If you both don't tell me soon what the hell has been going on the last fortnight, I'm going to lose my shit, OK? I am verging on the edge of a breakdown. Leave nothing out, OK? I need to know what we're dealing with here or, I swear to God, I'm going to radio you in right now. Start at the beginning. You wanted to leave Mark.'

Claudia nods. 'I had planned to leave for Canada over the two weeks that the Olympics were on. I had arranged for a story to be printed – about Mark – that would allow me a reason to leave him. And I banked on him being so absorbed with fighting the accusations of it, and with the diving, that he wouldn't have time to try to find me. That he would just leave me alone.'

'What was the story?'

'It was about a girl back in America that he'd become close to.'

'Right?'

'But I never sent the story. Instead, we had a huge fight on that Saturday afternoon and I knew I had to disappear for a while. I wanted to take my stuff but I . . . I couldn't.'

'Why?'

Claudia shakes her head. 'I . . . He . . . was too strong for me.'

'What does that mean?'

'It means violent,' Bill says. 'She just had to run.'

Violent, that word again.

'Did he hurt you, Claudia? On that Saturday when you fought?'

'Yes.'

'Where?'

'He hit me on the head.'

'You were in the garden, weren't you? You left through the fence panel.'

Claudia looks at her wide-eyed. 'How do you know that?'

'It's called forensics.'

'What do the police think happened to me?'

'They don't have a bloody clue,' Jen says. She turns to Bill. 'You didn't pick Claudia up from there though, Bill? You didn't go through the fence at that point?'

'No. Claudia rang me, we met at the water-meadows and then we came here, to my flat.'

'What time did you meet – that day?'

'About . . . six? And then we waited until it got dark and then Bill drove me back to get stuff. Mark wasn't at the house.'

'Wait, you went back? When?'

'About ten-fifteen, ten-thirty?'

'That makes sense. Your phone was last on then, Claudia. The police tracked it.'

'I switched it off after that. Bill bought me a pay-as-you-go phone to use so Mark couldn't trace me.'

Jen looks at Bill. 'And you were where at ten-thirty?'

'I waited up the lane in the truck.'

'Listen to me very carefully,' Jen says. 'When you went back to the house at ten-thirty, did you see anyone there? On the road? Walking a dog? Walking out by the water?'

Bill pauses a moment. 'No?'

'If you remember seeing anyone else there, now is the time to tell me.'

'If there was anyone there, we'd left by then. And I don't see why that's relevant now that we know Claudia is actually here?'

'Trust me, it's relevant.' Jen turns to Claudia. 'What then?'

'Mark wasn't at the house. His car wasn't there, so I thought it would be easy to get my things, and the money I had promised Bill, which was in the safe in the study. But I . . . I couldn't get into the house. Mark had changed the goddamn code to the gate and I couldn't . . .' Claudia starts to cry. 'I couldn't get into my own house.'

Bill reaches for her and Jen sees how tenderly his fingers wrap Claudia's arm.

'We got a few things together from my flat,' he says. 'Some of my clothes for her to wear and some other stuff. Mark had seen us together in that cafe, and we were worried he'd come to my place to look for her. I had the idea that Claud could stay in one of the houses on the building site and hole up until we figured out what to do. I had a generator and a fridge, everything she could need.'

Jen exhales. 'Why the secrecy, though? Why the lengths of silence when you've seen everything happening on the news? What was the story you were going to send to the tabloids? You said you'd found something out about Mark, so tell me why the fuck you would upend your life like this – all our lives – when Mark is the one holding all the cards about what happened at the barn?'

THIRTY-THREE

Bill wasn't even supposed to have been anywhere near the barn that day – that's what upsets him most of all. He was supposed to be at the cinema with a friend, but he'd been ditched last minute. Instead, he'd idled the morning away playing PlayStation with Jen while Fiona drank heavily through the morning as had become her habit when she was navigating a difficult phase of the dementia. Before long, she'd passed out face-down on her bed, and, after they had cleaned up the sick on the floor, he'd turned to Jen.

'You want to go swim at Cowell Farm?'

'Yeah.'

'Shall I invite Claudia?'

'Sure.'

They'd gone out at midday, in the thick heat of August through the bracken and the foxgloves, under a cloudless sky. Crickets sounded in the reeds, birds called from low thicket branches. Jen tore off her T-shirt, jumped straight in with her bikini top and her shorts still on. Bill sat on one of the stones, rolled up a joint, before a spray of water hit him in the face and then his sister cackled. They were fifteen and nearly seventeen, two teenagers on the cusp of adulthood, who wanted to spread their wings into the world but knew – with their mother the way she was – that they were clipped. But the river was always their salvation: to stress, to boredom.

'Get in, you muppet!'

He left the joint for later, and they spent an hour, maybe more, timing themselves against the current, bombing each other, and after they were spent in the water, they laid on the bank and drank the flat lemonade Bill had brought them from home.

'You think Mum is OK?' Jen asked.

'She'll be out of it for hours,' he replied.

'What will we do when it gets really bad?'

He shook his head. 'That's not for you to worry about.'

'In six months' time, it'll be the British Diving Championships,' she said. 'And then I'll show everyone what I can do. Then the European Championships. And then I'll get to the Olympics.'

He'd looked at her with pride.

'I'll get the money for Mum,' she said. 'Sponsorship will bring money.'

'You'll get there. I believe in you.'

But secretly he was worried. Secretly he was making enquiries into care homes, terrified of his mother's future, of what their lives would become without her, but he couldn't articulate this to Jen because she needed him to be the strong one, the one who made the difficult decisions even when they would inevitably cause heartache.

They stared up at the sky.

'I brought something,' he said.

'What?'

'I've got some mushrooms.'

'You brought mushrooms? From who?'

'A guy from college.'

'Have you taken them before?'

'Twice. It's like . . . nothing I've felt before.'

'Like what?'

Relief, he wanted to say. Escape from worry.

'You don't need that shit,' Jen said.

'You want some?'

'I'd rather be off my tits on sunshine, thanks. And I don't think you should do it.'

'You're such a granny, sis.'

'*And* someone could see you from here.'

'No one comes down here. Anyway, even if they did, who's going to care about seeing a teenage boy acting weirdly at a riverbank?'

She bristled. 'If you have a bad trip, being next to water is really bad planning.'

'Jesus. I'll go to the barn.'

'Don't come crying to me when you think you've got beetles crawling out of your eye sockets.'

He laughed, put his T-shirt on over his damp shorts, and didn't bother with shoes. 'Come and get me when Claudia gets here.'

'Whatever. I'm going to sleep under the tree, OK?'

'I'll wake you up and talk trash about the beetles crawling out of my eye sockets.'

'Please don't.'

He walked through the meadow, long dry grass tickling his skin, and the sounds of flying insects forming a cacophony now that he was away from the noise of the river until he reached the barn.

He tugged the doors open, the loud shrieking of wood against wood making him wince. He wanted to go up to the loft, thought it would be nice to be up there to do the mushrooms, but decided it was safer to stay down in case he had a bad trip. He climbed into the tractor cab instead and sat on the cracked leather seat, re-lighting the joint with his Rolling Stones lighter. That first drag washed him with calmness and he stayed like that a while, before carefully unwrapping two little mushrooms, smooth, with lightly glossy, caramel-coloured caps. He popped one in his mouth and chewed, and then leaned back in the cab, inhaled the sweet perfume of the joint, tasting that it had now taken on a strange flavour. Bill leaned forward, his hands on the controls of the tractor, thought how sick it would be going for a ride in it. Outside the barn, the meadow sounded like it was thrumming. A bug ball. He started to laugh to himself. Bugs in suits, bugs in hats, tiny monocles, twiggy canes. He could see them all.

He dragged again on the joint. His body felt heavy, rubbery, and he lifted an arm, then a foot, and noted with relief that he wasn't paralysed. His skin was slick with sweat, he could see the droplets running off his skin.

'My mind is coming away from my body,' he said aloud and closed his eyes.

His head was beginning to spin, it was too hot in the tractor cab. He opened the door, leaned, and fell straight out.

'Shit, you OK?'

Who had asked him that? Had he asked himself? Bill nodded in response, started laughing, but he knew that it should have hurt. He'd pay for it tomorrow – was it already now tomorrow? Time was sand through his fingers.

He rolled over on the ground and looked up at the barn ceiling, saw patterns and kaleidoscopic colours weaving snake-like through the dust he'd kicked up. Laughter was replaced by panic rising at the back of his throat. Was there a snake up there? He wasn't in control of his own eyes.

'I need some air,' he said.

'Sure,' someone said casually, but there was no one with him.

He looked around. 'Jen?'

He staggered out, his joint lost out of his fingers somewhere in the fall, but he didn't think about it. He needed to get out, wanted to be swallowed up into the vast sky, wanted to fly. He briefly wondered if he could.

He walked out of the barn, but kept stopping to watch the dragonflies criss-cross his path – huge, monstrous, but beautiful, so beautiful with their jewel-like shimmering bodies. He wondered if he should try to catch them and reached out but couldn't grab at any and the effort made him dizzy. He sat heavily, the tall grass coming up over his head, and thought that he could be in a horror movie when they run through maize and can't see who's chasing them. He closed his eyes.

'Bill?'

He sat up to see Jen standing over him, *glowing* in front of him. 'You've got pink skin,' he said. 'Like rainbow pink. No! Like a salmon.'

'There's something wrong in the barn.'

'Are you a salmon?'

She went to yank him up, but he was a dead weight and dropped down again.

'Shut up, can you smell smoke?'

He stood, wobbled, squinted back at the barn. 'What's that?'

'It looks like flames?'

Alarm sobered his mind. 'How long was I gone?'

'Like, forty minutes? I don't know? We should call the fire brigade.'

'Shit, my joint—' He shielded his eyes against the sun. 'I left it . . .'

'My phone is in my bag,' she said. 'We need to get it.'

He nodded, but then paused because something on the wind caught his ears.

'Did you hear that?'

'What?'

He started to laugh, hard and fast and breathless. 'I thought . . . Shit, that trip must be fucking me over. I thought I heard someone in there.'

'You are so fucked,' she said. 'Jesus.'

And then they both heard it. A terrible moaning from inside the barn. The hair on Bill's body stood up in fear.

'There's someone *in* there,' Jen said.

She grabbed his hand and they ran towards it but the nearer they got, the more nightmarish it became. Before they couldn't see flames, but as they rounded the back, they could see huge tongues licking at the wood.

Again, a voice rose up from inside, a discernible howl above the roar.

Bill moved forward. 'Can we open the doors?'

'No! Are you insane? The fire might be right behind them and we'd get blasted.'

'What do we do?'

'I don't know, but we can't *not* go in! I'll call the fire brigade—'

But as she turned, something cracked from within the barn and there was a terrific thud. The screaming from inside stopped abruptly and flames leapt upward.

'Can you hear us!' Bill yelled.

'We need to get over the other side of the river,' Jen said. 'I need to get my phone. If the fire comes down and spreads over this dry grass, we'll be in real trouble.'

Bill raked at his skin with his fingernails. 'We can't leave them!'

She took him by the shoulders. 'We have to cross the river, you understand? We have to cross and ring the fire brigade and wait for them. OK?'

Bill looked at his sister, her expression strong and authoritative at fifteen years old, and in that moment he knew he was seeing the woman he knew she'd become – a person you'd follow at the ending of the world because she'd know how to survive it.

'OK, shit.'

They ran – Bill stumbled – through the grass, made it to the river and swam across to their clothes.

'What's going on? The barn is on fire!'

The two of them turned to see Claudia coming towards them with a bag on her arm, and looking horrified. Jen picked up her rucksack, scrambled around for her phone.

'The joint,' Bill said. 'I . . . I think I left it in there . . . I don't know!'

'You did what?'

'I was smoking in there . . . I—'

'There's someone inside, Claud,' Jen said.

Claudia's face paled. 'What?'

'Someone is *in* the barn. We heard them shouting.'

'Who? Who is it?'

'We don't know!'

They watched in horror as the fire continued to soar with its joyful ferociousness, and the smoke blackened the sky, all of them numbed until they heard fire-engine sirens blare in the distance.

'Someone must have called them.'

'We need to tell them what we heard—' Jen started, but Bill pulled at her arm.

'But, Jen, they can't know,' he cried. 'They can't find out that I started the fire.'

She stared at him. 'Are you crazy? Someone is *in* there—'

There was a crack – a whip across the sky – and the three of them jerked backwards. The entire roof collapsed inwards and a plume of black burst up into the sky.

'Oh my God,' Claudia breathed. 'Oh my God. We have to go.'

'No! We can't leave, we're the only witnesses to someone *burning*!'

'But I *started* the fire!'

Claudia grabbed at her. 'Do you think whoever is in there will get out alive?'

'I—'

'Do you want Bill to go to jail for this?'

'Of course I don't—'

'The fire brigade are coming. Someone has seen the barn and called them. The same person might have seen us all here too.'

'We need to get home,' Bill said with desperation.

'We'll call Mark,' said Claudia suddenly.

Jen stared at her. 'What?'

'We have to put ourselves out of the frame completely and he would vouch for us.'

'We can't ask Mark to *lie* for us. What if he finds out where we've really been?'

'We'll tell him the truth,' Claudia said.

Bill shook his head wildly. 'What? No, he'd go straight to the police—'

The sirens were getting louder.

'We'll tell him we were here at the river when the barn started to smoke. We'll say you were worried the police would question you if you stayed because you'd been getting high in there *before* it went up.'

'But he'd think that I set fire to it, wouldn't he? And he'd ask us about the person! What would we say?'

'We'd say we didn't hear a person.'

Jen swallowed. 'This is insane.'

'We'll go to the dive pool, all of us. And even if Mark suspects later, he'll lie for us because I'll ask him to. I'm his biggest chance of winning an Olympic gold and that's what he wants more than anything.'

Bill took Jen's hand. 'I've done something really bad and in any second, the fire brigade are going to come down this lane. Think about Mum. We need to look after her, but how will I . . . Fuck, how would I if . . .'

She was silent.

'Claudia can help us,' Bill whispered.

'Run,' Jen said.

THIRTY-FOUR

They'd killed a man. Or, more accurately, they'd left a man to die, but the feelings attached to the split-second decision they'd made are still the same – unparalleled guilt, shame and remorse. Yet none of them have ever come forward to relieve themselves of the burden. Instead, it's been their secret for eighteen years, locked beneath the surface of the lives they went on to build themselves.

'Tell me what you found out about Mark.'

Here it comes then, Claudia thinks, the moment of truth. But will she speak the whole truth and nothing but the truth, or will she opt out of certain details? She glances at Bill, who has always been Team Claudia, and he nods encouragingly at her. Jen's eyes, however, are dark and her expression is guarded. Jen should know, though, Claudia thinks, what Mark is truly like. Maybe there's also a part of Claudia that secretly wants to hurt her. Jen made the decision to hurt Claudia, after all, in sleeping with Mark and having his son. How dare she, how fucking *dare* she.

She clears her throat. 'Mark and I have always had a strange power balance, which is unsurprising given how we started. But we never grew to be equals. He likes to be in control and stay in control. He likes to be admired, and dominant.'

'Did you mean physically dominant? Is that what you meant when you said he was violent?'

'Yes.'

'A lot?'

'For the majority of the time, it was emotional. I didn't even know he was doing it for years. Manipulating me. He controlled who I saw, what I did. What I wore. At first, I liked it – I liked that he took the decisions out of my hands. Maybe I let it happen.'

'No, Claudia,' Bill says. 'Don't talk that way.'

'She can speak for herself, Bill.'

'About four months ago, I found out that Mark rents a flat that I was never supposed to know about.'

There's a beat of silence. 'A flat, where?' Jen asks. 'Fording Hill?'

Claudia is surprised. 'How did you know?'

'I found the address on a receipt, in your work locker, Bill.'

'Do the police know about it?' he asks.

'Not that I know of.'

'It's *Mark's* flat,' says Claudia. 'I was suspicious of his behaviour because he started being erratic, not sticking to his schedule. He was staying out late, and sometimes he wouldn't come home at all.'

'You thought that it was an affair?'

Claudia laughs bitterly. 'As you know, he's got form for it. One night, I followed him and I saw him park up in front of the flats, get a key from his jeans, and go inside. I waited, I didn't know how long for at the time, and then a girl came knocking. *Mark* answered it to her in person, smiled at her and that's when the hairs on the back of my neck stood up. Because I knew, I *knew,* what that smile was.'

Jen frowns. 'What was that smile?'

'The one he reserves for those he wants to seduce. Or already has.'

Jen laughs. 'Are you serious? You don't know who the girl was. You don't know why she was meeting him in that flat.'

Claudia looks at Jen with pity. 'Of *course* I knew who the girl was.'

'Who was it?'

'Marie Cadorna. His golden girl from the swim team, Jen. A teenager, like I was.'

THIRTY-FIVE

Jen is confused. 'Wait, he bought her a place near the diving pool?'

'No, it's his place, and she visits. They're having a relationship.'

'You're sure about this? From one time seeing them at the door?'

'I'm sure. I saw them together once *that* way in our bedroom too. In Oak House.'

Jen takes in little sips of air, so many that her stomach begins to hurt. 'No—'

'I can still picture that little bitch's face in the mirror, the grip of her fingers on our bed linen. I smelt his limey aftershave mixed with all that sweat and chlorine, I heard his . . . his noises. I *watched* them, it was like I was transfixed there, and for the first time, do you know what? I saw clearly what my own life had become. Marie is exactly who *I* had been. I thought that all those years ago I was acting like a grown-up, living a dream, but I was a stupid child. *That* was the moment I realised that my life was all a lie, that I was like a piece of driftwood going along with the tide. I had no power.'

Jen grips the edge of the stool so hard that she's losing feeling in her fingers. Mark is the father of her *son*, but all these years he's been a predator?

Claudia clears her throat, the fury in her words obvious and raw. 'As you know, a relationship between an adult and a person under eighteen when in their educational care of an adult is illegal. Mark has abused his position of authority and exploited someone vulnerable, just as he exploited *me*.'

'But . . . but you were twenty when you got together? It's not the same?'

'Did you never think about when it started? I was much younger when he first kissed me, sixteen. I was only just seventeen when we slept together. All those late-night practice sessions, Jen,' Claudia says and her face twists into a smile. 'I was practising very different things.'

Jen feels sick. 'Jesus.'

'There was talk about our engagement in the media, but I was twenty when he proposed and twenty-one when we got married. I was an "adult", but can you imagine if they'd really known how long things had been happening? Twenty wasn't young enough for them to go viral about it, but sixteen would have been. And that was two decades ago. Things have changed now. If they had a story about Bella, *right* before the Olympics, they would absolutely hang him out to dry.'

Jen looks away from Claudia to try to escape her words, but, of course, she can't.

'Who is Bella? The girl in America?'

'Yes. She's the reason we left Chicago for Boston seven years ago,' Claudia continues. 'There had been rumours that Mark had been inappropriate towards one of his dive team there – Bella – and he was asked to leave. I ignored that when I shouldn't have done, but then I found out about Marie . . . it was history repeating itself and I . . . I got so angry. So upset that he could do this to me. And how many others have there been who *haven't* come forward? He obviously never loved me like I loved him. It was the right thing to do to blow it all out of the water, expose him for what he is.'

'So you had enough and decided to leave?'

'It wasn't as simple as just leaving him. He knows the truth about the barn so I needed to play the long game. I found Bella and wrote to her. I asked for her truth of what happened with Mark. She told me that Mark had tried to kiss her a couple of times and she'd initially kissed him back and then had freaked. She was fifteen. *Fifteen*. She had told her parents that he'd said something inappropriate and it caused enough fuss for him to move on elsewhere.'

'But she willingly shared the details of what happened with you?'

'She said she'd felt guilty all these years. Like it was her fault. So I wrote a document that I planned to send to a tabloid reporter anonymously with instructions to run a story on Mark the week before the Olympics. I wanted his reputation to be called into question and then I could have a public reason to disappear, to leave him, and he wouldn't have known that the story had originally come from me.'

'What went wrong?'

Claudia squeezes her eyes shut, looks like she's in pain. 'I didn't get a chance to send the email to the reporter. I drafted it on my laptop and Mark . . . Mark found it.'

Jen inhales. 'The police are looking for your laptop. Does Mark have it?'

'I have it here in the flat,' Bill says. 'It's under my bed.'

'That's why we argued on that Saturday. Mark knew by then that I knew about both Marie and Bella and he told me that if I was to say anything to the press about either of them, he would talk to the police about what really happened at the barn. He said we needed to come to an agreement that I needed to stay with him – be his *front* – and he would continue to say nothing. I was so *hurt* that he could use me like that. A smokescreen. I was someone he'd once *loved*. And who will it be next after Marie? How many others had there been that hadn't said anything? It's all about his ego, his control, his *golden* girls.'

Jen swallows. 'We have a duty of care towards Marie if we know Mark is having an illegal relationship with her. We can't just ignore that.'

'Do we need to go to the police?' Bill asks.

Claudia shakes her head. 'But if I go to the police with what I know about Mark, Mark could ruin Bill with the barn, and your career would go down with him, Jen. Have you told the police that you knew me? That we were friends, trained together? Bill says you hadn't, which means you're a corrupt officer.'

Her words slap Jen in the face because they're true. She sucks in her cheeks, thinks of the body which is now in the morgue. Being identified.

Focus, she tells herself. But fuck you, Claudia. Fuck *you*.

'Mark won't say anything against me because of Sam.'

'What's Sam got to go with any of this?' Bill asks, confused.

Jen closes her eyes, exhales. 'Bill, Mark is Sam's dad, OK?'

Bill stares at her, dumbly. '*What*?'

'Yeah. I didn't mean for you to find out like this, obviously. And obviously I *never* intended Claudia to find out, but you brought her, Bill, – the missing person that everyone is hunting for – to my flat, which is, understandably, covered with pictures of my son. And in the very small amount of time of her being there, Claudia has deduced that, yes, Sam is absolutely one hundred per cent Mark's son, while you, my lumbering gorilla of a brother, have failed to see it for six entire years.'

'How the hell didn't you tell me this? Oh my God, Jen? What happened?'

'Let's not have a discussion about the birds and the bees, Bill.'

'Christ's sake, I didn't mean that—'

'He's six?' Claudia interrupts. 'How interesting. Now I think about it, his trip to the UK to get away from all that bad PR with Bella, would have been the time that he would have seen *you,* Jen, am I right? That works with the timings of your *son*.'

Jen's mouth falls open. 'What are you—'

'You had once been a teenager that he flirted with, a girl he knew adored him. At his lowest point, he came looking for you.'

'Stop,' Jen growls.

'Don't you think that's a bit sick?'

Jen thinks about the drive on the bike to the coast, with the wind in their hair and the hum of the engine below her. The hotel afterwards, the way Mark undressed her and finally, after all those *years* of thinking about him, he kissed her and everything else besides. It's one of her most treasured memories.

'I'm sorry that Mark isn't who you thought he was. He wasn't who I thought he was either.'

'What do we do from here?' Bill asks. 'Jen? What do we do?'

'You think I know? I literally have no idea how to make this better. And it's not just this . . . the whole thing is way over our heads now.'

'What do you mean?'

Jen wonders how many punches a person can be hit with until they're down and will never get up. In the last forty-eight hours, she's been in a boxing ring. She takes a deep breath. Does she tell them about the body? Fuck it, they're going to find out in a matter of hours when it comes out in the press and she needs them to understand the gravity of what they're dealing with if Mark is serious about blackmailing Claudia, and potentially exposing Bill about the barn.

'They've found a body in the river.'

Bill gives an exclamation mark of laughter, sharp and loud.

'You think I'm joking? They think it's *you,* Claudia.'

Claudia's face has lost its colour, the skin around her mouth turning a sickly grey-green.

'And as it's not you, Claudia, then who the fuck is it? The body's been in the water long enough that it'll be in a state of decomposition. It will take maybe half a day to identify.'

Bill stops laughing. 'Are you . . . are you serious?'

'Deadly,' she says and realises too late her unfortunate wording.

It's like she's detonated a bomb. Bill and Claudia start asking questions over one another, shrill and high-pitched. Jen leans back, exhausted, as their voices rise and fall with the debate of what they need to do, of how to protect themselves. She thinks of Sam asleep in his bed and she wants only to go to him.

'Why didn't you say anything before now?' Bill asks.

'Because I wanted to hear what you both had to say first. Do you realise how this is looking, given what you've told me? You both ran away that night and you've been hiding all this time. And your phone, Claudia, was last on at your house, that night. And now there's a body.'

'What are you talking about?' Claudia gasps. 'I've not hurt anyone. Why would you think that? It could be someone who's been down there for weeks? Months?'

'It could be. But it looks very odd that the dog-walker phoned it in on that Monday evening. We need to sit tight for a moment until we know exactly what's going on and who exactly is in the water.'

'I feel sick,' Claudia says. She wobbles to her feet, reaches her hand against the wall to steady herself as she goes.

The bathroom door shuts.

'Jesus Christ, Jen?'

'I need to go to Sam.'

'No, you have to stay! You can't just—'

'I *can* just, actually. I've heard enough.'

She stands up and Bill stands too.

'But what do we *do*? If Claudia becomes a murder suspect in all of this, we need to go to the police, don't we? And clear her name?'

She walks to his front door.

He follows her out of his flat and she pulls the door closed.

'Ordinarily yes, but . . .'

'But? But what?'

'But that tie I asked you about earlier, the one you wore for the interview.'

'What about it?'

'It was found in the river. It's *Mark's* tie that I borrowed and gave to you. If Claudia goes to the police, it would mean that you, too, could become a suspect to murder if that's the conclusion from the coroner.'

His eyes grow wide with shock. 'What? So Mark *is* a suspect for someone *else's* murder?'

'He wasn't at the house that weekend.' She takes his hands. 'But possibly? And do you see how this looks for you?'

The realisation creeps into his face.

'Your DNA won't be on the police database because you've never done anything wrong . . .' She stumbles over her own words, because had it not been for Mark's alibi at the barn all those years ago, perhaps Bill's DNA would be on record. 'But it's also on the fence panel that Claudia went out of.'

'Oh, shit.'

'Who knows what anyone else might have seen. Someone might have seen your truck somewhere that night that could link it to this body.'

'Even if we don't know who the hell it is?'

'We need to wait. But you *cannot* tell Claudia about the tie. That information isn't in the public domain.'

'Nor is the information about a *body* and you just told us that?'

'News about the body will come out tomorrow, but the details of the case *won't* come out.'

'Why can't I tell her?'

'Because I don't trust her.'

'Jen, she's absolutely innocent in all this. It's a complete coincidence! You're being suspicious of exactly the wrong people. You *know* Claudia, Jen. It's Mark that you need to watch out for—'

'I haven't seen her for years, Bill! I *don't* know her and nor do you! We don't know either of them . . . well, Mark . . . God, it's complicated.'

'Why didn't you tell me about Sam? About Mark?'

She pauses. Why didn't she? Because her day at the beach with Mark – aside from it being adulterous – had been *wrong*. Even though at that point they were adults, being with him had been like fulfilling a teenage fantasy. It makes her sick to realise it given what Claudia has told her about Marie, about this Bella girl.

'Listen to me. Tell me how long Claudia was out of your truck when you went back to Oak House that night to get her stuff?'

'I don't know – no more than twenty minutes, twenty-five?' He pauses. 'You don't think *Claudia* managed to hurt someone in that time? Who? Why?'

'I don't know, and I don't know. I *do* know that I don't trust her. The water-meadows are the other direction to the lane. If you were parked up the road, you wouldn't have seen anything, would you?'

'No, but . . .'

They're silent together, staring into each other's eyes.

'Tell me what to do,' he says.

'Until I can figure this out, you need to lie low.'

THIRTY-SIX

Jen drives home, turns the key and the engine shuts off, zipping the Tranquil app into silence.

I will no longer fear what the day may hold.

Surely, she thinks, as she sits in the car, there is no more that the day can hold that could undo her further than this. She is wired and exhausted at the same time. It's eleven-thirty and she's come home so that she can go to sleep in her own flat and think about things in the silence without Kerry or Sam bounding in and wanting her to be a normal person, because she isn't one, not any more. Any hopes and dreams she had for a future with Mark – zip. Gone. Is this what grief feels like? A desperate ache of her entire body, a stabbed heart. But how can she grieve for something she never had?

She's about to get out of the car when her phone vibrates. She looks at the screen, presses Accept.

'What did the medic say?' Idris asks.

'I've got norovirus.'

'Seriously?' She can hear the dismay in his voice.

'I'm sorry. I'm out of action for a bit.'

'Why didn't you tell me? Didn't you go to the medic at base?'

Please stop asking me questions, she wills. Please stop making me lie to you.

'I wasn't thinking straight. I drove myself to the hospital and I've only just got home.'

'Is there someone with you?'

'My friend has Sam for me, so I'm going to sleep right now.'

'When can you dive, do you think?'

'I don't know,' she says. 'A couple of days?'

'I need you to come to base in the morning. Important briefing. Just stay away from people.' He hangs up without waiting for her answer.

She wanted to say that she wouldn't come in, that she wouldn't be there again, ever. All she wants to do is curl up in a ball and have her mother stroke her hair like she used to when she was much younger and remembered Jen's name.

She gets out of the car, practically falls into her flat, drunk with tiredness. She's going to be horizontal in bed as soon as she can crawl to her bedroom and she's never craved it more. She switches on the living-room light, shrugs out of her jacket and then snaps upright. Something is wrong. The air feels different. She turns to see someone standing in the corner of the room.

'Mark?'

He walks towards her. He looks completely different. His face is haggard and his hair appears long – the curls have fallen heavy with lack of washing, but it's more than that. He looks different now because she *feels* differently towards him. She knows something so terrible, and now so blindingly obvious about him. She thinks of all the times she's seen him over coffee these last few months, and felt blissfully happy, and smug – yes, smug – that he's been with her instead of Claudia, and it disgusts her.

'How long have you been here?'

'A couple of minutes? I don't know. I didn't put the lights on, I didn't want to draw attention. I called for you but you didn't answer, so I thought I'd wait. I thought maybe I'd stay.'

'Have you done this before? Come in when I've not been here?'

'I—' He pauses. 'Once. I came in once about a month ago when I'd seen Bill in the cafe with Claudia. I followed him back from his site and then lost him. I came here looking for you to tell me his address.'

She's angry. 'Why didn't you just call me?'

'I changed my mind.'

'But you still came in?'

He sighs. 'I know it's crazy. But you had given me the codes. Maybe getting Bill's address was also an excuse to see where you lived – where *Sam* lives and *how* he lives. I went into his bedroom. I loved his drawings, Jen. His duvet cover—'

She wants to throw him out. She also wants to ask him about the tie. Had she left it here? Had he taken it? Surely, it's the only explanation, but she can't ask him.

'You need to leave—'

'Jen, there's something big that's happened. That's why I'm here. You probably already know, but the police called me in before they put it out on the news because there's been . . . There's a *body*. I had to go over my statement again. Three times now, but they haven't told me anything more – I don't understand what's happening?'

'The night that Claudia disappeared, you were at your parents' house?'

'You *know* I was. I swear, Jen, I didn't hurt her. I didn't.'

'I know,' she says because she does. 'You can't be here. I'm an officer, I've been diving for Claudia. I'm connected with this case.'

'Why didn't you *warn* me that you'd found a body? I thought . . . I thought . . . What's been going on at the station?'

'You know I'm not involved directly with investigations.'

He claws at his hair, and she can see how desperate he is, how urgent. 'But what will I do?'

She waits until he calms, breathes shallowly. She thinks how boy-like he looks, like the young man he was when she first met him. But an innocent face can't mask innocence of the character that Claudia and Bill have made him out to be. His true colours have started to leak out – muddy and black.

'Tell me the truth,' she says. 'You and me, here. Me as a person, not as a police officer.'

'What's that supposed to mean? You *just* said you know I didn't hurt her.'

'I know you haven't hurt her, but you need to tell me if there's anything else.'

She sees him hesitate for a split second and then he shakes his head, eyes wide, like a fawn's.

'No! There's nothing to tell?'

He's not going to explain about the flat, about Marie, about the other girl Bella, about his argument with Claudia, so what does Jen do now? Does she really believe that Mark could be dangerous, and if so, how dangerous? She wants to sob, overwhelmed by the conflicting emotion in her heart.

He takes her hand. 'Can I stay here with you?'

She snatches it away. 'Of course you can't.'

His jaw trembles. She's never seen him so vulnerable and it's odd – their roles have reversed – and she doesn't like it because he's always been strong and capable, and now he's weak.

'Tell me what to do! I'm going out of my mind!'

'You need to get out of here.'

'I'm so worried.'

Before she realises what's happening, he's crying on her shoulder, heaving, wet tears bleeding into the wool of her jumper.

'And I'm sorry I've been so bad to you and Sam.'

'Please—' she says.

'But it's always been you, Jen. I've always loved you.'

Lies. Lies because he's scared. Even if he did actually love her, it's tainted, disgusting love.

She doesn't hold him and so he releases her and they stand, faces close.

'I'm sorry for what happened at the trials,' he says. 'It should have been you. I should have stood up for you when you were unwell for the championships and nominated you anyway.'

There – finally the admission that she's waited so many years for. That she was *better* than Claudia, and that Mark had failed her.

She's never liked to recall when she was forced to call him from the darkness of her bedroom on the morning of the British Diving Championships. It was a day that she had worked so hard for, and yet there she was, telling him that she had spent the night before it in the bathroom, vomiting and worse, and that there was no way that she could compete. She asked for him to make a plea for exceptional circumstances, that she could be seen by judges at another date or on video, but he said no. She asked him if he would put her forward for the European Championships instead, but he refused. He told her that if she was going to be sick with nerves, she would never cope with being an Olympian. He told her that she had let him down.

'It's not nerves,' she'd said, tears streaming down her face. 'I think I ate something funny.'

'Excuses like that are not going to win you any favours or any medals.'

He hung up on her.

Later that day, Claudia texted her and told she'd won the championships.

Jen had never felt so low and rejected.

'I let myself be second best. Over and over again, I did it. And I let *Sam* be second best.'

'I'm sorry. But I made it up to you, didn't I?'

'I appreciate the money you've given me for him. It's a lot and I never expected—'

'I don't mean that.'

She takes in his body language and pauses. She sees that he's scowling, his fists are balled, his jaw clenched. She knows at once that he's referring to the barn, that he's telling her that she's in his debt. Is this how he spoke to Claudia when she found out about the flat, when they argued about Marie Cadorna, and the girl – Bella – in Chicago?

'You helped Bill,' she says measuredly. 'And we're grateful.'

'Eighteen years,' he says. 'That's how long I've kept your secret.'

'I know.'

'And I didn't have to do that.'

She turns away from him, wants him gone. She busies herself with moving a cup from the table to the side, realises this isn't the cup she drank out of this morning and feels angry because it must have been Claudia who just abandoned it – used Jen's things and then left. Everyone just *using* her, time and again.

She turns back to Mark. 'I know you didn't have to. But you *did*.'

'You weren't being quite honest at the beginning, though, were you? She told me, you know. Claudia told me that you heard him inside. Burning to death.'

She pauses. She always thought Claudia might have told him – they got married after all – but the truth of it makes

Jen wants to weep. 'It was a long time ago. And we're all complicit now.'

'Where is he, Jen? Where's Bill?'

'I haven't seen him. I've been busy, unsurprisingly.'

'You don't think he could have done anything to Claudia?'

'There's no way.'

'How can you be sure? I told you that I saw them together.'

'You said you saw them together *once*.'

'I went to find him at the building site and the site manager told me he was away. Do you know where he is? Don't just protect him. If you know what he might be hiding—'

'He's not hiding anything.'

'Except the truth of what happened when you were all young and stupid.'

'Get out of my house.'

His expression turns. 'Hey, no, I'm sorry.'

'Get out.'

'I'm trying to deal with a lot of shit happening, you know? What am I supposed to be thinking? Doing? Saying?'

'You're not supposed to be here waiting for me, or threatening me. Please leave.'

'I think we need to find Bill.'

'I agree. I'll do my best.'

He walks to the door. 'If you hear anything before I do, will you tell me?'

She is silent.

'I love you.'

'You've never loved me,' she whispers, but he's already gone.

His departure out of the door causes a draught and she shivers with it. She's cold, and so she sits on the sofa, pulls the throw over herself. A humming starts up in her ears; like a wasp, an insect, something whirring.

She pulls her laptop towards her, and scrolls through the national diving team that Mark and two others coach. There are four girls between seventeen and twenty-three, fresh-faced, determined. She takes the time to look at each picture of each girl, wonders if Mark would have touched them inappropriately, *kissed* them, and the thoughts makes her heave. She stops at Marie. At the pool, Mark said that Marie had toiled through the foster system, and Jen wonders where it was Marie came from originally, and what her history is.

She now thinks that Bill had been watching a YouTube clip of Marie because he knew what Mark was doing because Claudia had obviously told him. Jen gets up without even bothering to shut the lid. She needs to go, now, to bed.

Before turning off the corridor light, she automatically glances into Sam's room, berates herself because he's at Kerry's, and turns to leave. But, she does so, she gets the shock of her life. Because Sam is in his bed. She gasps audibly. If Sam is here, it means that Kerry has brought him home. Which means that *Kerry* is also here. It was her teacup that was in the living room, and not Claudia's.

Jen's heart starts to thud as she walks slowly to her own bedroom. Inside, she can make out a bulk in her bed, and the dark tresses of Kerry's dark hair on the pillow. Jen holds her breath, creeps forward and looks down at Kerry's face. Her eyes are shut, her breathing is slow, her hand up by her chin, but is she asleep?

She bends to whisper. 'Kerry?'

There's no movement, no flicker of Kerry's eyelashes.

Jen turns to creep out, glances behind her as she nears the door. Just in time to see Kerry's fingers curl into a fist.

THIRTY-SEVEN

'We should sleep.'

Claudia nods. 'Yes,' she says, but she makes no move towards the bed.

They're in the bedroom and Bill is looking for something for her to wear, but she is blank, useless. The thought of a body down in the river that everyone thinks is *her* makes her feel like a living ghost. She can taste the horror of this coincidence too – thick and black like a swarm – in the back of her throat.

'Do you think that someone meant to kill *me,* Bill? Do you think that Mark was there that night? That he wanted to hurt me but instead got someone random? Maybe he asked someone else to help him get rid of me?'

'I think you're reading too much into this,' Bill says. 'We need to wait for the identification.'

'What if the body is one of the girls on the swim team?'

'But Jen said that no one has been reported missing except you.'

'But what if it's another young girl, Bill? What if it's not only members of the swimming team that Mark's picking up? Do you think we did the wrong thing? Do you think we should have alerted the police to what Mark's doing with the girls?'

He puts a hand to his temple. 'We don't know Mark has anything to do with this,' he says. 'We've watched the news the whole time, right? He has an alibi for that entire weekend.'

'I know but . . . it just doesn't make sense.'

'Nothing makes sense,' he says. 'We just need to sleep and hope that things become clearer tomorrow.' He throws her a clean T-shirt and clean boxer shorts from his chest of drawers. 'You take my bed, I'll go on the sofa.'

'Don't be stupid,' she says. 'Get in.'

He does so and they sit against the headboard, silent.

'Jen is upset with me for telling her about Mark. About the girls.'

'She's been upset with you since that night she got ill and couldn't compete for the championships,' he says. 'But she needs to know about Mark. If they have a son together, she needs to know. What if he's violent with her or Sam? God, I can't even imagine it.'

'I know. My blood is on the fence panels,' she says. 'And your DNA.'

'Yeah.'

'I know that I promised to help you with the money. I'm sorry. Now . . . now I don't know what to do. What to *think*.'

He turns to her. 'Regardless of the money, I would have helped you. That person in the river – whoever it is – it's not you. That's all that matters to me.'

She leans into his shoulder.

'Jen told me something weird, Claud. Right before she left and you were in the bathroom. She told me not to say anything to you, but she asked me about a tie.'

Claudia looks at him. 'A tie?'

'She gave me one for an interview I had. She was doing me a favour because I'd bought a suit, but I hadn't got a tie.' He pauses. 'And it . . . it was found.'

She frowns, feels like she's missed a point he's trying to make. 'What do you mean it was found? Found where?'

'In the river.'

She sits up straighter. 'Are you serious?'

'Yeah. She told me that it's Mark's tie.'

Shock pinches her throat and her voice is tight. '*Mark's*?'

'It could be coincidence – you don't live far from the river, obviously – but Jen's worried. *I'm* fucking worried. How did it get there? Why is it there? It can't be a coincidence, can it?'

'You told me that we couldn't read too much into this—'

'Well, I was trying to calm you down.'

'Did you . . . did you see anything?' she asks. 'While you waited for me up the road in the truck? Did you see a person?'

'No, of course not. Jen asked me the same question. Do you think that while I was sat warming the car for you up the road, helping you get out of a marriage you didn't want to be in, that I saw a random person, and then what?

Followed them and thought I'd push them into the water for fun? And then, threw a random tie in after?'

'I was asking if you saw anyone,' she says firmly. 'Maybe subconsciously?'

'Well I didn't! Did *you* see anyone?'

'I was trying to get into my own house! What kind of a question is that?'

'Neither of us saw anything.'

They both lie down and he switches off the light.

'I wanted to make things right from all those years ago when we ran away from our problems,' he says into the darkness. 'But we've run into something bigger.'

She squeezes his hand, says nothing.

Bill falls asleep quickly, but Claudia is restless, pulled to thinking about Mark. She wonders where he is, what he's feeling. Does he know now that there's a body? Is he worried, anguished, at the thought of Claudia being dead? Is he happy? She wants him to be devastated, to repent for all the horrible things he's done and said to her.

She thinks back to their argument on Saturday afternoon. She'd been sitting out in the garden on a deckchair, reading, ironically, an article about the dive team, and more specifically, the nation's hopes for Marie Cadorna. Claudia had been studying the shape of Marie's calves, the twist of her smile. Marie had become not just Mark's new obsession but hers too. She found that she relished the slow burn of passionate envy, of wicked thoughts. She fantasied about Mark touching that smooth, youthful skin. She thought about all the ways they might kiss, have sex. All those thoughts culminated in a rush of ecstatic fury.

God, she had stayed through his increasingly harsh put-downs of her in private over the years, had stayed through the occasional slap to her face when he'd got drunk, and the time where he had thrown a glass tumbler at her head which had knocked her out when she'd asked him about the rumours surrounding Bella. She'd stayed because she needed him, loved him, but realised she'd completely lost his heart and her hold over him physically. When she found out about Marie – when she *saw* them together in her very own bed, the humiliation was worth the effort to try to leave him. But she would need leverage, money, courage. Leverage came in the form of Bella Mitchell and her confession, money came from pawning her jewellery every week to save cash and hope Mark didn't notice. Courage came in the form of Bill Harper securing her a fake passport and offering her an escape.

She hadn't heard Mark come out of the house, shoeless across the grass, until he was right behind her.

'What's this?'

She'd whirled around in the chair to see him above her, a strange look on his face. The emotion wasn't anger or bafflement. It was something straight, quiet, measured, and she couldn't read it.

'What's what?'

'I found something interesting on your computer.'

He held up her laptop, which had been behind his back and out of her view.

She knew, instantly, that it was her email about Bella Mitchell. Had she left it up? Had he broken into it? She went to stand up from the deckchair and take it from him, but before she had a chance, he swung back his arm and smashed the laptop right across her skull.

Her hearing changed, one ear suddenly humming like she was under the water, and her eyes skittered. The green of the grass took on an odd fluorescence, and the legs of the deckchair appeared to be swimming. She realised that she was on the ground with her face sideways.

'What game are you playing, Claudia?'

She tried to lift her head, but it seemed to roll on her neck like something huge and heavy and unmovable. His feet came into her view. He was wearing the trainers she'd bought him for his birthday only a month ago – white and clean. Unblemished.

'When were you planning on sending this to the papers? This week? The day before the Olympics? When exactly was it that you were thinking of ruining my life?'

Something landed beside her with a thud and one of his feet moved from her view. She heard a crash beside her as he stamped on her laptop.

'I'm guessing it's also on your phone, so let's take a look at that too, shall we?'

She couldn't say anything; her mouth felt full of words, but they were scrambled.

'Where is it?'

She made a moaning noise. She couldn't remember where her phone was.

'Where's your phone?'

She raised herself to her knees, swayed, grabbed uselessly at the material of the deckchair, and then the wooden arm to support herself.

'You're disgusting,' she said. One of her back teeth felt wobbly. Her mouth was puffing up.

He grabbed at her then, his fist in her hair, tangling his fingers in it, wrenching it as hard as he could so that her neck was tipped backwards and the sun hurt her eyes.

'Where's your goddamn phone?'

'I don't know.'

He let go and she put her arms out to the lawn again, panting. There were little dark spots on the grass that she realised were made from her blood.

He turned around to stalk back inside and in that split second, she reached under the deckchair to where she'd put her phone when she'd come out – she always put it there when the sun was out. She got up, grabbed the smashed laptop too, and fled across the garden, disappearing out of the fence panel that was loose, and racing through the woodland towards the water-meadows and the river. She rang the one person she knew would drop everything to help her.

'I'm . . . I'm at Cowell Farm.'

'Claud?'

'Come, Bill. Please come.'

THIRTY-EIGHT

Jen needs to go into work today, needs to face the music, and – most importantly – the details of the body discovered. She glances at the clock on the wall – Sam's beloved *Transformers* clock – and decides that four forty-eight is almost five, which is almost six, so she might as well get up and into the kitchen now, wake herself properly with caffeine.

She goes to fill the kettle, relishes the quiet of the house, and wonders how she can slip out without a conversation with Kerry.

'Why did you not tell me?'

Kerry stands in the door frame and Jen debates playing dumb, but can't insult her best friend. Besides, Kerry knows her well enough to call out her bullshit.

'Which bit?'

'I know that Mark is Sam's dad, Jen, but I've known that since the second you got pregnant. I've been waiting for you to tell me for six years.'

'How did you know?'

'Because you've always loved Mark. Because there's never been anyone close to hold a candle to the way you used to talk about him. Intense training with someone who sees you basically naked the whole time must really warp your senses. And having Sam has kept you connected to him for all these years. I get it – it's easy not to move on when you have a real-life solid hope in front of you, that you put to bed every night. But obviously that's not the reason why I'm upset.'

'You heard everything.'

'They've found Claudia, right? In the river?'

Jen sinks her head into her hands, wants to tell Kerry that it's not Claudia, but how would that help anything? Kerry doesn't deserve to be dragged down any further than she already is.

'I *heard* it, Jen! There's a *body*. And then Mark threatened you.'

'No—'

'*Yes*. I know what I heard. Do you think I'm stupid? He's got something on you that happened eighteen years ago? What's it about? Diving?'

'We made a pact,' Jen says and it sounds so childish, so ridiculous. 'I can't talk about it.'

'Do you think Mark has killed Claudia?'

'No.'

'How are you so sure?'

'Because I am,' Jen says because she can't say that she's seen Claudia, only hours ago.

'And Bill?'

'Bill hasn't done anything bad, I swear to you,' she says. 'The thing that happened all those years ago, I thought was forgotten about, but it's all become . . . complex. Risen to the surface.'

'Is it to do with Claudia?'

'Sort of. Her family.'

Kerry scowls. 'Everything has always been complicated with that family. They're liars, all of them.'

Jen looks at her, surprised. 'Liars? You didn't even know them?'

'What happened then? Why can't you tell me? Do you not trust me?'

'No! I mean, of course I trust you, but I can't get you into any of this, do you understand?'

'I would have lied for him! I would have!' Kerry starts to laugh, but it's punctured with grief. 'I keep everyone else's secrets for them – why not Bill's too?'

'I told you, Bill has got nothing to do with—'

'Mum!'

Sam barrels forward at her into the room, knocks Jen off balance.

'Sam, it's so early, what are you doing awake?'

'I heard you!'

Jen catches Kerry's eye and at once they rearrange themselves into how they should be – Jen pouring hot water into cups, adding milk, all smiles. Kerry switches on the radio.

'Can I have toast and peanut butter?' Sam grabs her arm, swings it, does the same with Kerry. 'Why is it still dark outside?'

'Because it's five in the morning.'

'I'm not tired.' He bounds away into the living room. 'Can I watch *Ryan's World* on your laptop?'

'I . . . Sure.'

Kerry looks at Jen. 'I'm assuming you're going into work.'

'Yes. Idris needs me in.'

'I'll take Sam to school then, shall I?'

'Wait—'

'I thought we were best friends?'

'We *are.*'

'So act like it, Jen. Tell me what's going on.'

'I can't. I'm sorry.'

Kerry walks out of the kitchen, and Jen hears the bathroom door close and the lock turn.

'Mum?'

She turns and sees Sam through the open doorway, her laptop still open from last night. He's woken it and on the screen is a picture of Marie Cadorna.

'Why have you got a picture of the nanny?'

She frowns. 'What?'

'That's the nanny who comes to the park.'

Jen startles. It was *Marie* who spoke to Sam at the playground that day. Why was Marie talking to him about Jen being in the police?

'Mum?'

Jen smiles at him to mask her shock.

'Yeah. She's also a swimmer,' she says. 'What else did she ask you, Sam? This girl?'

'Nothing else.'

'OK—'

'Oh, no, there was something else. She said she knew my dad.'

Her heart leaps, screams against her chest. 'What?'

He shrugs. 'I didn't want to tell you. I know you don't like talking about it.'

'I . . .'

'I know I have one. But it's OK, Mum. I don't *need* one. I have you and Bill and Auntie Kerry. But it was weird she said that. How can she know him but we don't?

Jen wants to weep. 'Come and have breakfast.'

'But I didn't watch Ryan—'

'Come on.'

She snaps the laptop lid down.

Marie knows that Mark is Sam's dad. This is huge and frightening because Marie has the potential to blow everything – and Jen – open for investigation. She won't go straight to the base this morning. She goes instead to the dive pool.

No one yet knows about the body, but Mark must have cancelled the practice because it's six-thirty and no one is here, except the receptionist who lets her in and the two cleaners she saw in the changing room as she passed through to the pool. Now Jen will have to go and find out where Marie lives, which will take a lot of time and energy, neither of which she has in any abundance.

She stares at the dive tower, aches to climb it right up to the ten-metre platform, and jump into the water below, to lose herself in the depth of it, but all she can do is squat at the water's edge and dip her fingers in. How different life could have been, she thinks, if it had been her and not Claudia that had gone forward to the Olympics. How different Fiona's life could have been if Jen had got the sponsorship money and provided proper care. A burning anger courses through her body.

Jen should have fought off the sickness better the night before the championships. She should have become one of the youngest divers to win gold at the Olympics. She should have been successful, but then, how do you measure success? Is it by being the best at something? Is it by feeling like you have done nothing *but* your best? She's striven to be the best at diving within the force, but she's cheating them all. She thinks of Idris, of Joe and all the others, men that have become her extended family over the years, and imagines their crushing disappointment and betrayal if they knew what she's been doing. The whole reason she joined the police was to help relieve herself of the guilt she felt from running away that day at the barn. She didn't take responsibility then, so she's made sure that she's doing it now, navigating the murkiest places to retrieve beloved things, beloved family.

Without knowing why – a sixth sense – Jen turns her head to the viewing gallery. There's a girl sitting very still in the shadows, a hoodie worn up over her head, facing Jen.

'Hello?'

The girl stands quickly, and moves across the seats and up towards the door to the upper floor. Jen sees a whip of dark hair from the beneath the hood.

'Marie?'

But the girl is now out of the door and out of her view and so Jen starts to run, rounds the edge of the pool.

'Hey! Wait!'

The girl jumps up to the first level of seats and Jen runs through to the changing rooms to try to head the girl off before she disappears out of the building. But she corners the pool too fast, slips and falls on wet flooring, crashing down hard on the stone tiles, her hip bone taking the impact.

'Fuck!'

Her cry echoes around the dive pool. She hauls herself up to sitting, takes her phone to text Bill.

Does C know Marie's address? If so, give it to me NOW.

THIRTY-NINE

A few hours later, and Jen is sitting in the base briefing room with the others, waiting for Idris. There's a sweet smell of pastries in the air because Amir has brought some in, but she can't stomach them, or anything else.

Joe is sitting next to her, leans close to her and sniffs.

She jerks back. 'What the fuck are you doing?'

'Are you diseased?'

Jen rolls her eyes.

'You can't smell illness on a person,' Amir says from one side of Joe. 'Stop sniffing her.'

Liam leans in from the other side of Jen. 'Actually, there was a study in 2016 that shows dogs can pick up early-onset Parkinson's.'

'Joe isn't a dog,' Amir says.

'Out for debate,' Oli puts in.

'I really can't catch anything for Ben's wedding on Saturday,' Joe says. 'I'm the best man.'

'Why did you sit next to me then, knob?' Jen mutters and crosses her arms. She's hemmed in by them all and usually their proximity and banter wouldn't bother her, but today she feels claustrophobic. Today she feels like anyone could smell the fear on her.

'I've written a killer speech,' Joe continues. 'Do you want to hear it?'

'No,' they all say.

'I start by saying, "Ben's asked that I don't share any shit stories about him, or stag-do antics or whatever in my best man's speech . . . so that's it from me! Thanks for listening." Yeah? Do you like it?'

'Have you copied and pasted the same one as I did, mate?' Oli asks, turning around from in front of them.

'Best Man Speech dot com?'

'Yeah, that's it.'

Jen wants them to stop talking – can't they sense that she's different? She is feeling otherworldly, like she's living above her body and not in it. Today the body will have a name. She looks up at the strip lights. When was the last time she thought about anything other than Claudia? Claudia who is alive when someone else is dead. She shifts in her chair, wincing as the pain from her hip shoots down her leg.

Idris walks in, swipes up a pastry as he goes to the front of the room.

'We have identification.'

The others all lean forward, hungry for the confirmation, but Jen remains leaning back because she needs the physical support. The air in the room feels thick.

'It's *not* Claudia Franklin. It's Victoria Franklin, Claudia's mother.'

Victoria, Victoria. The name thuds in Jen's head like a dull heartbeat. Jen wrings the sleeve of her hoodie, a twisted sorrow sweeping over her. Her life suddenly feels magnified, exposed, because it isn't a stranger, it's someone connected to them all.

Joe whistles. 'Left-field.'

'Cause of death is likely to be drowning. But CID aren't ruling out suspicion of foul play, given how the chips have fallen so far. She's been in the water a long time, but there are marks around her wrists. There's a high probability that she died the same night as we think Claudia herself is likely to have disappeared. Given that Claudia is still missing, we can't rule out that something has happened to her too, or there is the possibility that she has killed her mother.'

Jen wants to vomit. *Is* that what happened?

'This just got really interesting,' Oli says.

'Victoria flew from Ontario to Heathrow that Saturday and the flight got in at eight in the evening. CID have worked all night on it, tracked her on CCTV. She goes to the taxi rank, gets into a taxi at ten-twenty.'

'What then?'

'They've found the driver, who said he dropped Victoria at Oak House at around eleven-twenty at night.'

Eleven-twenty. Claudia and Bill said they'd gone back at ten-thirty or thereabouts, and only for twenty-five minutes max, so did they just miss her or were they lying to Jen about the timings? Did they know she was flying over to the UK?

'Did the driver see anyone let Victoria into Oak House?'

'No. Apparently he left her at the gate which is coded. Mark Mason already told the unit from the get-go that he had recently changed the gate locks. He did this every so often for security purposes.'

Jen nods. Claudia had told her that Mark had changed the code on the gate so she couldn't get back in that night to pick up any belongings, so this part of the story is in keeping. Perhaps they had been back at the house at exactly the same time that Victoria was due to arrive, perhaps they had met her outside the gate and Claudia had led her towards the water-meadows. But what would have been her motivation for killing her own mother? Neither one of them have mentioned Victoria, except for the sale of Oak House. Bill had told her that Victoria had been unhappy about it. What if the two of them did something together to Victoria to free up the money?

'Is Victoria's DNA on the red tie?' Jen asks.

'Her DNA *is* on it – we'd put that down to being Claudia's because they're related. Mark Mason's DNA is on it, as we already know, and also two others, as yet unidentified. One of which matches traces on the fence panel.'

Fuck, Jen thinks. That's got to be *Bill's*.

'The driver didn't pass any other vehicles on the lane?'

'He can't remember seeing any other vehicles and there's no CCTV on those small roads to check. He did tell CID that Victoria seemed very drunk, and the airline have confirmed that she bought four mini bottles of white wine. There's a chance she could have fallen into the river. Either way, we're in the water again. We're also looking for a suitcase, a small handbag, and a coat, all of which were on the airport CCTV but *not* with the body. CID are now looking in Oak House for those items on the off chance she did get in somehow.'

'With Mark Mason being away? How would she have got in?'

'Don't forget Claudia in all this. She could have been in the house. That's where her phone signal was last located. Anyway, whatever the outcome, if we find the items, they might give CID a better idea of what might have happened.'

'How many other jobs are we ignoring for this?' Joe asks.

'We've got seven lined up for when this is done. We're going to be busy.'

'There goes my third marriage,' Gareth mutters.

'Here's a picture of everything we're looking for.'

Idris shows them his phone and they bend their heads to see a grey, pixelated security-camera footage of Victoria in motion, walking out of an airport terminal, a little suitcase by her side, and dressed in a smart black-and-white houndstooth jacket – the one that's hanging up in Jen's wardrobe at home.

She recoils in horror, stifles a gasp and disguises it with a cough.

'Fuck's sake, sick note.' Joe moves away from her with deliberate drama and covers his mouth with the crook of his arm. 'Are you going to throw up on me?'

She stares again at the picture until Idris takes his phone away, unobservant to her fright. She'd thought this jacket was Kerry's that she'd left at some point at Jen's flat while she was diving. How can it be Victoria's? Did Bill leave it there? Claudia? Did Mark? She can't hand it in, so what does she do? Does she burn it? Bury it?'

'Jen?'

'Yeah?'

'You ready to go?'

'Yeah.' She gets up unsteadily, forgets to be careful with her injury. Her hip roars with pain. 'Ouch, fuck.'

'What's happened to you now?' Joe asks as he passes her.

'I . . . I fell.'

'Like an old person? It's not your month, mate, is it?'

They all filter out, laughing, and she takes a few seconds to regain her composure – both physically and mentally. With shaking hands, she gets out her phone, sees that Bill still hasn't replied about Marie's address.

'Jen, you OK?'

Idris is in front of her. A blurry version of him.

'You look white, mate? You still feel like shit?'

'I . . . yeah.'

'You know what's really fucking strange?' Idris says. 'It's not the first time something bad has happened to that family around the water-meadows.'

Jen knows what he's going to say before the words leave his lips.

'Claudia's stepfather, Henry Barton, died in a fire eighteen years ago, not far from where Victoria Franklin turned up. His body was found in the ruins of a barn.'

She closes her eyes. The nightmare of their past has come knocking.

FORTY

It's always in the still of the morning that Claudia thinks of Henry. The way he screamed through the noise of those flames.

Regardless of who was trapped in the barn, they did the wrong thing by running away. Sometimes the enormity of what they did – shunning all responsibility, denying Henry of their help, even though their help would have been useless at the point of realisation – crushes the breath out of her, makes her curl up in a ball in her bed.

The police questioned Victoria as to why Henry was out there, but it was common that he walked around the water-meadows for hours at a time, smoking his cigars and pondering his work. After investigation, the police ruled it as a tragic accident – coming to the conclusion that Henry went to the barn for the shade but had tripped and fallen, and his cigar had lit up the barn while he was unconscious. There was no cigar, of course. There was Bill, as high as a kite, and a joint that he'd left there when Henry had come in and obviously hadn't noticed it smouldering. Possibly they had missed each other by minutes.

It was six months after Henry died when Claudia participated in the British Diving Championships and scored perfectly, which won her the place at the Olympics without even needing to do the Europeans, but she won that too, effortlessly. To the outside world, her story was one of heartbreak, but also fierce determination, and she was written up as a phoenix rising out of the ashes of a personal tragedy, championed by the sport and by her attractive coach. Diving was her salvation. But inside she was a frightened child.

Victoria Franklin had collapsed under the sorrow of losing two husbands. A few short weeks after the championships, she flew to Canada, telling Claudia that she'd be back after two weeks, but then emailing to tell her she was going to stay. She'd met a man out there apparently, on a grief therapy course. At eighteen, legally now an adult, Claudia was alone and suddenly without an authority figure except for Mark Mason. She had coped in Oak House, driven herself to school, to diving practice, to the shops for food. Abandoned. Paranoid too that her mother had realised that, somehow, Claudia had been involved with Henry's death.

When the day of the Olympics came, at twenty years old and newly engaged to Mark, Claudia had stood on that platform and felt the eyes of the crowd on her, had smelt the water in the air, heard the agitator below, and realised that a gold medal – or indeed, any medal – didn't matter. Nothing did. For three years since the fire, she had buried her head in the sand. She'd survived on autopilot, single-minded in her propulsion to make it there, but somehow, suddenly, all she could see was Henry's face.

She very nearly didn't even jump, but she just wanted it over. She wanted to close her eyes and fall and so that's exactly what she did. With each attempt, she didn't tuck properly, didn't roll with any grace. She simply fell.

The media were frenzied with the arc of her mental and emotional breakdown, wrote features about her stepfather's tragic death, her mother's obvious desertion. Claudia retreated back to Oak House and closed the doors, wanted to lie down and sleep forever. Only this time, Mark came with her. Their wedding had been planned for the month after the Olympics and even though he was angry with her for failing him, they went through with it. It would have been better, she now knows, to cut ties, but they were bound by then by their lies.

She touches the side of her head with her fingertips.

She sits up in bed with Bill and the bacon sandwiches and cups of tea he's made them both. It's nearly eleven now and the sun has moved to throw rectangles of light across the bedspread, casts shadows of the crumbs they've spilt. They have the TV on, have been glued to it, waiting to see when the news will break about the body.

Bill gets up. She notices that he's spread a little in the middle now, but that his shoulders are still strong, his arm muscles are built up. His hair is still thick and dark, his smell is still the same.

'I have to get ready,' he says. 'I need to go back to work and try to sort things with Andy.'

'It'll be OK, Bill. I'll get you the money.'

'He's starting to suspect. I haven't got long.'

'I'll get it to you.'

He smiles tiredly. 'Yeah. You won't do anything while I'm away, will you? Like, don't go out anywhere. Not until we know what's going on.'

'I won't.'

He picks up a bit of paper and then his phone. 'Here, I'll give you Jen's number—' He trails off, stares at the screen.

Claudia's heart starts to race. 'What? Is it something about the body?'

'I've got, like, nineteen missed calls from Jen and texts . . . She's asking about Marie Cadorna's address. You know it, right? You told me before you followed her once?'

Claudia has followed her, numerous times. 'She lives on Bridge Street, down from the common, in Upper Sombourne. Why does she want to know?'

'Do you have a number?'

'It's a flat. Number three. Ask her what she's doing?'

She watches him text Jen, wonders what can of worms she's opened.

'You still want the TV on?' he asks.

'Yes. Why haven't they said anything yet?'

'Jen said they'd wait for identification. Maybe the body is too . . . damaged?'

They've both seen enough crime dramas to know that prolonged time in the water means a body will be near unrecognisable; bloated and mottled, perhaps partly eaten by fish.

Bill goes to the en suite bathroom and Claudia flicks her eyes back to the TV. The news switches from one piece to another, a collage of gloom and despair, because bad news sells, and she eats the crusts of her sandwich that she'd previously left but now is hungry for. She listens to Bill showering, to the water on the glass pane, to the click of shower gel bottles and shampoo caps, and wonders what he's thinking in there, and if he regrets all he's done to help her. Bill has never let her down, ever. Forever her loyal dog whose nature it is to protect without question. But how could she know what would snowball?

She should have loved him. It would have been so much easier, so much better. But she had always chased the ones she shouldn't have – she loved the thrill of it, the attention. The therapist in Boston suggested that attention was the driving emotion for all her actions, both past and present, and that this need probably stemmed from childhood and her relationships with her mother and stepfather. She had rolled her eyes, but in the years since, she has come to the realisation that it's true. Attention, love. It's all she wants. Isn't it what everyone wants?

She hasn't told Bill everything. She never can.

The shower turns off, she hears the door slide, and then the news changes again, the flash of BBC red, *Breaking News,* and then a reporter who stands by a stretch of river that Claudia knows. Claudia sits up straight.

'The body found in the river yesterday, previously thought to have been Claudia Franklin, has now been confirmed as her mother, Victoria Franklin.'

The sandwich crusts become dry and somehow bigger in Claudia's mouth so that she can't swallow them. She's heaving, choking, and soggy pieces come out on the duvet, and then she is leaping over the bed to the TV, where she stands so close that the picture isn't whole, isn't clear.

Her mother, the body which is now unrecognisable; bloated and mottled, eaten by fish. Claudia vomits on the carpet.

FORTY-ONE

So far, the dives for Victoria's missing items have been fruitless. The team started as close to Oak House as they could get, on the assumption that when Victoria had been here and found the gate locked, she had drunkenly stumbled towards the river. Their job is not to question whether she slipped and drowned, or whether she may have been pushed, but it's all they're talking about as they trudge back towards the lorry which is stationed on the lane near Oak House.

'If it had been an accident, she wouldn't be missing her jacket or bag or suitcase. She wouldn't have fallen in with them, surely? And there wouldn't be that tie,' Joe says.

Jen is the last to get to the lorry, glances back at Oak House, and wonders who could be in there watching them and the search. Mark? Mark's parents? There were a few journalists hovering around before the police came in to cordon off the area, but she wouldn't be surprised if a couple have stayed to lurk in the tall reeds to snap for stories.

Idris has kept her on the surface because of her 'illness' but she's not been concentrating. All Jen can think about is the jacket in her flat, how it came to be there, and what she's going to do with it.

'How long are we going to be looking for?' Oli asks.

Idris takes the hosepipe from the back of the lorry. They're always grateful when it's a summer day – it's warm and they can strip off without feeling like their skin is contorting against their bones.

'CID are ramping up investigations with the Canadians. Access to Victoria's home, her laptops and phones, etc.'

'I think Claudia Franklin's done away with her,' Joe says, dripping wet.

'Or Mark Mason's done away with the both of them,' Liam says.

'Did you see that he was on the news this morning?'

Jen's ears prick. 'Saying what?'

'Saying that he's still planning on going to Paris for the Olympics with the dive team. They leave in two days.'

'Surely CID won't let him go at this point?' Gareth says. 'If he *is* involved, he needs to stay in the country. His mother-in-law is dead and his wife is still missing.'

'He'd be pissed if he didn't go. That girl Marie is the best chance he's ever had at gold.'

'I'm going in,' Oli says, stepping up to the lorry

'Tea all round,' Idris says.

Jen goes to get changed back in the lorry with them all, but Idris stops her.

'How are you feeling?'

'OK—'

He fires the hose straight in her face.

'Oh, fuck you.'

She takes a towel, grimy with use, and shakes the worst of the water off.

'You doing OK?' Idris asks.

'Sort of.'

'Need a break for a bit?'

She could hug him. 'I could do with some downtime at home.'

He nods. 'OK. Granted. A couple of hours.'

Her phone is flashing.

Here's Marie's address.

Marie lives not far from the dive pool. It isn't surprising: she came from Wales, and moved here for training, so it makes sense she would live close by. Jen knocks on the door and waits.

Marie is dressed in denim shorts and a yellow T-shirt when she answers, her long brown hair over one shoulder, damp from the shower, or a swim. It blooms across one breast, shows the outline of a pretty bra underneath. As soon as she notes Jen, she looks alarmed and goes to shut the door. Jen rams her foot against it.

'How did you get this address?' Marie asks.

'I'm a police officer.'

'The police can find whoever they want?'

'Well, yeah.' Jen shrugs. 'But you're not in trouble, OK? I just want to ask you a few questions. Can I come in? I don't think we should be talking on the doorstep.'

Jen can see discomfort on Marie's face. 'I'm packing to go to Paris.'

'It will only take a couple of minutes.'

Jen edges herself inside and Marie obviously decides to let her. She closes the door behind them and Jen follows her through to a small living space. There's a TV on a cheap-looking black stand, some shelves above it with pot plants, and a couple of landscape pictures in frames. Jen can't see any photos of family, but if Marie was passed from family to family during her years of being fostered, perhaps she didn't form any particular bonds. Jen feels a sudden empathy towards her. A drying rack stands by the window in the sun, adorned with haphazardly hung skimpy pants and tiny crop tops. A faded red shammy.

Jen sits on a sofa which is greasy at the arms. Marie hovers, uncertainly, by the door as if she's going to bolt out of it.

'Do you live here alone?'

'There's a housemate, but I don't see her much. She's older.'

'She here now?'

'No.'

Jen nods. 'Then let's cut to the chase, shall we? You were at the pool when I came. And you came to the playground and spoke to my son. Can you tell me why you wanted to talk to him and not directly to me? He told me it wasn't the first time and that concerns me. Especially given that you lied and said you were a nanny.'

Marie shrugs and Jen sighs.

'There's a lot going on around Mark Mason right now,' Jen says. 'Perhaps you could tell me about your relationship with him.'

'He's my coach,' she says finally.

'I think he might be a bit more to you than that.'

Marie's eyes narrow, reveal a crack in her otherwise rigid demeanour. 'How do you know?'

'Because I've been there,' Jen says simply. 'As I think *you* know.'

Marie nods slowly, and then sits down on a wooden chair opposite Jen. 'I saw the news. About Victoria Franklin.'

'Yes.'

'What do they think happened?'

'Honestly, I don't know. I'm never involved with the "why" and the "how". I'm involved only in searches. My job is full-time diver. I mostly get my information like the rest of the public.'

'In the news?'

'Yes.'

'Oh.' Marie sighs. 'I knew you were someone important when I saw the picture in his flat.'

Jen pauses, doesn't want to let anything slip. 'Mark's flat in Fording Hill?'

'Yeah.'

Jen frowns. 'He has a photograph of me there?'

'No,' Marie says. 'There was a picture of a boy. I asked Mark about him, he said his name was Sam.'

'What? Tell me about the picture?'

'It was a boy playing with Lego.'

Jen exhales. She *knew* there was a picture missing when Claudia was in her flat and she had been manically removing the photos of Sam. Mark had taken it, obviously the time he'd let himself into her flat.

'Mark told me he was a nephew.'

'Huh.'

'But then I realised he *didn't* have a nephew. He doesn't have siblings and nor does Claudia. And then I remembered that when I was at Oak House, I saw a photo on the wall of Claudia when she was younger.'

Jen swallows, remembers Claudia's story of seeing Mark with Marie at Oak House. 'How often did you go there? Did Mark and Claudia used to invite you over there?'

Marie looks at the floor. 'I went over a few times.'

Jen's insides roil. 'Carry on.'

'In their hallway is an old picture of Claudia, of when she was younger, when Mark had been her coach, a team photo. I thought that the boy from the flat matched one of the girls in the photo so I did some digging around who was in Claudia's old team, and I put two and two together. One of the girls in that photo was you – Jen Harper – which means Sam is his son.'

Jesus, Jen thinks. This girl is a good detective.

'That's why you came to the playground and spoke to Sam? How did you know we'd be there?'

'I followed you from the school one day. I wanted to know everything about Mark. He lied to me and I didn't like that.'

'Why did you run away from me at the pool?'

'Because Sam told me you were in the police. Everything was kicking off with Claudia, and I didn't want you questioning me about Mark.'

Jen pauses, studies Marie. 'You know it's wrong, don't you? It's actually more than wrong. It's illegal under The Sexual Offences Act. Mark holds a position of trust – he trains you, is in sole charge of you, and you're under eighteen.'

'But *Claudia* was in that position too, wasn't she?'

'I'm telling *you* so you don't make the same mistake. Mark will be charged for this. He'll likely serve time.'

'I'm not telling the police. I want to get to Paris and I don't need protecting.'

'I think you do.'

Marie is silent for a moment. 'Do you think Mark has anything to do with Victoria's death?'

'I can't comment.'

Marie's expression sets to one of determination. 'Let me *win* because I can. I'm eighteen in three months. Then it wouldn't even have to be an issue, would it? You could just pretend we've never had this conversation.'

Is Marie unwittingly throwing Jen a lifeline? How tempting would it be to feign ignorance and leave it all to time to sort out? If Jen doesn't declare her knowledge of this relationship, she wouldn't need to let her brother be pulled back into the past and face an uncertain future.

'To dive is all I've ever wanted and Mark has given me the chance. I feel . . . alive in the water. I feel *myself*. Only ever truly myself in the water.'

'I get it,' Jen says, because she does.

'If I don't tell anyone about your relationship with Mark, you don't let on about mine. Deal?'

Jen doesn't reply. How can she? Instead, she leaves the question unanswered and leaves, wonders how the hell she can untangle this mess.

She waits until Sam is in bed before she opens her closet and takes the houndstooth jacket from the hanger. She throws it on the bed and then paces around her bedroom, staring at it for answers it can't give her until she gives up and sits in front of *Midsomer Murders*. She starts to scribble notes, stopping only to drink hot tea and eat chips, both of which are too hot. She's ravenous, can't remember when she properly ate like this. The smell of the greasy chips wafts around her head like a glorious mist, settles over her hair and her clothes and her sofa throw, but she doesn't care; she doesn't care about anything right now except protecting the life that she's so carefully built for herself and for Sam.

Victoria's death hasn't even – to Jen's knowledge – been definitely ruled as suspicious but could it really have been an accident with marks on her wrist, with the tie in the river?

She longs to talk to Kerry and tell her everything. The weight of all this is oppressive and she's buckling beneath it and Kerry is the one person that can be relied on to make sense of things. She thinks back on what Kerry said this morning – that she was always keeping everyone else's secrets, that the Franklin family were all liars. It was a strange thing to say, but where Jen had always tolerated and accepted the differences between Claudia's upbringing and hers, Kerry seemed offended by them. She had always been jealous of Claudia – of her wealth, of the way she constantly seemed to land on her feet, of the way she treated Bill over the years.

Jen's phone rings and she jerks, spills the tea that she's holding in her other hand.

'Ow!'

She sucks at her skin, digs around for her phone at the same time, which has fallen between the sofa cushions. She presses Answer.

'I don't know where she is! Is she with you?'

'Bill? What do you mean?'

'Claudia! She's gone.'

Her stomach flips. 'Gone? How long gone?'

'I don't know? I've only come back from the site – Andy knows . . . I think he knows everything . . . God, she could have been gone for hours? She didn't leave a message, nothing!'

Jen can hear the agony in his voice, but she wants to scream at him. Like Claudia Franklin would leave him a note, a love letter like in a Hollywood movie, before disappearing into the sunset.

'Like Claudia Franklin would leave you a note, a love letter? It's not a Hollywood movie,' she says, deciding to voice her thoughts aloud. 'Where could she have gone?'

'She doesn't have any money and no car. And she hasn't taken anything of mine. My wallet is still here.'

'Your wallet would be no fucking use to her anyway. It's always empty.'

She hears him sigh. 'Please,' he says. 'This isn't the time.'

'Is she with friends? The pool?'

'I don't know. Where else? Come on, think!'

But she doesn't answer him because on the TV screen is blurred street footage of The Corner House Cafe, and on loop, is Claudia and Bill walking in together.

'Oh Bill,' she breathes.

'What?'

She turns up the TV, sees a young woman standing in front of the cafe.

'I think the man's name was Will?'

Jen's chest tightens.

'I think I . . . Maybe I'm not remembering right. It came to me, but . . . the woman – Claudia – ordered something, she called over her shoulder to him.'

'Jen? Hello?'

'We're in deep shit.'

FORTY-TWO

Bill's first thought was that Claudia had gone to the police. Like an animal that knew it was going to die, he thought she had gone alone to face fate, but it's been hours now – maybe longer because he's had to go to the site and have a meeting with Andy to bluff the accounts. She's still not back and she's not answering the phone he got her. It's switched off – he doesn't even know if she has it with her. He feels like invisible walls are closing in around him. He knows now that he's in deeper than he ever expected to be – his face is on TV, he's a person of interest to the police. This was never part of the plan.

It's nine in the evening and he's come to the only other place that he can think of to find her – the ruins of the barn at Cowell Farm. The sky is dark but adorned with stars and a pale moon which is enough light for him not to have to switch on the torch of his phone. He knows it all by heart anyway.

He walks down the verge, pauses at the bank, and shivers. To get to the barn he needs to cross the river and he walks up to the narrowest part where the stepping stones are. He knows which are solid and have grip, and which are covered in moss and might be slippery. He picks his way through the rushing water carefully, can hear its babble as its flow threads around the stones. He wonders at its language. Did the river know that it held Victoria here in the deep? Does it know all their terrible secrets? To think that Victoria was found only half a mile down from here, to think that his favourite childhood place is now the death place of two people he once knew.

The ruin of the barn is a black shadow against the skyline and grows more sinister as he walks closer towards it. He can hear the wind whistling through its rafters, the call of a bird before a flap of wings in flight, as he approaches.

'Hello?'

The barn is silent in reply.

He inhales deeply, still feels like there's the essence of fire in the remaining wood. What is it they say? Walls absorb, and buildings remember.

What if somehow Claudia has found a way to escape out of the UK? Would she really have gone without telling him, without giving him the money? He knows the pain of losing a parent, she must be devastated about Victoria. A thought crosses his mind. What if Mark has found her? What if he knows where Bill lives and dragged her from his flat? He stands in the silence, his heart thudding because now that feels like it can be the only explanation. So what does he do if she's held by Mark against her will?

Bill needs to finish what she had started. Mark's word against hers.

He goes to his bedroom and pulls out her laptop from under his bed. The screen is smashed, but he presses the on button anyway and it boots. It's alive.

He opens the word document and there it is. He copies it over into her email and then he presses send.

A message pings back almost immediately.

Is this from THE Claudia Franklin?? Where's your verification?

Bill writes back.

You don't have time to verify it. You have to print this now.

FORTY-THREE

Claudia is not with Mark. She is alone and moving towards the quiet darkness of Oak House, having walked hours through the fields, through the woodland. She is here for her belongings, to retrieve everything she needs now before it's too late, because from what she has seen on the news, there's a question mark over whether Mark will be able to get to Paris, and she cannot lose her opportunity to get out.

The diving team are travelling on the Eurostar tomorrow morning, and all of them are due to stay the night in a hotel in London beforehand. There was supposed to be a big dinner with speeches, and press taking photographs and Claudia knows that Mark won't want to miss it, even with this all hanging over his head. Her lips turn up into a sneer. She knows what he'll be telling them in his speech.

You will stand on the edge of that platform, and take the moment to look at the water. Tell yourself you are here, *that you can do this.*

She reaches the garden fence panel and pulls at it, expecting it to come away like it's always done, but to her surprise, there's a resistance and then a ripping sound. She inhales sharply, realises as she tugs that the fence panel has been taped. Yellow and black with writing from films and TV dramas.

Do Not Cross. Police.

She steps between the strips of tape, heart hammering wildly in her ribcage. What do the police think happened here? She slips through into the garden, and her body starts to convulse with panic. The grass looks freshly cut – did she bleed there? Did Mark wash it out, cut out the stains? But the deckchair is still on the grass, the birdbath is filled with water, the flowers are in bloom, and everything looks hauntingly normal.

She lets herself into the house with the key that she told Bill was in the Welsh dresser, and walks through the boot-room and then into the kitchen. She can't help but pause to touch the white quartz countertop, feel its cold smooth finish, catches the sparkles buried within the surface. As a girl, she used to gallop her toy unicorns over it, used to pretend that the sparkles gave them magic. Her mother always got cross with her for it – worried the little hooves would mark it even though they were plastic. Claaudia looks to the Aga, duck-egg blue, remembers that she used to stand in front of it when she came back from swimming, the lids both open and warming her damp hair. Above it is the huge oak beam that would have only the best Christmas cards tacked into it with pins. There are parts of the house that are built with old ship timber and so many times she wondered where her house had sailed. She would love it to grow wings now, enormous wings, and fly her up to the sky. She wonders where she would go, where she would feel safe.

She can't take the house with her, of course. She must leave it and all its memories behind. She treads lightly up the staircase to go up to her and Mark's bedroom. It used to be her mother and Henry's room, has enormous glass windows overlooking the garden and woodland beyond, an en suite made of white marble.

She reaches for a suitcase from inside the wardrobe and she swiftly puts in some clothes that Mark won't notice she's taken, and some toiletries. Have the police done an inventory for her belongings? She hopes not. She'll also take her precious shammy. She goes to the pillow, lifts it, sees that it's there, folded like always. Her mother had started that tradition for her. To wish on it, see if her dreams came true, because Victoria was big on manifesting destiny. She had been a dancer, she understood discipline and rigorous training. She was always the one that took Claudia to the diving pool and never Henry. She was always the one to drive her – and Jen too – to the numerous competitions around the country, regardless of where they were held, or what time of day they were. She would sit in the gallery with a coffee and her sunglasses on.

'She's probably asleep,' Claudia often said to Jen. 'She's only here for the outcome of possible glory so she can then go to the Ivy with all her friends and bask in their admiration.'

'That sounds a bit harsh.'

'It doesn't. The cocktails there are really nice.'

'I meant on your mum,' Jen said.

'Your mum and my mum are very different.'

'Your mum remembers your name at least.'

'But she doesn't ever use it.'

But if Claudia thinks about it – really thinks – she can recall that there were occasions when she saw Victoria tilt forward and purse her lips into a thin line as Claudia walked to the edge of the dive platform. But as she surfaced from the water, Victoria would be leaning back again.

Maybe she did care. Maybe she just didn't know how to show her love. Maybe Claudia should have tried to love her better. Maybe, maybe. Too late for any of that now.

There's a noise from downstairs.

She stops dead and straightens, and waits, poised like an animal. Perhaps she misheard, but no, there's another sound now. Slow footsteps on the staircase. The police? Mark?

Her head goes light with fear. No one can catch her here, not when she's so close to getting away. She looks around wildly for a place to hide because she won't be able to flee the room – the landing comes out where the stairs come up and she can't jump out of a window this high up. She can't hide under the bed because it has storage drawers, and can't risk hiding in the en suite because it has no lock. Her only real resort is to hide in the wardrobe and will herself not to make a sound. She grabs the suitcase she was filling, puts it inside as noiselessly as she can and then follows it.

It's awkward to stand; there are shoeboxes at the bottom of it and a couple of silky blouses that she's now displaced from hangers. She buries herself deep within the coats, and covers her mouth with her hand and waits. If it is Mark, then why is he here and not with the team? Did he see her across the lawn? Has he called the police already? She stifles a cry and an empty coat hanger sways dangerously next to her and she grabs at it before it clangs. She hears the familiar creak of the bedroom door opening.

She slips her hand into her pocket to turn on the phone Bill got her and text him, or Jen, but as she twists it to take it out, it slips from her clammy fingers. It thuds on a shoebox, bounces, makes another thud as it lands on the wooden bottom of the wardrobe.

Silence throbs in her ears.

And then, the closet handle turns. Mark's fingers curl around the edge of it the door and she could scream, she should bolt out, but she doesn't have time to do either.

FORTY-FOUR

He yanks her out by the hair and the pain of it almost causes her to black out. He shoves her down to the floor.

'I knew you were alive.'

Claudia cowers beneath him. 'Please—'

'Have you had a nice vacation?'

'I don't want any trouble.'

Mark laughs. 'Really? Because that's all you've been causing me since you've been away. What do you think would happen if I phoned the police and told them my wife is home and looking like she's about to do a runner when her mother has been found dead only a mile from her house?'

'I wasn't. I came home to be with you.'

'Liar. I found your new passport, Claudia. And an envelope with five *thousand* pounds in it.'

'You need to give them to me—'

'I don't think I will.'

He steps towards her and she skirts backwards like a small animal into the corner of the room.

'You sent that story about Bella Mitchell to the papers.'

'What?'

'It was suggested to my lawyer that I bow out of the dinner tonight and thank Christ I did. Because half an hour ago, your story broke. Can you imagine how that would have looked whilst giving my keynote speech about passion and love for diving?' His eyes are like storms. 'Is that what you wanted?'

'I didn't send—'

'I have no choice now but to tell the police about what happened to Henry.'

'Mark, I didn't send it—'

'And then I'll tell them I know that you came back to Oak House on the night Victoria drowned.'

She startles. 'What?'

'I have a security camera app on my phone. I know you tried to come back to the house, but I had changed the lock.'

Claudia's heart is in her mouth. 'Have you . . . have you told the police that I came back?'

'No. I deleted the app and I told them that the camera had broken.'

'But – why? Why didn't you tell them? Why did you delete it?'

'Does it matter now anyway? You're a murder suspect, Claudia.'

'But I didn't hurt her. I didn't hurt Mum.'

'But you always hated her.'

He moves closer and she is trapped in the corner. She thinks about jumping over the bed, but he would be quicker.

'You wanted to sell the house and she came over to stop you and you pushed her into the river.'

'Of course I didn't! I didn't know she would come back! I think she must have drowned—'

'And *I* think that you've sat pretty the last few weeks whilst your mother has been underwater and you've said *nothing.*'

A white-hot fury floods her body. 'I've sat pretty for years saying nothing about *you*. Predator.'

He comes at her then, with a roar that punches her eardrums, and for a moment she's rigid from the shock of it, and lets herself be taken by the shoulders and shaken like a doll.

'Take that back!' he shouts. 'Take it *back*!'

She tries to move her arms to struggle against him, but he's pinned them against her body, and she can only close her eyes as he rages in her face, spit flying from his lips and onto her skin.

'You bitch!'

The force of his shaking her makes her unstable. He stabilises her with a slap to the face and she opens her eyes.

'Take it back! You think you're better than me?'

'Please—'

'You're a *murderer*!'

The word rings in her ears and she slumps. Because he's right, she is a murderer. That day eighteen years ago, Henry hadn't gone to walk to smoke at the barn and slipped like the police believed he had.

Claudia killed him.

FORTY-FIVE

At seventeen years old, Claudia got herself a secret older boyfriend – Mark Mason – and for months they managed easily to spend time together. Claudia would stay behind at practice, fooling both Victoria and Henry in telling them that she was dedicating herself to diving. They agreed to pick her up an hour after everyone else had left, none the wiser that Claudia and Mark would use those sixty precious minutes to touch each other, kiss in the water, or lie on the trampolines when they were practising jumps, talking excitedly about their glorious future together.

Until Henry had discovered the note in Claudia's swim bag.

'What's this?'

Claudia didn't look up, was painting her toenails in the living room, with the TV blaring *Strictly Come Dancing*.

'Claudia? What's this note?'

She'd glanced at him then, and when she saw the folded piece of paper in his hands, and her swim bag in his other, a cold dread stole around her throat. She dropped the nail-varnish brush, which rolled on the coffee table and dropped to the cream carpet. One of their dogs sniffed at it.

'What are you doing looking in my stuff?'

'I was putting the washing in the basket for the cleaners,' he replied. 'And this was very nearly washed with it.'

She snatched it away from him, heart hammering, and opened it. Mark hadn't written his name in any of the previous notes he'd secreted inside her change bag, but what if this one was different? Her eyes scanned the bottom and relief coursed through her body. She looked angrily at Henry.

'It's *private.*'

'I agree and I apologise.'

'Did you *read* it?'

She glanced down at the first line.

All the places I can imagine my tongue – you are a forbidden fruit but I want to know the core of you.

She cringed, scrunched the note in her palm.

'Don't you think you need to be concentrating on diving now that you've been accepted by the board?' Henry asked.

'Don't you think you should be minding your own business? It's just someone from swimming.'

'I thought your swimming team were all girls. This doesn't sound like something from them.'

'Course it's not *them.* A boy. It doesn't matter, OK?'

'I didn't think your coach allowed people to sit in and watch the training sessions.'

She laughed then. 'He definitely doesn't. It's someone from outside practice. A guy I've been seeing for a couple of months. Don't tell Mum, OK?'

Henry had narrowed his eyes.

As calmly as she could, she had picked up the nail brush, and gone upstairs, and then sat on her phone and giggled to Mark about it in a voice-note.

But, of course, the cogs of Henry's mind had obviously started to turn. A month later, he came early to pick Claudia up, and the receptionist let him into the pool and he went to the viewing gallery. Claudia and Mark were on the platform, his hands on her waist when he stopped suddenly and pulled away.

'This position,' he said in a firm voice. 'So you're square, OK?'

She had laughed, utterly confused, but he'd pinched her and she quietened.

'Excuse me, sir?' he said. 'Can you wait outside?'

She followed his eyes to see Henry.

'Can you wait outside, Henry?' she repeated.

After that, there was an added sense of danger, but that made it feel even more exciting. They continued their affair, and started to meet in other locations.

On the day of the fire, Claudia had asked Mark to the barn, the perfect place for them to be alone for a couple of hours. They climbed the ladder to the old hayloft, the squeak of the wooden rungs under their shoes, the remnants of dried mud beneath their hands. Mark was behind her, told her that he'd follow her anywhere if her perfect arse in tight shorts was the view. She laughed, and reached the top, took a moment to inhale the romance of the afternoon light through the cracks in the roof, the shafts of which cast a golden hue onto his lustful face as he lay beside her. He kissed her and she thought she was the luckiest girl in the world.

They had only been up there a little while when they heard a noise outside the barn – a scrape of the wooden doors and someone coming inside.

She tensed.

'Who is it?' Mark hissed.

'I don't know?'

They stayed still, heard the clang of the tractor door below them and then the zip of a lighter.

'Who the fuck?' Mark mouthed at her and she could only shake her head in reply, her heart beating furiously.

Her phone vibrated in her bag, made them jump. She glanced at it and then at Mark, found that he was already looking at her with dark, suspicious eyes, like she had deliberately trapped him.

'I think it's *Bill*,' she mouthed to Mark. 'Jen's brother.'

He shook his head to mean he didn't understand what she'd said so she turned her screen round to show him.

Come to the river and swim with us? We're here now. Bx

'Why is he here?' Mark whispered and she could see he was angry. 'Why is he asking *you* here?'

'Sometimes we come here to swim—'

Mark's fingers tightened around her thigh, his nails sharp in her skin. 'Be quiet.'

She shut her mouth.

'Do you think he'll come up?'

'I don't know?'

There was laughter below, a low cackle, and Claudia's stomach dropped. A trickle of sweat fell down her cleavage.

'My mind is coming away from my body,' Bill's voice drifted from below them.

'Is there someone else with him?'

She shrugged helplessly. They stayed rigid as minutes passed until they smelt the sickly-sweet smoke of weed below them. She offered Mark a smile, but he didn't return it. His fingers were still clenched around her thigh, his knuckles white. She uncurled them, kissed the back of his hand. He didn't look at her.

They heard a noise, the tractor door was opening again, and there was a thud.

'Shit, you OK?' Bill's voice said.

Mark looked at Claudia. 'He's talking to himself? Who's with him?'

'He's high. I don't think anyone else is there.'

'Jen?'

'I don't think so.'

They waited five minutes before they heard a clank of metal again, footsteps and the groan of wood. Claudia risked leaning out.

'Has he definitely gone?' Mark said quietly.

'I can't see him anywhere.'

He pulled her back and kissed her hard, so hard that she could feel his teeth behind his lips, and she kissed him back. She could feel his heartbeat hammering against her chest, was sure he could also feel hers. He slid his hand under the waistband of her shorts and she bit down on his neck, and they fooled around for a while enjoying the relief from the tension, before creeping back down the ladder.

'Fuck me. That was too close, Claudia.'

'I know,' she grinned. 'I'll think of a better hiding place.'

'There's nowhere you could hide that I wouldn't find you,' he said and went to kiss her when suddenly he paused, as if stopped on a TV screen.

She pulled away, saw the horror on his face and turned to see Henry standing at the corner of the barn.

'Mr Barton—' Mark began.

Henry walked towards them, silenced Mark with a palm raised upwards. 'I am taking my daughter away from here, away from you, *right* this second.'

Claudia swallowed a hard lump of emotion. *Daughter*. He'd never called her that before. Why now? she'd thought. Why now when he was obviously so angry, so upset?

'It's not what you think,' Mark said.

'And what story do you think I will buy after seeing that? After hearing what you just said.'

'There's nothing going on.'

'Don't take me for an idiot,' Henry snapped. He looked at Claudia. 'The note from your swim bag. From him?'

'No—' she said, but the denial was unconvincing.

'It's *disgusting*.' He looked back at Mark. 'You'll be struck off as a coach and I'll make sure you're on the register as a sexual predator—'

Claudia stepped towards him. 'Please, Henry, you can't say anything! Mark and I can win gold together. Let us win.'

'You're a *child,* Claudia, and this is a serious violation.'

'I'm not a child! I love him. We want to be together—'

Henry gave a snort of laughter. 'Don't be absolutely ridiculous.'

His mirth, his dismissal of her truest feelings, made her heart feel wild with rage. Before she even realised she was doing it, she'd launched forward with her arms outstretched, and shoved him hard in the chest with a strength she didn't know she was capable of. In surprise, he fell backwards and his head took the brunt of the fall, catching the metal steps of the old tractor, with a sickening crack. His legs buckled and his body twisted at an unnatural angle as it slumped in the dirt.

The silence that followed was thick.

Mark knelt down. 'What have you done?'

'I . . . I didn't mean to.'

'I can't—' Mark moved his fingers to Henry's wrist. 'I can't feel a pulse.'

'What?' Claudia dropped, put her head to Henry's chest. 'No, I think I feel a heartbeat? Isn't there? Henry?'

Mark gripped her arm tightly. 'Don't scream – someone will hear you.'

'I didn't mean to – he made me so mad, but he's OK, isn't he? I didn't push him that hard, I—'

'He's hit his head.'

'I can't see blood . . .'

Mark pulled her up. 'Claudia. Listen to me. He's not *breathing*. I'm trained in first aid.'

'But—'

'I think he's dead.'

'No – maybe I knocked him unconscious or he's—'

'He's dead.'

She let out a howl and Mark drew her to his chest, to stifle her sobs.

'Shh, you didn't mean to.'

'We need to call an ambulance,' she cried into him.

He held her shoulders, stared straight into her eyes. 'We can't ring them.'

'What do you mean?'

'If we call an ambulance, then people are going to know that we were here together. The police would come and it would cause questions about how Henry came to hit his head.'

'But—'

'Do you want your mother to know what you did? You want the world to know? It would ruin your chances at diving, and my career.'

She looked down at Henry's motionless body. 'What do we do?'

'I don't know . . .'

He trailed off. His eyes were on the ground and she followed them to the floor where there was a lighter – Bill's – dusty on the floor.

'We need to pretend we were never here.'

She stared at him. 'What?'

'It was an accident, Claudia. You didn't mean for it to happen.'

Her eyes blurred. 'Of course it was an accident!'

He picked up the lighter, handed it to her. 'Henry smoked cigars, you told me that.'

'Yes?'

'We need it to look like he fell, that his cigar caught fire. This whole barn is dry. It'll go up.'

'No, Mark.'

'If Jen Harper and her brother are at the river, wait a while before you join them and pretend you've just got there.'

'I—'

'It's the only way, Claudia. Isn't it? I love you. OK? You didn't mean to hurt him.'

She took the lighter from him. 'I didn't mean to.'

'You need to do this.'

In pure panic, she did as he said. She lit the barn up in several places – on wisps of dry hay, the splintered wooden posts. She remembers bending to blow it, remembers the lick of tiny orange flames, the barn awakening. She remembers then walking back through the long grass, to the copse of trees, and throwing up there, the shock of it all pouring out of her, and crying so hard that she thought her lungs might burst. She had killed Henry, the one person who had always been so gentle with her, called her *daughter*. How could she have done it? She didn't know how long she waited, but it was enough, because when she managed to drag herself up and navigate her way towards Jen and Bill across the river, the barn was fully alight.

'The joint,' Bill said. 'I . . . I left it in there . . . I don't know!'

She stared at him. Bill thought the fire was *his* fault.

'You did what?'

'I was smoking in there . . . I—'

'There's someone inside, Claud,' Jen said.

She heard it then. Henry's screaming.

Mark releases Claudia in the bedroom and she slides to the floor, her body convulsing with the unutterable pain of the memory. Henry wasn't dead. She had knocked him unconscious, but Mark had got it wrong and they'd both panicked and that mistake is the worst torture of all. What kind of primitive terror must Henry have felt when he had woken and realised he couldn't get out? Had he broken his back in the fall, or his legs? What sort of abandonment must he have felt in those last moments as the heat grew to become a furnace? Had he known that Claudia had started the fire, had he thought she had wanted to hurt him?

Mark stands over her, panting, as she sobs. Then, a sound that echoes from the hallway, up to the bedroom. The doorbell rings.

Claudia stares up at Mark. 'Who's that?'

She sees him swallow, his Adam's apple move down his throat.

'It could be reporters,' he whispers. 'Or it could be the police. Either way, what should we tell them?'

FORTY-SIX

Bill lets himself into Jen's flat without knocking.

'I don't know where she can be,' he says as he walks into the lounge.

He can see that Jen wants to tell him he's been an idiot, but she doesn't. Instead she opens her arms to him, waits for him to fall into them. It was so often this way round when they were children; though he was older, she always supported him emotionally. Nothing has changed now.

'I'm sorry,' he whispers.

'I know.'

'Are you OK?'

'Not really.'

'I've done everything wrong.'

'I've also done some really shitty things if that makes you feel better,' she says.

'Do you have a lasagne or something?'

'I've got chips.'

'OK.'

She goes to the kitchen and he follows, shrugs his jacket off, puts it on the chair.

'Do you know if anyone came forward about the footage of me?' he asks as she goes to the freezer.

'I haven't heard anything if they have.'

'But you think someone will?'

'I think it's inevitable.'

'And then what?'

'I don't fucking know,' she says. 'We deal with it when it happens.'

She tips the bag of chips onto a tray. They're the thick crinkly ones, his favourite.

Jen closes the oven door, turns the dial. 'Why did you help her? Just because of money?'

'Not *just* because of money. Because I didn't want to be a coward all my life.'

'What are you talking about?'

'I should have listened to you. We ran away from a man who was burnt alive. Not just any man – Henry. He was always so nice to us and . . .'

'It was an accident, Bill.'

He holds his hands up, doesn't want to hear her try to justify the past. 'I've made a mess of my life, Jen. I've lost stupid amounts of money and I've been stealing from the company. Amending invoices here and there, shaving off payments. I do it because I can't deal with who I am. Henry and then Mum—'

'We didn't have any control over any of it.'

'I should have told the police about Henry. Admitted to my joint being lost somewhere in there.'

'The police report said that Henry banged his head somehow. They said that it was probably his cigar that started the fire.'

'But we *know* differently,' Bill says. 'We know it was my joint in there. I lost it – I was so high and I . . .'

She places her hand on his shoulder. 'He might have had a cigar in there. We'll never know, Bill. Henry was always smoking them.'

'I know I killed him and you can never convince me otherwise.'

She sighs, understands his need to bear the responsibility but wants to take the weight of it away for him.

'Andy is checking over all the finances. He'll know in a matter of days that I've been taking money.'

'*I* could have covered them.'

'Forty-five thousand pounds?' he asks.

She inhales through her teeth. 'Is that how much you owe?'

He is ashamed. 'Yes.'

'I have thirty thousand from Mark that's in trust for Sam,' she says. 'And if you swore on your life you would pay it back, that you would give up those apps and sort yourself out, I would give it to you today. Tonight.'

Her words make him choke with emotion. 'You would do that for me?'

'Yes, because I *love* you. Because you and Sam are all I have.'

'I'm scared, Jen.'

'So am I.'

They sit in silence. They can say nothing to console one another, but there is an odd comfort in the awful shared heaviness of it.

'Aren't you meant to be diving?' he asks.

'We go back in tomorrow,' she says. 'I—' She hesitates. 'I need to show you something. Wait a second.'

She walks to the bedroom and then comes back out again, holding the black-and-white houndstooth jacket.

He frowns. 'What's that?'

'This is Victoria Franklin's.'

His mouth falls.

'I need to know why it's here in my flat,' she says and her voice breaks. 'I need to know what happened that night.'

'I didn't bring it here,' he says. 'I swear to God.'

'Did Claudia?'

'I don't ever remember seeing her with it?'

She's interrupted by a thumping on the door. Not a knock, but a thump.

'Open up. Police.'

Bill stares at Jen, who stares back at him before she runs to her room, bundling the jacket under her arm.

'Did you hide it?' he hisses.

'In Sam's room – fuck, should I tell them I have it? I don't know what to do!'

He puts his hand to her shaking arm. 'You can't, Jen. You can't tell them. Stay calm.'

'Do you think they've found Claudia?'

'I don't—'

'Police! Open the door.'

Jen opens all the locks, and a man in uniform stands at the doorway, two officers behind him, a man and a woman.

'Are you Jennifer Harper?' the first officer asks.

‘Yes? What’s—’

The first officer looks over her shoulder at Bill.

‘Are you Bill Harper?’

‘Yeah?’

‘Bill Harper, you’re under arrest for the abduction of Claudia Franklin and will be questioned regarding the death of Victoria Franklin.’

Bill can only stare, dumbly, at them all.

‘What the fuck is going on?’ Jen growls. ‘Someone tell me what the fuck is happening?’

‘Claudia Franklin has come into the station,’ he replies. ‘She’s told us everything.’

FORTY-SEVEN

Jen is stunned. 'Told you what? What's she told you?'

The officer ignores her, starts speaking to Bill.

'You do not have to say anything. But it may harm your defence if you do not mention when questioned something which you later rely on in court. Anything you do say may be given in evidence.'

Jen puts herself in between the officer and her brother. 'Hey, hey, what are you doing? He's done nothing wrong, you hear me?'

'We're not at liberty to discuss this with you—'

'Then you can get out of my house and come back in the morning when you've had your chance to fact-check,' she snaps. 'How dare you come in here and—'

The other male officer steps forward, starts to steer her into another room.

'Get off me,' she starts, but then freezes.

Sam is standing in the door frame, his pale face illuminated by the light of the living room. He looks frightened.

'Sam,' she whispers.

The officer hears the panic in her voice and releases her immediately.

'Mummy? Why are the police here? Are they your friends?'

'That's right, bub. Some of my friends from the station,' she says, plastering a smile to her face. 'Can you be an angel and grab Uncle Bill's coat from the kitchen? He's going to watch a game of football.'

Sam's face lights up. 'Can I go, too?'

'No, bub.'

Sam looks to the officer.

'Another time, mate,' he replies gruffly, not meeting Sam's eyes.

'Here, I'll go with you to get your uncle's coat,' the third officer says, appearing beside Jen. She smiles down at Sam. 'My name is Jaina.'

'On the back of the chair, OK?' Jen says. She's trying to sound as normal as possible, but on the inside she's screaming. Please, she thinks, do not go back into your room. Do not let Jaina into your room. What would happen if they found the jacket? What mess would she be in then?

Jen moves back to the living room, where the first officer stands grim-faced beside Bill. 'Bill's not done anything, I swear to God.'

'Your superior has been notified of your involvement with this case, and has given his permission for us to retrieve your badge, your radio and your ID.'

This is the moment where her heart breaks. She's kept it together until this point but now it's unravelling. Idris already knows that she has lied to him, that she is corrupt. The shame runs so deep that it physically cripples her. She steadies herself against the door frame.

'But I know things,' she tries. 'We both do, about Claudia! Whatever she's said, I can tell you that it's wrong—'

He ignores her.

'Jen, it's OK,' Bill says. 'I can straighten this out.'

'She's set you up, Bill, that fucking bitch!'

'No,' he says. 'She wouldn't have done that. It's a misunderstanding—'

'Are you stupid? Didn't you hear the charges?'

'I've found something.'

Jen turns to see Jaina, holding Bill's coat and another. The houndstooth jacket.

'Sir, I think this is Victoria Franklin's missing coat.'

There's a beat of silence.

'Wait—' Jen says. 'Please. It's not . . .' But she falters because to deny it will be worse.

'It's OK, Jen,' Bill says. 'I'll explain it all.'

She wants to grab him, hold him to her and never let go, because how can he possibly explain it? The jacket, the tie, the blood on the fence. All circumstantial evidence that will put him away. Her brother who has always tried to do the right thing but somehow always manages to come off in the wrong light.

'I'll come with you, hang on—'

The first officer looks to Jen. 'You know that is not possible,' he says. 'The investigation team will be talking to you in the morning. From this moment, you're suspended. Please get me your badge, your radio and your ID.'

'Please—'

'Please retrieve them.'

Heart thrumming, Jen goes to her jacket for her badge, the kitchen drawer for her documents and radio. This can't be happening, she thinks. Any minute and she'll wake up from this nightmare.

'Mum? Are you OK?'

Sam is behind her.

'Yes, bub.'

But she slams the drawer shut, makes him jump, and marches back to the living room, where the officer now has Bill's hands behind his back.

'Have fun, Uncle Bill!'

'Thanks, Samster,' he says and then looks at Jen. 'It's going to be OK.'

'You will get a call tomorrow morning to come to the station,' the officer says and then they're all gone.

Jen presses the bell, and keeps her finger on it so hard that the tip turns white. She knows how it'll trill inside the house, echo around that huge hallway, but there is no answer.

'What have you done, Claudia?' she shouts. 'What have you done!'

She picks up a stone, hurls it as hard as she can over the black railings and then watches it land, ineffectually, nowhere near the house.

She screams as loudly as she can, wants her voice to reach where the stone couldn't. 'I know you're in there!

Sam is in the car down the lane, sitting in the warmth of the heaters and with the radio on. He's asleep, but if he was to wake up, he could probably hear her screaming. She shouldn't have brought him here, but she's so angry, so vengeful. Claudia has betrayed them, but why? And what the hell can Jen do about it? Bill will be at the station now, will be giving his fingerprints and his DNA for elimination, except she knows that his DNA will be a match to the tie and the fence, and what then?

'Come out and talk to me!'

She picks up another stone and launches it. It doesn't even go as far as the first one. Nothing can ever touch Claudia Franklin.

And then, the shadow of a person in the window. The front door opening and then someone runs out.

'You're sick!'

It's not Claudia or Mark. Jen blinks. It's a woman who sounds furious and Jen watches as another figure chases her down the driveway. There's shouting, but Jen can't make out words. She suddenly feels very strange – dizzy and unanchored, like she's floating. And then there's humming, that same humming sound that's been in her ears for weeks.

Jen gasps, and then she wakes up.

She's been dreaming that she's screaming at Claudia through the railings, but she hasn't yelled, hasn't thrown stones. But she *is* here at Oak House. The dawn is creeping in and she can see that no one is on the driveway and no one is at the window. She's walked the loop yet again, has stopped here again at the railings. She looks to the lane and there's no car there, no Sam.

He's at home, alone. She has no phone, no nothing. She runs as fast as she can, panic in her chest. And that humming in her ears.

FORTY-EIGHT

Bill sits in a room that is heavy with heat and his own anxiety. The chair is plastic, uncomfortable, and his back is sweating against it.

It's morning – he's spent the night in a cell – and for the last hour, the two officers in front of him have taken it in turns asking questions, but his brain is turning too slowly to answer them – the cogs are sticking, and he can't formulate words. He can't formulate a *defence*. His lawyer – he can't remember her name – asked for a break and got him a cup of tea in a plastic cup. It's too milky, but he's in no position to complain about it, or indeed anything.

There's a part of him that is laughing at the absurdity of this, the other part is howling with the pain of it. Because why would Claudia do this after all he's done to help her, after all they've been through? Is it to buy time so she can get away, is it because Mark has forced her hand? Or is it because this was always her plan? Perhaps she's always harboured hatred against him for what happened to Henry.

He swallows. His mouth is dry and he wants some water but doesn't dare ask for any. He wants his sister too but definitely can't ask for her. He's ruined everything that she has worked towards – has utterly failed her. All those years ago, he fucked up her Olympic diving dream and now he's fucking up her diving career. He's done so many wrong things.

His hands clench; he wants to bite his nails, wants to grab at his phone – though the police have that – and disappear into the murk of his gambling addiction but he's impotent to do anything to make himself feel better. He doesn't deserve the temporary relief of it anyway.

'Mr Harper?'

Bill refocuses his eyes.

'You've given us your version of events as to what has been happening the last few weeks.'

'Yes.'

'And now I'm going to tell you what we're looking at here, direct from Miss Franklin, and you can see where we're having some issues.'

Bill swallows. 'OK.'

'When Mark Mason and Claudia Franklin returned to the UK, you and Ms Franklin had struck up a friendship again, yes? You had offered to help her with selling her home, as she'd expressed an interest.'

'Yes?'

'You also offered to help her with managing real estate in Canada. In fact, you emailed some, am I right?'

'Yes—'

'You also corresponded directly with Victoria Franklin.'

'Claudia asked me to—'

'Bill,' the lawyer says. 'You don't need to say anything.'

'On the twentieth of June, you and Claudia met up at The Corner House Cafe, I gather, to finalise some of these plans.'

'I gave her a new ID that day,' Bill says. 'Because then Mark wouldn't track her. She wanted to start again.'

'We have never found an alternative ID in our searches of Oak House.'

'Ask her! Ask Claudia! Ask *Mark*.'

'Ms Franklin has told us that during this meeting at The Corner House Cafe, you told her that you were in considerable debt. She felt sorry for you. You asked her to lend you some money when the house sale went through. She felt bad, but she said no.'

'That's not true—'

'Bill, you don't need to counter this.'

Bill looks to the lawyer. 'This isn't what happened.'

'Claudia told us that you were angry – that you had helped her with getting things going with the sale and felt you were owed. You demanded money for the sale of Oak House to pay off your substantial gambling debts which we have since looked into. You owe a *lot* of money, Mr Harper.'

'You don't have to comment, Bill.'

'Yes,' Bill says at the same time.

'Forty-five thousand pounds. More than twenty thousand of which you owe to Andy Bowman's company, who you currently work for on a site as foreman.'

Bill closes his eyes. 'Yes.'

'On the twenty-ninth of June, in the afternoon, you broke into Oak House via one of the fence panels. You used to come through there as a teenager, Claudia tells us. Ms Franklin was in the garden on her laptop – the same laptop that we have since found in your flat. Claudia has said your argument got heated and you hit her on her head with the laptop.'

'That's *not* true. I've told you—'

'Bill, I advise you not to comment,' the lawyer says.

'Then you dragged Ms Franklin back through the fence with you in case her husband returned.'

'That's not what happened,' Bill says and sees his lawyer's shoulders heave with a sigh.

'You took her to your building site, held her against her will at the only finished house – number ten – until she agreed to give you the money.'

'No.'

'You then left the site and drove to the Lake District with Claudia.'

'Yes. I mean, it wasn't against her will. That's where we decided to go to be as far away as possible—'

'Bill,' the lawyer tries, but Bill keeps talking.

'I told you, we went there because the investigation had taken a turn we didn't see coming and we needed to get away and figure things out.'

'Or you just wanted to cover your tracks. You stayed there a couple of days until you were called by your site manager because something had been discovered in the pool of number ten, hadn't it? Claudia had managed to write a message on the bottom of the pool, a message that you later tampered with. We have a photograph given to us by the site worker that originally found the note. Jonny

Kilby. He'd taken a picture with his phone before you were back on site.'

Bill is silent.

'When the police officer you met with came and took pictures, the message looked different. Your site manager told us you had gone down there alone and when he came to join you, you were *in* the pool, and told him that the liner had come away. He also confirmed the original message because he had seen it.'

'I told you that I was worried . . . I was worried that, police would think I was perverting the—'

'Bill,' his lawyer growls.

'You *were* perverting the course of justice, Mr Harper.' The officer looks at his notes. 'You then drove to town, where you are seen on CCTV going into Tea For Two. There you saw your good friend Kerry-Lou Westbrook there.'

He feels sick.

'Her manager, Mr Ricky Prior, told us that you tend always to sit on the same table. Both you *and* your sister, Jen Harper, sit there because apparently it's tradition. *Apparently*, as teenagers on the dive team, your sister and Claudia Franklin used to sit together at that table. There's a very long history between the three of you.'

Bill swallows. Has Claudia told the police about Henry? How deep has her betrayal run?

'Mr Prior showed us the table. And what did he tell us? That there used to be a message on it, but it was changed recently, but that he remembers the original and it's the same as the one in the pool.'

'I was worried.'

'You were right to be worried, Mr Harper. Because now we come on to Victoria Franklin's death. The tie that you said you borrowed from your sister for an interview was found in the river. You know this already, of course, because your sister *told* you about it, and you in turn told Claudia and gave her cause for concern. This, as you'll understand, is another huge violation and won't look any good for Jen Harper.'

Bill shakes his head. 'I don't know why it was there. I don't know what to say.'

'Say nothing,' the lawyer says. 'Christ.'

'Ms Franklin told us that you made her go back to Oak House on the evening of the twenty-ninth of June, to get any money she had in cash and her jewellery. Mark Mason wasn't there by that point, but you waited up the road while she tried to get in. However, by chance, Mark Mason had changed the locks and clearly had forgotten to tell her the new code. This was something neither of you had foreseen, so you panicked and decided to think of a new plan. You got Claudia back into your truck and you drove down the lane again.'

'That did happen, but not how you're describing,' he says. 'Why would she come back to my truck if she'd wanted to get away from me?'

'Claudia tells us that it was when you were driving down the lane again that you saw headlights.'

'What?'

'You pulled into a dark lay-by, under the treeline, and switched off your engine. You both saw a taxi pass and saw Victoria inside. You had been communicating with her directly from Claudia's laptop for quite some time, haven't you, Mr Harper?'

'Because Claudia asked me to. So that Mark Mason wouldn't suspect anything—'

'We have accessed her emails and she wasn't happy about the sale. You could have manipulated Claudia, but not Victoria as well and now here she was, back in the UK for the first time in eighteen years.'

'No—' Bill says.

'I admit that this is where it gets a little blurry for us,' the officer says. 'We're not quite sure if you waited until the taxi had dropped Victoria off and then went back to talk to her about the sale, or if you drove away and she just happened to fall into the river. There *are* marks on her wrists, and they'll be matched against the fingerprints you've given us. But, aside from that, the tie you were wearing for the interview was picked up from the river. Victoria Franklin's *jacket* was in your sister's flat. Her handbag and suitcase aren't anywhere to be found. And when you discovered that Claudia had managed to escape your flat where you had taken her whilst on site with Andy Bowman – you then wrote an email from her laptop to the media, to divert attention from yourself onto Mark Mason.'

'What happened to Bella Mitchell is *true* and you wouldn't be doing your jobs if you didn't look into it—'

'I think my client could do with a rest,' the lawyer interjects. 'And we should have a chance to speak privately, Mr Harper, yes?'

Bill is about to say no, about to argue further, but stops when he sees the look in the woman's eyes. Disdain, hopelessness.

'OK,' he says quietly.

'Interview terminated at ten-thirty a.m.'

FORTY-NINE

In the light from the huge hallway window, Claudia sits on the bottom step of the grand staircase and listens to the grandfather clock which counts down time, and counts up all her lies.

She has ten minutes until the press conference at midday and she has all her make-up on, her hair is washed and curled, and her clothes pressed. She looks the part, as she always has done, but she feels like a husk and the house seems to echo it. The dusky pink tulle of her long pleated skirt is edged with grey dust and so she stands hurriedly. The cleaner clearly hasn't been coming over the weeks Claudia has been away; soil, gravel from the drive, ancient plaster dust from the ceiling and strands of hair, all whisper across the stone tiles.

She tells herself that she's detached emotionally from Bill, but he's all she can think about. She could see herself reflected in his trusting eyes that evening when he met her at the barn and took one look at her bleeding head; he held her so tightly, she felt she couldn't breathe. She could see love in his face when he delivered and set up a little fridge-freezer for her at number ten. And now she has framed him for murder. What a bitter thing it is to discover about yourself – that when the chips are down, you're someone who will betray others in order not to face your own demons. Mark knows she's a murderer. She knows he's having an illegal relationship with Marie. The only way of keeping this truce, for them to both escape, is to place blame elsewhere. She cannot have the world know that she killed her stepfather, a man she had come to *love*, in cold blood.

'I've let Emily in through the gate.'

She looks up, sees Mark coming down the stairs dressed in smart navy trousers and a crisp white shirt.

'OK.'

Claudia doesn't want to let Emily in. She knows that a family liaison officer isn't merely a friendly face for a family in the middle of a shitstorm situation, but an investigator, a recorder of all the things that they say inside the house, and all the things they don't.

'Finn is already outside prepping the reporters.'

Finn is Finn O'Reilly, Mark's lawyer.

'We stick with our statements.'

'Yes.'

He goes down past her and the stench of his cologne makes her insides curl.

'And we limit the damage.'

She is silent.

He leans to the side of the door, glances out of the window, and then opens the door. She can hear the clicking of cameras from where she sits, like a swarm of crickets, and the sound alarms her.

'Hello, Emily,' Mark says.

'Are you ready?' she asks.

He looks back at Claudia, and she gets up, smooths her skirt, and walks towards them. He holds out his hand to her and she takes it, locks in the promise they've made each other. So different to their vows of love. Now they have vows of secrecy.

'We're ready,' he says.

They stand side by side on the gravel outside Oak House. A few choice reporters have been allowed access inside the gates – others are beyond the railings. All are calling out to them, clamouring for their attention, snapping their cameras for photographs before they speak.

Mark squeezes her hand. He's already holding it too tightly and Claudia can barely feel her fingers. She wonders if anyone can see it and if they can, if they'll mistake it for support.

The media on the front drive are quiet as Mark reads out their statement.

'Three weeks ago, on the twenty-ninth of June, my wife experienced something no person should have to. She was physically attacked, forced from her home, and then hidden away in a building site by a man she used to know, and used to trust. And, during this horrific trial, she found out that her mother, Victoria Franklin, had been found, dead, less than a mile from our house.'

He sticks to their script, and to the facts that are already in circulation and approved of by the police. He's doing most of the talking because he always has done; he's used to interviews and is good at them, but everyone knows that it's Claudia that the nation wants to hear from. They want to know the terror she incurred, the violence she might have been subjected to, the horror and upset that her mother has been found dead in the river. People love bad news, love to absorb all the gritty details. Only Claudia knows the absolute truth of it all, save what really happened to her mother.

Claudia doesn't know what she believes happened to Victoria – she can only think that she came, drunk, to the gates of Oak House, and on finding them locked and the taxi having disappeared down the lane, that she decided to cut through to town the quickest way, following the river through the water-meadows. To think that Claudia must have missed her mother by minutes, after living years of her life without her, is too much for Claudia to bear. She was going to go to Canada to start again, had hopes of rebuilding their relationship. She was going to try to be a good daughter. Impossible now to be a good person.

'We are helping the police with their ongoing investigation into Victoria Franklin's death,' Mark finishes, 'but this news was obviously extremely distressing on top of what was a hideous ordeal to go through. We appreciate empathy and respect towards my wife and I at this difficult time. Thank you.'

Immediately there are flashes of cameras.

'Can we hear from you, Claudia?' someone yells. Claudia sees that it's a woman dressed in a powder-blue suit, her lanyard close enough for her to read it. The *Sun*. 'Why did the man arrested take you away? What was your connection?'

Finn O'Reilly steps towards the microphones. 'Mark has told you all he can at this present time.'

'Are *you* going to comment about the article printed by the *Mail* last night, Mark?' a man asks.

'That email was sent by the man arrested, from Claudia Franklin's laptop,' Finn says.

'Which he *stole* when he physically abused my wife in our own private garden and dragged her through the woods,' Mark chips in. 'Those allegations are unfounded.'

Claudia stands still, listens to the lies trip off his tongue. The way he says them, with such conviction, makes her wonder if he's come to believe their story himself.

'But you don't deny that Bella Mitchell *was* a diving pupil under your care in Boston—'

Claudia knows without looking at him that the muscles in Mark's jaw will be working hard to contain his angst.

'Mark Mason will not be answering questions about Bella Mitchell,' Finn says firmly.

'When is the arrested man going to be named?'

'What relationship did you have with him, Claudia?'

'Is it the man from the cafe on the news?'

'That is all, thank you,' Finn says.

'One more question! Claudia!'

Mark turns them and Claudia is forced to face the woman from the *Sun*.

'Do you believe the man who abducted you could have killed your mother?'

She waits for Finn to jump in, but he doesn't. Out of the corner of her eye, she sees Mark appraise her. They *all* appraise her. There is only one answer here.

'Yes,' she says quietly. 'I do.'

FIFTY

Jen lets out a scream at the TV. She wants to launch herself at it, wants to go through it, and scratch out Claudia's eyes, pull out every strand of that golden blonde hair and stuff it into her mouth so she chokes on her lies. How can she have betrayed Bill so viciously? With every moment that passes, Jen is more convinced that Mark and Claudia planned this together all along. She doesn't know for what reason they might have killed Victoria – perhaps it was an accident – but, either way, they needed someone to frame. And who better than Bill, who thought he owed Claudia everything.

Jen has written everything down – her and Claudia's shared history of diving, Jen's own complicated relationship with Mark, her limited knowledge about Bella Mitchell. She's written down what Bill and Claudia told her on the day Claudia disappeared and what happened after, she's even written about the barn – written that it was a dreadful, horrible, mistake, but it's what Mark Mason holds against them. She's going to lay everything bare, because what does she have to lose? Bill can't be sent down for something he didn't do, Jen will be damned if she lets Claudia screw him over.

She needs to get this all to someone – no, not just someone, to a person who knows her best, who cares about her, or at least used to. She needs to get it to Idris – but why would he listen? She is a wild animal, locked in the cage of her flat, sick with anger.

The front door bangs opens and Jen whips round, the subconscious part of her confused that it must be Bill somehow. But it's Kerry standing there, wide-eyed and with inky-black mascara tear tracks running down her cheeks. Jen stands and they fall into each other's arms.

'Oh my God,' Kerry breathes into her ears. 'I listened to it on the radio. I couldn't even drive properly. Is it true, Jen? Tell me it's not true! Claudia is alive and Bill – Bill abducted her? Did he hurt Victoria Franklin?'

'None of it is true. None of it.'

'The police have interviewed *me*,' Kerry says.

'What did you tell them?'

'They knew about you and Claudia and the diving team. They knew about Mark. And Sam. They asked about Sam.'

Jen closes her eyes. She's thankful Sam is at school, away from all the news, and away from Jen's rage. It was all she could do this morning to put a face on at the school gate without bursting into tears.

'Fuck.'

'I'm sorry – I'm sorry. I said I'd lie for you but I couldn't. I *didn't*. I was scared.'

Jen holds her friend tightly. 'I don't blame you, OK? I've never *wanted* you to lie. I've written it all down. Everything that I've never told you, never told anyone. The thing Mark threatened me about. I'm going to go and tell my dive supervisor, though anything I say will be severely discredited after everything that's gone on.'

'When are you seeing the police?'

'They haven't called yet, or come. I guess soon.'

'Why did you keep all this from me, Jen?'

'Because I had to.'

Kerry nods, wipes her eyes with the back of her thumb. 'Let me make you tea,' she says.

'You're not at work?'

'I quit,' Kerry says, getting mugs out. 'When Ricky spoke against Bill. How could I stay?'

The loyalty is unwavering.

'Oh, mate.'

The kettle boils and Jen sits.

'I always said she was a bitch, Jen,' Kerry says.

'You were fucking right.' Jen pauses. 'You said something about the Franklins, Kez. About keeping their secrets. What did you mean?'

Kerry pours the water. 'Oh, God, you know what I meant. It's water under the bridge now anyway, isn't it?'

'What?'

'The dinner.'

'The . . . the dinner?'

'I know I didn't tell you about what Victoria did for a while, but I *did* tell you. It made me so mad that she lied, Jen. That she could have done that to you.'

'What Victoria did?' Jen shakes her head. 'I don't follow.'

Kerry looks at her like she's lost her mind. 'Are you crazy? The dinner before the British Diving Championships. You were at Claudia's house and you got sick. How have you forgotten about this?'

Jen nods, the bitter taste of disappointment still sharp on her tongue even after all these years. 'Of course I remember *that*.'

'Yeah. And Claudia told me – about a month after she'd been accepted by the Olympic committee – that Victoria had put something shitty in your food and made you ill.'

Jen jerks back like something has shocked her. 'What?'

'Jen – why don't you remember this? I told you when we watched Claudia dive at Beijing on the TV.'

'Victoria made me *sick*?'

'I always thought how convenient it was. I confronted Claudia about it before she left for China and she was shocked I'd asked after all those years. She told me her mum had basically poisoned you. She didn't know her mum would do anything like that, that's what she said. She'd found out – I don't know how – what Victoria had done and they'd had a huge row about it.'

Jen holds up her hands. 'Wait. Victoria made me sick before the trials so that Claudia could go forward?'

'*Yes*. The championships were only months after Henry Barton had died in that fire. Victoria admitted to Claudia that she'd done it to give Claudia purpose; she was worried that Henry's death would have held Claudia back from achieving big things. Victoria saw you as an obstacle in the way.'

Jen's heart has started to race. 'But Victoria – she wouldn't do that. She liked me?'

'That's what Claudia told me.'

'But I . . . I can't remember? How can I not remember you telling me this?'

'We never talked about it again. You went really quiet and I thought maybe I'd made a mistake telling you.'

'Was I properly awake when you told me?'

'Yes.'

'Are you sure?'

'I . . . well, we were in my bedroom. We'd been drinking, and it was late, and we'd switched off the lights. We laughed in the dark about how awful Claudia had been up on the platform. We said that it should have been you up there. And that's when I decided to tell you what I knew.'

'I don't remember.'

Kerry puts her hands to her head, rakes her fingers through her hair and Jen knows there's more she wants to say.

'What else?'

'I . . . no. Nothing.'

'What?'

'You said that you were glad Victoria had left for Canada,' Kerry says. 'Because if you were ever to see her again, you'd kill her.'

Jen runs to the bathroom, retches. Everything is closing in on her. The night Victoria was dropped off at Oak House, the night she disappeared, Jen had woken up with her feet in the water-meadows. She had walked her loop but hadn't thought anything of it because she had been doing it since Mark and Claudia had moved back again, but now . . . now she is terrified. What if she has harmed Victoria? Is that why she had Victoria's jacket in the flat?

She keeps her head down in the toilet bowl, tries to steady her heartbeat, but there are fireworks in front of her eyes. Memories flash sharply in vivid colour.

A woman leaves the gate of Oak House, walks at fast pace in the grey of an early morning before dawn, her feet making a clattering noise because she's on the wooden boardwalk of the water-meadows.

'Wait!'

Jen's calling to her, can hear the urgency of her own voice, but the wind whips her words backwards and behind and the woman ahead doesn't hear her – or chooses not to. She carries on walking, disappearing and reappearing from Jen's view as the boardwalk weaves through the tall reeds.

'Stop!'

Jen's shout disturbs a bird only metres from her feet – an enormous white swan that lifts its head and then beats its wings because she's startled it. Jen sidesteps it to pass but unbalances herself and falls off the boardwalk, her boots immediately sinking into the swampy marshland, and her feet soaking up the sop. She steps out of it before she can sink any deeper and hisses back at the swan who is nonplussed and back to sitting again, but during her imbalance, she has lost sight of the woman.

She's sick in the toilet, and with each hurl, tears come and sweat gathers in the creases of her elbows, the backs of her knees.

'Jen?'

'I was there that night. At Oak House. I thought I'd woken up because I had walked my loop, but I had been there *hours*. I had been there in the dark – at night-time – and there was a woman coming out of Oak House, shouting. Lots of voices, but I can't remember if it was just her and me – or other people – I don't know. I followed someone.'

Kerry kneels next to her, hands her toilet roll. 'Are you sure about this? Was the woman Victoria?'

Jen can only shake her head. She wouldn't have harmed Victoria Franklin, would she? If anything, Victoria became like a surrogate mother for those years she knew Claudia. She drove Jen to dive practice along with Claudia in their enormous four-by-four as opposed to Jen cycling or getting three different buses to get to the pool. She cooked for Jen – and Bill – huge meals – and gave them leftovers in Tupperware because she knew Fiona was unwell. She let them both sleep over on Claudia's bedroom floor some nights, gave them each their own 'Franklin' blanket – cashmere, of course – to drape over themselves.

Perhaps Victoria had stumbled and Jen had been there at the same time and seen it, tried to help her? But how could she have forgotten what Kerry told her about the dinner and her reaction to it?

She looks at her friend. 'When I woke up, I was standing in the silt and it was dawn, so how long was I there for? My feet were fucking freezing. There was no one around – just silence. I put my boots back on, I pulled a jacket around myself. Victoria's jacket, I'm sure of it now, and then there was this weird humming in my ears.'

'Like a bird singing?'

'No. Like an insect. Something constant. Low.'

'A lorry?'

'No,' Jen says, but she pauses. Kerry's suggestion has triggered something. The hum *was* mechanical. 'It was a motorbike.'

FIFTY-ONE

How could Jen have forgotten it? A detail so obvious to her but which she'd completely overlooked, and so had the police. At some point that night, she'd heard a motorbike and for weeks since, the sound of its engine has been ringing in her ears. But why would Mark admit to it now? Mark's dad owned a motorbike and Mark had a licence to drive it. The same bike she'd ridden on behind him, to the cliffs that day.

She sits in her car, looks at the house across the road. Anna and Rob Mason live thirty minutes' drive from Bourne in a pretty village with houses made of sandstone and fields with grazing livestock. Jen knows the implications for having driven here, and she knows that being away from her flat, today of all days when the police are due to question her, adds to an increasing list of violations. But she needs the evidence to prove her theory, and it needs to be *now*. How else is she going to bury the dread inside her mind that *she* had done something to Victoria?

She parks up, rings the doorbell.

The door opens, and a woman – Anna – bends to look at Jen through a crack. She's dressed in slacks and a navy blue gilet over a pastel pink cotton shirt. By her side is a Labrador who noses the door wider.

'Are you a reporter?' she asks suspiciously. Her voice is like Mark's – a smooth, Chicago accent. 'Because you can leave this road immediately if you are.'

'I'm a police officer,' Jen says. She's dressed in uniform, though she no longer has a badge to flash. She can only hope that her demeanour and the pressed shirt and trousers make enough of an impression. 'I'm Jennifer, one of the officers on the unit investigating Victoria Franklin's death.'

The woman hesitates. 'Come in then.'

'Thank you.'

Jen had once or twice imagined coming here with Sam and being welcomed by Mark's parents and now that thought makes her sick with relief. Thank God they don't know about him, but for how long? If the media get hold of it, she is doomed.

The house is small, characterful, cheerful and smells of casseroles cooking, and of dog hair.

'Please, come to the kitchen,' Anna says.

She is a retired sports teacher, and Rob – Mark's father – is an engineer, born in Hampshire. Both are in their eighties now. Jen remembers seeing them interviewed on TV at the Beijing Olympics – they were so proud of him, their only son, and were devastated for him when Claudia messed up, as was the nation. But Jen wonders if they are so charmed by him, or protective over him, that they might lie for him? They've always maintained his statement that he was with them on that Saturday night, but do they know otherwise?

Jen follows Anna through to a kitchen with a huge range the same blue as the front door, a beamed ceiling and walls. The texture between them is bumpy, whitewashed.

'Can I get you tea? Rob is out at the moment.'

'I'm fine, thanks, Mrs Mason. And I don't want to keep you. I had to follow up on the night Claudia disappeared for a complete picture.'

Anna Mason nods gravely. 'I saw on the news about the man who has been arrested. Someone Claudia knew a long time ago? William someone.'

Jen grits her teeth. 'Apparently so.'

'Do you think he killed Victoria? I'm a big believer in innocent before proven guilty, but it's not looking good for him, is it?'

'Innocent until proven guilty,' Jen mirrors.

'Will you sit?'

'No, but thank you. I'll only take a few minutes of your time. You can confirm to me that Mark stayed with you on Saturday, June the twenty-ninth, from around six in the evening through to the next morning.'

'Yes. He left at around eleven on the Sunday. I've been through this?'

'Did you at any time in the night wake and he wasn't in the spare room as you have already stated?'

'I didn't wake.'

'So it's conceivable that he could have left and then come back?'

'The police have already asked me,' she says. 'Why are you here asking the same questions?'

'Sometimes we revisit statements and ask the same questions. Especially when there are new developments in the investigation.'

'New developments?'

'Mrs Mason,' Jen says. 'I need you to tell me where Robert's motorbike is.'

Anna blinks. 'His motorbike?'

'He has a blue Nighthawk, correct?'

'Yes?'

'Where is it kept? Is it here?'

'I don't understand why—'

'And your son Mark also has a licence to drive it?'

Anna Mason pales. 'Yes?'

'Can you please show me the bike?'

'It's . . . it's gone to the garage for repairs.'

'When did your husband put it in?'

'Mark put it in for Rob.'

'When?'

'It was—' She pauses. 'It was that Sunday morning.'

'The thirtieth of June? Yes? And have you also told this to the police?'

Anna has begun to shake. The dog bats her hand, agitated. 'No, I didn't think . . . I didn't . . .'

'What's the name of the garage, please?'

Anna gives a bleating cry. 'He wouldn't hurt anyone. You don't think so, do you? Mark didn't go anywhere that night, I would have heard the motorbike engine?'

'Not if he walked the bike out.'

The dog starts barking now.

'But he would never have hurt *Victoria*? Why would he?'

'Please give me the name of the garage, Mrs Mason?'

'Jones and Sons.'

'Thank you,' Jen says. 'I'm sorry to leave so abruptly, but in light of this new information, I'm afraid I must.'

'Please,' Anna says. 'He would never harm anyone.'

Jen doesn't reply. Instead, she walks out of the house, back to her car, leaving Anna dumbstruck behind her.

She's a long way off alleviating the claims against Bill, or even herself, but now she's got something that could put Mark back in the picture that night. Could he be a murderer on top of everything else she's been told he is?

Jen wants to sob, but the tears won't come. Perhaps she's becoming numb to all of these shocking revelations, or perhaps the gravity of this horrifying possibility hasn't settled yet. Or perhaps she's cried enough over him.

She pulls over, five minutes from Anna Mason's house, and calls Idris.

'We shouldn't be in contact,' he says without hesitation. 'You shouldn't be calling me.'

'Idris, wait – don't hang up! You need to tell CID to seize Rob Mason's motorbike from Jones and Sons garage.'

'I'm *sorry*?'

'And then to arrest Mark Mason.'

'Are you kidding?' He's enraged. 'Who the hell are you to talk about any of this to me? I'm going.'

'Wait, Idris! For *fuck's sake*!'

'You didn't declare your connection to Claudia Franklin, or Mark Mason, you discredited evidence: it's gross misconduct, can't you see?'

'Of *course* I see.'

'You've let down the team and you're a good diver so it's a fucking crying shame.'

'I know but—'

'The boys are pissed at you and so am I. You never had norovirus either, did you?'

'No.'

'You're a piece of shit.'

'I know I messed up, but can you throw the rule book out for one second? Are you listening to what I'm telling you? I think Mark drove Robert Mason's motorbike back to Oak House the night he went to his parents' house. Which places him back at the scene of a possible murder. You have to tell CID about the motorbike, get them to run the registration plate and see if it comes up on any of the roads that night.'

He is silent and she is worried he's hung up.

'Idris?'

'How would you know that?'

'I can't—'

'Did he tell you something?'

How can she explain how she suspects this – she doesn't dare place herself at the river that night, tell him about the humming, so how is she going to convince Idris? She's just going to have to ignore the question.

'He must have taken it out of the garden, out of sight of the camera on his parents' driveway or whatever. Maybe he went back by chance, or maybe he knew Victoria was coming, I don't know. But you need to get the team to seize it, Idris, like *now*.'

'I'll remind you that you're suspended, Jen. You can't go around conducting your own private investigations like some sort of maverick.'

'I know but—'

'Your brother's been charged for abduction and suspicion of murder.'

Jen inhales sharply. 'Bill's no murderer. Don't let them put his name out there, Idris, or his face – *please*. I should have told you all this before and I didn't. It's my fault – I was only trying to protect the stupid decisions he made.'

There's silence.

'Send me the registration of the bike,' he says.

FIFTY-TWO

Claudia sits in silence as Mark drives them to St Pancras International. It's six-fifteen in the evening and the roads are stuck with traffic and Mark is cursing that they'll be late for the train, but Claudia doesn't care if they make it there or not. She doesn't know if she cares about anything any more. No, that's not true, she cares about not being outed as a murderer.

She relives the press conference from earlier today over and over. She blamed Bill for her mother's death. She didn't even need to, but she's too gutless, too afraid to speak the truth, that she did it anyway.

She stares out of the window at the passing buildings of the city they've been diverted through. She knows them all well because she used to come here all the time. The dive pool is around the corner. She remembers that she used to get excited on this stretch of road at the thought of seeing Mark. Now she's in a car with him with years of history and secrets between them and wishes she was anywhere but.

'If you talk,' he says out of the silence, 'then all of this is going to get ten times worse for you.'

She continues to stare out of the window. 'And for you.'

'We agreed.'

The car slows. She sees a woman driving in the lane next to her. In the back is a toddler in a car seat, who sees her looking and holds up a *Mr Man* book for her to see. *Mr Tall*. She smiles and nods at the little boy.

'Will you see Sam again?' she asks.

'Don't talk to me about Sam.'

'You have a *child*. Were you ever going to tell me?'

Mark honks the horn and she jumps.

'Fucking cars need to start *moving*. We're going to have to change the tickets to the next train.' He looks at his watch. 'The last one is at eight. Shit.'

'We won't make that one either,' she says and waves at the little boy as they move off.

From below the Satnav screen, Mark's phone rings and connects through to the speakers.

'Finn?'

'There are a few more articles doing the rounds, Mark. About this girl, Bella Mitchell.'

'Tell them I'll sue.'

'I've been telling them.'

'Get the UK Olympics committee to put pressure on the media – do they want to be responsible for screwing up our chances next week?'

'The *Mail on Sunday* is trying to get hold of Bella. They all are.'

'But they haven't found her?'

'Not yet.'

Mark jabs a button on the steering wheel to hang up, takes the phone from its holder, and throws it at Claudia. She gasps in surprise, and in pain, as it hits her elbow.

'Book us a hotel overnight. We'll go to Paris first thing in the morning. I'm not missing any more of the competition than I need to.'

She looks at him coolly. 'You don't want to miss Marie.'

'She's going to win me the gold medal that you should have won.'

'I could have done it,' she said. 'If it hadn't been for Henry.'

'You fell apart.'

'I was *traumatised*.'

'You want to go to the pool? Is that it? Relive your youth? Show me what you *could* have been?'

'Of course not,' she whispers.

'No, come on. Why don't we go to the place we started out. It'll be *romantic*.'

He indicates, and swings the car out to turn at the junction that approaches. A horn blares behind them.

'Mark—'

'Come on, Claudia – for old times' sake.'

'I don't want to.'

'I don't give a *shit* about what you want.'

He turns off the A-road, and she grips the seat, even though they're barely doing thirty miles an hour.

'Book a hotel,' he says again. 'Two rooms because I don't want to sleep next to you. I can't look at you.'

Tears spring to her eyes. She's surprised that his unkindness still affects her. The screen blurs. She goes to open a web browser but pauses. She goes instead to his contacts and there – thank God – is Jen Harper.

FIFTY-THREE

Jen is snarled in traffic, drums her fingers impatiently on the wheel. She wonders if the police have called for her at the flat and if they have, how much more trouble she'll likely be in. She has ignored a couple of calls on her phone, perhaps it's been them, but the only person she's waiting on to call her is Idris.

When he does call, fifteen minutes from when they last spoke, she pulls over to take it.

'They ran the registration on the bike.'

'And?'

'And CID want you to come in and talk to them. They came to your flat. Where the hell are you?'

'I'm . . . just getting Sam from his after-school club.'

'You couldn't have got your friend to get him?'

'I'll come in, Idris, Jesus, of course I will. Just tell me, did they trace the motorbike?'

'I can't impart any information to you, Jen. You know that.'

'*Did* they, Idris? Have they arrested Mark?'

'I can't tell you—'

'Are you fucking joking? My brother has been detained on suspicion of murder! Have they arrested Mark, or not?'

Idris pauses. 'The police can't find him.'

'You what? Claudia then! Get Claudia in!'

'They've both gone, Jen. CID says that Eurostar tickets were bought on Mark's card. They were due on the 7 p.m. train tonight to Paris but they never boarded.'

'Fuck.'

'If you know where they might have gone, you need to tell me right now.'

'I don't know, I swear.'

'And if you know who might have been on the motorbike with Mark that night, I suggest you also tell me.'

'Someone was *with* him?'

'CCTV shows someone riding on the back.'

'It wasn't Claudia – she was with Bill.'

'CID are expecting you at Bourne station.'

He hangs up, and she sits in silence. It's then that she realises she has a message on her phone.

DIVE POOL

It's come from *Mark's* phone and was sent two minutes ago. Why has *he* sent her this? She calls Idris again but he doesn't pick up.

'Son of a bitch.'

She throws the phone down on the passenger seat. The dive pool is eleven minutes away from where she is now, but does she risk going when CID have been at her flat already, when she should be defending herself? She grits her teeth – she's not got the police officer badge or the licence or a radio to call in for help, but, fuck, she's still got the heart of an officer, still got the courage, and she needs to confront Mark. She dials 999 for backup, and then she puts her foot down on the accelerator.

FIFTY-FOUR

Mark opens the doors with his key fob and steers Claudia forcefully into the reception. There is no one behind the desk, and the lights are off, but the evening sunlight filters through the huge glass windows. She hasn't been in here for years – since her Olympic training sessions. The smell of it, the warm chemicals, are as emotive as her own perfumes. They've upgraded everything; it's all sleek and expensive and branded.

'Where's the receptionist?' she asks.

'Not needed because everyone who might have been at practice is now in Paris. *We* should be in Paris.'

He walks her through the labyrinth of the empty changing rooms, which are also different to when she came, and then out of the door that leads to the pool. The tower is enormous, still and silent, its three platforms jutting out like arms. The water of the pool beneath is deep and dark blue, with the sun shimmering on the surface of it.

He prods her in the back. 'Let's go up the stairs. See it for all its majesty.'

'No,' she says. 'Let's leave. I've booked the hotel and they'll be expecting us for dinner.'

'Up the stairs, Claudia.'

He grips her bicep and she cries out in pain. Perhaps if she goes with him, he'll remember the good times here with her and she can convince him to leave again.

They start to walk up the stairs and she grips the rails with fingers that slip. When she was younger she used to skip up these steps, now she feels faint with each one that she takes.

'Do you remember how we would kiss up there?'

She could weep with the shame of it all. 'Yes.'

'Do you remember how good you were at diving?'

'Jen was better.'

'But she got ill.'

Claudia is mute. Only she knows the real reason behind Jen becoming unwell. After what had happened to Henry, Claudia had to be the best and the only chance of being the best was to fell her only real opponent. Before the championships, Jen had come for dinner and Claudia had put laxatives in her food. It was Kerry that had approached Claudia one day after school, suspicious, and untrusting, as she'd always been, and Claudia had blamed Victoria.

'You had such drive and ambition, Claudia. It was what I loved about you.'

She looks up at Mark. The sunlight through the glass gilds the side of his face.

'Do you still love me?'

'No,' he says, the smile on his face wiped suddenly. 'How can you love someone you don't trust?'

He walks her to the edge of the platform. She holds on to the side railing tightly, but feels his fingers curl around her wrists.

'Look down.'

'I . . . I don't want to.'

'You're not scared, are you? Look at that water, remember how you loved it. I loved the curl of your body, the smile on your face when you approached the platform. You *owned* it, Claudia.'

'If I'd won, would you have been happy with me? Loved only me?'

'No doubt,' he says.

She looks at the water. 'It was my life.'

'Show me,' he whispers. 'Show me what you could have been.'

She stares at him. 'I'm not going to dive.'

'No?'

She laughs because, even after all this, he can't be serious that she would attempt to dive from this platform? She hasn't dived since 2008. She can't remember how to do it, and more than that; she's afraid of being up here with all the screaming memories.

'You show me,' he says softly.

'No.'

'You can do it.'

'I . . . I can't, Mark. I'm in all my clothes. And the agitator isn't on . . .'

'You don't need it on. You could always time your body perfectly.'

'But not now—'

He shoves her head forwards suddenly and she cries out. Her nightmare spins at her – where she's turning in the air, faster and faster, towards a glass sheet of water, where she can't tell where the bottom of the pool is, and she's going to smash through it at the wrong angle. If she jumped, she'd break her neck. He knows that surely?

He whispers in her ear: 'Do you know why I wiped the security camera app from the gates? Why I told the police that the camera had broken? Because I had *also* come home that night to teach you a lesson for running away from me.'

She looks at him in horror. 'You went back to Oak House?'

'I came back, but by then, you had gone.'

'Did you see my mother?'

'Oh yes. I saw her. I thought she was *you* so I opened the gates and she came in.'

Claudia's head swims. 'Did you *kill* her, Mark?'

'You're going to jump now, Claudia, and I will jump in after you. But you're going to drown here, and I'm going to live.'

Her eyes grow wide with understanding. 'No, Mark – please.'

'When people ask, I will have to say that I stopped here for you because you wanted to relive your own youth. I'll say that you ran up to the tower and I followed, that you told me about Henry. You told me that you drowned Victoria, and before I realised what you were intending to do, it was too late. I'll say that I tried to stop you, but you ran to the tower, and then you fell.'

He goes to push her, but she ducks out of the way, and kicks him hard in the groin before dodging past him. He grabs at her again as she runs, spins her around, and she trips, is on the edge of the platform, clinging to it, but he is coming at her and she won't be able to stop him.

FIFTY-FIVE

Blood drips from Jen's knuckles. She's had to wrap her jacket around her hand so she could punch some of the glass out of the reception windows and a shard has caught her skin and has ripped it. A siren within the building screams at her break-in, and she's glad of it – the police will come because she's called them, but this will add to their urgency.

She runs through the changing rooms, leaves the alarm behind her, and goes through to the pool, skittering on the tiles in her trainers. She can't see Claudia and Mark now, but she can hear them – scuffling and shouts.

'Claudia!'

She runs up the steps of the tower, three at a time, and reaches the top, her lungs burning in her chest, her vision blotting with sparks of light. The two people in front of her are barely recognisable. Claudia is laying on the platform, her hands tight around the railings and Mark is trying to haul her up by the waist. Both of them are panting, sweating.

'Mark! What are you doing?'

'She wants to jump, Jen! I have to save her!'

'I don't want to jump!'

'She wants to end it all! She's lied to you, Jen—'

'You *both* lied!'

Jen swings a punch, whacks Mark round the head and he staggers backwards. She stands between the two of them, outstretched, a human shield.

'You took your motorbike from your parents' house that night,' she says. 'The police had only looked for your car on the CCTV cameras.'

Claudia lurches to a stand, her hair wild across her face. 'He went back to Oak House! He was there! He admitted it – my mother rang the bell and he let her in!'

Jen looks to Mark, who pushes back his hair from his forehead. It glimmers with sweat.

'Is that true? You saw her? Did you hurt her, Mark?'

'No.'

'You'll be put away!' Claudia spits. 'For my mother! For all your disgusting behaviour with Bella and Marie.'

'You've publicly denied that story about Bella,' he roars. 'And you've framed *Bill* for all the rest. You even let him think the barn was *his* fault for all these years.'

Jen startles. 'What?'

'I don't know why you're protecting Claudia from me, Jen. Claudia has protected herself well enough all these years.'

Jen glances behind her at Claudia. 'What's he talking about?'

'Jen knows about Marie!' Claudia shrieks. 'She knows what you've done and she believes it about Bella, and it'll only be a matter of time until your reputation is ruined.'

'I was *there* that day at the barn. Claudia and I were in the hayloft when Bill was as high as a fucking kite below us. He fell out of the tractor and then he left the barn and we came down ten minutes later.'

'*Stop it!* We agreed! We agreed!'

Claudia goes to barrel towards Mark, but Jen shoves her away.

'What we didn't know was that, at the same time, *Henry* had come looking for Claudia because he was suspicious of her meeting up with a boy and Claudia hadn't covered her tracks. He saw *us* together. She pushed Henry so hard that he hit his head against the tractor.'

'Mark!' Claudia exhales, sounding like she's deflating.

'And then she set the barn on fire.'

Claudia puts her hands over her ears. 'You told me he was dead!'

'She set the barn alight with Bill's lighter.'

'His . . . his lighter?' Jen stares at Claudia in horror. Why had they never thought about what happened to his *lighter?* 'Is this true?'

'You really believed that the stub of a joint could have caused a blaze like that? Claudia went around setting light to whatever tinder she could find.'

'You told me to, Mark!'

'Take some fucking responsibility.'

'I was blind to what you were! What you *are*!'

Mark flies at her again, and before she thinks, Jen lunges forward to intercept them. But Mark's hands are already outstretched, he's going too fast for her to stop him, and she has no time to brace herself and they fall from the platform.

Immediately, her ears are filled with water and little clicks of bubbles that stream up in front of her eyes. Her body is a different weight, her eyesight is prickled with the chemicals of the pool, and she can hear muffled shrieks above the surface. She then feels pain, realises that her left arm is heavy and useless, the impact of the fall has shattered it because she didn't have to time to position properly. It's blinding agony, but she hasn't fallen from a height like that for so long and she's lucky not to have landed head first and done more serious damage.

She needs to rise for air, to address the shooting pain and fucking *howl*, but as she kicks, and the bubbles clear, Mark comes into her view. She expects him to swim to the surface like her, but instead, his hands are on her again, pinning both her arms and dragging her downwards. In shock, she struggles against his strength, terrified because his face doesn't look like it belongs to him – there's malice in his eyes, a determination to hurt her, and this is all that she's thinking as she looks at him now, how badly she's misjudged him. Because now she realises – that he *meant* to lunge for her. He means to hurt her, because she now knows too much about him. His relationship with Marie, that he was at Oak House the night Victoria died, that he was there the day of the fire, that he *told* Claudia to light the barn. If he was responsible for Henry, was he also responsible for harming Victoria? He wants to make sure that no one ever finds out.

She tries to twist her body and make contact with his groin, or his ribs, but he's as deft in the water as she is – after all, he spends hours of his days in the water just as she does. She thrashes against him, manages to free her one good arm and try to propel herself upwards to breathe, but he's one step ahead. He's used the opportunity of her managing to free herself to take a breath, and then come down again, on top of her once more and with his hands around her throat so that she can't surface.

I can hold my breath for longer than he can, she thinks. I'm trained for this. But in her peripheral vision, the water starts to turn black and the thud of her heartbeat in her ears is like the galloping horse that she imagines beside her on her dives. Is it now a friend? Or is it Death coming for her? She never thought her life would end so violently, or at the hands of someone she once admired, loved even. As the darkness takes over her eyes, the remnants of a deep-rooted memory seems to swirl above her head in the water like smoke.

It is the memory of that Saturday night. Jen stood by the railings of Oak House, looking at the empty eye socket windows that were dark, save for one – a bedroom light was on, and the curtains were ajar and Jen saw movement. The front door opened and a woman came out into the night, through the gates, and passed Jen – unnoticed – by metres. Jen caught her blonde hair, the tang of alcohol on her breath as she walked briskly.

Victoria.

The emotion that Jen felt at seeing her was almost physical, a slap to the face, a jump into ice. It felt like heart-break, like fury.

Then there were people behind talking – shouting – a man and a woman.

'I can't see her! Where is she?'

'Put some clothes on, I'll help you look.'

And then Jen was walking at fast pace, her feet making a clattering noise because she was now on the wooden boardwalk of the water-meadows. She was calling to Victoria ahead of her – was it Victoria? She couldn't see clearly any more, only knew she had to follow.

'Wait!'

There was a note of desperation in her voice, but the wind whipped her words backwards and behind and the woman didn't hear her – or chose not to. She carried on, disappearing and reappearing from Jen's view as the boardwalk wove through the tall reeds.

'Stop!' Jen called again, and raced on because she couldn't let it go, the feeling of anger towards Victoria. She wanted to talk to her about something, *confront* her.

She rounded a corner, to the darkest part of the meadows, where the riverbank fell away to deep water, and there she saw a black-and-white jacket lying on the boardwalk. She picked it up, ran on.

'Hello?'

Metres from her feet, an enormous white swan lifted its head and opened its wings to beat. She sidestepped to pass it but unbalanced herself and tripped off the boardwalk, sinking her boots into the swampy marshland. Her feet soaked up the sop before she could jump out and carry on running, but she had lost sight of Victoria.

Was it Victoria? The woman she was following now looked smaller, was wearing a white top, not a shirt, and was not blonde but dark-haired. Like Kerry. But it wasn't Kerry, no. It was Marie Cadorna.

'Hey!'

What happened then? Jen's mind cuts to a distant splash of water, a shout, and then it wasn't dark any more but dawn, and she could hear a humming in her ears. Something properly woke her; she thought that perhaps it was a bird's cry in her ears, or the pink of the sun that edged over the horizon and into her eyes. Or maybe it was pain because her feet were hurting. She blinked, looked down and realised that the feeling of needles was because she had submerged her feet in the icy shallow silt of the riverbank. How long had she been standing there without her boots on? When had she taken them off? There was a distinct feeling that she was looking for something.

She lifted her feet carefully, shivered against the cold, and absently pulled the black-and-white jacket around herself for warmth. It didn't fit properly; she didn't notice. She knew that she needed to get back to Sam before he noticed she had gone.

Sam.

Jen's eyes snap open. She's still in the water, and Mark is still on top of her, his hands around her throat. All she can do is stop struggling against him and, while she still has the conscious thought, she looks him straight in the eyes. Through the silence of the water, she mouths one word in despair.

'Sam.'

Suddenly, his eyes change, he looks like Mark again – shocked at what he's doing – and his hands loosen.

There's a roaring noise above her head, and a jet of bubbles suddenly obscures her vision. His hands release completely and Jen claws to the surface for breath, chokes to get the air into her lungs.

There is screaming in her ears, the noise is back to normal frequency, and Jen realises that it's Claudia screaming. Is Mark still behind her? She treads the water instinctively, turning to try to see where he might be, and that's when she sees it – ribbons of red around her body. In her confusion, she checks herself for injury.

'Get out!' Claudia shrieks.

Jen jerks her head to the side of the pool, sees Claudia standing, holding a metal pole.

'Where's Mark?' she pants.

Claudia drops the pole, which clangs to the stone flooring, and points to the water. Jen looks beneath her to see Mark limp in the water, slipping downwards, the red of his blood drifting like vapour.

'I . . . I hit him,' Claudia says.

'Help me get him out.'

'No, we should leave him here. He attacked you.'

With her lungs burning, Jen takes in a huge breath and dives down for Mark, who is suspended, dreamlike, in the pool. He's unconscious or worse. She wraps her good arm around his body, her feet find the pool's floor and she yanks him upwards, pushing up from the pool floor.

She breaks the surface, leans Mark back against her and swims with him. Her hands on his body feels so intimate, and she wants to choke with sadness at this mess.

'Help me, Claudia. My arm . . . I can't—'

Claudia is sobbing. 'We have to leave – or . . . or if the police come, we have to pretend it was all an accident and—'

Jen pulls Mark to the side of the pool where the steps are, and stays there for a second to get her breath back.

'The police are already on their way.'

'I can't tell the police about Henry! Oh my God!'

'You have to tell them *everything*. You have to come clean about Bill, for Christ's sake! He's charged with murder! You betrayed him, his trust. *My* trust. I can't believe you fucking lied for so long about the barn. How could you?'

Claudia is mute.

'Call the ambulance and then come here and help me get Mark out of the water.'

'OK,' Claudia whispers. 'OK.'

She scrabbles in her bag, her fingers shaking, and while she starts to speak on the phone, Jen looks down at the wound on Mark's head, which seeps blood in a thread down one side. It gathers where her leg is positioned on the step like a barrier. His blood in the water is pink now and disappearing and Jen wishes she could make all the wrong decisions she made disappear also.

'They're coming,' Claudia says.

'Help me.'

Together they lift Mark out of the water and lay him on the tiles. Mark's eyelids are fluttering and then he leans, is sick over the pool ledge.

'Mark?' Jen says. 'Can you hear me? We're getting you an ambulance.'

He vomits again.

'Don't tell Sam,' he says.

'Trust me, I won't be telling him anything about you.'

He nods, squeezing his eyes closed in physical pain. Perhaps emotional too because she really believed that he wanted to know Sam but now knows that he never will. Sam is her golden child, and hers alone.

'You have to tell me something.'

He stares up at her, but his eyes aren't focused.

'Was Marie with you that night at Oak House?'

'Yes.'

'Did Victoria find you together? Is that what happened?'

'We went looking for her,' he says. 'But we couldn't find her.'

FIFTY-SIX

SIXTEEN HOURS LATER

The horizon to Marie Cadorna's career sparkles with promise.

She is in her navy swimsuit and standing at the very edge of the platform, composing herself before her dive. Below, her team is her only audience – they are in their practice sessions – but in a few days' time, she'll be up here with millions of eyes on her, and the hope of a nation. She's going to claim Paris as *her* city, the one where she wins gold for Great Britain.

Early this morning, the team arrived in Paris and it's as beautiful as everyone says it is. It so very nearly didn't happen, but she can't let herself think about that night at Oak House, or what might be happening to Mark right now. There are whispers going around the Olympic village – people are talking about the team, but the other British coaches are telling them to keep focus, keep away from rumours. You are *here*.

Take the moment.

Marie took that fucking moment.

Since Claudia went crawling back to Mark, and then the article started to circulate about Bella Mitchell and catch fire, Marie has panicked that Mark might be forced to break and tell the police about the two of them. But it would be career suicide for him, surely. She has to tell herself that he'll make it here to Paris, that he will fulfil his promise and the two of them together will win gold. She owes it to him, he gave her this opportunity. But the price of it is mounting. Bill Harper is arrested, charged, but the truth may yet gain momentum.

She closes her eyes to steady herself but immediately regrets it because whenever she closes her eyes, she's catapulted back to that moment where she received Mark's message from the phone that Claudia never knew he had.

I'm going to pick you up on the bike and take you to Oak House. Be ready for 11 p.m.

She went with him – of course she did, because he was exciting and spontaneous, even though she would have no idea what was in store that night. She didn't know at that point that he was planning on having Marie there because he had seen Claudia on his stupid gate camera, that he wanted to taunt Claudia by letting her see him with Marie, naked and spread out on the bed. But it was Victoria Franklin, not Claudia, who opened the bedroom door and she was a different, and very real, threat.

Marie remembers feeling the waves of panic radiate from Mark as he stumbled up, as he grabbed a shirt, and placed it in front of himself, as he started offering excuses to his mother-in-law, who stood there, rigid and horrified, before she started to scream.

'How old is she? How old?'

The alcohol from her breath stung Marie's nostrils.

'Come out of the bedroom—' Mark started to say.

'In *my* house! Oak House is *my* house!' Victoria slurred. 'Where's my daughter?'

Marie said nothing. She slipped from the bed, her heart hammering in her chest, grabbed her jeans and white top and fled to the adjoining bathroom, listening to them shouting through the door.

'Let me explain—'

'You *can't* explain! I'm calling the police—'

'Victoria—'

'Is this what you did with Claudia? Is this how it started?'

There was the sound of a hard slap then – of skin connecting with skin.

'You hit me!' Victoria's voice was shrill.

Then, there was a door slamming, the thud of shoes down the staircase, and Marie opened the bathroom door, ran to the bedroom window to see Victoria storming out of the house, the black-and-white of her jacket stark against the front lawn and gravel drive. Mark, who was semi-dressed in a random suit jacket and shoeless behind her, caught up with her and wrenched the bag from her hand, knocked it to the ground.

'You are sick!' Victoria yelled.

She swung her arm out at Mark, and he lashed out at her once again, and she started to run this time – suddenly realising that he was panicked, afraid, and would hurt her. He went to go after her, tripped over the bag he'd knocked out of her hand. In that split second, Victoria ran through the gate that was still open and disappeared into the night.

Marie saw her turn left, away from the lanes. Towards the water-meadows. Would she run to town, tell someone? Marie's dreams of Olympic gold were fading before her eyes. She needed to act, now. If Victoria managed to tell the police, then her chance for Olympic gold would be ruined. Her name would be splashed over papers for being involved in scandal, she might be thrown out of the team. The team was the only good thing she had in her life.

She ran down the stairs, put on her trainers and went out of the door.

'I can't see her!' Mark cried at the gate when he saw her running over. 'Where is she?'

'Put some proper clothes on, I'll help you look.'

He looked down, registered what he was wearing. 'I just grabbed it on the banister . . . I—'

'You've not got *pants* on, Mark. Get some trousers, and then you go down the lane, and I'll search the meadows.'

He went back to the house and she went to turn when she saw that a red tie had dropped out of Mark's jacket pocket. She picked it up, wound it around her wrist, and then she ran out of the gate to follow Victoria.

Marie caught up with her in minutes, but she stayed at a distance following as Victoria stumbled along, moaning to herself. Her little heels kept catching in the cracks of the wooden boardwalk, her arms were wrapped around her thin body, and in that moment, Marie made a decision. Victoria Franklin would need to be stopped. Silenced.

Marie came up behind her, pulled at her black and white jacket, and it fell down Victoria's bony shoulders, and Victoria turned then, and, upon seeing Marie, she sighed so hard that the jacket fell cleanly to the ground.

'You silly, silly, girl,' she whispered sadly.

Marie had never been called silly in all her life. She had been called a bitch by her mother, high-maintenance by most of her foster families, headstrong at school, beautiful, but never *silly*. Silly implied careless, stupid, imperfect and she was definitely not any of those.

She reached out her arms and shoved Victoria so that she staggered backward and tripped over the little wooden lip that was between the shallow water and the boardwalk. Victoria made a gasping sound and plunged into the dark murk, and Marie crouched beside her and before she had even thought about what she was doing, she grabbed a fistful of Victoria's hair and held her head down into the water. Victoria thrashed against Marie's grip, but she was disorientated, drunk. Muddy bubbles erupted, a low guttural moaning but she couldn't pull herself free. In less than a minute, Victoria Franklin was motionless in the water.

Marie cried out then, at the pure terror of it, the pure elation. She'd extinguished a threat. She'd extinguished a life.

'Wait!'

A voice called from the boardwalk some way behind and Marie froze. Because it wasn't Mark's voice, but a voice belonging to a woman. Was it Claudia? Marie grasped a tighter hold onto Victoria, stepped over the shallow lip and sank low into the reeds beside her.

'Stop!'

Her heart hammered so hard. Any second now she would be discovered and what would she say? How could she hide what she had done? Victoria had been unstable, drunk, and Marie could say that she was trying to save her but would people believe her?

'Hello?'

The footsteps stopped and there followed silence. Through the reeds Marie could see a woman stood on the boardwalk, and looked around blankly. She was dark-haired with a heart-shaped face, but even in the gloom, Marie knew that she looked familiar. She looked like the *boy* in the photograph Mark kept in his flat – the one with the Lego. Who was she and what was she doing here? How much of Marie had she seen, what had she seen her do?

The woman was taking off her boots. A shiver ran through Marie's body with the realisation that she needed to get Victoria into deeper water where the current was stronger and could take Victoria away with it. As soundlessly as she could, Marie slipped further into the water and took Victoria by the wrist, dragging her into the wider part of the river, supporting her beneath her ribs, and looking desperately around for somewhere to hide her. Marie's own face sank down many times with the effort and the weight of Victoria's lifeless body, the earthy water filled her mouth, and chilled her eyeballs.

At some point as she heaved through the water, the tie that was wet around her wrist, began to unfurl into the water, and she noticed only as it drifted away, dark red, blood-like. She didn't even know why she'd picked it up, couldn't possibly comprehend what it would come to mean later on.

Victoria's body was beginning to sink now, her white shirt billowing, ghost-like, from under the black of the water. Marie guided her down through the river, and when she thought she could go no further from sheer exhaustion, she let her go. She worried about her DNA on the body but what could she do now? Her only hope was that Mark would protect her if and when Victoria's body was found. They would protect each other. That's what he'd told her after they'd slept together one time, fingers laced. They were in it together – the Olympics, everything. Come hell or high water.

She swam back against the current, past where she had seen the woman she didn't know, and only once she was convinced that she was safe, she heaved herself out from the water, and ran, sopping wet, back towards the house.

She must have been gone only ten minutes, but ten minutes – ten seconds – is enough to change the course of a life forever. Several lives. Outside the railings, she bent forwards, put her hands on her thighs and panted with fatigue and shock as droplets rained down her clothes. Mark's footsteps echoed from up the lane and she straightened.

'Did you find her?' he asked.

'No.'

'You have to help me look for her!' He paused, stared at her. 'Why are you wet?'

There was a second where she thought she'd tell him. But what would it achieve at this point?

'Because I missed my footing and fell in the fucking river trying to find her. Drive me home.'

'What the fuck are we going to do?'

'You're going to drive me home.'

'Marie, she'll tell the police! All we've worked for, it'll go up in flames! Is that what you want?'

She looked at him without expression. 'Get the bike, and drive me home.'

Did Mark suspect her of wrongdoing when Victoria's body was found in the river? He never said so. Perhaps he trusted that she would never do something so wicked, so primitive. Perhaps he never knew exactly what diving meant to her and what she might do to protect it, because his own want and ambition for gold and glory was as strong. Or perhaps he *did* know and kept her secret because he would have done exactly the same thing as she had.

Marie jumps high, arches backwards into a three-and-a-half somersault inward tuck, before extending her arms above her head in the downward dive into the water.

She hears it – the rip – the sound of a perfect dive, and she rolls down and drags the splash down with her. When she surfaces, she is like a phoenix, reborn of water and not fire. Her team cheer for her as she gets out of the pool and she allows herself to smile because she is Marie Cadorna and she will be unblemished, golden, and titled the queen of British diving.

Until her eyes come to rest on two men coming down the stairs. They are dressed in police uniform, and one of them points to her.

FIFTY-SEVEN

SIX WEEKS LATER

Jen's name is called just as the rain has started to lash against the windowpane. She stands. Momentarily, the door in front of her is going to open and she's going to step inside a room where the fate of her career will be decided by police tribunal. Most likely, she will be found guilty of gross misconduct, but she lives in secret hope that her good discipline record will be taken into account, and an allowance might be made for her dishonesty.

'You OK?'

Idris is beside her. She asked him to be her police support but never expected him to agree. The fact that he's here after all her lies speaks volumes to the strength of their relationship before she went and screwed everything up. She can never repay this kindness, whatever the outcome in that room.

'I'm OK.'

He nods, and faces forward.

She thinks of Mark and Claudia, both in prison on remand, deemed flight risks. Their trials are scheduled for

November; Claudia charged for the manslaughter of Henry Barton, for perverting the course of justice in the investigation of Victoria Franklin, and Mark for his role in the manslaughter of Henry, for his abuse of a position of trust under The Sexual Offences Act, and for also perverting the course of justice. Marie Cadorna is also on remand, charged with the manslaughter of Victoria. The evidence against her – her DNA on the red tie, the CCTV of her on the motorbike with Mark, holding Victoria's suitcase that she apparently then hid in her flat, the finger marks on Victoria's wrist matching hers – will mean a quick trial. Her lawyers will suggest that Mark manipulated her, get some years off a sentence. Perhaps he did, perhaps he didn't. It's not for Jen to think about now, but she thinks about it all the time, and dreams about it. She has walked the loop again, over and over, and wakes in various places around it. She wakes most of all at the black gates of Oak House.

The three of them are now famous, but for all the wrong reasons. Perhaps Jen is also famous too within the policing world, but she has no idea because she's not been allowed contact with any of her team. She has, however, received a picture message from Joe of a woman eating a nectarine the size and colour of a bollock, which made her laugh and then cry, because it's all gone so wrong but yet he has still reached to bridge the gap.

'Whatever happens, I valued you on my team,' Idris says, staring at the door. 'We all valued you.'

She's so grateful for his words, but she continues to stares ahead of her in case she completely falls apart. 'Thanks.'

The door is opened. The panel look up at her.

'Come through,' the Chief Superintendent says.

The decision will be made within seventy-two hours and in the time between, Jen goes to the only place she finds comfort, and where she is truly herself – to the water.

She is in the river, a mile up from Oak House, away from the barn and Cowell Farm, and from where Victoria's body was found. Away from the bad memories. She is in the part where there is fast-flowing water, where she and Claudia and Bill used to race under the canopy of trees, where they created happy memories. If she really was to listen, perhaps she could hear the memory of Claudia's laughter here, but allowing herself to remember it would bring her sorrow. That Claudia then is not the same as Claudia now.

The leaves on the trees are beginning to turn, some have already fallen and succumbed to their destiny, are curled golden boats which race down with the current. From his cross-legged position on one of the black rocks, Sam commentates on them, pokes at a few of the slower ones with a stick he's found. Jen's boy, her pride and joy. Kerry is on the bank, pouring hot chocolate from the flask she's made. There is mud on the soles of her feet.

Upstream, Jen and Bill swim together against the flow to warm their blood. Bubbles arch from their hands, which are white against the mirror black, and beer-like foam gathers where the reeds jut from the surface. They reach out for one another, smile as their hands touch, because no words are needed between them. They know more retribution is to come for the both of them, but they will stand up to it, accept it.

Jen dips her head under to hear the rush of the current and her heartbeat in her ears, opens her eyes into the dark. There is nothing to see, but yet it is there in front of her – the galloping winged horse.

ACKNOWLEDGEMENTS

Firstly, an enormous thank you to my contact within the police dive team (and thank you also to Graham Bartlett, who directed me to them!). I have been asked not to name names, but this contact was incremental to the writing of *Silent Waters*. After lengthy phone calls and numerous messages, I can verify for absolute certain that diving is one of the toughest jobs within the police. It requires such grit and determination and patience. A thank you also to Catherine King for my many rambling messages and queries. (Please note that any police procedural inaccuracies in the book are my mistakes alone, and / or due to artistic licence. This also applies to any of the Olympic diving references.)

Thank you to Camilla Bolton at Darley Anderson Literary Agency for always going above and beyond in all aspects of agenting – I thank my lucky stars to have found you! To Jade who is eagle-eyed, to Mary and the rights team, to Sheila, and to everyone at Darley Anderson, thank you so much.

To my editor Rosa Schierenberg for your wisdom and fun (I will miss you!), to Jon Elek, to Jennifer Edgecombe, to Rob Cox, to Annabel Robinson and to James Horobin,

Nico Poilblanc and Carrie-Ann Pitt, and to the entire, wider team at Welbeck who I know work so incredibly hard to produce these books and put them out to market. I hope this one blows it out of the water – pun absolutely intended! Thank you also to Cat Camacho for her copy-editing skills, to Simon Michele for the striking book cover, and Emma Dowson at EDPR for getting me such amazing exposure, I am truly grateful. To Celine Kelly who is the most precious jewel in any author's crown – your insights never fail to amaze me, and you may be across the Atlantic now, but we will always have LEON on The Strand!

To my husband and my boys – I love you beyond words. You make me laugh, you are my most favourite and best. To my parents and brother, to my wider family, and to my treasured friends – thank you for your humour, and your love. Plim, to you especially, because I've come to realise that so much of my writing voice has come from the films we used to make. So much of me is down to *you*.

To the writing friends I've met but a special mention to Emma Christie, Karen Hamilton, Sophie Flynn and Mira Shah for making a solitary writing life sociable, and to Jen Hawkins, who straddles both sides of the coin – half a sister, half a mentor, and always one hundred per cent with nailing writing problems.

To the bloggers, and reviewers, and bookstagrammers – you read and review books with such furious passion that it leaves me breathless. Thank you for your relentless encouragement. This leads me to say that two of the female characters in *Silent Waters* are named after women who have championed me since *The Prank* was published – Kerry-Lou (@bookbeforeyouleap) and Jen (@diaryofabookmum), thank you for your ongoing, unfailing support. I hope that you love Jen and Kerry as much as I do.

To all the many bookshops and booksellers here in the UK, and beyond the seas, thank you so much for supporting my writing. I cannot tell you of the unparalleled joy an author feels when a book that's been so toiled with and sweated over, is eventually on a shelf.

And to you, the reader, for everything. This was the hardest book I've ever written, but I think it's my best. I hope that you love it.

ABOUT THE AUTHOR

For over ten years L.V. Matthews worked both in domestic and international sales for major publishing houses, before leaving to pursue a career in writing.

THE TWINS was a Richard and Judy Book club pick in 2022. Also available, *THE PRANK*, both from Welbeck Publishing.

Find her on:

@LV_matthews
@lv_matthews_author